TWO
HUNGERS

OF

PRINCE
FIERRE

THE
TWO
HUNGERS
OF
PRINCE
FIERRE

DARCY ASH

SOLARIS
NOVA

First published 2025 by Solaris Nova
an imprint of Rebellion Publishing Ltd,
Riverside House, Osney Mead,
Oxford, OX2 0ES, UK

www.solarisbooks.com

ISBN: 978-1-83786-477-5

A CIP catalogue record for this book is available from the
British Library.

Designed & typeset by Rebellion Publishing

Author's Note: Trigger Warnings

A full content note can be found at the back of the book

One

Fierre

"Do you think I look pretty in a crown?"

The echoes chased each other around the throne chamber like bolting horses. Aiven halted in the middle of the moonstone floor while I draped my legs across the throne.

I suppose I shouldn't have spoken so dashed loudly, but if you can't exclaim about how pretty you're feeling in a crown, when *can* you be loud? I gave my behind a little wiggle and tilted my chin up so that the jewels caught the light from the chandelier.

Aiven gazed at me. If it were anyone else, I would have said that he gazed *up* at me, but this was Aiven: all six-and-a-bit feet of Aiven. The last time he'd looked up at anyone had been at his own birth.

"Tell me how I look. Don't be frugal with the adjectives, Aive. I want to hear your best work. Splendid, magnificent, polished…"

"You know perfectly well that you look good."

"Good? Stirring saints." I tsked. "I thought you'd at least pretend to butter me up."

I climbed to my feet and descended the steps from the throne. I couldn't resist a glance at the mirrored wall as I moved. The pale pink folds of my enserre tightened around my body, while the hem sat at mid-thigh; the sleeveless, skirted garment revealed just enough leg to invite murmurings, while a small cape in matching pink silk dangled down my back. Gold straps curled up from my sandals to my knees and layers of rose-quartz and pearls dripped from my neck, glimmering in the chandelier's light. I wondered if I'd checked my outfit for long enough before I left my bedchamber. I looked expensive—no doubt about that—but maybe a silk belt would've accentuated the narrow shape of my waist. Maybe I should've tried on a sash, tying it with a double bow to rein myself in.

Aiven looked at me for a very long time. "You shouldn't be playing dress-ups with the crown, Fierre."

"That's *Prince Regent* Fierre to you."

"Not yet." Aiven shot a glance at the sundial outside the window. "In fact, not for another quarter-hour."

"That's plenty of time to tell me how exquisite I look," I said.

I twirled around in the centre of the room, letting the coronation cape billow from my shoulders.

"You look like you're wearing half the coffers."

"I can hear your disapproval, you know." I halted in front of the mirrored wall, trying to catch a glimpse of my back. "Something's not right. Is it this shade of pink? Does it make my skin look sickly? Or it could be the way I tied the bow—"

"Fierre."

As I turned, a pair of strong hands grabbed me by the shoulders, and I leaned into him without meaning to, drawn into the embrace. His chest felt warm and comforting. Suddenly, I was rising: Aiven lifted me up and set me down again, plopping me on the moonstone with an embarrassingly easy movement.

"You're going to be perfect in there," he said.

I could feel myself blushing. I had no firm idea why Aiven's voice made me blush on occasion, but I suspected that it was because we had been friends since childhood. There were only so many times you could be scolded by someone who had seen you skin your knees and work yourself into a blubbering mess without feeling a little self-conscious.

"If you can stop preening for a moment, that is," Aiven said.

I sighed. Did he think it was an accident I'd managed to fit into this enserre?

If anyone else had been standing before me, they would've appreciated the way my enserre emphasised my narrowing waist. If Laird Rossane had been getting a preview of my coronation outfit, I was sure that the crown would scarcely have been off my head before he would have been peeling off his gloves and running his fingers down my spine, trailing a path lower and lower. But Aiven didn't feel a thing... well, except for a desire to scold me for trying out my crown.

I was dashed well sure he felt that.

"Here." I tossed the crown to him. "Catch."

Aiven grabbed at it. "Fierre! You're twenty-six, not twelve!"

I smirked. He shot me a reproachful look before holding the diadem up to the light, letting the full glow illuminate its points and band. On the near side, a slender deer grazed, its pearl body curved above a few blades of emerald grass. On the other side of the crown, I knew, a saint tree would be rising above a cloud, its sapphire branches extending from the circle of blanched pearls. Aiven frowned as he perused the motifs.

"I wish the artisans would fashion different pictures," he murmured.

"Why ever should they?"

"I just don't think it's right." He tapped the pearl head of the deer. "The divine tree and the deer of perfect elegance. Reminding us all that the ruler must show their fitness for the job through a daily performance of delicacy and…" He paused. "Fragility." His forehead wrinkled into a subtle frown which, from Aiven, was the equivalent of another man's rage. "You shouldn't have to starve yourself to fit an ideal of spiritual beauty cooked up by a bunch of old men. It's unjust."

"But then how would the court know if I was a deserving ruler?" I kept my voice deliberately light. "If I don't show up looking divine, how will anyone believe I'm god's instrument on earth–the blessed sky that proffers sun and rain? Chin up, Aive."

"None of *them* have to suffer to prove their lairdship."

"Well, none of them is a prince," I said, patiently. He was being rather obtuse, even for this hour.

Aiven looked at me and seemed to bite down on what he was about to say.

"Shouldn't we be heading into the corridor?" he managed.

A shrill voice rang out from beyond the door at the end of the room. "Guards attending the Prince Regent, gather in the throne room immediately! Not you, MacKenshie! Nibson, look alive! Household, to your posts!"

Brilliant. Right on cue. As if they knew I was trying to

have a moment with my best friend.

"Fierre!" Aiven hissed. "You didn't tell me they'd arrive so soon!"

Before I knew what was happening, he had me by the arm and was steering me across the room. Somehow, in the flurry of movement, he managed to lay the crown back on the throne and smooth my hair until it was simply its usual soft sheath of midnight black, almost reaching my eyes. He brushed away the ruffling from the crown so easily, as if he were stroking the coat of one of his parents' sheep. I let him drag me to the side door and bustle me through it, without fighting; Aiven's hands were quite soothing when they were bustling me, the unhelpful part of my mind noted.

His big palms pushed me through a low doorframe and into a corridor, where we both stumbled over cracked stones. The staff passage smelled like roasted barley with a sprinkle of raven pepper tossed in. I'd only ventured here a few times, on quiet afternoons when the corridor had yawned before me, but today the passage teemed with kitchen-hands carrying plates. Aiven nodded to an elderly man in an apron and exchanged greetings with a sharp-nosed woman as he led me through the cramped space.

He hurried us on, past more staff and around the bend in the hallway. A few kitchen-hands gawped at me. Was it just the recognition of their prince? Or was it my enserre? Had I wound it too loosely—or too tightly?

We stopped just outside the brass door at the end, and Aiven let go of my hand at last, facing me.

"We shouldn't delay a second longer... but..." He reached into his breast pocket. "Happy coronation, Fierre."

Nestled in his palm, a red acorn glimmered. My breath swelled and filled my lungs.

"You remember?" Aiven said, his voice wavering. "The day we ran away—"

"And hid in the back of your parents' farm, under that obscenely large oak tree. Yes, I remember." I pushed back the wet tide behind my eyes. I was determined not to let tears drip all over my enserre, after I'd worked so hard to wrap it just so.

"Let me guess." I took the acorn from his hand. "So that I never forget my humblest moments?"

"So that you know I'm always by your side."

I swallowed. Closing my hand around the acorn, I leaned in and pecked Aiven on the cheek, then threw my arms around him and hugged him close.

"You're very cold," he said.

"No, you're awfully warm."

Aiven smiled. We pushed open the brass doors together and Aiven's hand slipped into mine, the acorn clasped between our two palms as we walked in. I tried not to dwell on what Aiven might be thinking about my body temperature, or its causes. The bronze panels of the Summoning Chamber enclosed us in a cool new world, its windowless design blocking out all traces of heat; I nodded to the guards along the wall, and then to the knots of nobles who looked up from their conversations. Everyone bowed, and a silence fell.

I remembered that I was still holding Aiven's hand.

I let go and slipped the acorn into my pocket. In the mirror on the opposite wall, I glimpsed myself wrapped in tight pink silk, and Aiven clothed in the dark brown garments of his job.

You could hardly avoid thinking about the gulf between

our two positions when one of us was decked out like a plank and the other one was dressed like a strawberry tart.

"Prince-in-waiting! And Master of Compliance! Welcome!"

The high notes of Mistress MacLyon cut through the air with all the elegance of a rusty saw. I smiled tightly.

"Welcome." The Chief of Household looked me up and down with an eye that was about as soft as her voice. "Almost on time. But exactly in style."

Aiven and I watched as she steered the nobles into lines, arranging the group so that the lairds from the most influential clans were interspersed with nobles from the less powerful families. I had to hand it to her; it was an impressive display of tact and balance, even though every nobleman knew where they stood in the court's ranks. The guards knew, too. I suspected that the mice under the floorboards knew, if they'd been listening to any conversation in the staff quarters in the last couple of hours. They were probably squeaking about hereditary titles and the hierarchy of estates.

Halfway down the line of nobles, I saw Laird Rossane lean out and stare over his shoulder at me. He swept his gaze over my figure and made a small kissing motion. I pretended not to see it. If I noticed Aiven's fists clench, then I pretended not to see that, too.

MacLyon rapped on the double doors at the end of the Summoning Chamber. Her cane echoed against the brass. The doors creaked open a sliver, then an attendant on the other side heaved a bit harder and the windowless chamber gave way to a vast, airy hall.

As MacLyon led the way down the aisle, the Gilded Roses started to play their instruments. I craned my neck to catch a glimpse of the musicians; I could see only a few cymbals and a pair of trumpets near the dais at the far end, but I was sure that there were more players out there with brass and strings, concealed by the heads of the crowd. My face and neck suddenly felt warm.

Ceremonies were nothing new in the palace, yet this grandeur had been assembled for me alone. I wondered if the court would think I deserved it. Maybe that wasn't the right question. As I looked around at tables of well-dressed people dripping gold from their necks and ears and saw not a commoner among them, I wondered if anyone could deserve this.

Aiven stopped as I did.

Just as we agreed. Side by side.

Only I'd never guessed that my heart would be beating like a drum with a short attention span.

"Don't tarry, or you'll miss the summer-rag pudding," Aiven murmured.

I smiled, and took a step forward, moving with him behind the long procession. We filed further into the Heart Hall, over the smooth parquetry, and fear rose inside my chest.

This was really it. I'd done it without father, and without a retinue holding my hands and shepherding me into place. I let myself take in the ivy wreaths on the hall's plinths and the dishes on the tables. Plates greeted my eyes, piled with golden tate scones and tureens of coolan soup, a spiced apple cake, and yes, a vast, impenetrable mound of summer-rag pudding, black and sweet-smelling, sitting resplendent on its traditional cloth. A pang hollowed my stomach; a moment later, I recognised it for what it was.

I was supposed to be hungry.

The familiar burn of deprivation was good.

Wasn't it?

Other men strive to be rugged and strong. The voice of my tutor echoed in my head. *You will be slender like a deer. Slender means beautiful–and beautiful means divine.*

I watched the guards file into the tiers that led up to the right side of the dais and the nobles file into the tiers on the left, and kept my pace going. As we reached the platform, Aiven made to join the main crowd, but I grabbed his hand and squeezed it.

"Give me some courage, Aive."

"You have every second man staring at your arse right now." His whisper barely reached me. "How's that for a pick-me-up?"

"Just what was in order." I smiled, hoping that it looked like a beatific and stately smile to the nobles watching.

"Who'd you pick for Star?"

I tensed. Ever since we passed through the doorway, I'd known that this was coming, but that didn't make it any easier.

"Ah," I said. "So your gift was a bribe, after all."

"You know I wouldn't—"

"Just kidding. I thought you knew me better, though." I squeezed Aiven's palm again. "I'm not going to drop a single hint into your lap."

"Am I going to be mad at you after the ceremony?"

Of course he was going to scold me; that was what Aiven did. He was the only one who could reproach me without fear. But I couldn't help hoping that once he had digested my choice, he would forgive me. If Aiven accepted my decision, then everything would be all right… everything would feel safe.

I touched the acorn in my pocket and gazed at the tiers

on the left. The lairds shot glances in my direction, and I could feel the stares of the crowd behind me, no doubt every second man still perusing my arse. Yet Aiven's hand was warm and firm. Aiven's smile made a familiar curve, real and true.

Drawing a deep breath, I marched onto the platform and took my place in the middle, right in front of the golden altar, where everyone in the Heart Hall could view me: scrutinise me and appraise my body... weak, thin, and hopefully perfect.

Two

Aiven

I HATED EVERY man in those four tiers.

They thrust out their chests and tilted their faces towards Fierre. Across their ranks, I tallied the number of those who had talked about Fierre behind his back and those who had spent a night with him—sometimes, the two things overlapped. And sometimes, they hadn't waited till night. I still remembered the summer afternoon that I had discovered Laird Crawshall on top of a slender figure in the palace orchard, and my sinking feeling when I realised that it was Fierre being pinned to the grass.

I reminded myself that I was no laird.

I was a sparrow facing a room full of peacocks.

I looked up at Fierre on the platform. He was taking the ceremonial staff from Mistress MacLyon, smiling brightly, saying something that I could not make out, which would no doubt turn out to be a polished gem of small talk. Fierre was talented at small talk. He was good at everything that I wasn't.

I watched him bow to MacLyon, beaming. Before I

could take a seat, Fierre's gaze fell upon me. He beckoned, then pointed to the only spare place on the four tiers below the dais, next to Laird Rossane. I could think of species of plague vermin that I would rather stand next to than Rossane, but I couldn't refuse—not when Fierre was smiling at me like that. It was a soft, sparkling smile; a sun-touched smile; the kind of smile that no one in the palace received except for me.

Gritting my teeth, I took my place.

"Who did you bribe to get in here, Grian?" Rossane whispered.

His breath gusted hot against my ear. I didn't give him the satisfaction of flinching.

"Goodness, I'm forgetting. You couldn't afford a bribe. I suppose it was weaselling your way into the Summoning Chamber, was it, then? A pretty trick for a farm boy."

"Former farm boy," I murmured.

"Well, you know what they say... once a man smells like hay, he can never quite get it off." Rossane's laugh tickled my ear. "Even if he stands inside the Heart Hall."

I fixed my gaze steadily on Fierre's person. He looked devastatingly beautiful in that shade of pink, his black hair falling softly to his eyebrows, complementing the enserre. I wished I'd had the courage to tell him so.

"You're very good at getting inside places, aren't you? The irony does seem rather delicious." Rossane's voice had grown louder, and I was sure that others could hear.

"Irony?" I shot him a glance.

"Well... as far as I can see, you're the only man on these steps who's never been inside the prince." Rossane flashed me a smile.

I wanted to grab him by the shoulders and something very inappropriate for a courtroom setting.

Maybe I'd punctuate it with my right fist.

MacLyon called the priest to the dais, and I concentrated on the robed woman as she moved across the platform. There was enough pressure in my jaw to explode something, but I kept my eyes on the priest, watching her touch Fierre's forehead and cheeks, following the paths of the blessing across his skin. In truth, I told myself, it wasn't the fact that Rossane had slept with Fierre that pricked me deepest. It was the way Rossane threw Fierre's experience around in conversation like a soiled cloth, desiring and disrespecting him in the same breath. All his ilk behaved the same way.

But Fierre deserved someone who would cradle his heart softly in their hands; someone who would tell him that he didn't need to check his reflection in the mirror so often, nor cinch the fabric around his waist.

"I now proclaim you to be the Sky of Eilean-òir! Not only Prince Regent, but he who stands above all of us in Eilean-òir: he who nourishes the soil with wind and rain and sun, who makes all things grow in their season." The priest stepped back, facing Fierre. "Do you vow to protect your people?"

"I do—with arms and laws in turn."

"Do you vow to provide justly for your people?"

"I do—with food and coin in turn."

"Do you vow to uphold the realm's expectation of a ruler, endeavouring to become a symbol of grace, elegance, and beauty for the people to aspire to?"

"I do—with body and soul in turn."

"Then I crown you Prince Fierre Dannatyne, the thirty-fourth Sky of Eilean-òir!"

Cheers ripped through the hall as MacLyon lowered the band of the crown onto Fierre's head. The jewel-encrusted sides stood out starkly against his hair. I saw several noblemen smirk on the tiers above me—most likely calling up memories involving Fierre which I didn't want to think about—but I pushed their satisfaction aside and allowed myself to take in Fierre's beaming face. The priest accepted a leather-bound book from her assistant. She waited a long time, until the cheers and applause had died down, before opening the book and reading out the virtues of the crown one by one, keeping up an impressive drone.

"Of course, it's all a bit of a lie, isn't it?"

Rossane's remark slithered into my ear like a snake nesting.

"Provide for the people, with food and coin? The last time I checked, that was the lairds' job. You ought to give the priest an amendment, Grian. That's your speciality, isn't it—checking little details and scratching out things with common ink?"

"Common ink is far more reliable than rare dye."

Rossane chuckled. "You have to admit, though, she's got it wrong. We clan leaders provide for our people. The Sky reaps our taxes, and grants us favours in return. And don't you think it's a neat twist of an arrangement?"

There was a long pause, during which Rossane watched me, obviously expecting me to ask what he received from Fierre. I kept my lips pressed shut. I wasn't a minnow waiting for a hook.

"I said, don't you think it's a neat twist of an arrangement?"

"There's a flaw in your working," I replied. "You claim you provide for the people."

The priest held up the holy book, pointing to an illustration of a throne. Beside me, Rossane managed a chuckle that was almost convincing.

"Who works the fields and reaps the harvest? Who pays taxes to the clan chiefs? How do you get that money to pass on to the crown, Rossane? Remind me, do you provide for the people… or do they provide for you?"

"I don't recall asking for a farmer's opinion."

"And here I thought we were going to have a nice, friendly chat."

I cast my gaze deliberately out across the dais while Rossane settled into silence. The priest looked up for a moment, allowing her pause to fill the hall.

"And now for a short passage on elegance, from the Book of Silver Deer…"

If the lairds of this realm wanted to hear a sermon on thinness and purity so that they could pat themselves on the back for encouraging their ruler to starve, it was their right, but I didn't have to listen to it. I used my time to study the nobles around me, sizing them up. Out of twenty-four men on the steps, I counted only five who I considered real contenders for Star of the Sky, and I examined them one by one.

Hattray always boasted about his investments to anyone who would listen. Red-headed Kinnaid spoke quietly, perhaps because he didn't need to brag about the number of mines his family owned. I didn't care for either of them, but I had a much stronger feeling about the next two candidates.

MacArlay and Rossane had an armoury apiece and a record of crushing their enemies in the field—yet only a fool would ignore the frequency of their visits to Fierre's bedchamber. Most suitors only managed a single night.

And then there was Crawshall… the man who had famously slaughtered a rival's horse in the royal hunt so that he could gallop on to kill the bear. He had gutted the stallion with his dagger, the stable-hands reported. No one had been willing to contest the result.

"Thank you, Your Excellence," Fierre said, his voice ringing through the Heart Hall.

I glanced up.

"It is now my honour—I should say, my privilege—to make the royal appointments. For the position of Moon of the Night, the Treasurer, I choose a man whose skill with figures is known to us all…"

"Skill with *his* figure, I hear," someone muttered behind me.

"Laird Hattray!" Fierre finished.

Scattered applause welcomed Hattray to the stage, where Fierre pinned a stag's-head pin onto his mantle. I heard Rossane clapping loudly beside me. He didn't look jealous. When you were rich enough that counting your own money took several days at a time, the role of treasurer probably didn't seem like a lure.

Hattray smiled unctuously and descended the tiers again. I noticed Fierre waver a little on the spot. Had he eaten enough this morning? When he'd told me that he would drink only snowfruit juice for two days before the coronation, I'd assumed it had been a jest… maybe I'd heard what I'd wanted to. Or *not heard* what I'd wanted to.

"For the position of Foam of the Sea, the Chief of Diplomacy, I choose the pride of one of our most ancient families: Laird Kinnaid!"

If any of the nobles were surprised, they hid it well. Kinnaid received Fierre's pin with a little nod and left the platform with a swaggering gait, his red hair blazing around his face. He was the least obnoxious choice of the lot, I supposed. Thanks to his mining profits, he had only over-taxed half of his peasants. It was like selecting the most pleasant viper from a nest.

"For the splendid role of Rock of the Glen, the Commander of the Armies, I choose the well-known breaker of shields, Laird Rossane!"

Rossane knocked me with his elbow as he pushed past me. I was pleased when he stumbled as he climbed the tiers, nearly tripping over the last one. He whispered something that, judging by Fierre's tight smile in return, seemed more of a joke to the speaker than the hearer.

Fierre shook Rossane's hand and pressed the silver stag's-head to his mantle. As he fastened the pin, Rossane's palm fell over Fierre's and rubbed the back of the prince's fingers.

Murmurs ran through the crowd.

Somehow, without intention, my hand flew to the hilt of my dirk.

Fierre looked coolly at Rossane and announced:

"And with him, to act jointly as Commander of the Armies, I appoint my second Rock of the Glen, the battle-hardened Laird MacArlay!"

If I could have painted the look on Rossane's face, I would have done so.

I noted the flush of anger that infused his cheeks. It was perfectly done: Fierre could not have timed it better, and when he caught my eye, I gave him a little wink, hoping that he understood how pleased I was. When Rossane returned to his position beside me, he wore an ugly scowl.

I resisted the urge to make a remark about the difficulty of sharing a role.

In the excitement of the moment, I hadn't considered what the appointment of two army commanders implied. Now, it sank in. If both Rossane and MacArlay shared the position… and if the other two positions were taken… that left only one true contender for Star of the Sky. I looked up to the first tier, where Crawshall's lips were twisting into a smile.

He had realised it too.

"And finally," Fierre said, taking the final pin from MacLyon's outstretched hand. "To the greatest and most glorious position in my court—the person with whom I will work closest of all—the trusted right hand of the ruler—"

How could he appoint someone as boorish as Crawshall?

"The first gentleman to the Prince of Eilean-òir…"

The kind of man who killed an innocent horse to win a prize was not the kind of man I wanted near Fierre. But Fierre had pondered over this decision for months, in his private hours. He must have reason for it, and it was not my right to demand it. I would simply have to accept it.

"I appoint Aiven Grian as my Star of the Sky!"

All around the tables, nobles gaped at each other. Someone knocked a glass over, but no one moved to sweep up the pieces.

I raised my hand very slowly and pointed a finger into my chest. Fierre nodded, beaming. My body seemed to move like an oil slick; I didn't know how, but I managed to slide out from my place and stand in the gap between the guards and the nobles, looking straight at Fierre.

"Me," I said.

"That's right, Aive. You."

"Fierre." I heard a susurration of voices, and remembered that we were in public. "I mean, Sky of Eilean-òir, and Prince Regent." I took a deep breath. "Is there a mistake?"

"None at all."

He spoke so blithely. As if the words weighed nothing to him. As if he didn't know how much they meant as they settled upon my shoulders.

The first step seemed to stretch for an eternity. The second step was easier. I didn't dare to meet the nobles' eyes as I made my way onto the platform.

"You wish to make the Master of Compliance—the man who handles the palace accounts and checks legal obeisance—your Star of the Sky?" MacLyon said.

In her voice, I heard the echo of reason. Everyone was going to object, now, surely. Fierre would be forced to overturn his decision and hand the position to one of the remaining lairds, and they would all laugh it off together. I would go back to standing on the floor below the tiers, in the last empty space.

"I believe I said it loudly enough." Fierre raised an eyebrow. "Don't you think so, Mistress, as Chief of Household?"

"Is it legal for a son of farmers to accept this position?"

MacLyon shot a glance at me after she had spoken, and I saw the tiniest smile curl her lips. Her usually sharp glance softened slightly. I wondered whether Fierre had slipped a few coins her way before he asked her to pose these objections.

It must be bittersweet for her. A woman, trying to elevate a man to a position she could only dream of holding.

"You ask the right question, Mistress MacLyon. The most apt query. I quote the original text: *The Sky shall choose the most deserving candidate as their Star, to guide and serve them*. That's from the Book of Pearl and Sapphire—the book of royal laws itself—Chapter

V, Page XXII." Fierre gazed defiantly around. "Not a damned trace of anything about birthright. Any habit of choosing a laird has merely been custom." He inclined his head to MacLyon. "I shall be pleased to create a new custom today, because Aiven," he shot a glance at me, "is the most deserving person I've ever known."

He extended his hand towards me.

A silver stag's-head pin gleamed in his palm. Taking in its perfect sheen, I wanted to back down; to agree with the part of me that believed I could never be Star of the Sky; to accept the declaration in my head that a farmers' son could never rise higher than I already had.

A cornstalk cannot grow above its station, a voice muttered in my mind.

But Fierre… Fierre was the one I would be serving, not some nameless, unfamiliar prince. And if I couldn't tell him how much I cared about him, I could at least stave off the wolves in furs and mantles who snapped around the crown. I could put my body between their jaws and his tender skin.

"Come near me, Aive," Fierre said, his hand still outstretched.

Yes. I could come closer. Step by step. Heartbeat by heartbeat.

I know you're only offering me this as a friend, and you only want me to guide you in politics, I added in my head. *But I'll take that. I'll take what I can get to be near you, and to make your life happier.*

I closed the space between us, stopping just inches from Fierre. My heart seemed to beat louder when Fierre reached over and pinned the silver stag's-head on my brown doublet. We looked into each other's eyes.

He grinned.

I lifted my right hand and brushed a strand of hair that had fallen to the side of his forehead, beneath his crown. Behind me, I heard the whispering of many voices, but they might have been speaking a southern tongue for all I cared: all I could hear was Fierre's breath. The whole horizon was Fierre's smile.

"Congratulations, Star of the Sky," he said.

I allowed myself to smile back.

"You're supposed to kneel," Fierre whispered.

"Oh. Right, yes." I dropped to the platform, feeling the hard parquetry beneath my trouser legs, ignoring the murmuring that continued behind me. I looked up at Fierre. The tension left my body, and I realised that I had been bracing myself for no reason. It felt good, to be sworn to him. It felt like the unnamed emotion that swelled in my breast whenever I watched the pale orange light glossing the hills behind my parents' farm.

A moment later, I felt the tip of a sword against my neck.

"Stand up now," Laird Crawshall said, "and you'll regret you ever clapped eyes upon that pin."

Three

Fierre

THERE ARE SOME things you can time perfectly. A six-course breakfast service, a sword dance, and a hammer toss at the highland games all rank highly among them.

A violent tussle in a court room is trickier—especially when your best friend's neck is on the line.

Over the top of Aiven's head, I saw Crawshall mount the steps of the dais, taking them at a stride. I made sure to keep my face expressionless, but on the inside, I felt a warm surge of satisfaction. As soon as I made the appointment, I had expected a challenge from any one of the lairds. The fact that it was Crawshall pleased me greatly.

He would stride up to Aiven. He would throw a punch at the man who I had dared to elevate above the oldest families. And Aiven, with his height, muscle, and courage would knock down Crawshall, warning the rest of the court with a single blow not to challenge my decision. It couldn't have worked out better if I had invited Crawshall to step forward myself.

Trenches carved themselves into Crawshall's forehead as he crossed the platform. At any moment now, I was sure, he would challenge Aiven to face him.

He drew his sword from its sheath and swung it down to Aiven's neck.

No. I couldn't be seeing this with my own eyes. To draw a sword on a man with no matching weapon, in the Heart Hall, of all places—the most honoured hall in the whole palace—I hadn't even considered that Crawshall would dare it.

"Stand up, and you'll regret you ever clapped eyes upon that pin."

I opened my mouth to call for the guards, but Aiven pushed the sword off his neck, prising it up with both hands, and a rivulet of crimson trickled down his left palm where the steel bit into his flesh. Crawshall reeled backwards. Aiven's right hand flew to his belt, and something metallic and sharp slid from a sheath.

Crawshall lunged. Aiven rose and threw himself sideways. He pivoted to come up behind Crawshall, grabbing hold of Crawshall's arms and pinning them behind his back with his left hand. It all happened so fast—so dashed fast—that I didn't dare order the guards to close in. A flash of a blade. Aiven's right hand shifted, and then his dirk was at Crawshall's neck.

"Careful, my laird. Attacking me while I take the prince's command, in the Heart Hall—that is not peaceful behaviour. Now this..." Aiven pressed the short dagger against Crawshall's skin. He looked like an ancient warrior from a painted scene, with his whole body strained. "This could be peaceful. I press here, like so, and you'd sleep serenely." He gave a slightly harder push of the blade. "Without interruption." Crawshall struggled, but Aiven held him in a vice-like grip. "Are you weary, my laird? Would you like a nice, long sleep?"

"Let me go," Crawshall grunted.

Aiven threw him to the floor. Crawshall landed roughly on his knees and slumped forward, scrabbling to avoid landing face down. Crimson flushed his cheeks. The whole hall was watching, I realised; every member of Eilean-òir's nobility had witnessed this.

Crawshall would not forget it.

I looked at Aiven's face, tense with concentration, and his defensive stance, dirk pointing out, poised for another assault. Something about his focused expression made my stomach flutter, and I couldn't say why.

"Guards," I said, making sure to project my voice, "please take Laird Crawshall to the water-garden. He is overly excited about the coronation. He needs to cool down."

A long, tense pause followed. The guards moved to encircle Crawshall, waiting. Crawshall shot a look at Aiven and contorted his face into a silent snarl, but then he stood up and strode from the hall, the guards trailing him into the corridor.

I met Aiven's eyes. A look of horror crept across his face, as if he was just realising what he had done.

I knew my buoyant mood must have shown on my countenance, because I saw Aiven's shoulders relax a little and his hand lower. I nodded to him. He wiped his bloody palm on his doublet sleeve, dark red trailing over brown.

"My lairds!" I shouted. "Let's not be wasteful! We have a hall full of scones and cake—and attendants to bring you more! Let's give some love to our cooks and roar their praises! Why not throw back a dram and sing your hearts out to the Gilded Roses' thumping tunes? Why not chatter of crowns and princes from ages past, and make this hall ring with fair Eilean voices?"

I might have asked them to talk of hay carts and asses, for all that they listened. After a round of dutiful cheering, the sound of Crawshall's name reached me from every corner and nobles began gossiping about the drama of my coronation. I waited for the lairds to descend the dais before stepping down, feeling the weight of the crown upon my head. Then I unfastened my cape, and let the swathe of silk drop to the floor.

Several lairds scurried over at once to pick it up, and the one who succeeded locked his gaze on mine as he offered it to me. *Maybe I* am *beautiful enough*, I thought. *For now.*

With a wave of my hand, I sent the man off clutching my cape.

MacLyon approached me with an inquisitive look. I grasped Aiven's arm and steered us clear of her, strolling around the edge of the crowd.

"Fierre," Aiven said, softly. "Can I still call you Fierre?"

"I'd prefer it to 'royal prat,' and your face says that's what you're learning towards."

"You should've told me."

"Darling Aive. I make you the first gentleman of Eilean-òir, and immediately you scold me."

"It's an honour I don't deserve."

He lifted my hand, gazed at it for a moment, then seemed to think better of whatever he had been about to do. Why did I feel strange, all of a sudden—as if someone had pulled a rope around my chest and tightened it?

"Listen, if I'd told you, would you have accepted my decision?" I said.

"Well—"

"Of course not. You would've said the very same thing: that you didn't deserve it. Do you remember the day I fell into the river on that trip through Skailcross? All of the guards were riding back with father, too far for us to call." I still remembered the moment I realised that no one was coming to rescue us. "The water was so damned cold, I thought I was going to freeze to death before I drowned. I kept thinking about warm cherry cake as I tried to stay afloat." I chuckled. "I remember I was disappointed that my last thought was going to be of pudding."

Aiven covered his mouth with his hand, but not quick enough to hide his smile, and it bolstered me to speak on.

"And then you tore off your shirt and dived into the water; you grabbed me around the waist, pulled me over to the bank, and carried me up into the fresh air. My teeth were knocking so hard that I was certain they'd come loose and start raining down on the grass, like little pointy hailstones. I asked you what I should say to father when he arrived, but you said I didn't need to speak." I blinked back a tear. "When he rode up, all red-faced and shouting, you dropped to your knees and asked forgiveness for pushing me in." I ran one hand over his back, trailing my fingers across the region between his shoulder blades, where a calcified scar remained from the beating that father had doled out to him. A beating for a lie. A beating that had diverted the course of father's rage away from me. "Serving me, an honour you don't deserve? Aive, you're the only man in this hall who deserves to be Star of the Sky. I'd make the same choice ten times over." *On my knees*, I thought.

He hugged me, then. It wasn't a long hug, like the one he had given me when I first told him that my father's body was failing, but it was enough. I didn't say anything else: not about how I wanted his big hands to wrap around me again, nor about how dangerous he had looked when he was wrangling Crawshall; not about my rising hunger.

"You didn't look surprised," Aiven murmured.

"I'm sorry?"

"You didn't look shocked that Crawshall laid his sword to my neck. Did you know that you were putting me in the line of attack when you chose me as Star?"

"I didn't know it'd be Crawshall," I said. "Or that he'd use a sword."

"But you knew I'd have to fight someone."

I glanced away for a moment, but there was no hiding from Aiven's stare.

"I knew you'd win," I said.

We stared at each other. The moment stretched on and on, like thinned glue. At last, just when my nerves were about to snap, Aiven reached over and ruffled the strands of hair that were peeking out below my crown.

"Let's eat," he said, and it was as good as forgiveness.

PLATTERS LEERED AT me from every side, thrusting their scones and soups and puddings in my direction, begging me to come nearer and snatch a morsel from their gleaming silver. I tried to numb myself to the burn in my stomach, but it was growing by the minute. Striding to the closest group of nobles, I proffered greetings and smiles, scattering compliments about the lairds' kilts and tartan sashes, calling up the names of their spouses and children in my head all the while. I charmed the group with questions about their kin, then moved on to the next cluster with a nod and a smile. If I kept talking, I wouldn't have to look at the food. I wouldn't have to think about girdle tarts and thick blackberry sauce.

Aiven popped several tate scones into his mouth and ladled a liberal serving of soup into a brass bowl. He ate two slices of summer-rag pudding next, and washed it all down with a full cup of honeyed whisky. Where on earth did he get the stamina?

I considered asking him if he was going to leave any appetite for the next fortnight, but I was cut off by a woman tugging at my wrist.

Her riding cloak stood out in the milieu of bright tartans. I stared, and she dropped her hand.

"Forgive me, Sky. I worried that I might not reach you in time."

"And your name is…?"

"Browne, Sky." She bowed her head, but I motioned for her to speak on. "I work in your father's household, in the old palace on the Isle of Hairstin, off the northern coast."

"Ah." I drew back a step. "Did father pass on any formal message? Or was it merely a handful of taunts and curses about my waistline?"

"Neither, Sky. I came of my own accord."

I glanced from side to side. The nobles on my left were leaning towards each other as they chatted, waving their tate scones and cups of wine enthusiastically. On my right, still attached to my arm, Aiven wore a look of deliberate indifference, which I knew to be a sign of deep nosiness.

"No more chatting here, Browne. Come and see me in my chamber at twilight. Ask Mistress MacLyon to escort you—I'll tell the door-guards to expect a woman in a riding cloak with a scar on her cheek."

Her right hand twitched. I wondered if she wanted to clap her palm to her cheek and cover the scar. I also wondered how old it was, and who had cut her so deeply.

"Thank you, Sky." She bowed and retreated, slipping away between the groups of nobles.

Before Aiven could ask me a question, I heard a familiar drawl.

"May I offer you a cherry tart, Prince Regent?"

Rossane added my title lazily, after a pause. I knew that he had done it to remind me that he could address me in an informal way, in different circumstances. I also knew that the gaze he was trickling down my body must be leaving any onlookers with no doubt as to what those circumstances were.

On my left, I heard Aiven's inhalation, short and sharp.

"No, thank you, Laird Rossane," I said. "I'm quite full."

"As you please. You must be busy, after the coronation." Rossane leaned against my side. "Perhaps later you can find room for me."

I heard whispering from around us, and saw a group of lairds darting glances in our direction. I hated Rossane, suddenly. I hated the way that he could humiliate me with just one mouthful of words. I hated myself more, however, for the way I felt when I ran my eyes over his hard jaw, his playful mouth with its sadistic twist, and the bulge of his muscles beneath his shirtsleeves and tartan sash. He had been born without an ounce of kindness in his marrow, like the highland wolf. Whenever he looked at me with such confidence, something inside me wanted to be mauled.

"Perhaps you could visit—" I began.

It was strange. The room had begun to spin. I did not remember the Heart Hall ever spinning before; was the room drunk, or was I?

"Fierre?" someone called.

I threw one hand out, trying to stabilise myself. My fingers closed on the empty air.

"Fierre?" someone shouted again, and I realised that it was Aiven speaking; his voice seemed to come to me from a long distance, even though I could have sworn he was rushing towards me. Above me, I saw Rossane's face twist into an expression of discomfort. *Above me?* When had I begun falling? And more to the point, was I about to crack my skull?

A pair of arms caught me. A pair of big hands wrapped around my back and bore me upwards, propping me into an upright position. I slumped, and Aiven gripped me harder.

"MacLyon." He addressed Rossane. "Get MacLyon."

"Watch your mouth, Grian. Just because he pinned a stag on your chest doesn't mean you're a noble animal."

"Either put your pride aside for a baker's minute, or get out of my way. Can't you see he's fainted?"

Aiven waited a few seconds, then gave a sharp exhalation and turned away from Rossane, hefting me as he did so. My legs swung out, but it was all right, because Aiven's hands moved me into a horizontal position, and then his right hand was beneath my knees and his left hand was supporting my back. I was propped in Aiven's steady arms.

He carried me through a sea of elbows and hips and forearms, moving carefully so that my head didn't bump anyone. I tried to look to the side, but the hall started wobbling again, and I decided quickly that that was a bad idea. I gazed up into the arches of the ceiling. Along with the dizziness, my stomach felt oddly swollen beneath my enserre. I hoped that no one noticed.

"Is he hurt?" MacLyon's voice reached me as if through a wooden door, muffled and distant.

"May we speak in his suite? I think he needs to lie down, mistress. And quickly."

The journey from the Heart Hall to the Skyward Suite passed in a blur, the clop of Aiven and MacLyon's boots ringing off the stone walls. I heard the creak of the door when we reached my suite, a familiar sound that, during my inspection of the chambers, I had insisted I liked. I had never told anyone that the creak was there to alert me to potential intruders. I suspected that MacLyon understood, however; she had always paid attention to what I didn't say.

Right now, as Aiven lowered me onto the bedspread and laid me out on the pink-and-silver check of my family colours, MacLyon's face loomed over me. I tried to find the strength to speak, but a reddish darkness overwhelmed my mind. I closed my eyes.

"Unsteady sits the crown on an ailing body." MacLyon sounded genuinely concerned. "The lairds might start getting ideas if he's taken ill right now. Do you think he'll manage the rituals tomorrow?"

"Your guess will do as well as mine. But our best chance is to let him sleep." A warm hand pressed against my brow, and I knew that it was Aiven's. "He's suffering."

"You misunderstand me, Master Grian. You are Star of the Sky. I'm not seeking your opinion; I'm asking for your command." MacLyon pronounced each word slowly. "You're the one who decides what happens if the prince is unconscious."

I wanted to speak up and tell her that I was not asleep. But more so, I wanted to hear what Aiven would say. A long silence filled the bedchamber.

"It was a sudden collapse," Aiven said softly.

"Some toxins work very suddenly upon the body, I hear. I make no accusations, you understand. I am Chief of Household, a minor lady born, nothing more. But I think it bears noting. Some of them can put you to sleep within minutes, if ingested in the right dose, and I hear that newly-crowned princes have a bad habit of eating the wrong food at parties—scooping up a tainted slice of cake from a platter, the poor lambs."

Another silence fell.

"Impossible," Aiven said, at last. "He didn't touch a thing after the coronation. Not so much as a bite of a scone."

"Wine, perhaps?"

"There was no time. He was bustling from group to group, charming them all and asking after their families, the way only Fierre can." Aiven's voice wavered. "I would've noticed if he'd stopped to take a drink."

MacLyon made a clicking noise with her tongue. Aiven's hand pressed against my forehead again, and this time, he ran it down to my neck, keeping it there for a while, as if feeling my pulse.

"You don't think…" MacLyon trailed off. "Something in the air?"

"No. I don't."

"Was there anyone near him?"

"Laird Rossane." Aiven's voice sounded strained. "But if Rossane wanted to kill the prince, he could've done it several times over, in private."

I was glad that I couldn't see Aiven's face right now.

"Well then, Star. Shall we wake the Sky of Eilean-òir, before anyone takes advantage of a fainting Regent?"

"Let him rest," Aiven said, firmly. "Have someone check

on him every half-hour, and when he wakes, send for the very best doctor—the one his father used to employ. I'll deal with the lairds in the meantime."

"He's lucky he has you as his Star." MacLyon's voice had softened.

"I'm sure the son of a noble house would have known what to do faster than I did."

"If you'll pardon the correction… any laird in your position would have looked to seize the moment and flex their new authority once the prince fell. You thought of him, and him alone."

"Always." Aiven's voice dropped so low, it barely reached me. After a long moment, he added, "Thank you, Mistress MacLyon."

MacLyon's boots clopped out of the room. I felt a hand brush my hair upward, and then a pair of lips pressed against my forehead, holding their position for a long time. As Aiven kissed my skin, I thought that I agreed with MacLyon. I was lucky to have Aiven as my Star of the Sky. I was lucky to have him near me at all.

He removed my crown and necklaces so gently that I barely felt it, and I heard a clink—no doubt the jewellery dropping onto a cabinet.

My head grew heavier by the second, and the reddish haze over my eyes faded to deep indigo. A scent of light floral sweetness reached my nostrils. The last thought that passed through my mind before I feel asleep was that Aiven smelled like fior-chridhe, the flowers that grew on mountaintops, sustaining each other through tempests and snow. Once, on a trek with my father, I had seen them dancing in a headwind.

No matter how strong the gales blew, they always grew in pairs.

Four

Fierre

THE MIDDAY SUN had ceded place to the soft gold of late afternoon by the time I woke, and light poured through the high windows, gilding my bedspread. I gazed around at the cabinets, the ghost-oak table, and the Dannatyne family crest of two prancing deer that loomed over the stone fireplace. It felt strange to be waking in the Skyward Suite and sitting up in my father's old bed for the first time, especially since I'd been too dizzy to take it in last night.

I trailed my hand over the spare pillows on my right and caught the faintest trace of a floral scent.

Aiven. I remembered now. Aiven's strong arms holding me, supporting me... Aiven's large hands laying me down in the bed. Aiven's warm lips pressed against my forehead like a seal.

I rose hastily and began to unwind my enserre. In my dizziness and exhaustion I'd forgotten about its tight embrace, but the lines on my upper body showed me a maze of red creases: the reward from lying on my front.

It was a good thing the coronation rituals were a day away, or I'd have been bathing while looking like a poorly drawn map.

It wasn't the creasing that I was truly worried about. A full-length mirror waited in the bathing nook next to my bedchamber, and I did what I always did after waking: checked my body from head to toe. The polished glass reflected my arms (too fleshy), my calves (too wide), my stomach (utterly disgusting with its scant covering of fat), and all the rest below. Everyone might say that I looked beautiful, when I'd crammed myself into fine silk, but the sight of my naked body always hurt to behold. No matter how hard I tried, I could never lose those last few pounds, those bits of fat that would make the difference between *slim* and *perfect*.

I wrapped myself in a pink-and-white tartan and slid on a pair of white stockings. I was in no mood to dress myself carefully in formal garb, so I padded to the window in my bedchamber, ignoring the cold stone of the floor. Why was it so dashed frigid all the time? Opening the left window, I drew a deep breath of salty air.

You were never far from the sea in Eilean-òir. The realm's name meant *the golden isle*—emphasis on the *isle*—after all. Yet sometimes I wished to be closer to the water, to move the palace to the land's edge and climb from my chamber directly into the sea where I could float, weightless, on the waves. My body would move with the briny tide. I would forget about the shape of my hips and the unpleasant softness of my arms; I would become a creature of seagrass and foam, unblooded.

I closed the window and strode to the bells in the antechamber, seizing the pull-rope of the largest one. Minutes later, MacLyon rapped at the door.

"I believe there was talk of sending for a doctor," I said.

"Ah." She glanced down quickly. "I wondered if you were really asleep last night. I suppose that's my answer. Shall I call him now, Sky?"

"If you please." I smiled as warmly as I could, trying to convey how grateful I really was. "And there's a little matter I would have your help with. A woman named Browne will be coming to see me at twilight. She has a scar on her cheek. Admit her to my chamber, and tell the guards not to ask her any questions." I leaned closer. "She's to speak with me alone."

As the sound of MacLyon's boots receded, I returned to the mirror and examined myself once more. The tartan and stockings covered enough of my body, surely; if the doctor was going to examine me, there was no point slipping on a shirt and a sash. I fidgeted for a few minutes, then paced to the window.

Dr Galar swept his cap off his head as he entered. He crossed the floor at a stride, stopping with a crisp bow. "It must be four years at least, Prince Regent. I trust your father is keeping well?"

"As well as a dying man can be," I said.

Galar bowed and set down the wooden chest he was carrying, looked me over, and pressed a hand to my forehead, examining me for signs of fever. If he was at all unnerved by the thought of assessing the Sky of Eilean-òir, I could see no sign of it. I suspected that I was the nervous one, for every calm movement of his hands reminded me that this man was an expert: clever, objective, and ruthlessly honest.

It wasn't the tap of a potential hammer or the scrape of a possible scalpel that bothered me. It was the thought of what he might discover about my body as he poked at it.

"Describe your symptoms last night, in clear terms, if you please."

"I'd been talking to some of the lairds in the Heart Hall when I came over dizzy. It was as if the whole hall was spinning—wobbling from side to side. I'm not sure that I can say I fainted, because my mind didn't black out at first… but my body lost its fortitude." I thought of thatched houses, toppled by a headwind. "I collapsed."

"I see." Galar eyed me down the length of his nose. "I will need to inspect your body, Prince Regent."

"Shouldn't you check my head, first? Search whatever made me dizzy?"

"It is for me to decide upon my methods, and upon my physic."

I flushed, and began to unfasten the knot on my shoulder. As it came free and I made to shrug off my tartan, Galar said hastily: "Just the upper body, Prince Regent."

I rolled down the tartan and tied it around my hips. I wasn't sure why I was still flushed—I had let enough men go further. Maybe it was just that the sight of Galar made me think of father, and for a moment, I could feel his reptilian gaze sweeping my flesh, picking out places where a little padding had built up.

Then Galar moved, and I was back in the present, shivering in the stone room. He produced a set of ropes from his doctor's chest—four ropes of different sizes, which he used to measure my neck, chest, and waist, making notes with a quill on a piece of ink-splattered parchment. He motioned to me to roll up my tartan again. I stood, watching him check his notes.

"I see you are keeping up with the demands of your position. That is no easy task, saints know, and without your father to aid you... well, you are doing admirably. Elegant. Slim. You drank only snowfruit juice on the days before the coronation, I gather?"

"Yes," I said.

"I inferred as much by the swelling in your stomach. Did it feel swollen after you collapsed?"

"That's exactly it. Swollen. Like I had been stuffing myself—only I hadn't been, I promise."

"It is your body's effort to compensate for a lack of fuel. A build-up of fluid beneath the skin." Galar nodded to himself, as if this was entirely expected. "You've done admirably, Prince Regent, as I said. Now you will need a little nourishment."

Still he gazed at me, and still he made no effort to check my head or to ask me further questions. Slowly, I realised that it was not a question of laziness or reticence. He knew that my dizzy spell was a symptom of something else.

"Was it wrong to starve for the coronation, Dr Galar? Is that why I'm sick?" I kept my voice steady.

"No. Starving is necessary, for a monarch." He spoke without hesitation. "Now you must give yourself a little more food, to make sure that you do not have another such... incident. Be careful that you keep it to a small ration, though. A few spoonfuls of porridge or half an oatcake will do. It will be easy to go too far."

"Doctor, if I may be honest..."

"You may always be honest with me. I was your father's doctor, after all."

"I'm desperately hungry. Do you think I could eat a large meal, perhaps? To balance out the last few days?"

"How may I put this?" Galar's cold eyes raked over my face again. "We all have our roles in this realm, Prince

Regent. Yours requires an extraordinary regime. Your body needs energy, but if you eat more than a little ration of gruel or oats, you will gain weight, and quickly. You wish to fit into your enserre and look graceful—to look as divine as you did at the coronation, do you not?"

"Of course."

"Then here's what we will do." He reached into his medical chest and took out a stoppered bottle. Its tapering neck winked in the morning light. Within it, a cerise liquid sloshed. "If you find yourself eating more than my recommended amount, take a thimbleful of this immediately after eating."

"If it's not rather impertinent of me to ask, doctor… what will it do?"

Galar closed the chest. It snapped shut with a firm click. When he spoke, his voice reminded me of a priest's, filled with the calm grace of stained glass.

"It will put things right," he said.

THE ATTENDANT PLACED my food upon the table, gave a neat bow, and scurried out. The single oatcake separated under my knife, its warm interior fresh enough to part without leaving a trail of crumbs. I threw one half into the fireplace and watched it burn. When it had disappeared, I returned to the table and took a tiny bite of the remaining half.

I chewed the baked oatmeal carefully, making sure to taste every bit of it before I moved on to the next bite. My eyes closed as I tasted a trace of honey. Was there any word that could describe this? Could any heaven ever compete with the taste of solid food after three days?

I slowly chewed several more bites, and had a quarter of the oatcake left when a knock broke my reverie.

Really? I slammed the plate down and regretted my force as the piece of oatcake crumbled. I marched through the antechamber, opening the door.

"Yes?" I snapped.

Browne's face gazed back at me, swaddled by the hood of her riding cloak.

"My apologies, Sky."

"No. The apology is mine." I rearranged my face into a smile. "I'm afraid the suite is rather lacking in refreshments, but I'll see to it that the kitchen provides for you later."

"No need, Sky. My tale will be a short one."

I led her through to the table and pulled out a chair. She hovered for a moment, readjusting her cloak. I sensed that she knew what she wanted to say, but could not tell how it would be received.

"Your father is dying, Sky."

My throat prickled.

"The whole court has been aware of that since he left the throne," I said.

"I do not mean from a long, slow ailment. I mean that he has a month left to live. Perhaps less, if he is unlucky."

We stared at each other, and I saw her fists clench and her back straighten, poised to defend herself.

No one ever asked why my father had begun to show signs of ageing before his time. I didn't ask why. There were certain things you weren't supposed to ask about a man who had held divine right—a certain dance you were meant to perform, ducking and weaving, sidestepping any details that could make you think of him as a man with a heart that could quieten, lungs that could strain, bones that could chip like well-used flutes. *Say nothing about the king.* Everyone knew their steps.

This felt awfully close to slipping out of the dance.

"You can speak safely here, Mistress Browne," I said.

Swallowing, she took a seat. "He forbade us to speak of it—the cooks and the cleaners, the guards, and myself. He did not want word to reach you in the palace. But I have a son myself, Sky, and a daughter nigh on sixteen years. I couldn't bear the thought of a parent dying without saying goodbye to their kin."

My mind whirled, but I didn't want Browne to notice. Walking to the window, I gazed at the courtyard below, taking in the branches of the ghost-oak tree without really seeing them. Their dark forms twisted outward, as if reaching toward me.

"Describe his symptoms," I said.

"He clutches his stomach and writhes. His legs struggle to bear his weight. Sometimes, he wakes in the night and cries out for water, but when we bring it to him, he cannot drink a drop. And…" Browne dropped her voice. "He claims to feel a chill even when the fire is blazing in the hearth: a cruel and bitter chill, which we cannot sense. We wonder if he already feels the grasp of the grave."

I hear that newly-crowned princes have a bad habit of eating the wrong food at parties, MacLyon had said, last night. What about ailing kings who had given up their crown?

"Thank you, Browne," I said, returning and placing a hand upon her shoulder. "You showed courage in bringing me this news."

"If I may ask, Sky… we are all very concerned for he who was king…" *More like concerned for your future employment*, I thought. Father had inspired many emotions in the staff who served under him. Tender concern was not one of them.

"What do you intend to do?" she said.

"I mean to think upon the matter." I smiled, as if we were speaking of highland games. "The evening's not getting any younger. I invite you to lodge in the palace, Mistress Browne. Mistress MacLyon will set you up with a bed and garments and bring you dinner. Meet with me tomorrow, after the rituals, and I'll give you my thoughts."

She rose, bowed, and offered her thanks. She did not linger. Perhaps a woman who had earned a deep scar knew to get out of a noble's chambers before anything interesting could happen. I disliked that thought, just as I disliked the thought of my father writhing, calling out for water, and shivering in his warm chamber: for all the words he had fired at me over the years, he was still my blood. This land was stitched together by the binding threads of blood.

I listened to the door of my suite swing shut.

I could avoid finishing the oatcake, now. And whatever I had told Browne, I had no intention of thinking about her matter until the morning. The air was cold, my stomach still burned with hunger, and I was lonelier than I had been in weeks. If I summoned Aiven, he would ply me with food until I was full.

Was I not a Dannatyne? A prince, to become king when my father died? I was supposed to deny myself nourishment, especially when fear and stress tempted me to indulge—but there were other pleasures to take.

I sucked in a deep lungful of chilly air and walked out, muttering an order to the guards.

Back in my bedchamber, I took off my tartan and looked through my wardrobe for the dressing-gowns at the back. I chose the one with tiny diamonds sewn into the black trim. *Soft-cut highland diamonds. The kind you'll have to trade with the ambassador for Sarleven in return for a parcel of ships*. I didn't want to think about diplomacy, or my duties, or which clan I owed the most favour for digging diamonds out of the cold earth. I didn't want to think about anything except how I looked in the mirror.

For one moment, I wanted to feel beautiful.

The sheer fabric showed everything underneath *very* clearly, and I twirled in front of the glass, testing out the gown with only my white stockings underneath.

It didn't take Rossane long to arrive. He set a bottle of wine down on the table and stared his way down my body, his lips parting in a soft whistle.

"That's quite the ensemble."

"A bit colder than an enserre, but worth it—wouldn't you say?"

He moved to stand before me, his figure coming into the light of the torches and the hearth. The plain shirt he wore guided my attention up to his face. As he placed one hand upon my left hip, his mouth twisted into a wolfish smile.

"I can help you with the cold," he said. "Take that off, and I'll warm you up very thoroughly."

"And if I don't?"

"I'll tear it off with my teeth if I have to."

That brutal smile reminded me of the moment when I had begun to fall: of the reluctant expression on Rossane's face as he waited for someone else to step in. My jaw clenched.

"You know," I said, "I'm Prince Regent now. Not the prince-in-waiting. If a man gives me an order, I can have him whipped on the palace steps for insolence."

"You could throw me in the dungeons and slit my throat, too." Rossane's expression did not flicker. "I suppose a wise man would say that I should be docile in your chambers from now on." He perused my face. "Is that what you want, Dannatyne?"

I ran my gaze over him, from the jutting point of his chin to the hard swell of his biceps. Slowly, I took in the sadistic set to his features.

"No," I said.

He ripped the gown off me and threw it onto the bed. I leaned into him, letting him run his hands down my shoulder blades and the length of my back, feeling his fingers ghost over my hips and move lower. The heat of his palms on my skin made me suck in a breath. I pulled away, prompting a little snarl from Rossane.

Before he could reach for me, I began to lean down. I trailed my face along his shirt front, untying the laces as I went, admiring the thick muscle of his upper body. He smelled like musk-roses. I wanted to smother myself in that scent, but I focused on undoing his kilt instead, folding the tartan and the belt and placing them neatly on my bed.

"Good boy," Rossane murmured.

I was dangerously close to licking his hand, like a dog.

I kept sliding down until my knees hit the stone floor. I could feel the fine material of my stockings rip as I edged closer to him. I ran my hands slowly up the muscle of his thighs, taking my time.

Even though I'd never been one for gossip, I'd overheard the attendants of the bedchamber talking often enough, and I knew that some women disliked doing this. Some of them, the staff said, hated the thought of taking a man into their mouth, especially if they couldn't be sure whether he would gossip about their efforts later. It was whispered that Lady Dairn had created a list of excuses to use on her husband, to protect her reputation.

Perhaps I should have acquired her instinct for self-preservation.

Personally, I wanted nothing more than to suck Rossane's cock, and the thought of him talking about how well I did it made me hasten.

When my lips were halfway down the length of him, I looked up and saw him shiver. Rossane liked being worshipped under any circumstances. Over the course of a dozen or so encounters, I'd noticed that he liked it most of all when I made eye contact, and I held his stare now until he gave a small gasp. He exhaled shakily. I guessed that this was the difference the coronation made—it was probably a whole new experience, having the ruler of the realm blow you in his own suite.

I'd have to be sparing with my glances.

Two fingers worked their way into my hair. A few seconds later, his other fingers followed. Rossane twisted one of my locks hard, sending a thrill through my body, and I wished I could ask him to pull harder: to really make me feel it. I couldn't bring myself to be that shameless. I kept sucking him slowly, using my hands to caress him, and when I glanced up at his face, our gazes met again.

I tried to etch the moment into my mind. I wanted to enjoy this later, when hunger burned in my stomach.

A moment later, he shoved my head down.

Warm pain blazed at the back of my throat. I widened my mouth, trying not to choke. Sliding up, I tried to free myself from the pressure, but Rossane forced my head down again, with both hands this time. I felt his cock abrade my tonsils. The pain was nothing. I could handle pain. But I couldn't get enough air, and for all that I was gagging, I was going to start choking soon.

If I bit down and hurt him, he might strangle me on the

spot. I tried to pull back harder. Two strong hands held me in place.

"Speak up," he said. "I can't hear your orders."

I did the only thing that I could think of. I punched him hard on the thigh.

Rossane swore and let go of my head. I pushed him backward, and he stumbled on the stones. I rose, wiped my mouth, and stared at him. My face must have told him exactly how I felt, for he teetered a little on the spot.

"Did you know that if the Prince Regent chokes to death on your cock, you've committed high treason?"

"Come on, Dannatyne. I was just having fun." He shifted into a low, wheedling tone. "I'd never let it go that far."

"And yet you wanted to show me you could." I was burning with a cold fury. I didn't even try to temper my feelings.

I walked around Rossane in a semi-circle, waiting. He was going to grovel and apologise. He was going to beg my forgiveness.

"You look pretty with your mouth full," he said.

I wasn't cold with anger any more. I was fucking incandescent.

"I want you to call me Prince Regent," I said.

"In public?"

"Right now."

Our eyes met. Rossane gave me a dangerous smile. "You look pretty on your knees, Prince Regent. I hope you don't forget how long you were on your hands and knees, last time—or that you begged me for it."

"Get dressed," I snapped.

Judging by the sulky look on his face, he could see that he had pushed it too far: that even his brand of feral grace wouldn't work on me now. He dressed with the speed of a hare, doing up his shirt laces and belting his kilt.

"Splendid Rock of the Glen." I dripped out each word. "You share every duty with MacArlay now. You know that, don't you?" I circled back around him. "Go and tally the armouries of the allegiant nobles."

"MacArlay's doing that," Rossane said.

I spread my arms in a half-shrug. "Take over. Send MacArlay to me."

"To your chamber?"

I folded my arms and waited. It took a moment for the implication to click into place.

"To your chamber, *Prince Regent*?"

"As I told you." I gazed at him without blinking. "You and MacArlay will be sharing everything."

I relished the look on Rossane's face for a few seconds before closing the door.

I picked up my gown and wrapped it around myself again, staring at the sheer fabric in the mirror. For a moment, I could believe that I was beautiful. Even if I wasn't quite slim enough, I could allow myself to feel like a rightful prince. It helped me forget about the throbbing soreness in my throat, and even about the feeling of gagging—the force of Rossane's hands upon my skull—the struggle to get enough air.

I was calm by the time MacArlay arrived, and I let him peel the gown from me, not with Rossane's speed but with the deliberate slowness of a man who'd just received an unexpected gift. His powerful frame pressed against my chest. I remembered a highland games, once, outside the palace; remembered watching MacArlay's biceps strain as he flung the hammer into the clear sky; remembered how the size of him had frightened me.

"May I?" he said, inclining his head towards the bed.

I nodded, and when he made to lead me, I snatched my hand away. "Carry me, please."

He picked me up as if I were a sack of barley and deposited me on the bed. He gazed at me for a moment, while I was lying on my back, as if waiting for my permission. I turned onto my front and rested my chin against the pillow.

I was glad that I couldn't see his reaction.

"Gently, Prince Regent?" he said, at last.

"No," I murmured.

As he moved on top of me, I pushed back against him with my body, taking him all the way in and forcing myself not to cry. His fingers tugged my hair. I knew that he must have remembered our last encounter, and that he had noticed how I liked it when he pulled my head backwards, as if he owned me.

If the power of his thrusts made me feel weaker, and if the muscle of his arms and thighs made me feel smaller, I didn't say it aloud. If the feeling of his big hands reminded me of Aiven, I kept it firmly to myself. And if I inhaled a lungful of floral scent when he ground me down against the pillow—the smell of fior-chridhe, still lingering unmistakeably on the cloth—I didn't allow myself to indulge in memories. I shouldn't be thinking about my best friend while one of my army commanders was deep inside me. I shouldn't be dwelling on Aiven's gentle manner and the steady grip of his hands.

More to the point, I shouldn't be thinking about the man I had made Star of the Sky in that way, at all.

Five

Aiven

I WAS STROKING the lamb when sunrise broke. As I
trailed my fingers through its cloud-soft wool, the first
rays of dawn bathed me and the little animal together:
gold, orange, and pink washed over our faces. The lamb
bleated in my arms and wriggled closer to my chest. I
kept stroking it while it cried, until suddenly it fell silent
and turned its face upwards, letting the morning gild
its white head. In the silence, I couldn't help smiling. I
supposed that an artist might have said that the moment
was beautiful.

Beautiful. I had heard so many men use that word
to describe Fierre, over the years. Most of them meant
physical beauty, because that was how people understood
that elusive quality which drew their gaze back again and
again; yet that wasn't enough. Fierre wasn't beautiful
because of his body. Not to me, anyway. It was what
animated him that made him so special.

The way he twirled in his enserre. The way he giggled
conspiratorially after doing something below a prince's

duties. The way he frowned when he was assessing himself in a mirror, as if worried he would fail to please everyone. The way he cried when he was upset—a passionate and loud sobbing, the kind most men were afraid to try.

Most of all, I cherished the way he had beamed when he named me as Star, gazing at me alone, as though no one else's opinion mattered.

My mother's voice broke through my thoughts. I looked up to find her striding towards me. In the field behind her, my father dug down with his foot plough, pushing until he turned over a clod.

"How're you coming along with the runty one?"

I held the lamb up, so that my mother could see its peaceful expression. "It won't be making any complaints."

"Unlike your old man." She jerked her head at my father, who was swearing. If the volume of his voice was any guide, he'd just hit a stony patch. "He's been howking around all week with that thing. Beats the horse plough any day."

That was as direct a thank you for buying the foot plough as I would ever get. I smiled and handed the lamb to my mother. "Time for breakfast?"

"Aye, you're raring to get back to that fine palace, I know."

"You *know* very well I'd sooner tend the farm all day with you, and keep dad from dropping that plough on his toe."

She laughed. "I'd take you up on that if it weren't for your fancy new role. It's not every day a Whyte becomes first gentleman to the Sky. Your old man and I said a prayer last night, for the rituals."

"A Whyte?"

"Och, well, a Grian, in your case. But born a Whyte,

and don't you go forgetting it." She tapped the ground with her boot, as if to remind me of the colour of the soil beneath the grass: the white earth for which our family, and so many others, had been named. "Help me with the sacks on the way. Or I'll drop your show-name and call you a Whyte again."

Lifting heavy bags of barley was one of my favourite tasks on the farm, though I didn't let on to my mother. I didn't want her to know how pleased I was to be useful to her. The grey sprinkled in her hair and the white taking over my father's sandy head reminded me that they needed my help more than ever. I carried the barley from beside the fields to the dim recess of our barn, counting the sacks as I did so and reporting the tally to my mother. We trudged back to the farmhouse, depositing the lamb back in its pen along the way, and I felt the pleasant burn from the lifting: the satisfying feeling that came from using my muscles.

My father came in just as I was setting down the girdle-cakes and porridge. "Leaving us early?"

"Now, dad, I wouldn't give up the sight of the sunrise over these hills if I had the choice."

"Aye, that's what I like to hear." He took the ladle from me and served up the porridge. The way that he and my mother could share every job seamlessly, from tilling the fields to cooking and doling out meals, always impressed me. They moved like fingers on the same hand.

"Any message for Fierre, on the day he officially becomes prince?" I said.

My mother frowned. "I thought that was coronation day."

"Ma, I've told you before. The coronation marks the ceremonial transition. The rituals make it law."

"It's all a mouthful of neeps and gravy to me. Just tell him I miss him about the farm. And I've a big bag of potatoes waiting for when he next visits. Eilean Black. His favourite."

I chuckled, and turned to my father. "And you?"

"Don't 'you' me, now, boy. Tell that prince he's not to go stealing you away for too long. I mean it, Aiven." My father looked me in the eye. "He's dear to me, but if he thieves you away once too often, he'll get a skelped behind, courtesy of my right palm."

"I'd like to see you catch him!" My mother laughed. "Boy's as nimble as a river salmon. Eat up, now, Aiven, or you'll be riding on empty stomach. We're not rich in porridge, you know."

We carried on chatting until the last bite was done, and I walked to where Lassie, my dun mare, was tied to a pine trunk. At the foot of the tree, pairs of flowers danced in the breeze. I cupped two of the purple blooms in my fingers, as I did every time before I rode to the palace, savouring their light scent and brilliant hue. I thought about definitions: about the word beautiful, again.

"You'll be needing this."

My father's voice reached me from across the fields.

"For the poor market." He held out a small sack, tied with a sturdy rope. I took it from him and nodded, my fingers brushing his calloused palms as I grasped the offering. Tying the sack onto my saddle, I made to say goodbye, but he pulled me toward him.

"We're proud of you, Aiven. Bursting our sacks with pride."

He wrapped me in a strong embrace.

I gripped him back, nestling my face into his neck for a moment. When was the last time he had held me like this? Five years ago? Or more?

"See that you don't burst any real sacks," I said. "Ma will use your guts for twine to sew them back up."

He laughed, but as I let him go, I glimpsed the tears in his eyes.

Lassie pawed the ground, urging me to get on my way. I guided her slowly along the barley and potato fields, skirting the fertile land. I waved to my father, and to my mother, too, who was standing outside the farmhouse; she always waved until I was out of sight. Once I had ridden out of our farmland, I put a hand to my right eye and was surprised to find it wet. Perhaps my father wasn't the only one whose emotions had suddenly welled.

The sunrise had given way to pastel gold as far as the eye could see, as if the sun were embossing the land especially for me. I loved this time of the morning, before the day was bright, when the goshawks and kites were wheeling in the sky and the corncrakes were rasping from the bushes. Every so often, a rabbit hopped across my path, twitching its nose and taking its time to scamper off. I didn't mind stopping for them. It gave me more time to feel the breeze on my cheeks and breathe in the scent of wild heather.

Not long after the farms, a tiny square emerged at the crossroads of four paths, a stone building rising behind it. I had scarcely slowed Lassie when a gaggle of children descended upon me, shouting my name and stretching their arms towards me.

I swung myself down and untied the sack. One girl grabbed hold of my palm, and I ruffled her hair, prompting giggles from the others. They lined up in turn to receive their gifts: two hard-baked oatcakes and one bannock apiece, prompting whoops and hugs. I wished I had more. Every single time, I wished I had more.

With the poor market behind me, I rode faster. Maybe it was the thought of performing my duties as Star of the Sky for the first time, or maybe it was the thought of seeing Fierre walk out of the ritual chambers, officially a prince, beaming and twirling around. Whatever the case, I reached the forest like a shot, guiding Lassie through the black arms of ghost-oaks and emerging from the cool darkness into the pastel light. We trotted down the winding path to the palace.

Each morning when I left the forest, I knew that I was leaving half of myself behind. My usual twinge of regret didn't arrive today. I rode on without sneaking a glance backward or trying to imagine the backdrop of the fields behind the ghost-oaks. The path narrowed in the final stretch to the palace, and where it ran alongside a low stone wall, I dismounted, leading Lassie behind me; I wasn't about to risk bad luck on the day of the rituals by riding a horse along the Old Kings' Road.

A red-faced woman walked toward me, carrying a basket of cooked fish. "How d'ye do, Master Grian?"

"Cheery enough. But you know me, Unar. No time to be scunnered." I saw her smile, and was glad that I'd used *scunnered* instead of *discontent*. I'd chew through a mouthful of horse-trodden hay before I became embarrassed to talk like a farmer. "And yourself? Disposing freely of trout, now, are you?"

"Orders of the new Prince Regent." She beamed. "We're to take any spare food from the kitchens to the poor, instead of throwing it out. And I can't say I'm sorry about it." She gazed down at the trout. "There's plenty who could use a bit more breakfast."

Fierre, I thought. *Already making me proud.*

I waved to Unar and led Lassie onward. Several more

people passed me on the way up to the palace: a royal messenger, a cloth merchant, and a doctor's assistant, and I greeted them all by name, inquiring after their health. Names were useful. Once you were on a first-name basis, you could get to know someone better, and once you knew them better, you could figure out the context for their deeds.

Context was everything to a Master of Compliance. Were they purloining cloth to make a fancy new doublet for an upcoming ball, or were they taking it for a blanket to keep their children warm in a draughty hovel? Were they permitting a visitor by accident, or were they helping their friends to slip into the palace for a night of card games? Were they clean out of barley in the store-room because they had miscalculated, or did they have the kind of keen mind that would submit a wrong tally because they were covering something up?

I was thinking about sums and checks, about names and personalities, as I reached the palace. Sunstone walls rose high above me, emerging from a slab of raw black rock: a reminder that clay and soil, peat and root held us all in their power. Even kings prayed for the mercy of the land when they built their homes, and I had been taught in the village school that Eilean-òir's land hummed with a magic that you defied at your own peril.

Greeting the guards, I took Lassie to her usual post in the small stable and entered the palace. The eastern staff door buzzed with gossip. I elbowed my way through the kitchen-hands and attendants to reach the wooden door further down the corridor that marked the entrance to my cramped office; I tried not to notice the way my body relaxed at the familiar smell of ink, or the way I eased myself into my chair to check over my final reports.

The place was like home to me—a smaller home, in which I could do my bit for the realm, and within whose walls I had conducted interviews and offered second chances, working to set things right with the accounts and the law, and above all, with the people affected by them.

MacLyon knocked on the door within the hour. I handed my reports to her.

"Thank you, Master Grian," she said.

"You don't sound overjoyed by my promotion."

"Are you sure you want to be Star?" She jerked her head at the reports. "I'll never find another man whose time at the counting house made him kinder, not stricter."

"Aye, you will. I'm not one of a kind, like a magic pearl."

"I think it's precisely because you are that Prince Dannatyne chose you. You don't think it's funny that the moment he gains power, he gives you a much fancier position with full access to his resources?" She sighed. "If the old king had retired as soon as his health started to decline, I'd wager you wouldn't have been Master of Compliance for more than a week. But it would've been my loss." This time, her sigh was more resigned. "Well, you'd better put these on."

She whistled, and a boy scurried in and handed her a pile of gold. Or so it seemed to me, at first, until she held it up and I realised that it was a silken garment, of the kind that only princes and kings wore. Beneath the golden enserre, I spied a pair of golden sandals. MacLyon handed both garment and shoes to me.

"Don't go squalling about it, now," she said. "You've no choice. The Star of the Sky must wear an enserre to match the prince, for this ceremony—and since you're a Star, you must shine like one. He's a symbol today, especially when he greets the people. You're to be a symbol too."

"I'm not in line for the throne, mistress. I've no idea how to tie an enserre."

"You're a smart man, Grian. You can learn quickly." She shooed the boy out again. "You've got a quarter-hour until you're due at the ritual bathhouse. See that you look sharp."

The door closed behind her before I could reply.

I set down the sandals and gazed at the golden fabric of the enserre. This was all wrong. Enserres weren't meant for farm boys who hefted sacks of barley around. The Sky of Eilean-òir wore his garment to remind the world that he was delicate, beautiful, and holy—three words that no one would apply to me unless they'd been smoking the choicest herbs from a midnight market. Besides, I wasn't *meant* to look like Fierre. The whole point of the Sky's look was that it placed him above the rest of us.

Emulate him, and you were tilting at the throne.

But Fierre had chosen me as Star, had he not? He knew that I had no background in politics and no noble blood. He must have wanted me to stand by his side, as I had done all my life, and I couldn't fail him because I was afraid of being wrapped in a long piece of shiny cloth.

Before I could attempt to tie the enserre, another knock interrupted me. The burly form of Laird MacArlay pushed through the door.

"Do you know he's making Rossane and I share duties?" He strode across the room and stopped before me. "Take *turns*?"

This seemed a strange question from someone who had just been publicly appointed as joint Rock of the Glen.

"Everyone knows," I said.

"He made you Star of the Sky. Are you part of this too?"

"Part of what, my laird?"

MacArlay gave a snort of frustration. "Want me to fucking spell it out, do you? Are you the third turn?"

Something was going on. I could guess what. But for a moment, I took in the way that MacArlay's eyes were searching my face, and the unsettled look on his countenance.

"I might be," I said.

"Stirring fucking saints alive. I thought it was strange he picked you. Listen, Star of the Sky—twinkle-toes," he hissed, nodding down at the golden sandals, "just remember. Whatever he's giving you now, some of us have been working at this for longer than you. We've earned our prize."

I couldn't think of anything that the rich lairds of this realm had earned that I had not worked harder for myself. Resentment, maybe. Or contempt. Yet as I met MacArlay's rock-hard stare, I had the feeling that I knew exactly what he meant.

"I'll bear that in mind," I said.

"You'd do well to." MacArlay leaned close enough that I could feel his breath on my cheek. "I'm going to beat Rossane and have that sweet little cherry tart for myself. You should pick the winning side."

He stormed out, his boots clopping loudly in the corridor until he was out of earshot. I drew a deep breath. Not only could I guess what MacArlay thought he could obtain from Fierre, I had a sinking suspicion that he'd been obtaining it last night.

After an encounter with an angry MacArlay, the task of putting on an enserre seemed less daunting. Mine didn't come with a ceremonial cape—perhaps they were worried I'd damage any billowing parts, or perhaps only Fierre was worth the price of the extra silk. I managed to wind the fabric correctly after four tries, putting the two strings at the waist to good use, and I tied the bow at the back to finish, hoping that I didn't look as ridiculous as I felt. Like Fierre's enserres, the garment came to mid-thigh. The golden sandals were a much simpler matter, their straps crossing over twice and then tying behind the ankle. They were made for the bathhouse, I realised—they weren't meant to emphasise the shape of my legs, like Fierre's knee-high straps.

I gave my chamber a last glance, pushing down any sentimental urges.

Today was the grand day. The official day. I needed to make sure that it all went smoothly and stick by Fierre's side as he greeted the people. The rituals alone weren't the end of it; he'd never met a crowd of commoners before, and I suspected he wouldn't be prepared. And I didn't like the way he'd collapsed at the coronation.

I would be ready, I told myself, if anything happened.

I walked swiftly to the ritual bathhouse, but as I neared the door to the antechamber, my feet slowed. Voices echoed off the walls. The word *prince* drifted down the corridor. I slipped into a nook a little way down from the antechamber, poked my head out, and caught a glimpse of a group of guards standing close together.

An old maxim declared that staff should be seen, not heard. My time as Master of Compliance had taught me that it was better to be neither—especially if you wanted to learn something interesting. I pressed my body flat against the side of the nook and strained my ears, waiting for any mention of Fierre.

Six

Aiven

"LET'S HAVE A little bet, lads. Which part do you think he's doing right now?"

The voice of the guard sounded low and gravelly.

"I'll take that bet," another guard said. "There're three rituals, aren't there? Physical inspection – by a doctor. Soul inspection – by a priest. Then bathing in the ritual bath, and being dressed, before the Star presents him to the people."

"You forgot the first part, you daft loon. The bit before all of that."

"What bit?" The second man's voice rose in bemusement.

"The prince has to confess all his past lovers to the priest. That way, he can be presented all brand new and anointed as a virgin, to love and serve the people."

"That explains why he's taking so long." Raucous laughter, and the sound of someone slapping their thigh. "We'll be here all day, lads. Prince Dannatyne's knees will get sore."

The laughter that followed this was so loud that it filled the corridor, and my fists clenched. I knew that there was no hate in their banter—that they were just low-paid men, looking to have a good time during their long and boring wait—but I wanted to leap out and chastise them, all the same. I reminded myself that a disruption might cause a delay for Fierre.

"Wouldn't you like to have a go, though?" A third guard spoke, this time, and I heard the wistful note in his voice.

"The likes of you can only dream of kissing his pretty ankles."

"I'd be charmed enough by that." The third guard sighed. "He's the most beautiful man I ever clapped eyes on."

"Aye, a true Dannatyne. No one can doubt it."

"Did you see him at the coronation, gliding across the platform? All smiles and poise in that pink enserre? I tell you, it was like a dream. Like a waking dream."

A moment of silence followed as they reflected on this, perhaps calling up their own memories. I took the opportunity to walk out from the nook and make my way over. The guards straightened, and several of them looked nervously at each other.

However I might look in my golden outfit, my new title had not escaped anyone.

Or maybe they had all witnessed my tussle with Crawshall.

"Good morning," I said.

The guards echoed my greeting warily. We were saved the awkwardness of further conversation by the opening of the door and the emergence of MacLyon.

She beckoned me in. As I followed her through the door, passing from the corridor to the golden glow of a candlelit world, my nerves jangled inside me. I'd been all over the palace in my ten years working here, and I knew the stables and corridors inside out, but I'd never entered the ritual chambers. It was just like MacLyon had said. Fierre might've kept me close enough for our friendship to flourish, one conversation and one stomach-clutching laugh at a time, but his father would never have allowed him to throw a man who bore the name of Whyte into the royal orbit.

Only once the crown sat on Fierre's brow could he cross that line.

And that had been scarcely two days ago. No one had told me exactly what to do today, or how the final stage of the rituals would unfold, and I felt sure that I was going to put a foot wrong, somehow—that I would move out of turn or speak at the wrong moment, and ruin Fierre's most special moment.

MacLyon crossed the round antechamber and seized a bundle of cloth from a chair. When I made to touch it, she dumped the whole bundle into my arms.

"For the Prince Regent," she said. "He's in the ritual bath now, and I expect he'll be there a few minutes longer. You've enough time to practice the shoulder wrapping." She eyed my right shoulder, where my enserre hung slightly loose.

"I think you mean to give these to the staff, mistress. To the attendants of his chamber, perhaps?"

"This isn't a morning routine, Grian. These are the ceremonial rituals of the Sky of Eilean-òir, and you'll dress him yourself."

"*I'll* dress him?"

"Are you a parrot, man?" She took in my expression. "You didn't know, I gather? Usually, the Star of the Sky

70

knows their duties; but then, usually, the Star is a laird. I didn't think…" She sighed. "Well, you've proven you can tie an enserre. It'll be all right. There'll only be the retinue watching, and the priest, and the doctor. And myself. It'll be quite a small party."

I gaped. I couldn't speak any more. The thought of wrapping Fierre's clothes around him in front of an audience was even more horrible than the thought of doing it in private. I stared down at the gold ribbon and the sky-blue enserre in my arms, and I was about to ask MacLyon a question when she marched off into the main bathhouse. "Wait here," she called out.

The antechamber suddenly seemed cavernous, and deadly silent, as if it were judging me. I picked up the gold ribbon. Where did it go? Was I supposed to drape it over the top of the enserre once I was done winding the cloth, or was the ribbon meant to tie around Fierre's waist like a sash? Did it go in his hair? Maybe I was supposed to wrap it around his upper arm, like a bracelet…

I wondered how MacLyon felt about overseeing this. I wondered how she felt about being permitted to do it. Women did what the law said it was okay for them to do, my mother had often observed, in a voice that made her opinion clear. It was acceptable for women to be cooks, attendants, and seamstresses—all the things that kept a noble's personal world running. It was permitted for them to be farmers, cobblers, artisans, and ferrywomen— all the things that kept a noble's wider world running. Everyone knew that it was okay for them to be priests— how better to elevate a man as king? How better to raise men as the inheritors of estates? How better to draw up the lines of Eilean-òir than to have both sexes gripping the brush?

What better wisdom than to have women announce their own submission?

MacLyon did plenty of running around after her prince. I wondered if she resented Fierre.

I wondered if she resented *me*.

"All right," MacLyon said, opening the door again. "We're ready for you."

I drew a deep breath. Slowly, I crossed the antechamber, my steps echoing around me. As I passed through the doorway MacLyon whispered into my ear: "Best of luck."

Beams of sun crossed the marble floor of the ritual bathhouse, falling from the high windows in the domed ceiling to meet at the centre of the room, vibrating with warmth. Behind the pool of light, a group of people waited before a ramp that led up to a bath: a deep creation of black stone with a small ledge for climbing in and out.

I knew it by reputation. The ritual bath looked less wondrous than I had expected from gossip amongst the staff. I searched for some special feature, some jewel or embellishment on the sides. I found none. Moonstone didn't need any decoration, for everyone in the realm knew how expensive it was to purchase from the quarries—I could hear the bitterness in my own thoughts. The candles flickered on their stands around the bath, giving the black moonstone a sheen.

I edged around the blaze of sun and made my way to the group. They introduced themselves in murmurs, too soft for my unrefined ears to pick up, but I knew the faces before me. The doctor was a quiet man, well-reputed for his role as the practicing doctor to Fierre's father—Galar—that was his name, I remembered. He smiled gently at me and made space for me to join him.

On his far side, a hard-faced woman in a long robe greeted

me, and I recognised her as the priest, though she was a higher rank of official than the priest at the coronation—one of the few high priests allowed to conduct the rituals. She gave me a minimal nod.

A laird and a minor noble stood on the other side of the ramp. With them were a poet, who I expected was tasked with composing a song, and an artist, who I hoped wasn't going to use my attempt at dressing Fierre for a painted scene. I endeavoured to return their smiles.

"Lucky eight," MacLyon said, as she joined me.

Had Fierre accepted that all these people would be watching him? If I felt nervous, how on earth did *he* feel about the prospect of climbing out naked before an audience?

"Indeed, the number of god and his angels," Dr Galar said. "Speaking of which… Your Eminence, might it be time?"

The priest gave a brusque nod and began to climb the ramp. We all watched her silently. She murmured something in the direction of the bath and I saw Fierre's delicate hands grip the sides, before he pulled himself into a crouching position. He rose so suddenly that I almost gasped aloud. The priest descended the ramp again, leaving us with a clear view.

And what a view it was. Every part of him was slick with water, droplets clinging to his hair and ears. His thighs and calves shone. He stood out in relief, even in the dim back of the bathhouse, and as I looked at him I felt my insides shift.

He was slimmer than I liked. A little worn-looking, too, from the recent days of fasting on top of years of careful restriction, and I wished for a moment that he had never been born a prince. I wished that I had met a fellow farm boy on that day he came to my parents' house, and that we had grown to be friends by ploughing the fields together, happily eating fallen apples side by side.

And yet there was so much of him that was more than his size—so much that spilled out of the confines of his role. As I looked at him, I saw exactly who Fierre Dannatyne was. His eyes sparked with the vibrancy of a man who loved to laugh. There was no shield in his gaze, and in that very absence of a defensive barrier, I felt the power of the yielding tenderness that had lured so many men to want him with a frightening sense of entitlement. Unlike them, I understood who the prince was as a person; I understood who he was as a friend.

It was that friend who stood before me now, entirely naked.

I was meant to be calm, I told myself. Steady. Strong. But my body was rearranging its pieces and setting them in new positions, as if everything I felt had solidified into an awful, terrible truth.

I *had* to hold it down. Push it down, and press it, and knead it.

I watched Fierre descend the ramp. He smiled brightly at all of the retinue before turning his gaze on me. "Thanks for coming, Aive."

As if I could just shirk the ceremonial rituals like a farmhand slouching off to the village! I felt a warm surge inside my chest when he smiled at me.

"Let the Sky of Eilean-òir show his majesty in the light," the priest declared.

She led the way over to the centre of the room, where the sunbeams poured down in a wash of gold, converging in one spot. Fierre followed her, and the others began to trail after him. "Stand just outside the light," MacLyon whispered to me.

She needn't have bothered. The others were already encircling the pool of sunlight, keeping a short distance from it, leaving an obvious gap for me. I took up my position between MacLyon and Dr Galar. Together, we waited as Fierre stepped into the circle of brilliant sun.

The light gilded him at once; turned him into a statuette from face to feet; revealed the contours of his waist and the lines of his pelvis. It took a moment for my eyes to adjust. I hated how the reminders of fasting were written everywhere on his body, so I guided my gaze up to his face, and felt my breath drain and my chest tighten; I should have been observing the scene calmly, but I almost forgot to inhale.

The way he looked right now… with all the grace and elegance of a Dannatyne king, that posture that made the people believe he was an instrument of god, but with a softness and vulnerability quite unlike his father's manner… I knew I was not gazing upon a transformed Prince Regent, but upon the same boy who had brought me ten sacks of oats on the back of a mule cart the year my parents' farm was robbed. I was looking at the same boy I had comforted when we were eight years old, after he had stumbled and scraped his knee while sprinting. The same boy who had sobbed on my shoulder until my shirt was wet through. The boy who leaned on me, and who always let me lean on him.

As I looked at the boy before me, and saw him as a man again—twenty-six years of age, the same as me—the truth that I had been trying to ignore surged through me and burst into my mind.

"Let the Sky of Eilean-òir be dried!"

The priest's voice echoed off the stone. My own realisation echoed in my mind, but I forced myself not to focus on it.

Dr Galar hurried forward with a vast tartan blanket in the pink-and-white colours of the Dannatyne clan. He wrapped it around Fierre, who patted himself down and handed the blanket back with no hint of discomfort. I glanced around at the rest of the retinue, and wondered if any of them were undergoing the same strain as I was to avoid staring open-mouthed; they all seemed to be gawking at Fierre's body, but it was his smile that worked upon me. It was subtle and moderate, so unlike his usual grin, yet tinged with the promise of warmth: a fire that had just begun to crackle at the edge of a hearth.

"Let the Sky of Eilean-òir be dressed by his Star, as befits his state!"

Before I could step forward, MacLyon grabbed my arm. "The ribbon goes first. Break it into three pieces, and do as the priest says," she whispered. "Kneel behind him until she tells you to rise."

The ribbon went *first*.

That meant that the ribbon went on Fierre's naked body.

That also meant that I had to tie the ribbon on Fierre's naked body right here, right now. It was fine. Those two facts were completely fine.

I felt as if someone had struck me in the head and left my ears ringing. I edged forward.

Fierre's expression brightened as I drew near. I hadn't seen him look so happy all morning. I followed MacLyon's instruction and moved around to kneel behind him, laying the sky-blue cloth on the floor and lifting up the ribbon, then folding it into three even lengths. The golden cloth resisted my force at first, but after brief contest between myself and the ribbon, it broke and broke again, until I had three smaller ribbons.

It was unnerving, completing my task with the stares of the retinue upon me. Judging by the priest's silence, I hadn't erred. All the same, I was glad when she spoke.

"Let the Sky's right ankle be bound in cloth of gold!"

Suddenly, I was aware of Fierre's body just inches from my face. I had been focused on tearing the ribbon cleanly, but now, I concentrated on looking downward, not looking straight ahead to where the curves of Fierre's buttocks filled my eyeline.

Determinedly, I focused on his ankle. I wrapped the first piece of ribbon around the narrowest part of the ankle, slowly winding the cloth until it came to an end and tying a bow. My fingers brushed his skin as I worked. How was his ankle so fine and so soft? For a moment, I thought about kissing it, making an oath of fealty with my mouth, but I stayed still, kneeling a tiny distance behind him. I wasn't completely mad.

"I bless the lowest place on your body, Sky. Here I name you friend and guide to the lowest in this realm, protector of the poor. Now let the Star bind your waist in cloth of gold, to wrap the midpoint of your being," the priest declared.

I leaned upward, reaching around Fierre's waist and winding the ribbon until it came to an end behind his back. The size of his waist worried me. If I'd been winding the ribbon around my own middle, I would have made no more than one circle, but I wrapped it around Fierre with plenty of ribbon to spare. For a moment I wished that I could shout at the priest: scream at the top of my lungs that if her religion demanded this from him, it wasn't worth it. My fingers slipped for a moment as I tied a large bow on Fierre's back—was I sweating?

"Here I bless the centre of your body and name you the

centre of this realm, the beating heart of Eilean-òir, the place from which its justice and truth will come. Now let the Star rise and stand before you. Let the Star bind your neck in cloth of gold."

I wound the final ribbon around Fierre's neck very slowly, making sure that I didn't exert too much pressure. He didn't make a sound, nor move an inch. I walked around behind him to tie the bow at the back of his neck, then returned to face him once more. Standing with gold ribbons tied around his neck, waist, and ankle, he looked even more like a statue—an alluringly decorated statue—but then he grinned, and the statue came to life.

"Nice job, Aive," he whispered. "Sorry I forgot to tell you about the trimmings."

I searched for the right reply, but the priest interrupted.

"Here I bless your neck and head and name you the head of this realm, the mind of Eilean-òir, the one from whom our wisdom and values flow." A long pause followed, in which I wondered if I was supposed to do something. "Let the Star of the Sky inspect you, and kiss the place below each ribbon," the priest said.

I shot a glance at MacLyon. She jerked her head towards Fierre, giving me a what-are-you-waiting-for look.

Oh god, I thought. *Please don't let me think about how he looks right now. Please don't let me think anything at all.*

Tentatively, I bent down and kissed the skin of Fierre's ankle, a half-inch below the golden ribbon that encircled it so handsomely. That soft skin felt just as I had expected, like silk itself, but it was cold, too. How was his body so cold? I had felt the skin of starved animals during our more desperate years on the farm, but those sheep usually came over cold suddenly, in a steep decline. Fierre seemed to exist in a perpetual state of lowered temperature, like a lamb that had learned it would never be admitted to the barn.

Slowly, I brought my head up to Fierre's waist. I couldn't avoid looking at everything along the way. As Fierre watched me, I wondered if my blush painted my cheeks, or if the blaze of sunlight had obscured it.

I kissed the skin just below Fierre's navel. It felt just as soft as his ankle, but my mind was fully occupied with trying not to lean too far against him and brush him below the waist. Once the kiss was done, I rose and faced him. The inches of height difference between us must have been blatantly obvious, for I had to bend down to place the last kiss below his collarbone. Here, too, I felt the coldness of his body, and the fine texture of his skin, like very thin paper that could be ripped with one tug. I didn't like how far that skin stretched to cover the bone.

"And now," the priest called out, "the garment of state!"

Saints be dazzled. I had entirely forgotten about the enserre. To my relief, it was still intact on the floor where I had left it, having somehow avoided trampling as I tied the ribbons. I picked it up now and unfolded the sky-blue cloth.

As MacLyon had noted before, I'd learned how to fasten an enserre, but trying it out upon myself in private was entirely different to garbing Fierre before an audience. Every eye seemed to burn into me as I crossed the cloth over and around Fierre's body and tied the strings behind his back. At last, it was done, and I eyed my handiwork: the sky-blue garment set off his dark hair and eyes, bringing out their depth through its bright contrast. He was born to wear colour, I thought.

"Now for the protecting of the Sky's feet!" the priest announced.

MacLyon scurried forward, placed a pair of gold sandals at my toes, and scurried away. Where in the dim recesses of the room had she been hiding those? I picked them up and examined their long straps. Not allowing myself to hesitate, I held out the left sandal before Fierre, and he placed his foot into it. I nearly messed up the crossing-over of straps, but I managed to wind them around and tie them neatly just below his knee, repeating the process for the right sandal, making a pattern that reminded everyone of his delicate beauty.

As I rose, I made the mistake of glancing upward. My position afforded me a view directly up Fierre's enserre. Somehow, it felt more shocking than when I'd knelt behind his naked body; an enserre was supposed to remind you that the prince was out of bounds, showing only a swathe of thigh.

"All kneel," the priest intoned.

We lowered ourselves quickly. The priest recited a prayer for health, long life, and peace, which seemed to go on for an eternity, though perhaps it was the drone of her voice that made it dull. She led the way out of the bathhouse when she was done, and Dr Galar and the rest of the retinue followed in pairs. I made to walk after them, but MacLyon nudged me.

"The Prince Regent has requested that you walk with him."

She bustled off before I could say a word.

I turned and found Fierre approaching, his face unreadable. He took my hand in his. After a moment, he squeezed my palm. "Was I terrible?"

"You did an excellent job of standing still while I did all the work."

"You're making fun of me."

"Never." I smiled. "You look every inch the prince, Fierre. But you would anyway, whether you'd been bathed and dressed up or not."

"You always know what to say." He squeezed my hand again. "As soon as I stepped out of that bath, Aive, I felt everyone's eyes upon me, and all of a sudden… I knew where every inch of fat was on my stomach and thighs, on my arms, even on my face. I was this horrible, disgusting, fleshy thing. The sunlight exposed every single flaw. But then you knelt and fastened my ribbons, and you didn't look at me funny or make me feel that I was just a body: just a sack of flesh to so many people. I knew I'd get through it." He let go of my hand and hooked his arm through mine. "Let's do it, Aive. Let's go and greet the people."

As he walked out of the bathhouse and into the antechamber, a wave broke inside me, and I knew two things with absolute clarity.

One was the same revelation that I had experienced when he stepped into the pool of radiant sun on the bathhouse floor, the thing I had repressed because it was too searing to contemplate, the sort of realisation that could tear your guts in two.

I was in love with Fierre Dannatyne.

I had always been in love with him, but I had only realised now that my passion was never going to fade. It would flare brighter and higher, showing me no mercy until I was charred.

The other revelation was simpler, but more painful to face. It rose inside me in a new tide, sweeping every speck of hope out to sea, and it was driven by the words he had just spoken. *Just a sack of flesh to so many people.*

He could never know how I felt.

Seven

Fierre

THEY CAME CARRYING baskets, boots, and belts—wearing homespun cloaks, plain white shirts, and patched-up kilts—walking with a limp, a soft step, or a stride. They knelt on the grass of the palace winter-garden in front of the rows of pink and white roses. They placed the fruits of their trade before them, and as I looked down at their offerings, I thought that the whole procedure had a votive quality. A woman at the front of the group of commoners whispered something to herself, and I wondered if it was a prayer.

"Are you sure they'll like me?"

Aiven put his hand over mine and rubbed my palm gently. "They're going to love you. Look at the way they gaze at you, Fierre. You're the only reason they're here."

"I haven't earned it," I whispered. "It's not real love, to love a prince. They'd look the same way at anyone wearing this enserre."

There were papers I should've begun drafting. Laws I should've been researching, to address the conditions in the countryside. But every time I thought about the smarmy words I'd receive from the lairds when they inevitably declined to help, I found myself wondering if it wouldn't be better to focus on what I *could* control. Or at least, what I *should* be able to control. My gaze dropped down to my stomach, tracing the shape of it.

"You think they don't know the real you?" Aiven let go of my hand. "Then show them who you are."

I looked across at him. He gave a small jerk of his head towards the group in the winter-garden.

I took the first step slowly, as if I was stepping out of the ritual bath again. My body seemed to remember its vigour after a few steps, and I faced the crowd with a smile, gesturing to them to rise. The artisans and tradespeople held out their gifts, watching me as I moved along their lines, and I greeted an old woman in a cloak who pressed her thatched basket into my hands and informed me that she had made it doubly strong for her prince. A bearded man presented me with a handful of horseshoes, which I slipped into the basket, thanking him for his hard work. A serious looking brother and sister team handed me a pair of leather boots and explained how they had hammered in the soles together and chosen the most durable cord for the laces. All these people, labouring away in the cities and towns. All these people, fashioning their best items for me.

"What's your name?" I asked a tall man, after he had passed me a leather belt. An engraving of two prancing deer glinted on its pewter buckle.

"Tavish, Sky."

"And do you enjoy your vocation, Tavish?"

"I don't know about vocation, or a'that." He smiled nervously. "But it's my pride to carry on my father's work, god rest his soul, and to serve the people of my village."

Don't know about vocation. I was careful not to voice my thoughts on that. "Was your father a good man?"

"Six days out of seven, Sky. As they say."

Rather the reverse of mine, then. I smiled, pretending I knew the saying. How many casual phrases did the common people have? I wondered how Aiven would respond if I asked him to teach me some of them. Would he laugh at me?

"Tell me more about yourself, Tavish. What are your hopes for the future?"

"Well, Sky, it's my goal to open a shop in Coldcross, the bigger village north of us, if I can find some apprentices willing to work for me…"

We talked easily of leather and fabric, until I noticed a blonde woman a little way along watching us, and I thanked Tavish for the Dannatyne buckle and moved on to her. It was supposed to be quick, this ritual of meeting the people, but I found each conversation so fascinating that I couldn't hurry. By the time I finished, Aiven was hovering at the edge of the winter-garden, eyeing me. The group of commoners beamed as I gave them a bow, and MacLyon swooped in to escort them away. I realised that Aiven had been right: they *did* love me. They wanted to press their gifts upon me. Even though I was no longer a hallowed statue but a man who spoke and listened, they cared what I thought of them.

You will be slender like a deer, my tutor's voice reminded me. *Your body tells them who you are.*

But hadn't every one of these people looked me in the eyes?

"You've got company," Aiven murmured.

On the steps of the palace, a gaggle of figures in clan tartans stood glossed by the mid-morning sun. I counted seven lairds.

"Not the kind who brings crafted belts." I sighed. "Though they're always crafting something."

They closed in as I made to enter the palace, jostling to get near me, and Laird Kinnaid emerged as the winner, drawing near my right side. Aiven did his best to fend him off, but Kinnaid ignored his remarks about rest and peace and pressed close to my elbow.

"Honoured Sky, would you favour me with a chat this afternoon? As Chief of Diplomacy, I have matters I would raise."

"I'd be happy to speak with you tomorrow," I said.

"But the ambassadors—"

"Will wait another day." I stopped, and smiled tightly. "Give them a seven-course dinner and pick their brains for the dispositions and desires of their rulers. Use your time well, my laird."

Kinnaid bowed and smiled, withdrawing. The sun turned his red hair into a fiery blaze as he walked away. Voices swelled on my left as several lairds petitioned me at once, and I tried to dispense with Cairnross, Dalston, and Locharnott before Aiven steered me through the entrance and led me into the western corridor, pushing the doors shut behind us.

He bolted them quickly. A clamour of voices came through from the other side of the wood, and Aiven shot a glance at me. I held his gaze for a long time.

We burst into laughter at exactly the same moment.

"I think I need to get away from here," I said.

"If I'd been starving myself for a stupid ceremony, I'd take a break, too. At least until tomorrow."

"Stupid?"

"I'm sorry." Aiven looked mortified. "I didn't mean that. I know you've been labouring away to satisfy the court. And I'm honoured by what you've made me."

"It's all right, Aive." I detatched my hand from his. "I think you make a point. No work until tomorrow sounds like paradise."

A thump sounded on the door. I sighed.

"Let's go somewhere they won't find us."

"Where?" Aiven said.

I grinned. "Somewhere you know well."

OUR HORSES BURST out from the forest at a canter, leaving a dark world of ghost-oaks and brambles behind us. The fields rolled on ahead like golden cloth, stitched with the black and white thread of sheep, the pink and yellow trim of roses, and the brilliant blue buttons of tiny lakes. I could almost pretend that we were boys again and I was riding to Aiven's family while father was in court, free of my running and dancing regime for a few blissful hours. This time, however, I had to ignore the clopping of four large stallions behind us. My royal escort seemed to have chosen the loudest horses in the stables.

There was no fence to bound the farm we were approaching, nor even a hedge. Every farmer in the countryside knew their land's borders, Aiven had told me, because they used natural landmarks to separate their territory. An ancient oak here marked the line where one farm gave way to another, and a dip in the ground there signified the back of the fields. When it came to animals wandering, farmers negotiated the exchange, but incidents were few and far apart; most farmers grazed their sheep and cows close to their farmhouse and kept the younglings in pens.

"Couldn't the farmers steal from each other at night?" I had asked Aiven.

"They could. But they get the jitters just thinking about it. In the old times, farmers chopped off the right hand off anyone who thieved their crops or sheep." He'd smiled at me. "There was no such thing as jail, back then. People up here still remember the old ways."

"I imagine most farmers wouldn't feel sorry for a thief who ended up with a stump for a hand." How many nobles had spoken to my father, over the years, about the savagery of farmers?

And yet I couldn't help wondering how angry I'd be if I had little food to spare. Who taxed the peasants, after all? Who made sure that there was just enough to survive, and never enough to prosper?

How much of that *savagery* was the savagery of the crown's laws?

"It's more than that, though," Aiven had added. "My grandmother says that if you do wrong by a neighbour, the devil will strike you down. Some claim he haunts these fields, waiting."

There was no sign of the devil today, but as we tied up our horses in front of the farmhouse, a familiar figure strode out, beaming from ear to ear.

"Rhonar!" I cried.

Aiven's mother picked me up and whirled me around, set me down, and wrapped me in a hug. Her arms smelled comfortingly of sheep.

"Beautiful boy. Are they feeding you enough?"

"I'll let you know if I have any complaints."

"You tell me quickly, mind. I'll be up at the castle, swinging my skillet before you can say *aim*."

"Any warrior would give in to you." I ran my hand over her firm shoulders.

"Let me make you some potato stew," a steady voice

said. I looked up to find Aiven's father stepping out from the doorway. The white in Finlaye's hair gleamed brilliantly in the sun, but when he passed into the shade, I glimpsed pockets of the same sandy blonde strands that covered Aiven's pate.

"I couldn't tax you with boiling potatoes on a summer day." I beamed, to show that this was not an insult. "Just a bite of an oatcake would do, Finlaye." I turned to Aiven's mother. "Would it trouble you both if Aiven and I spent some time in your fields?"

"Not in the slightest," Rhonar said, quickly.

"Well…" Finlaye said.

"Finlaye could use a break from that foot plough at last."

"Hmm." Finlaye glowered at her.

We walked slowly around the side of the farmhouse and into the first field. Sheep turned their dark faces towards us but didn't deign to wander over, keeping to their soft grass. A few rams baaed at me. I baaed back.

"Honestly," Aiven muttered.

"Can't let them go around thinking they're superior to me. They'll start demanding a place at court, next." I skipped down the narrow path to the next field. "Why do your parents keep the white sheep further away?"

"They're worth less at market. Everyone wants one of the rarest sheep in Eilean-òir." He jerked his head back at the black-faced flock, who were still eyeing us.

"I would've thought people would be less inclined to eat our national animals."

"Then you don't know people."

I thrust my tongue out at him and walked down to the pen a little further along. A few lambs were sleeping in the centre. Aiven climbed into the pen and scooped up the smallest lamb, carrying it back out. He cuddled the animal to his chest as we made our way to the spreading oak that rose at the border of the grazing land, where the barley fields began. I sat down at the base of the oak and Aiven followed suit, resting his back against the trunk beside me.

"I'll have you know I'm rather miffed." I shot a glance at him. "I thought we were going to talk alone, and here you are, bringing company."

Aiven stroked the lamb's head. "This little girl's been restless for a while. She needs some love whenever she can get it."

"Did something happen to make her jumpy?"

"We think her father's rejection hurts her. The ewe died during the birth, and the ram… well, you know how rams are." I assumed an expression which suggested I did. "What this little one needs is someone to give her warmth—any warmth, she'll take it. I try to comfort her when I can, otherwise she won't grow up strong."

I wiped my eyes. I wasn't sure at what point tears had begun to trickle down my cheeks, but I felt the wetness now. Aiven caught sight of me, and his face fell.

"I'm so sorry, Fierre. I didn't think…"

"Perhaps we're more alike than we know, people and animals." I smiled weakly. "I think father would have made a good ram." I drew a deep breath and exhaled, little by little. "That's why I wanted to talk to you, actually. I had a messenger from the old palace last night."

I told him all of it, then: Browne's report on father's sickness, her fear of a rapid decline, even the very phrases she had used. *He clutches his stomach and writhes. His legs struggle to bear his weight… We wonder if he already feels the grasp of the grave.*

89

When I was done, Aiven's frown had deepened to a sea trench. He stroked the lamb in silence for a long moment.

"I've known you ever since you visited our farm as a boy. Do you remember that day?"

"I could hardly forget."

I'd never had a friend until the day father decided I should visit a nearby farm. He'd told me I needed to understand the lot of the people. None of the lairds' children had liked me, during our meetings in the palace, and it had never occurred to me that a farmers' boy could—not until Aiven was holding my small hand in his big palm and leading me around the fields, pointing out the potatoes and barley, checking for my approval. I made up my mind that night. Aiven was going to be my friend.

And I was going to beg father for an opportunity for him.

"I know you well enough to know what you're going to do next." His words drifted from beside me.

"Do you?" My voice sounded squeaky. "I mean, I don't doubt you, Aive, but I hardly know what I'm doing myself, most of the time."

"You're going to ride to see your father," Aiven said.

The statement hit me like a highland cow barrelling downhill.

"Yes," I murmured.

"And you're going to make your peace with him. Whether he accepts it or not, you'll feel at peace yourself, after that, and when the day comes…"

He hesitated.

"When he dies," I finished.

"Yes. You'll be ready."

I drew another deep breath. I wanted to tell Aiven that it was not for love of my father that I was in pain. I wanted to tell him that losing my father would be like losing a burden I had hefted up a long slope; a relief, but at the same time, a loss of something I was used to carrying with me, something I was used to bearing without complaint. I couldn't say any of that, though. Aiven was the responsible one, and it was his job, now, to keep me in check.

"I think it's an excellent idea," he said.

My gaze snapped up. Aiven's forehead had smoothed out.

"You do?"

"It's the perfect chance to drive two horses with the same reins. You can see your father and make your peace, and on the way, you can meet the people of Eilean-òir."

"I thought I just *met* the people."

"That selection of artisans and smiths and merchants? Do you really think that was the entire peasant class—that poverty goes no lower than a belt-maker with a flourishing shop?" He drew a breath. "You want to be a good prince, Fierre; I know it. You want to do what the Sky is truly meant to, and nourish your people. So you have to know how their lives unfold—not just the ones with a happy ending, but the lives that begin in hard scrabble and end in hard scrabble. You have to look subsistence in the face."

I looked down. "You're right, of course."

How often had I sought advice about what a newly crowned Prince Regent should consider when making his laws? And how quickly had the lairds closed their lips about any matter concerning the working people of the realm? But whenever I'd tried to begin work by myself, I'd felt an immense sense of fatigue—as if I could barely lift my head without the room spinning. The duties of presenting myself, the battle to forego food, the feeling of my own inadequacy all seemed to coat my skull, dragging me down.

I became aware of the silence.

"But…?" Aiven said.

"But you didn't have to say it like that."

"Don't sulk at me, Fierre."

We gazed at each other for a moment.

"I'm only telling you what MacArlay and Hattray and all the others won't," Aiven added.

I wondered if MacArlay would ever tell me to ride through the villages and countryside, surveying the people. I wanted to believe that he would. In truth, I suspected that he wouldn't tell me to do anything that brought me too far from his cock.

In Rossane's case, I was certain of it.

"I'm not sulking," I said, getting up and brushing off my enserre. I turned away and made it a few paces before Aiven grabbed me. I fell awkwardly against his chest. He held me there, brushing his palm over my back. The same surge of desire that had distracted me during my time on the bed with MacArlay returned now, rather inconveniently, in a stronger swell.

"The court will be waiting for my new laws," I said. "You know that I'm supposed to announce them as soon as possible. What will they do if I take off and ride to the Isle of Hairstin? I can't tell them father is nearly dead."

"No." Aiven patted my head. "I don't think that would be wise. A few too many hungry lairds to go snapping around the crown… and I wouldn't advise telling them that you're interested in surveying the lives of the poor." He rubbed my hair gently. "Tell them you'll be taking a spiritual journey, to prepare yourself for the great task of ruling. When you come back, your mind will be clear as a new day—thanks to god's grace. Paint a deer on your cheek. They love that sort of thing."

I laughed. His chest felt so warm against my cheek, like a new-baked bannock.

"You might just be right," I said. "And whether they like it or not, they can't protest if I'm doing it for god."

"Blasphemer."

I pushed him softly in the chest, levering myself off him. As I did, something fell from above and bonked me on the head. It whizzed past my eyes, and I shot out a hand to catch it; my fingers closed over something small and smooth.

"Look," Aiven said, smirking. "God's sent you an acorn, as a sign."

I tossed the acorn toward the oak tree. It bounced off the trunk and rolled across the roots to nestle in the dirt.

"I don't need it," I said. "I've got this one."

I pulled Aiven's coronation gift out of the pocket of my enserre and held it in front of his face.

He stared. In the wash of sunlight it looked golden-brown and blemishless, a blessed relic.

"There are plenty of acorns on the tree, but there's only one acorn in the world I'm keeping." I patted him on the shoulder. "You'll be coming with me on the journey. If you want to, that is. I'll make sure you have every comfort, if you decide to ride out."

"I'll be with you every step of the way." He smiled. "And every canter."

We walked back to the lamb pen and Aiven lowered the little lamb back into the corner, and we both leaned over the rail to watch it settle in. My head felt light. We took the path on the opposite side of the fields, until a patch of stony ground threw me off; I stumbled and flailed, and Aiven grabbed me as I fell. The world wobbled. A sudden dizziness made me close my eyes, and I knew that it had been waiting all along to rush up and claim me, the same weakness that had unbalanced me in the Heart Hall.

"Here," Aiven said, crouching.

He motioned for me to climb onto his back. I mounted him and wrapped my arms around his chest, holding on like a bear cub, and he lifted me up easily. I clutched the acorn in my palm as Aiven carried me all the way back to the farmhouse, and with every step he took, I felt sure that I had made the right decision.

I would ride to father. I would learn about the people on the way. And I would decide on my laws with a better knowledge of what Eilean-òir's peasants were going through.

If I was happy that Aiven had promised to ride with me, what of it? I could think of him as my best friend and as my Star. I wouldn't quiz him about his feelings, nor sleep in his tent. MacArlay and Rossane and as many other lairds as I liked could come along to keep me warm at night, and Aiven would never need to know how I felt.

On this journey, I might lose my only living parent. The pain of it might pierce me like a battle-lance.

I couldn't afford to lose Aiven too.

Eight

Aiven

WE RODE AT daybreak, and the eye of the sun opened slowly on the horizon, melting away the chill too gradually for my liking. Fierre shivered on his stallion in front of me. I tried not to worry, but it was like telling myself not to breathe. I could pass him my own riding cloak, but would it do any good? He was wrapped in a thick cloak already and still shaking.

After a while, the hoofbeats of the riding party fell into a gentle rhythm, the palace territory giving way to the peaks and dales of the western countryside, and I dared to bring my horse up beside Fierre's. I didn't bother to check over my shoulder for the stares of the noblemen. I knew that they would be trained on my back.

"Do you think we've brought enough people?"

"Very funny." Fierre rolled his eyes. "They're all here for a reason."

"All of them? Even the second stable-hand?"

"Two dozen of the most skilful guards in the crown's army to defend us. Attendants to set up the tents and drive the carts. Dr Galar to provide physic for me, and to help if anyone falls sick. Laird Kinnaid to deal with the ambassadors, as my Chief of Diplomacy. And the ambassadors join us because... well, because they're annoying gits, and I haven't the patience to delay this trip to entertain them each for a week."

"That doesn't explain why MacArlay and Rossane are tagging along," I said.

"Lairds MacArlay and Rossane have the two biggest armies in Eilean-òir." Fierre's voice rose in pitch. "I need my Rocks of the Glen where I can see them... as a matter of respect."

"Ah," I said. "Well, each to their own, but if I ever held anyone hostage on a ride, I'd at least pretend it was some special mission. A lucky reward for their hard work. Give them a title: the Prince's Honour Guard, or something. Otherwise, you may as well just tell them you don't trust them for five seconds in the palace without you."

"I can assure you," Fierre said, "they both feel lucky enough already."

My fists clenched. Here I was, thinking I was being clever, and Fierre socked me in the mouth with his reply. The worst part was, he didn't even know it.

The clouds cleared above us but despite the unblemished blue of the sky, the morning failed to warm. Eilean-òir was mild at the best of times, and this was hardly the best of summers. I resented the clank of armour from the guards around us, for I wanted nothing more than to talk to Fierre freely, like we did when we were alone. If only we could stop in one of the orchards along the side of the road. He would like the wild apple trees that grew in the west. I would pass him a ripe apple and watch the juice flow down his chin... I could imagine it already.

We slowed as we passed a stone pillar, and I recognised the marker of a large family's land. Fierre motioned for the group to stop, and Rossane came galloping to us.

"Let me fetch us some food, Sky. The bannocks in these parts are divine."

"How much coin do you need?" Fierre said.

"Not a single piece." Rossane smiled. "This is Duncaldy land."

Duncaldy. I traced through the clan trees that I had memorised when I became Master of Compliance. Duncaldy... that family name had been written below Clan Rossane, connected by a sept-line. It took me less than five seconds to recall the exact wording of the law. *Any family declaring themselves a sept of a clan may draw upon the protection of the larger family, and in turn, the clan may demand taxes and duties.* In other words: benefit from clan armies, and you'll have to pay.

How many coins did Rossane and his riders snatch each year?

And judging by the set of Fierre's jaw, how long had he been dissatisfied with the arrangement?

"All right," Fierre said, "but see that you don't force anyone to part with their food."

"Oh, I won't have to. Allow me to demonstrate."

Rossane dug his knees into his horse's sides and sped away towards the nearest farmhouse. We all pulled our mounts up and stopped in an awkward gaggle, waiting. The guards murmured to each other. At last, Rossane returned with a bag swinging from his saddle. He passed it to Fierre.

I didn't need to peer across Fierre to count the number of bannocks inside. A glimpse told me that there was more bread in there than any peasant family could afford to give away on the spur of the moment. Fierre reached to the bottom and pulled out a small, back ball.

"How on earth did you persuade them to part with a neartfruit? One seed from this, and a man can make it through till nightfall, I've heard."

"As you may remember, Sky, I have a firm hand."

A look passed between Rossane and Fierre. I didn't like the way Rossane smirked afterward.

"Be careful how you use it," Fierre said.

We rode on, deeper inland than I was used to going, into a colder terrain where the trees dropped hard berries. Even though I knew that Fierre was following the route to the smallest villages in the western hills, I checked the land as we turned onto the hillside road, making sure I read the signpost. I couldn't be the only one who noticed the silence that shrouded us, yet the guards kept their thoughts to themselves, their eyes fixed on the road.

The rustling began at noon. I stared into the trees, searching for movement. The others stared too. Nothing emerged, but we slowed our pace and rode cautiously, a few guards moving to flank Fierre and the lairds.

Another rustle—from the firs on our right. Steel scraped as the guards drew their swords.

"Get down," I whispered.

"Why?" Fierre said.

"There's someone out there. Lie flat against your horse, and don't move."

"But—"

His reply was cut off by a scream as a man charged from between the firs, swinging a sickle and sprinting toward the guards at the front. A second figure rushed out behind him, howling, her sickle raised above her head. She flung herself at the belly of the nearest horse and sliced a line down its side. The animal bucked and neighed, sending its rider to the ground. The woman hacked at the rider, and he rolled away just in time.

Out in front, the man who had charged first was taking on two guards; having dismounted, they were pushing the man backward, coming at him with swords raised.

"Enough!" Fierre shouted.

The two attackers ignored him. Blades flashed through the air. The woman's sickle came dangerously close to slicing another horse and clipped the arm of a guard.

"I am your prince, countrymen!"

Fierre shrugged off his riding cloak and draped it over his horse. My heart leapt and lodged itself in my throat. The move exposed him, even amongst the other riders; I wanted to shout at him to cover up again, but the hard set to his jaw told me that he wasn't going to listen. His blue enserre sparkled in the midday sun. A ray of light caught the thin diamond choker around his neck and set it ablaze, showering white light over his chest.

"Let us speak in peace, friends," he cried.

"You stand before the Sky of Eilean-òir. Put down your weapons," Rossane snapped.

The sickle-wielding pair shared a glance. They stared at Fierre for a long time, then at last, the woman lowered her weapon, and the man followed suit. Their chastened faces told me that they hadn't recognised Fierre before. Indeed, they had run straight at the guards—any assassin would have been aiming for the prince.

"State the reason for this attack," MacArlay said.

"We're farmers, my laird. Defending our land," the man replied.

"Defending our *food*," the woman added.

"I see. And why do you think *we* would come for your stores?"

"Begging your pardon, my laird, but we have no stores. We've precious little to see us through this season, and no one ever rides into these parts. I thought you were raiders from Clan Rossane, and I asked my brother here"—the woman jerked her head at her companion—"to help me fend you off."

Fierre clapped his hands together, and everyone turned to look at him.

"Let us be merry then, friends, for this is all a simple mistake. Your prince and his entourage are here to survey the land. We would like to visit your farm and see how you live and work, maybe ask you a few questions. What say you?"

"Our honour, Sky." The woman knelt. "So long as we are safe, we welcome you."

It was an artful reply, asking a question of Fierre in return. Yet if he was perturbed, I couldn't tell.

He smiled and nodded, and this seemed enough for the pair of them, for they led the way down the road, walking side by side. The rest of our party dismounted and Fierre and I led our horses as quickly as we could, turning right at the end of the firs.

I shadowed Fierre as he approached the potato farm, and I took in the meagre crops, the tiny farmhouse, and the mangy hound that trotted warily out to sniff at my fingers. Our hosts introduced themselves as Cameron and Annis, and after a brief discussion about types of potatoes, they left us to inspect the farm at our leisure. The lairds and retinue gathered near the farmhouse, covering themselves in as much shade as they could.

Fierre made for the potato fields, but I could see no

side-path, only dirt and potatoes fringed by some scrubby bushes. I rushed to grab him as he bumped against a bush.

"Allow me," I said, crouching down.

I brushed bits of leaf off the bottom of his enserre, smoothing down the garment until the hem sat unrumpled against his thigh. I tried not to stare at that fine skin.

"Can't have you poking holes in the garment of the Sky," I said.

Fierre was looking at me strangely. I tried not to panic. I was only doing what a friend should do, and what a Star of the Sky should do for his prince—wasn't I?

Thankfully, Fierre was soon diverted by the sight of creamy potatoes a little way down the field. I scooped some of the dark earth from around the potatoes to help him view them.

"White potatoes grow in black soil," I explained. "These people will bear the surname Blacke, after their land. In the same fashion, black potatoes grow in white soil, and the farmers there are called Whytes."

"I'm not quite as ignorant as that." Fierre touched the earth tentatively with his forefinger, as if he were building up the courage to scoop a little soil. "We have brown soil in the far north, too. Next thing, you'll be telling me brown potatoes grow up there." He winked.

"Yes." I smiled. "And those farmers are called Browne. No contrast there."

"Tell me something, Aive." Fierre stroked the side of the largest potato before us. "Why would these people run out with their sickles, prepared to die just to keep their food?"

"I thought you weren't quite as ignorant as all that."

"I've heard of the basics of farming. It's the struggles of farmers that the lairds won't discuss with me." His voice dropped. "And my father wouldn't hear a word about it."

"Well, you see…" How could I break it to him? "Cameron and Annis can't take food from attendants. They can't give orders to a staff kitchen—a kitchen that has all the supplies of the crown. These people must grow their own food. If their crops fail, they have no dinner. No breakfast. No luncheon. They must feed themselves, and they must also grow enough potatoes to sell, to raise the money for taxes. They must drop coins into their laird's pocket. And their laird passes some of those coins on to you." I drew a deep breath. I hadn't realised that I was speaking so quickly. "These people must feed themselves *and* you. That is why they take up their sickles and chase off raiders. They cannot afford to lose a single potato."

Fierre's lips had parted slightly as he listened. He stared at me now, yet his eyes were glazed, as if he didn't really see me.

"You must think me terrible," he whispered. "And my father, and his father before him. You must think my whole family are wolves."

"I think you're the best chance this realm has of seeing change, and knowing plenitude again."

"Maybe you're right." He rose, and his voice shifted to a lighter tone. "Plenitude. Where'd you get such fancy words, Aive?"

"I read a lot."

"On your parents' farm?"

"In the counting-house, I read books in my breaks. And then, as Master of Compliance, I had to read a lot of scrolls. I don't expect I'll stop now."

Fierre waited for me to stand up and join him. He took my arm and walked me back towards the farmhouse, and though I was aware of Rossane shooting me a dirty look and MacArlay staring intensely at me, I didn't mind. Fierre's arm held mine. That was all that mattered.

"I think it's time for a talk inside with our hosts," Fierre said, softly. "See to it, will you, Aive?"

"Anything for you," I said.

He smiled, and it was as if the sun had never risen until now.

THE SINGLE TABLE in Cameron and Annis' kitchen fit eight people at a very tight squeeze, so I sent the guards to wait outside the farmhouse. They grumbled at first, but once I promised them a fair share of the food, they quietened down.

That left enough chairs for Fierre and myself, our two hosts, Rossane, MacArlay, Kinnaid, and Dr Galar. The two ambassadors asked to join us, but catching Fierre's slight shake of his head, I fended them off with promises of a discussion later. I sent one of the guards to ferry plates of potatoes and barley-cakes to and from the farmhouse.

This afforded me the pleasure of keeping an eye on Fierre. He chatted brightly to Annis and charmed everybody with an anecdote about cherry picking. Shortly afterward, the topic turned to the effects of frost on farming, and Fierre glanced nervously at me. I stepped in with some questions about crop diversification, leading Cameron to argue passionately with me about the benefits of single-crop cultivation, and we had progressed to a discussion on the law of water-sharing when Annis stood up and spoke across us.

"Sky, is the food not to your liking?"

Everyone turned to stare at Fierre.

He glanced down at his plate. A full serve of luncheon remained.

Fierre blushed and met Annis' gaze.

"It's perfect, mistress."

"Can I find some herbs for you? Some more salt?"

"None at all. I'm merely a little tired from the ride, and my appetite is lacking. Your food restores my vigour, mistress, with just a few bites."

The table resumed talking, and everyone seemed to forget about the matter, and I was quite sure that I was the only one who saw Dr Galar lean over from Fierre's left side and whisper something into his ear. Perhaps he was encouraging the Sky to eat more.

We let the lairds leave first when the luncheon was done, and Dr Galar trailed after them, leaving Fierre and I to thank our hosts alone.

"Don't worry about the food you've lost today. I intend to repay you three times over," Fierre said. "I'll be exempting you from taxes this year."

"Sky!" Cameron knelt, and Annis copied him quickly, the two of them gazing up at Fierre, disbelief painting their faces.

"Rise, friends. I mean this from the heart. I shall pay your dues to Clan Rossane personally. It's not a gift, just the beginning of righting a very deep wrong." He beckoned the pair up, and they rose slowly, still eyeing him as if they were expecting the promise to be taken back at any moment.

Fierre smiled. Even the most sceptical person could not have missed the sweetness and kindness in that smile. He took Annis' hand and pressed it between his own. "Remember this. By the time your taxes are due again, we may have new rules in Eilean-òir."

We were almost at the door before Cameron rushed after us, puffing, and held a raw potato out to Fierre.

"It would be our pleasure to give you a parting gift. One blessed potato in every hundred, they say—you can tell by the black spot on the top. Usually, we mash it and give it back to the earth, as a thanks to god for blessing our farm, but we would be honoured if you would eat it, Sky."

Fierre froze, his hand half-outstretched to Cameron.

"Now?" he said.

"I should say it needs cooking, first." Cameron grinned. "Whenever you please, Sky."

"It's a pact." Fierre looked palpably relieved. I glanced over at Dr Galar and noticed that he was frowning, but he didn't speak, only glowered in Fierre's general direction.

We left Cameron and Annis with many thank-yous and waves, turning back onto the narrow hillside road. The encounter weighed on my mind all afternoon, and as the sun changed from a pale yolk to a salmon-pink ball, I couldn't stop thinking about Fierre's words. *It's not a gift, just the beginning of righting a very deep wrong… by the time your taxes are due again, we may have new rules in Eilean-òir.*

Could he do it?

And if so, would he risk the ire of the lairds?

You didn't need to be a noble to know that cutting taxes would mean cutting money to the lairds. That meant fewer feasts and dances in the castles; fewer fine clothes for the clan leaders and their families; fewer orders of expensive dyes and exotic plants from Archland when the trade days came around. I'd often observed that the lairds of Eilean-òir weren't used to having less of anything.

I didn't have long to mull on the possibility, for we stopped early to make camp. Fierre declared that we would ride to our next destination in the morning, and the group murmured its relief. I directed the guards to hunt, gather, and fish in the nearest stream, while the attendants began to set up the tents.

"Don't like the look of my food, Grian?"

I turned to find Rossane sneering at me. The bag of bread he had taken earlier was swinging from his hand.

"It won't hurt to add to our meal. The guards need something substantial for supper."

"Watch yourself," Rossane said. "Remember your place, Grian. Always remember where you were born."

"I know my place very well, my laird. It's at Prince Dannatyne's side."

Rossane opened his mouth to reply, but Fierre ran into our midst and took me by the arm. "I'm frightfully cold, Aive. Do you feel a chill?"

"Not terribly. Let me take you to the doctor," I said, relishing the fact that he had completely ignored Rossane.

"Perhaps I could warm you up."

Rossane was not shy—I granted him that.

"No, my laird, I need your nobility at my service. You see the ambassadors in their foreign clothes?" Fierre said.

We all looked over to where a tall woman and a debonair man were leaning against a horse, bent in conversation.

"Help Kinnaid to fend them off for me, just one more night. Entertain them with gambling or whatever you please. Hint to Ambassador Rince that I'll go one price level lower for garment dyes, and drop an implication to the ambassador for Sarleven that I'll throw in a few more chests of gems. I need someone of your clan prowess to keep them at bay."

Rossane looked pleased, through he threw me another dirty look as he walked away.

"Are you really cold?" I said, turning to Fierre.

"Freezing." He nestled against me. "I don't think I can fall asleep like this."

"Come on." I slipped my hand into his and felt the icy temperature of his fingers. "Let's see what Dr Galar recommends."

I left him in his tent with the doctor and waited outside, fixing a steely gaze on anyone who approached. After a long time, Galar emerged.

"How is the prince?" I said.

Galar donned a smile. "Didn't expect you so close by, Star."

"Do you know why he complains of the cold—is it a malady of some kind?"

"A malady… no. I suspect that he was born with a weak constitution."

"Would food help? An instruction to eat more, perhaps?

"The Sky is an extraordinary man, Star. He's lived his whole life eating carefully. I suspect that with the grand change of his coronation, his temperament has been driving him to a slight hysteria. Some noblemen are very unlucky. He bears it well, but I am attending closely to his condition, as I did with his father. I have prepared a regimen for him. Tonight, he should keep warm and insulated, as much as possible. A fire outside the tent. Tartans to swaddle himself in. All the body heat he can get. I do not wish to see him shivering for too long, and I have warned him not to sleep alone."

"Thank you, doctor."

I watched Galar amble off to his tent. That had been a very thorough explanation. As a medical man, he owed me no confidence about his patients, but he had been willing to put Fierre's health above all else—perhaps I had been wrong to eye him suspiciously.

I found Fierre lying on the floor of his tent, resting on a blanket, with a thick pink-and-white tartan wrapped around him. He gave me a pained smile. Cocooned in the tartan, he looked even smaller than usual. I knelt beside him and ruffled his hair.

"Still cold?" I said.

"You must think me an idiot."

"I could never think that." I hesitated for a moment. "Galar told me that you shouldn't sleep alone. Shall I send for one of the lairds?"

"No, I want you, Aive." Fierre's fingers closed around my wrist. "Come and hold me until I'm warm. Just for a little while. You were always like the damned sun, hot enough to fry me, even when we were boys. Give me some of your heat, will you?"

I wavered. There was absolutely no way that this was a good idea. I gazed down at Fierre's fine cheekbones and his big, pleading eyes, underneath that sweep of soft hair.

He looked so pitiable. What if he shivered all night?

"Please, Aive. Just cuddle me under the cloth, for a while."

My fingers found their way to my cloak. Somehow, they were untying it, and then I was removing my boots and setting them aside.

I pulled up the edge of the tartan. An expanse of pale white cotton greeted me. Of course, he had taken off his enserre—of course, he was wearing a night-shift— no prince would crease his royal garment by lying in it all night. I knew that. Yet I'd hoped that he'd be fully clothed, all the same.

"Not like that!" Fierre gestured at my doublet and trousers. "I was hoping to actually feel the heat. Can you take it all off?"

I turned my face away from him as I undressed. The laces on my shirt usually took forever to untie, but for some reason, they undid quickly now. I tried to roll down my trousers inch by inch, avoiding Fierre's gaze.

When I turned back, he looked away and shifted onto his side.

I climbed beneath the tartan and pulled it over myself, swaddling the two of us. Fierre was silent for a moment. His hand grasped mine, and then he was pulling my arm around him, bringing my right hand to rest over his stomach.

"Don't let me go," he whispered.

The scent of his skin filled my nostrils. Apple blossom and cinnamon: the echoes of late spring. I pressed myself against his back and tightened my arm around him, and he wriggled back against me, pushing his buttocks against my groin.

I tried to think of rancid milk; rotten fruit; anything repulsive and abhorrent… any image that would stop me from feeling his delicate body pressed against me. Clenching my jaw, I wondered if god would answer a prayer for me.

Please, Holy Father, if you're listening, divert all my blood away from my cock.

Whether it worked or not, I never found out. Fierre's smell was calming… so sweet, with just a hint of fragrant spice… and I drifted off to sleep with my arm still encircling him, a smile curving my lips.

Nine

Fierre

A FAINT GLOW penetrated the cloth of the tent, washing my sandals, jewellery, and garments in a golden sheen. I smiled lazily at the filtered sun. How was I warm, despite the early hour of the morning? I was sure that I'd been shivering last night.

Something shifted against me, and I looked down to see Aiven's arm wrapped around me. Suddenly, the heat took on a different feeling. The warmth along my back and legs seemed to increase; with every second, I was painfully aware of Aiven's muscular body pressed against me. He sighed. I tensed. The rise and fall of his chest told me he was still asleep, and I allowed myself a deep inhalation.

He smelled *so good*. That hint of fior-chridhe perfumed the air, as if it emanated from him. Sighing again, he pressed closer to me, and I prayed for my body to stay still.

Oh god. I could feel one part of Aiven, in particular, pressing against me.

It wasn't even hard. Sweet merciful god… I couldn't imagine what it would feel like if it actually *were* hard…

except, no, I kind of could, because my mind was running to all sorts of places. What had I been thinking, asking him to take off his clothes and climb under my tartan?

As usual, I had totally neglected to imagine the consequences of my own lust. Now they were waking me up and bonking me over the head like a deranged washerwoman with a wet towel.

I wanted to move.

I didn't dare to move.

Aiven sighed and rolled slightly backward, and I seized my chance and climbed out of bed. I snatched up the tartan and wrapped it around myself. For a moment, I froze, but Aiven only murmured and rolled over on the blanket to lie flat on his back, exposing everything that had been pressed against me.

I tried to divert my gaze, but whatever the courtiers and the common people might think, I was only mortal.

I looked. After a while, I started to wonder if I could do anything *but* look.

Holy Father, I implored, *grant me the power to resist getting down on my knees and putting Aiven Grian's cock in my mouth, right here, right now.*

I was pretty sure that if god could turn a stone into honey, like the Hymn of the Saint Tree said, he could turn my unrestrained thoughts into princely ones.

It must've worked, because my legs found their strength again and bore me out of the tent. The breeze hit me like a cavalcade and I bent, trying to shield myself. A pair of guards ran over. They seemed to be the only other people awake.

"Escort me to the river, if you please," I said.

They fell into step beside me, marching in a peaceful silence to the little tributary that trickled through a patch of briars. They might've known that the water was close enough for me to reach safely alone, but I suspected that they also knew how important it was for the Sky of Eilean-òir to be shielded from unwanted eyes, even if it was all a bunch of claptrap.

"I'm going to bathe."

I felt rather silly, announcing it. If I walked into the water with no warning, however, the guards would be duty-bound to fish me out.

Once I had folded the tartan and placed it on the grass, the guards looked awkwardly at me. "Turn around," I said.

"I beg your pardon, Sky," the man on the left said, "but one of us must watch you. To ensure you do not drown."

"Very well. One of you can watch for wild animals, and one of you can watch me."

I pulled my shift off over my head and folded it up. One man turned his back. The other guard kept his eyes trained on my face, and his expression told me that it was taking him quite a lot of work to do so.

The river greeted me with an icy kiss, and I regretted my decision to plunge in at once. For a moment, I thought I was going to die. But it passed, and I cupped my hands over my groin, as if I were doing a magic spell. *Calm down. Please, god, let me calm down before I see Aiven again.*

The cold water shocked my body into compliance. By the time I climbed out of the water, I was walking easily.

The camp came slowly to life, awakened by the scent of the attendants' cooking. I slipped back into my tent and almost walked straight into Aiven—a fully dressed Aiven, fastening his belt.

"Where were you?" he said.

"I was bathing." Oh no. I sounded like a cat caught with its tail in a door.

"At this hour of the morning? I thought you were cold."

"I needed to settle my... humours."

We looked at one another for a moment. Aiven shifted on the spot. "Did you, ah... did I, last night... that is, did we..."

"Spit it out, Aive. No point saving it for later."

"Did I touch you at all, in the night? If I did, Fierre, I'm so sorry."

I had expected to hear the opposite of that. It felt a bit like getting your hand stuck in a jar of sweets, and then having someone else walk in and apologise for stealing.

"Not that I can remember. But then, I was fast asleep. I wouldn't know." I grinned. "If your hands went wandering in the night, you probably kept me warm, so... thank you. Or not. Depending on what happened. Which we can never know." I picked my enserre up off the ground and held it before Aiven. "Now, there only one man in this riding party who's qualified to help me put this on."

"Shall I fetch him?"

I sighed. "It's you, Aive."

"Oh. Of course." He seized the cloth, and I began to take off my night-shift.

With the help of the river water and a lot of determination, I managed to keep calm while Aiven wound the fabric around me, until I was covered in the sky-blue cloth. He fixed a sapphire necklace around my neck, on my request, and two sapphire earrings shaped like teardrops in my earlobes. I wished I could dress him up, too, in that golden enserre which set off his sandy hair so brilliantly. The tight binding had shown just how well his farm work had shaped him. But I was sure that he would have only brought a bunch of dull shirts with him. Aiven hated anything fancy; he'd probably never wear that enserre again.

The smell of cooked game drew us outside, and as I emerged from the tent, Rossane and MacArlay began speaking over each other. They stopped as they took in Aiven's figure.

"Goodness." Rossane scowled. "You're a dark horse, Grian."

MacArlay did not look remotely surprised, but he *did* look like he was swallowing a bitter fig.

"The Star of the Sky has been kind enough to keep me warm." I didn't realise how suspicious the words sounded until they were coming out of my mouth. "Anyway, lairds, shall we break our fast? I'm so famished, I could eat a small horse. Or maybe a large one. There's only one way to find out."

MacArlay and Rossane competed to serve me portions of meat from the cookfire. They argued with each other over the best cuts, and over the best portion of bread to offer me. The ambassadors weighed in with questions about the kind of bannocks made in the western hills. It was just as well, because in the ruckus of voices, I was able to pass most of my food to Dr Galar, keeping only the portion that he had advised; my breakfast might not be a laden plate, but it was a little more than my dinner, and for that, I was grateful. I nibbled a little at the bread, which seemed to satisfy my Rocks of the Glen. Neither seemed concerned with how much I ate, only with whether or not I accepted what they handed me.

"Get back, MacArlay," Rossane snapped. "Do you think he wants another ill-cut piece?"

"I think the Sky can choose which piece *he* prefers."

I happened to look straight across the cookfire to where red hair gleamed in the firelight, and caught the eye of my Chief of Diplomacy. Kinnaid smirked. He glanced at MacArlay, then back at me, and raised an eyebrow. I couldn't help grinning. Something about Kinnaid told me that he understood very well why other men strove to please me, but his quiet amusement rippled unexpectedly over me. It calmed me.

We moved quickly on the road, but a layer of tension remained in the party, simmering. At mid-morning, MacArlay threw his dirk into a wolf's side and wrestled the animal to the ground, pulling out his weapon and slashing its throat with a single blow. Rossane made a comment about desperate show-offs, projected in a faux whisper that was loud enough for the whole group to hear. At the sight of the next farmhouse, Rossane galloped off, returning shortly afterward with another bag of food.

I saw how the system worked, and I didn't like it one bit. The peasants gave to their lairds. The lairds gave to me. It was just as Aiven had told me on Cameron and Annis' farm: the common people of Eilean-òir fed themselves *and* all those above them, and yet we looked upon them as weak and inferior. We were the useless ones. Perhaps my father had avoided this topic with me—and threatened to beat me over a table for bringing it up—because he had known the reality of it all too well. Or perhaps his mind had been as fuzzy as my own, when he too was occupied with the regime of the Sky of Eilean-òir.

I leaned over to Aiven, close enough to whisper. "I don't want to eat here, Aive."

He glanced ahead. The next farmhouse loomed on the horizon, breaking the pastel of the barley fields with its dark stone.

"I thought you agreed to look subsistence in the face."

"I promise to look. I'll inspect the whole farm, if you like. But I won't take another morsel of food from these people. They'll give their barley to us, out of hospitality, and then they'll go hungry for weeks, even if I exempt them from taxes—they'll still have a gap of food to make up. They have so little, Aive! I don't want to make them starve."

"No." Aiven's voice dropped. "Only yourself."

"What?"

"Nothing." He patted his horse's mane. "You're right, of course. But if we skip a meal here, it'd be wise to ride to the next castle by nightfall; the ambassadors look like they'd murder someone for a soft bed and a serve of pudding."

"How many farms before the next castle?"

"At least a half dozen, I'd say." He took in my determined expression. "You don't mean to stop at them all?"

"That's exactly what I intend to do."

I greeted farmers, patted dogs, inspected potatoes and barley and wheat, discussed plough types and seedlings and coops. The farmers greeted me with broad smiles, some of them falling to their knees, others uttering a blessing in the Salt Tongue, a native language of the hills. As I shook their hands and beamed back at them, the thought occurred to me that any one of these people could have desired my death. Any one of them could have resented me for bleeding them of their coin and food, yet they were all joyed to meet me.

One couple ran out carrying heavy iron bars, in the manner of our former sickle-wielding hosts, but I revealed myself quickly this time, casting off my riding cloak and calling out to them before a blow could be struck.

In a strange way, it felt good to be learning how peasants lived. It was a brutal knowledge, but without it, I would

116

have been stumbling blind through my law-making. Now, I could see the choices I had to make.

Aiven and I rode slowly after the last farm, carrying the weight of all our conversations. Castle Aonar arose from the marshy land next to a lake, jutting toward the pale sky. Its starstone façade became a silhouette with the pink rays of sunset falling behind the building—silver walls transmuted into a black barrier—and I had to squint to make out the ramp that led up to the door.

"We welcome the Sky of Eilean-òir to our hearth!"

The deep voice rang over the marsh. Only when I had nearly reached the door did I recognise Lady Sabernethy and her two daughters, clad in tartans of scarlet and emerald.

"Grateful to see you at last, my lady," I said, bending my head in a sign of respect. Lady Sabernethy bowed low, touching her hand to her forehead. Her daughters presented me with a dirk apiece, which I kissed and passed to Aiven, acknowledging the ritual with a small bow in return. I could hear Rossane, MacArlay and Kinnaid shifting on the spot behind me, eager to get inside.

The guards tied up the horses while the rest of us took a tour of Castle Aonar, and Lady Sabernethy showed us family swords and described her clan's battle honours while I pretended to be deeply interested in the details of steel weight and shield strength. The wooden hallways of the castle creaked at our every step. I hoped that I hadn't gained any weight—were my steps heavier this week? I didn't want to think about it. At last, we were shown to our rooms, and Sabernethy's Chief of Household pushed back a pair of creaking doors to reveal a chamber stuffed with dark oak furniture.

"For the Sky and his Star," the man announced.

My shock must have shown on my face, for the Chief of Household frowned.

It was an outdated ritual, to pair the two of us in rooms on the road. As far as I knew, it was a northern custom to protect the Sky's virginity, dating from some ancient religious idea about the ruler's inviolable body that had never caught up to the workings of court politics. But I'd forgotten about it when I invited Aiven on the ride. If the Chief of Household noticed the nervous look I cast at Aiven, he made no observation upon the matter, and Aiven didn't voice any objections.

"Make sure you put Laird Rossane and Laird MacArlay in different rooms," I whispered to the Chief of Household.

He gave a tiny nod.

Aiven and I unpacked, leaving the guards to settle the horses in the stables. I lay my clothes, jewellery, and shoes out on the cabinets, while Aiven added his spare dirk, a comb, and a book with covers tied by a leather strap. I picked up the comb. It didn't have a pretty pattern on the handle, like the combs I had been given since childhood, but its tines looked sturdy enough.

"Looking after your hair?" I said.

Aiven walked over and took the comb gently from my hand. "It's for you," he replied. "I wasn't sure if you'd need me to comb your hair in the mornings, before we ride."

"Well, I wasn't planning to ask you, but now that you've mentioned it…" I flicked my hair with one hand. "It could do with some love. And as Star of the Sky, you know, you have the right to attend to me."

"Yes; it seems I have all kinds of duties that I didn't know about."

A long pause followed this remark, during which the double bed in the next room seemed to loom larger.

I wanted to ask him if it had been a chore, keeping me warm last night. I wanted to ask him if he had felt annoyed when I asked him to take off his clothes and hold me. I wanted to know why he had worried about touching me in the night—but before I could shape a question, Lady Sabernethy's eldest daughter knocked and invited us to dinner.

The banquet hall welcomed us with mingling smells, and it took a moment for me to pick out the individual scents of kippers, game, tate scones, creamed soup, and a dozen other hot dishes crowding the long table. My chest tightened at the sight of the silver platters before me. I remembered too late that the families of the hills and highlands prized hospitality above all else—to feed your guest well was to show your influence, up here, and guests were expected to indulge. What if your guest didn't want to be fed, though?

Lady Sabernethy seated me opposite herself and her two daughters, and her widow's garland slipped down her arm as she pointed to my chair. The black ribbon hung from her wrist like a bracelet, reminding us all conveniently who had charge of this castle. I flashed her a smile that I hoped looked convincing. As I sat down, Aiven took the chair on my right, and there was a scramble as the lairds hurried toward the chair on my left. Rossane reached it first, slipping his backside onto the wood.

"Whoever tied that enserre around you knew what they were doing," he whispered.

"I appreciate the compliment." I took a sip of my wine.

"It's exquisitely tight. Just like you."

I coughed. I nearly choked on the wine, before Aiven

patted me hard on the back, and I swallowed the mouthful, spluttering.

"Try to focus," I hissed at Rossane.

"I'm focusing on you, *Sky*."

I looked deliberately away from him. Lady Sabernethy seized the opportunity to ask me about the possibility of raising taxes on the farms, and I tried my best to fend her off politely. Within a minute, I felt a hand on my left thigh. Rossane's fingers slid up beneath my enserre, moving towards my groin.

"Let go of me," I murmured.

His forefinger crept ever so slightly closer to my cock.

"Rossane, I'm not joking."

He didn't move. Aiven leaned across me and brought his face close to him.

"If you don't take your hand off the prince right now, my laird, I'm going to drag you on top of this table and beat your face until it's so soft, they'll mistake it for another stew. And if you think you can take me on, I should warn you: I can you throw you across this room without straining a muscle." Aiven's expression didn't flicker. "It'll be a nice bit of exercise before the next ride."

My thigh was suddenly cold again. Rossane had never removed his hand so quickly, in all the years I'd known him.

"Thank you," I said, smiling brightly as I turned to Rossane, as if we had all been talking about the weather. "See that you don't make any mistakes again."

I took a tiny bite of a scone. The conversation meandered on around us, and I waited until Rossane had directed his attention elsewhere before I dared to sneak a glance at Aiven. His eyes locked on mine.

He leaned closer, until I could see the flecks in his eyes:

the tiny specks of black within his hazel irises. *Thank you*, I wanted to say. *I wish I could hug you.*

"How long have you known about Rossane?" I said.

"As long as anyone." He shifted closer. "MacArlay said something to me before the rituals. Have he and Rossane been visiting you too much?"

"Too much?"

We looked closely at each other. Aiven leaned back and sat stiffly upright. "Never mind," he said.

"You're snippy with me."

"I only wondered if you'd spent a lot of time with them lately. I mean… if you'd descended to some familiarity with MacArlay and Rossane, right before we left."

Ah. I sat back in my chair. My face felt warm all of a sudden. I checked to make sure that no one else could hear us.

"Descended," I said.

"Fierre?"

"The answer to what you're struggling to ask is: yes. I let them both stick their cock in me. As soon as the crown was on my head, Rossane wanted to choke me for a little fun, so I made him send MacArlay to my rooms." I straightened in my chair. "Go ahead and whisper about it, if you like. Everyone else does."

"Fierre, I didn't mean—"

I took a large bite of scone and pointedly sipped at my wine. Aiven looked down, and didn't speak to me again.

The food seemed suddenly more tempting, with the mixture of humiliation and anger running through my mind, but I managed, with great effort, to keep to the small portion of scone that Dr Galar had advised. As soon as the plates were cleared, Lady Sabernethy raised her glass.

"Please take a slice of the finest puddings from the cooks of Clan Sabernethy, Sky! We hope you will honour us with a taste."

Kitchen-hands streamed through the doors in a procession of platters, placing their offerings down as soon as the table was cleared. A river of dread ran through my body. Sugared biscuits, a mountain-pudding, potato macaroons, a log of golden dawncake and the black domes of raven buns all gleamed in the candlelight, taunting me with icing and pastry. The clarion call of sugar sounded in my veins. I tried to resist it, but it was hard… so hard.

"You must try the dawncake, Sky. It's our clan recipe. My father would've been proud to offer you this," Lady Sabernethy said.

I was doing the right thing, I told myself. It was expected of me. If I took a bite now, I'd make my hosts happy.

I could feel the eyes of the whole party upon me as I took a forkful of dawncake and raised it to my lips. The cake crumbled in my mouth and a sensation of honeyed sweetness exploded on my tongue, and I closed my eyes, concentrating entirely on that taste. How long had it been since I had eaten a sugary cake? Six months? Maybe longer?

When I opened my eyes, the entire group was staring at me.

"Perfection," I said.

Lady Sabernethy beamed and her daughters clapped, and several of the nobles began to serve themselves dawncake. Lady Sabernethy began to recommend the other dishes in turn, and I took a bite of them one by one, savouring every mouthful. The biscuit was bland, but I had gone without sugar for so long that it tasted exquisite, as if a harp were playing on my tongue. The mountain-pudding's thick constitution suited my hunger, for I chewed my bite so long that it gave me twice the satisfaction of the biscuit. I scarcely tasted the macaroon; its light texture seemed to evaporate in my mouth like a cloud, leaving a faint aftertaste of potato. Lady Sabernethy indicated that I should taste a raven bun last, and I eyed it cautiously, knowing how strongly my father had warned against its buttery filling. *You can get fat in a day on raven buns,* he had informed me, as he turned the palace cook away with a piled platter.

I cut a tiny slice of the bun before me, now, and held it up on my fork. It looked so harmless. The Sky was supposed to give pleasure to his people by approving and applauding their work… and how could I approve their work if I never tried it?

Besides, nothing could really make you fat in a day— could it?

Slowly, I lowered the fork into my mouth and slid the piece of bun from the tines onto my tongue. I tasted the combination of pastry and filling, in that mouthful. I tasted something rich and creamy, and something sweet and crunchy, and a flavour that I had not tasted since childhood: something almost like cinnamon, but stronger. I wanted to cry. It was harmony in a single bite, that piece of bun. It was everything I had forgotten I loved, and in that moment, I felt the ache of all I had missed out on in my years of slimming down, the pain of all the joys that I had never had.

"My lady," I said, "your clan knows the way to bake a bun. This would delight god, if he had time for dessert."

Lady Sabernethy smiled wider than I had thought possible, and I took the bun on my plate and held it in both hands. This was it. There was no going back, I knew.

We were in love, that bun and I. It could have been a languorous affair, but I lost my restraint after the third bite and began to eat quickly, devouring the rest in greedy silence. I didn't want to speak to Aiven, for I knew he would either question me or apologise, and I wanted to think about nothing but the taste of pastry and buttery cream. The last bite almost hurt, for I didn't want to see it go, but I ate it all the same and licked my lips. It was as I was wolfing the crumbs from my plate that I looked further down the table and caught Dr Galar's eye.

He didn't speak. He didn't have to.

I pushed back my chair and rose. Lady Sabernethy and the lairds scrambled to rise, too. I motioned for them to stay sitting.

"Excuse me. I feel a little fatigued. A short rest should do the trick. I do implore you all to finish Lady Sabernethy's marvellous repast," I declared.

Gesturing to the guards to open the door, I hastened from the room, and as a buzz of talk spread behind me, I did not look back. The floorboards creaked under my feet. I made my way through the corridors, passing dark wooden cabinets, stuffed deer, and bracketed swords, until I strode into the guest wing of Castle Aonar where a single torch burned outside my suite door. The guards looked past me, as if wondering where my entourage was.

"Lock the door behind me, if you please," I said.

I strode across the first chamber and seized the wrapped object on the farthest cabinet. Carrying it in both hands, I passed through the bedchamber and into the room where the bath and chamber-pot shared one half of the tiled floor.

On the other side of the bath chamber, two cabinets flanked an enormous mirror set in a gilt frame. I set the package down on one cabinet and unwrapped it. The stoppered bottle gleamed before me. The cerise liquid inside still looked as beautiful as it had when Galar presented me with the bottle, and as I tipped it to the left and watched it slosh, I heard the doctor's voice inside my head.

It will put things right.

The taste of sugar and cream filled my mouth.

I pulled the stopper free from the bottle and held the open end to my lips. The reddish-pink liquid slipped toward me, making a direct line for my mouth, as if it knew the way.

Tilting my head back, I began to drink.

Ten

Fierre

AT FIRST I felt nothing but a sweet sensation, like the cloying effect of raspberry wine. It took a moment for the medicine to glide down my throat. Stars exploded inside me: small points of heat blew out into incandescent flares, making my stomach swell until it threatened to burst, and I slammed the bottle down and clutched at the corner of the cabinet. My insides crackled and hissed. A storm raged inside me, showing no sign of abating.

The floor gave me a cold and sharp welcome as I sank to my knees. My palms trailed over the tiles and scraped against hard edges.

Galar's face swam in my vision. Though he was nowhere to be seen, he filled the bath chamber, calling out to me. *It will put things right... it will put things right... it will put things right.* The churning in my stomach grew. Something rose inside me, and I realised too late that it was my dinner.

I crawled to the chamber-pot and gripped its silver handles, drawing a deep breath through my nose.

I threw up directly into the middle of the pot. A mash of black food landed on the base, and I recognised the raven bun that had tasted so sweet just minutes ago. For a split second, I thought that that was enough.

A few shuddering breaths, and I grabbed the pot again and threw up harder, pieces of masticated biscuit and cake flying from my gullet into my mouth and bursting out. A small mouthful, then an explosion of food—I couldn't control the speed—the potion inside my stomach churned my innards, sending convulsions through my gut. At last, I tasted acid and rocked back onto my haunches, clutching my emptied stomach.

The smell of vomit pervaded the chamber. My forehead seemed to burn. In my throat, I felt a raw ache, as if someone had stripped the lining away. I tried to breathe slower, but my chest was pulsing, and placing a hand over the left side, I felt the *knock-knock-knock* of my heart.

Was I going to die?

I rushed to the tiny window and opened the shutters. Cold air streamed in. I gasped as it hit my cheeks and neck. There wasn't enough of it to flush out the smell of vomit, I thought, dumbly, before remembering the large window in the bedchamber and running back. Once the big shutters were open, a faint perfume of flowers wafted in; I peered out to find a bed of roses below the window ledge. Letting the scent fill the air, I brought my chamber pot out to the guards at the door and asked them to dispose of it.

After one of them carried it away, I closed the door firmly. I stood with my back against the wood, just breathing.

It was all gone. Removed. Purged, as if I had never eaten it. I would still be beautiful, after all. At once, I felt lighter and calmer.

The guilt hit me minutes later, when I was scrubbing the spattered food off the tiles of the bathchamber with a strip of cloth. What had I been thinking, eating freely? How did I have the stupidity to stuff my face and think that I could get away without paying for it? Had I ruined my body?

And why was I so thirsty, all of a sudden?

I finished scrubbing and got up. The jug of cold water beckoned to me from the table, and I poured myself a glass and sat down on the bed, sipping it slowly. I wanted to cry. Somehow, I couldn't: I just sat there in shock, drinking.

It was hard to say how long I sat there, but a knock broke my reverie at last. I walked to the door and opened it a crack. Aiven pushed it back the rest of the way.

"Is everything okay, Fierre?"

"Yes." I stepped back, hoping that my breath didn't smell like vomit. "Fine."

"I'm sorry about what I said, before. I shouldn't have asked. I was curious, but no matter what, I don't judge you for sleeping with anyone you like. And I know you must have so much on your mind without me interfering—your father's illness, the duties of your office, the concerns you have about the farmers and the realm... I shouldn't have bothered you."

Wonderful. Now I felt even more ashamed. Here Aiven was, listing all these big things I should have been considering, and I had been focusing on the petty matter of my own body. I was a narcissist. And a terrible person.

"Thanks, Aive," I said, softly.

"Would you like me to hold you, tonight?"

He stepped further inside, into the soft light of the candles, and his sandy hair glowed at the edges. He reminded me of a warrior in a classical painting, one of those selfless and powerful men who saved a deer from a highland wolf.

"No... I think I'll take a walk around the castle. Explore a bit. You should sleep, Aive. Get some rest."

The last thing I saw before I closed the door was the hurt in Aiven's eyes.

I tried to keep my walk slow so that my heartbeat could settle into a relaxed rhythm. It had about as much effect as an empty medicine jar. My heart simply refused to stop throwing itself against my ribcage, and I wondered if there was a quiet nook in the castle where I could sit. The thought had scarcely occurred to me when I turned the corner and saw Kinnaid walking towards me, his collar rumpled, a spattering of scarlet on his shirtsleeves.

"My laird, has something happened?"

"It's only wine. If you ask me, a waste of a good northern red." He glanced at his right sleeve. "After dinner, MacArlay shared some of his most colourful thoughts about Rossane... and Rossane shared the contents of his glass with MacArlay. At least, he tried to. Most of it ended up decorating me."

"I'm glad it's not blood." I stopped an inch away from him. "Did they come to blows?"

"MacArlay got a few hits to Rossane's ribs, and Rossane landed a couple of blows on MacArlay's head, but I think the only thing dented, really, was their pride. I sent them off in opposite directions and warned them that if they start another fight, I'll clang their heads together like a pair of bells, and I'll not mind how loud they ring."

"Thank you, my laird. I'm sorry your shirt had to suffer for your good deed."

"Oh, I don't mind about keeping it neat."

"Not fussy?" I said.

"I tend towards a little roughness, myself."

In the flickering light of the torch, Kinnaid's eyes looked like pieces of dark glass, opaque but glinting on the surface.

"Would you care to walk with me, my laird?" I nodded to the hallway extending behind him. "I was looking for a quiet nook, but as far as I can see, this castle seems to be made entirely of corridor."

"I think I know just the place," Kinnaid said.

We climbed the stairs to the next level and he led me through an even longer corridor, moving at a gentle pace so that I could keep in step with him. At last, the hallway opened onto a small alcove to the right, where twin torches lit up a bench and a small table offered a vase filled with black roses. I sat down and wriggled back against the cushioned padding of the bench. Kinnaid joined me. The softness of the seat felt welcoming after the cold tiles of the bathchamber, and I couldn't help closing my eyes for a moment and trying to block out the memory of bending over, of gripping the chamber pot, of vomiting until I tasted acid.

Kinnaid didn't ask if I was tired or sick. He simply let me relax, waiting in silence. I opened my eyes and found him holding out a glass of water; I hadn't noticed the jug beside the vase, and I drank thirstily, draining every drop.

"Your hair," Kinnaid said.

I ran my hand across my brow. Nothing seemed to be out of place.

"No need to worry, Sky. I was just observing how fine it is."

"Oh." My tongue stuck to the bottom of my mouth.

"May I touch it?"

We locked eyes. That dark, glittering stare of his gave nothing away. I felt the rawness of my throat, the empty pit of my stomach. I didn't want to feel any of it.

"Yes," I said.

His fingers lifted a few strands from my brow and pinched them, holding them up to the light. Slowly, he ran his forefinger and thumb along my hair, to the root, and slid them back down to the tip again. His gaze trailed from my face to my chest, and then lower.

"Is it fine all the way down?"

I swallowed. "I wonder if yours is that coarse everywhere."

"Oh, I may seem quieter than some of the other lairds, Sky, but I'm coarse in all sorts of ways."

He leaned close to me. The red of his hair turned molten in the full glare of the torches, and I felt its brightness like a firebrand.

"I'm going to kiss you, Sky."

He could have made it a question. In a way, it was a question, with a long pause after he spoke, but he had made it sound like a firm statement. This way, we could both pretend I wasn't his master. We could both imagine what it would be like for him to take control.

I closed my eyes and leaned towards him. A hand wrapped around the back of my neck, and then his lips parted mine and his tongue was in my mouth, exploring as much of me as he could reach. He kissed me like a hungry animal, and I liked the way all other thoughts disappeared from my mind. The hard pressure of Kinnaid's chest against mine drove my shame away for as long as I needed.

"We should head to a room," I whispered into his mouth.

"Yours?"

"No. Yours will do nicely."

The suite that Lady Sabernethy had given Kinnaid was considerably smaller than mine, but the bed was just as imposing. The doorway faced the bed, and I followed Kinnaid in, trying not to stare at the silken pillows. Kinnaid watched me for a moment, then wrapped his hand around my neck and kissed me again, a little harder this time, as if he were testing to see what I would tolerate. He slid his hand down my back as he kissed. After he let go, he gave me a gentle slap on the arse.

I didn't say a word.

"Can I take off your clothes, Sky?"

"If you think it wise."

Kinnaid smiled, and began to untie my enserre. He made short work of the ties, unwound the silk quickly, and placed the fabric on a cabinet. After untying and ripping off my sandals, he stared at me without even the slightest restraint, his eyes running all over me. "Stirring saints," he said. "I don't think I've seen anything this beautiful in all the paintings in the realm."

"There's no artistry involved."

"Are you sure? You look like a very detailed picture to me, Sky. If the painters were allowed to depict our holy lord, I think he'd look like this."

My title sounded too formal on his lips: a reminder that I was supposed to wield power.

"No need to call me Sky in here," I said.

"How should I address you?"

Dannatyne was what Rossane called me, and I didn't want to be reminded of him... there was my first name, of course, but that was for Aiven. *Fierre* was special. Only my best friend had the right to call me that.

Kinnaid was looking at me like a hound that hadn't been fed.

"Call me some coarse names," I said.

Kinnaid, it turned out, had no short supply of them. He walked around me in a circle, testing a few of them on me, his gaze sweeping my skin all the while. I tried to keep cool, but my body was determined to show that I was enjoying every word.

Kinnaid's right hand found the hair below my abdomen and stroked it. He looked into my eyes. His fingers closed around a few hairs and yanked them, making me yelp.

"So it *is* fine all the way down."

"Wait." I shot a glance at the doorway to our right.

Kinnaid looked inquisitively at me.

"Stay here until I come out of the bathchamber," I said.

"Is something wrong?"

"I, uh…" Oh god. My cheeks were hot, all of a sudden. "I need to prepare myself."

Kinnaid's expression was that of a man who had just won a lottery. Not the small, rural kind, either.

I shut the bathchamber door behind me and looked at the shelves, searching for a bottle or a jar. I nearly exclaimed in relief. The tiny amber bottle sat between two pieces of cloth, and I unstoppered it and smelled the familiar oil. Carefully, I slicked my fingers.

It wasn't that I was shy. I just couldn't bear the thought of someone seeing my body's imperfections, seeing that I needed to cleanse and oil myself like any other man… I was supposed to be a finished object: a masterpiece to be presented. Hadn't Kinnaid called me beautiful? The illusion would fall away if he saw me doing this.

Once I had made myself thoroughly slick inside, I walked back out to find Kinnaid taking off his clothes.

He threw his kilt onto the cabinet once he saw me. We walked towards each other, and I knew that I was walking into another mistake, but I kept crossing the floor.

"If you were anyone else, I'd be telling you exactly what to do. Looking like that…"

I stopped right in front of him.

"Well, I'd be giving orders."

"What would you say?" I asked.

Kinnaid's jaw twitched. He stepped away, then circled me, taking painstakingly measured steps. Finally, he halted in front of me again.

"I'd tell you to touch your toes, like a good little whore."

I turned to face the bed, putting my back to him. Ignoring the ache in my calves, I bent over until my fingers touched my toes.

I heard Kinnaid's intake of breath, clear even from a distance.

A second later, his fingers were on my buttocks, pulling them apart, opening me up wide, and I felt so humiliated that my face burned anew. He inspected me slowly, and to my shame, I felt myself getting hard. It was as if Kinnaid knew that this would be his one chance, and he wanted to see every inch of me—even several inches inside of me.

"Did someone make you specially for this?" he said.

"You tell me." I could feel the blood going to my head.

"My god. I've never seen anything like you. You're perfect."

"Can we stop talking, my laird?"

He slapped my arse, harder than before, and the sound was like a warning. I didn't pay it any heed. When something cold and hard pushed into me, I gasped and held onto my ankles. Kinnaid shoved harder, and a few more inches of cold metal slid into me, until I felt a horizontal bar rest against my arse. I recognised the guard of his dirk, and thanked my stars that he had used the harmless end of the dagger. The metal pommel hurt inside, but after a moment, my body adjusted to the round shape, and I could feel the dagger-hilt's length.

"Do you cry?" Kinnaid said.

"Not easily."

"Good." He shoved the pommel in and out of me quickly, making me suck in a breath. "I like a challenge."

He pounded me with the hilt until I wanted to cry. I kept silent, biting my lip. I didn't want him to know how sensitive I was, even though I could take the pain. He withdrew the dirk slowly, making me feel every inch as it came out, and I felt my head spin as I stood up again. Kinnaid didn't seem to notice how dizzily I moved to grip the bedpost.

"I'd say you're warmed up, now," he murmured.

I didn't need to confirm it.

"Come here."

I walked into his arms, feeling the room spin a little. My arse hurt, and my throat still felt raw from vomiting, and my stomach was a churning mess. It occurred to me that I should probably leave. But Kinnaid's body pressed me into the bed, and he felt powerful, like Aiven. For a moment, I pretended that it was Aiven stroking me.

Everything changed, then, in a heartbeat.

"Will you call me Fierre?" I said.

Surprise flared in Kinnaid's eyes. "If you like."

We looked at each other for a long moment.

"Call me Fierre when you hold me down," I said.

That was all the encouragement I needed to give. Once I was on my back, he held my legs behind my head and pinned my arms back as he fucked me, and god, it felt good to pretend. I shut my eyes and heard him breathing hard. My stomach felt fragile, and I hoped that my body didn't collapse. When Kinnaid slapped me across the face, I moaned. When he pressed his entire, muscular form down on top of me, sinking into me, I felt tears leak from the corners of my eyes. I wanted to wipe them away, but he had a firm grip on my wrists.

"Fierre," Kinnaid grunted.

It wasn't Aiven's soft murmur, or Aiven's scent around me, but with his big hands on me, for a moment, I could make believe. I shut my eyes. In the blackness, I imagined Aiven pinning me down.

"God," Kinnaid said, "Fierre—"

It was a second too late when I realised what was about to happen. I didn't have the heart to refuse, and as he came inside me, I watched the vein strain in his neck. I let him moan into my mouth, shuddering his way to the end. Rich men were always so vulnerable when they came. It was the main reason I was glad that it took me so long, each time; I liked watching each lover lose his hard shell and become limp in my arms.

Or in this case, limp on top of me.

I shifted slightly, and Kinnaid took the hint and climbed off me. He wrapped his hand around my cock and moved it mercilessly. The rubbing drove me to the edge until I cried out and came across the bedcover. We both lay back for a moment.

A few seconds later, I felt Kinnaid's fingers push into me.

I looked down. A rush of shame ran through me. Worse than the feeling of him cleaning me out was the experience of watching, and seeing how easily he did what he liked with me. I had never been able to resist men who treated me like the dirt beneath their boots, but in that moment, I wished I was stronger.

"Good boy," Kinnaid said.

And it was like Rossane, like all the others merging into one in my head: *good boy, good boy, good boy.*

He kissed me again, and studied me, as if he didn't quite know what to do. Silence filled the space between us.

"Shall I keep you warm for the night?" Kinnaid said.

"You've done enough already."

"Did I fail to satisfy you, Sky?"

There it was: my title, the end of our little rendezvous, and a reminder that no matter what Kinnaid did to me, he was still my subject.

I wished I could tell him, and MacArlay, and all the others, that sex wasn't the problem. They were all capable of being as cruel to me as I liked, in bed. But I wanted someone who would kiss me afterward and hold me because he wanted to—because he cared, not because it was a chore or a duty, or a way to ensure that I left their clan basking in the glow of coin and privilege, unchecked.

"You did perfectly," I said.

Once I had used the bathchamber and dressed, I slipped quietly down the corridor. The guards watched me, and for once, I was glad of the distance between prince and commoner. I didn't want to know what they were thinking. At last, I reached my suite and slipped inside, peering through to the bedchamber, where a mound beneath the bedsheets showed me that Aiven was asleep.

I untied my enserre awkwardly and exchanged it for my night-shift. The air swirled around my ankles, frightfully cold, although I could still feel the heat inside me where Kinnaid had been.

I crawled onto the bed and slid beneath the sheets, pulling the upper blanket high up to my neck. Aiven shifted onto his side. His eyes blinked open slowly.

"Fierre."

I didn't know exactly when I began crying. It was somewhere between Aiven sitting up and his hand finding my shoulder, but I felt as if I had wanted to cry for days, and when Aiven offered me his embrace, I didn't refuse.

His hand stroked my head, caressing the locks one by one.

"Whatever it is, it's okay," he murmured.

I could almost believe it was true. I could almost forget about the cerise liquid sloshing and my stomach convulsing; about Kinnaid opening me up and pushing his dagger-hilt in deep; about the way I had imagined Aiven's face while Kinnaid came inside me. I could almost pretend that it would be okay, because Aiven kissed my forehead and pulled me close to him.

"It'll feel better after a night's sleep."

I was sure that he was right. And yet, as I rested my back gently against him and let his arm curve around me, I wanted to stay awake forever in this moment: to trace every detail of this warm comfort into my mind's paper, so that I would always remember what it felt like when Aiven held me close.

I fell asleep quickly. In my dream, I ate as many raven buns as I liked, chewing the black pastry, letting the cream linger on my tongue. Nothing happened: I didn't take any potions, and I never gained any weight.

Eleven

Aiven

WE SAID OUR thank-yous, made our bows, and mounted our horses, and we were just turning to ride when Lady Sabernethy's cry of "Wait!" rang out.

It wasn't Lady Sabernethy sprinting towards us, however, but one of her daughters, carrying a bunch of highland roses down the ramp. The blue ribbon around the stems matched the blue petals of the flowers. I couldn't help but admire the distinct colour of the blooms, rich and bright as a midsummer sky.

"It would be my honour if you would pass judgment on our roses, Sky," the girl said. "We grow them carefully in the pleasure garden of Castle Aonar." She stretched her arm up to Fierre.

Fierre smiled as he took the flowers. He didn't seem to realise how easily his smile could pierce someone through the heart, but judging by the rapt look from Lady Sabernethy's daughter, he had accidentally struck another person down.

"I named these blooms Sky Roses, in your honour," the girl said.

"That's most gracious of you... er..."

"Sorcha, Sky."

"Well, I find them exquisite, Sorcha. I can smell their fragrance, but it's gentle, like a hand caressing my brow and leaving a floral memory where it has passed."

He drew a deep breath, then passed the roses back to her. Sorcha gazed down at the roses in her hands.

"You gave me flowers," she said.

"I'm happy to return them to you. As beautiful as they are, we can hardly take them on the ride."

"You gave me flowers, Sky."

Something about her tone of voice made me tense. It was shy, but artfully so, and she looked very satisfied to be holding the blue roses. Lady Sabernethy strode down the ramp towards us, coming to a stop behind her daughter.

"You know the law, Master of Compliance," she said, looking at me. "We are honoured to receive pride of place."

Of course. How had I missed it?

"And you must know that *she* gave the flowers to *him*," I retorted.

"What I saw just now was the Sky honouring my daughter by handing her a bunch of roses. Did you see otherwise?"

It wasn't fair, I wanted to say. It wasn't honourable to trick the Sky of Eilean-òir like that. But Fierre was smiling, and I knew by that bright smile that he didn't wish for trouble.

"Excuse me," a man said, "but can somebody explain to me what is going on?"

We all turned to find the ambassador for Archland perched on a grey mare, leaning over to catch a glimpse of the flowers.

"Ambassador," Fierre said. "I'm so glad we can speak at last. Allow me to illuminate this little surprise. We have a law in this realm that if the Sky gives flowers to a woman, he must consider her for the Quickening."

"The Quickening?"

"I think it's time for a chat. What do you say, Ambassador Rince? Shall we talk while we ride?" After Rince's nod, Fierre turned back to Lady Sabernethy and beamed at her. I was close enough to see the strain in his neck that accompanied the smile.

"I shall honour the law, and be glad to report my answer within a year's time. Until we meet again, Lady Sabernethy!"

"Until we meet again," Lady Sabernethy echoed.

I remained quiet with great effort as we trotted away, keeping my horse on Fierre's right. The ambassador brought his animal up on Fierre's left, and we rode in an awkward trilogy at the head of the party, just behind the first group of guards. The riding party found an easy pace, allowing us to talk.

"Master Rince, you're new to your post, aren't you?" Fierre said. "My father only spoke of a Mistress Rince as ambassador to Archland."

"I've been in this post for five years, Sky."

"You shared it with a wife, perhaps?"

"Er... no... that is... Sky..." Rince drew a deep breath. "I was Mistress Rince, before. Now I am Master Rince. I completed a course of physic, to aid me with the change."

A silence hung tautly over us all.

"Then, congratulations," Fierre said, slowly and firmly. "For being more yourself."

Rince blushed. "Thank you, Sky."

"I'm so glad you spoke up about the Quickening,

Ambassador Rince," Fierre added. "I've been longing to converse with you ever since we left the palace, but I've been frightfully busy."

"This Quickening… is it a ritual of some kind?" Rince studied Fierre.

"More of a necessity. It's the reason Eilean-òir still has a line of kings." Fierre flashed him a smile. "You see, the Sky must choose a few women from noble families who he will consider making an heir with. He must meet them to see that they are worthy, and present them with flowers to mark them as his choices. By the year's end, he must announce which woman he will choose—and if she agrees and joyfully consents, they will lie together with full ceremony, being blessed by a priest and observed by four witnesses. If her womb quickens, her child will be the next king of Eilean-òir."

"And what if she fails to quicken?" Rince frowned. "Or quickens, but bears a girl?"

"No matter. They can always try again. If the Sky feels they have tried too many times without fruit, he may ask another woman." I heard the note of disapproval in Fierre's voice, even if no one else did.

"I see." The ambassador pursed his lips.

"Something troubling you, ambassador?"

"It seems like an enormous amount of rules and restrictions and bother, when you could make the whole business easy. Take a wife, lay with her every night, and make a child faster that way. Indeed, make many children! It would be much simpler than waiting until a special occasion and meeting only for the purpose of congress."

"Do you not think language is revealing, sometimes?" Fierre said.

"Sky?"

"We are always *taking* women. Taking a wife. Taking a woman to bed. Taking a partner for the Quickening."

"Er..."

"Sometimes, I wonder what might be done about that." Fierre cleared his throat. "But, to the point: it is generally understood that the Sky shouldn't frequently lie with a woman. If he did so, he would have no time to make himself..."

Fierre's sudden trailing-off prompted the ambassador to lean slightly to his right, as if he might glimpse the reason written on Fierre's face. "Yes?"

"Er... it's customary for the Sky to make himself available to certain noblemen at court. The lucky ones."

"We have a king who consults with his court, too, Sky. But that does not prevent him from taking a wife."

"It's a little more than consultation."

"Sky?"

Fierre glanced desperately at me. After a long pause, in which Rince looked increasingly bemused, I cleared my throat.

"If you'll allow me to explain, ambassador: the Sky of Eilean-òir is traditionally seen as the pinnacle of elegance and grace in our realm. His body emblematises the perfection of our divine lord. His disposition must be equally perfect. As such, his favour is always sought by men of influence and power, and he gives his favour sparingly, to those who are luckiest of all."

I heard Fierre splutter as I said *sparingly*, but I pretended that I didn't notice.

"Now, if the Sky were to have a consort, he couldn't lie with a nobleman when it pleased him. He wouldn't have those favours to grant," I added.

Rince didn't ask any more questions, but stared at

Fierre with a new interest. I guessed that even a foreigner could not fail to understand my meaning, now. I hated myself for saying the words, for if there had been a way to change that custom in the speaking, I would have altered it at once.

I wondered what my mother would say if she were here now. Something about the implied value of women as brood mares, no doubt.

It wasn't only the Sky of Eilean-òir who held complicated feelings about the Quickening.

THE HORSES GALLOPED over the downs and cut a smooth path through the last of the hills. We pressed into the northernmost part of the realm, following the pale blue ribbon of the East Highland River into a tapestry of mountains and lakes that stretched all the way to the northern shore. On our right, the snow-dusted tips of peaks stood out against the charcoal of the sky, and on our left, the river's surface glittered more brilliantly than a royal crown. I liked the sight of it, but the very drama of the landscape reminded me that I was far from home. The gentle slopes around the palace were my home: low hills, not soaring mountains, were my comfort.

We didn't stop at any more farms, though there were plenty scattered across the highlands. Perhaps Fierre had seen enough, or perhaps he kept his father's ailing health in mind, for he only paused to let the horses drink and the riders eat, and we flew over half the territory in one day. I didn't bother to set up my own tent when we camped, for I knew that Fierre would want me to sleep in his. Kinnaid hung around the entrance to Fierre's tent for a while, but Fierre sent him away, and once my petty wave of satisfaction had subsided, I was left wondering why the Chief of Diplomacy had been so confident of his chances.

I'd tried not to think about where Fierre might have gone after he disappeared from the bedchamber in the castle, but thoughts of Rossane's sneering face and MacArlay's aggressive expression had popped up every now and then. Maybe it wasn't Rossane or MacArlay I should've worried about.

In the morning, we struck an even pace, trotting up the steeper slopes between mountain passes, and I measured our distance from the sea by the smell of salt in the air—faint at first, then stronger, and finally a strength of brine that none of us could miss. We lodged our horses in the stables at the last town before the shore, while the minor laird stumbled over his compliments to Fierre, dazzled by the sight of the prince.

After that, we walked. A curve of white pebble beach came into view from the cliff, and it was with some excitement that we took the narrow path down to the bay. I looked around for a boat and found a litany of small craft bobbing in the water, their wooden sides tied to tiny posts along the shore. As we set foot on the pebbles and began to move towards them, a woman strode out from next to the cliff, her face possessing the unmistakeable texture of a person who worked exposed to the afternoon sun.

I glanced over at Fierre. He didn't look surprised.

"Honoured to guide you across, Sky." She bowed low. Her voice was the creak of an unoiled door. I liked her at once.

"We're honoured to have your expertise at our call. How many years is it that you've been ferrywoman? Twenty-two, Laird MacBrae said, but that would be astounding…"

"Twenty-two years rowing to the Isle of Hairstin. Eight

years ferrying boats back and forth from the Reedy Isle afore that. It's not fancy work, but it's steady, and few can do it—or maybe there's few who want to."

"Father told me that you can pick your way through the shoals. And that you're a deft hand at navigating the still water."

"Aye, I don't know that I'm a deft hand, but I'll put my mind at your disposal, Sky."

They led the way to the posts together. Only Fierre, I thought; only Fierre could charm a woman who looked as if she lived in a world that the word *charm* was afraid to enter.

We paired up for the boats, since the little craft could only take two people at a time, and the ferrywoman took Fierre into her boat. MacArlay, Rossane, and Kinnaid each paired with a guard, with Dr. Galar courteously asking the ambassador for Sarleven if she would accompany him. (The ambassador for Sarleven was so tall that her legs could scarcely fit in half the boat.) The attendants hurriedly paired with each other. That left Ambassador Rince and I with one guard apiece, but Rince beckoned me over, and we climbed into the same craft, leaving the last two soldiers to sail together.

Blue waters lapped at the vessels, lightening from a navy blue near the beach to a clear sky-blue in the open sea, and eventually, a bright turquoise colour. I'd always imagined the Isle of Hairstin as a windswept crag where dying kings went to retire, but the sight of that water gave me the impression that I was approaching a place from a faerie tale.

Even though I knew that such stories weren't real—that tales of meddling fae and prideful giants and fire-belching dragons were merely slivers of poets' imaginations—I pictured something wonderful beyond the horizon, all the same.

We glided along with just a little rowing, the ferrywoman standing up in her boat and leading the way, her eyes fixed on the sea. Rince said little. I kept my silence, too, watching the rose-pink coral just below the water and the schools of glinting fish that darted amongst the strands of seagrass. Once we entered choppier waters, we barely needed to row; the wind propelled us onward, and I took the opportunity to watch Fierre, sitting a little way ahead. I tried to figure out if he was enjoying the journey or not.

"You look preoccupied, Star."

Rince's voice cut through my focus.

"It's just my face," I said. "My mother says it's a serious one."

He smiled tentatively. "I did not wish to disturb you, but I wondered if you could tell me… how many islands lie ahead?"

"Just the one. The Isle of Hairstin sits alone off our northernmost coast. We call it the sacred isle, for it marks the topmost point of our realm. But twenty-four islands lie to the north-west, and a great many small islands float off the eastern coast."

"Thank you." Rince's smile warmed. "I'm sorry for asking so many questions today. We're not allowed to ask many questions, back home, but we're expected to know the answers."

"Is the king of Archland so demanding?"

"Demanding? That's one way of putting it."

"Perhaps you'd honour me with another," I said.

Rince exhaled. "His disposition is quite narcissistic. He is happy, himself, all the time, but cruel to others. We obtain good prices for dyes, and he asks for them to be twice as high next time. We sell all the cloth he requires, and he tells the court we have stone feet—that we're dragging ourselves along, trailing the market. He smiles as they all laugh." He trailed a finger through the water. "Your prince, I think, is the opposite."

I straightened against the side of the boat.

"I've been watching him on the ride. I had plenty of time to," Rince added.

I felt a little awkward over the ambassador's neglected position, for I was very aware that Fierre had still not treated Rince to a private audience, but Rince's voice cut across my thoughts again. "He shows kindness to others, Prince Dannatyne, but when he is alone... he looks sad. Why is Prince Dannatyne sad, Star? The way I see it, he has the world at his disposal."

"It's not that simple," I said. "A whole mantle of expectations sits upon a prince's shoulders. He must create an image that the whole realm venerates, through his manner and way of speaking, and through his body's shape, his way of walking, his every gesture. He is tasked with inspiring hope and desire by turns." Too late, I heard the ring of defensiveness in my voice. "I expect you've heard that Clan Dannatyne has divine right to rule. In this court, rights are purchased with the eyes."

"I see," Rince said, in a voice that told me he did not.

"When the Sky glides through in his enserre, in a physical form that no man here can emulate, he is truly, then, god's vessel on earth."

"But still, I think he could easily find comfort," Rince said. "He could have his pick of courtiers... or any bride he chooses."

"We say *consort*, not *bride*, in Eilean-òir. Any subject may marry a man, a woman, or a person of other nature—

but a royal marriage is rare. The Quickening makes it easy for a king to keep his state alone. Why commit to one person, when you can give your favour as it suits your purpose each week?"

If there was a trace of bitterness in my voice, I hoped Rince didn't hear it.

"I see." Rince paused. "I understood you, before. Has it always been this way?"

"Since the Dannatynes assumed power. An untouchable divine vessel is one thing. A potentially touchable vessel… that is even more to be desired. Favours may be granted. As the lairds desire; as the Sky permits. Push and pull. Pull and push."

"Perhaps rights are not only purchased with the eyes, but with the hands," Rince said.

I smiled tightly.

"But from certain gossip, I have the impression that many men have sampled Prince Dannatyne's… shall we say, favour?" He paused again. "So, I must return to my original question. Why, then, does he look sorrowful? Can he find no man who makes him happy?"

I checked the distance between our boat and Fierre's. Judging that there was no way we could be overheard, I turned back to Rince. "Do you know of the scarlet bee?" I said.

Rince's forehead wrinkled. "I don't believe I have made its acquaintance."

"A small species of bee with a dark red marking on the back. It is unique amongst bees, in that it has no sting. It goes about pollinating and working whilst entirely vulnerable to attack; yet while the scarlet bee should be more cautious, it is, in fact, more reckless."

"You know a lot about bees."

"I'm a farmers' son." Rince looked surprised, but I pressed on. "When I say that it is reckless, ambassador, I mean that it befriends a very dangerous creature. I think you will know of the midnight spider in Archland."

"All ambassadors to Eilean-òir are briefed on your most venomous spider." Rince shuddered. "I hope to never see one of those things."

"If only the scarlet bee were half so wise as you. The hapless creatures are fascinated by their predator. When they come across a midnight spider, they sense it as a danger, yet they cannot help approaching it. They have been known to lie down before the spider, on their knees... or on their backs."

"I enjoy this scientific interlude, Star, but are we not drifting a little off track from matters of princes and kings?"

"Are we?" I said.

Rince glanced across at Fierre. The waves rippled around us, and our boat began to drift slightly off-course. I took up the oar again and rowed gently, pulling us back into line. After a very long moment, Rince returned his gaze to me.

"I see," he said.

"Do you?"

"I see that there are some people who choose the open flower to offer themselves to, and others who choose the midnight spider."

A long pause followed, in which I felt the ambassador's eyes on me. The wind blew sea spray into our faces.

"But perhaps there is still hope," Rince said.

"Hope?"

"That in time, he will be pulled towards the right one, like a boat pulled to shore."

It was my turn to stare.

"You understand me, I think," Rince said.

I looked over at Fierre. The breeze was ruffling his hair, sending a few strands flying, and the sun highlighted the fine sheen on the deep black. Very slowly, I looked back at Rince.

"I think we understand each other," I said.

The breeze gave way to stillness and the boats began to slow. The ferrywoman stood up and pointed to a patch of water ahead. Squinting, I could just make out the shape of a sandbar beneath the water's surface.

"Stillwater," the ferrywoman said. "And not before time. We're coming up on a shoal, so everyone follow me, and row quickly now. Dawdle, and you founder."

None of us were eager to be beached and to suffer an ignominious rescue, but Rossane and MacArlay rowed so fast that their boats surged ahead, rounding the shoal and passing Fierre and the ferrywoman in the process. Judging by their faces, they realised this too late. I saw Kinnaid smirking as the rest of us caught up to them and Fierre's boat glided ahead, restoring hierarchy.

"If you two lairds can bear to wait, we'll be coming up on the isle soon." The ferrywoman's voice had a touch of humour to it, but Rossane looked furious. I feared for the ferrywoman's life for a moment.

No one spoke, and I guessed that Rossane had the good sense to know Fierre wouldn't be pleased by another round of fisticuffs.

Once we had cleared the sandbar, the water became shallower, its bright turquoise giving way to a translucent section, and I leaned over to gaze at something leaping beneath the surface. Purple and pink scales moved in and out of focus, sharpening and blurring as the fish jumped.

Fins churned, but amidst all their excitement, the island minnows failed to leap high enough to clear our rail.

"I'll be pulling the boats up to the posts, now." The ferrywoman stood up and climbed out of her vessel, stepping into the thick of the fish. They darted around her legs like dogs welcoming their master back home. She unwound a rope from beside Fierre and ran it through a sturdy wooden loop at the front of the boat, ready to tow the craft forward. "If you don't mind, Sky, you can climb out and walk."

Fierre took off his sandals, laid them in the boat, and swung himself tentatively over the side, steadying himself on the sand. The pink and purple fish leaped towards him at first, before slowing down and circling him in a more measured motion. I heard him giggle, and the sound was pure sunlight.

"Are you all right, Sky?" Rossane called out.

"The fish seem to like me!" Fierre beamed. "What colours they have! Do you think island minnows can bite?"

They're not the ones whose bite you need to worry about, I thought, as Rossane leaned to the side of his boat to stare at Fierre's bent-over figure.

The ferrywoman began to tow her empty boat towards a post on the shore, while the rest of us crouched and readied ourselves to climb out. Ignoring the bustle of movement, I kept my eyes on Fierre. I was watching as he clutched at his head, teetered, and fell forward into the water.

"Fierre!"

I forgot all about the correct title to use as I jumped from my boat and splashed towards him. His body floated, face down, like a fallen log. I could hear the splashing of others behind me, but I reached Fierre first and pulled him upright, moving without hesitation. He felt light and limp in my arms, even with his enserre waterlogged. I patted his cheeks, and he opened his eyes and gasped.

"Aive! What happened?"

"You fell."

"I don't feel so brilliant, Aive."

"Let's get you to the shore, then." I wrapped one arm around his shoulders and grasped his right hand in my left. Taking one step at a time, I led him up the gentle slope from the shallows to the sand. He gripped my palm hard. We had almost reached the shore when he sagged against me and I quickly caught him, propping him up. His eyes closed again, and his hand lost its grip.

"Fierre!" I cried.

This time, no answer came. I pressed my fingers to his neck and then to his wrist. I felt no pulse.

"What is it, Grian?" MacArlay shouted. "Is he sick?"

I didn't reply. My hands moved before I knew what I was doing, and I scooped Fierre up and lifted him before me, placing my left hand under his knees and my right hand against his back. I held him as firmly as I could. The small rocks amongst the sand scraped my feet as I climbed onto the shore and carried him up to the nearest patch of grass. Nothing else existed, in that moment— not the dark trees, not the curve of the cliff to our left, not the distant turrets of the island's castle above the ridge of low hills. Fierre's limp body filled my vision.

When a man in a black cloak knelt by my side, it took me a while to notice that his face was unfamiliar.

The man jabbed a finger at his chest. "Lighiche."

"I don't know that word," I said.

He pointed at Fierre, then back at himself, and repeated:

"Lighiche."

"Excuse me, Star." One of the guards stepped forward. "It's an old word from these parts, *lighiche*. It means doctor."

Slowly, the man in the black cloak nodded.

There are some times when everything rests on a quick decision. I looked back at the water and saw Galar still floundering amongst the fish, struggling to reach the shore. I returned my gaze to Fierre and placed my hand on his chest, feeling for a pulse.

When none came, I looked across at our new doctor.

"If you can save his life," I said, "do it now, man."

"Dunhairstin," he said.

He jabbed his finger at the castle on the horizon. I hefted Fierre up again, swinging him into the same position, and turned towards an approaching MacArlay. "Get Galar to follow as fast as he can," I said. "We're going up right now."

The man in the black cloak began to walk, and I followed, toward the ridge of hills, through the fog and mist, making a direct line for the only fortress on the island.

Twelve

Fierre

THERE ARE SOME mornings when your head feels like it's had a small knock with a light hammer. There are other mornings when you're sure that someone has been tapping on your skull all night with an iron bar. There are even some mornings when it feels like an elephant has been dancing on your head in steel boots, doing a vigorous jig and smacking you with its trunk.

Today was definitely the latter kind of morning.

I stretched woozily and sat up against the pillows, taking in the large bed and the pink-and-white tartan blanket laid over the sheets. Two chairs stood near the left wall, bathed in the light from the window. The Dannatyne crest on the cushions looked faded, its prancing deer a pale brown, and the hanging on the far wall offered a blotched tapestry of an ancient battle, the clashes partly overlaid by black mould. Either my father hadn't had guests in a while, or he'd offered me this room to punish me for having any shred of taste.

My instinct to head to the bath chamber and examine

my naked body kicked in—who knew how much damage I had done with that feast on the ride, even after the vomiting?—and I threw back the blanket and sheets. My head protested with a sudden dizzy spell, and I gripped my forehead. A cough drew my attention to my right. I looked across to find Galar eyeing me from a small wooden chair.

"I take it that you are disoriented, Prince Dannatyne?"

"No," I said. "Unfortunately. Do you think you could knock me on the head for a bit, and make me forget that tapestry?"

Galar's smile didn't quite reach his eyes. He rose from his seat and leaned over the bed, holding out a glass. Emerald green liquid swirled inside it, and little crystals settled in the bottom of the glass, like sediment coming to rest on a riverbed. A faint aroma of brine rose to my nostrils.

"This will restore your energy, Sky."

I screwed up my face as I sipped at the potion. Whatever it was, it hadn't been made as a dessert. My tired brain reasoned that if it tasted this bad, it had to be good for me. I swallowed the lot.

"There. Restorative, and no buns or biscuits needed."

I stared down at my hands, folded in my lap, and tried to look as if I wasn't embarrassed.

Galar's cold eyes raked my face, and he seemed to see that there was no need for further reproachment. My shame was probably writ in bright paint on my forehead. "Do you remember the man who rushed to your side as you lay on the shore, Sky?"

Now it rushed back: my head spinning, and my vision dimming; the splash of water; Aiven scooping me up and carrying me through the shallows, his big hands propping up my back and legs; and a man repeating a word somewhere above me. A strange word. A word in the local dialect, most likely, by the sound of it.

"*Lighiche*," I said, rolling it around my mouth.

"Yes, that is what he calls himself. *Lighiche*. Doctor." Galar exhaled sharply. "He is no such thing. A charlatan dabbling in the savage ways of his family, with no regard for the respectful distance between himself and his prince."

I considered pointing out that you couldn't really keep a respectful distance when you were trying to revive someone who had swallowed a lot of sea water, but Galar's flared nostrils told me that he wasn't in the mood for it.

"He may have revived you, but it was a happy chance, not a matter of skill. As your royal doctor, I advise you to avoid the so-called doctors of Clan Sethune. A long time ago, they dared to pour their words into your grandfather's ear, before the king sent them on their way. They come from the Isle of Hairstin, this very far-flung rock, and let that be a warning. The further north you travel in this realm, the more science flies out the window: if the Sethunes were appointed to care for you, they would destroy your body in days."

I gave a non-committal cough. What did you say to that, really? Galar could be right—he certainly knew what he was doing with his potions, for I felt as if my heart was beating faster already since drinking that emerald concoction.

"Did father send for me?" I asked.

"Your father stated that he is resting this afternoon. He requested that you join him for dinner. He also insisted, in no uncertain terms, that you bathe in the Fae Pools in the island's interior before you see him." Galar looked as if he were perilously close to rolling his eyes. "Something about cleansing yourself of favours."

It would probably take a few months of bathing in magical pools before the faeries could even make a start on scrubbing off all the favours I'd given to men whose alliances I needed. It occurred to me that my father must know that I had confessed my string of lovers to a priest in the rituals. He'd probably ordered me to bathe in the Fae Pools so everyone else knew that in his eyes, no matter how well I fulfilled his expectations, I still deserved a cleaning.

That sounded like him.

"Where's Aiven?" I said.

I saw Galar's eyebrows leap and knew that I should have asked where *everyone else* was, or where *my retinue* were.

"In a pavilion with the lairds and ambassadors, eating lunch," Galar said.

"Well, then. I think we should take a stroll."

It didn't take me long to dress and put on a diamond necklace while Galar waited outside. We walked together through Dunhairstin Castle's long corridors, working our way down to the ground floor and emerging from a dim world of tapestries and busts into a misty garden. Rows of bright purple flowers flanked the path to a pavilion. Beneath the pointed roof of the little structure, Rossane and Kinnaid were talking with Rince, while the ambassador for Sarleven towered over MacArlay. On the end, standing apart from the others, Aiven was conversing with the guards over the edge of the pavilion. I watched him smile and lean further towards them, ignoring hierarchy so that they could hear him.

"Gentlemen… and lady," I said.

The conversations broke off at once.

"Sky, I'm relieved to see you well!" MacArlay cried.

"You look splendid," Rossane added.

Kinnaid merely nodded, and the ambassadors bowed. But Aiven walked out of the pavilion and stopped just inches from me, taking my hand and kissing it.

"I'm so happy you're okay," he said.

I almost blushed. Unfortunately, there was too much grey mist swirling above us to pass it off as a touch of heat.

Pretending not to notice the death stares that were being levelled at Aiven, I faced the group.

"I hate to bother you all while you're eating, but I have a mission to complete. I must ride to the Fae Pools, bathe, and return in time for dinner… that means a journey into deeper mist than this, to the centre of the isle." I looked around the group. "Our family holds those pools to be sacred, and the Fae are said to permit only two travellers at a time. It will be safe to ride without guards on the Isle of Hairstin." I paused again, teetering awkwardly on the spot. "I can only take one of you."

Rossane stepped forward. "It would be my honour to aid you, Sky."

"And mine," MacArlay said.

Kinnaid moved to the front of the pavilion. "As you require me, I will serve."

I waited for another voice to chime in, but Aiven only gazed at me. His jaw clenched, and I considered that although Aiven had been Star of the Sky for less than a week, he had been Master of Compliance for several years, and a farm boy for much longer than that.

Did he know how to put himself forward amongst a group of lairds?

"You all make such sparkling company." My gaze swept Rossane, MacArlay, and Kinnaid. "And that's why I can't choose you. So perfectly matched—I couldn't pass judgment between those of equal title and merits. But the Star of the Sky shares his position with no other, and in choosing him, I think I risk no offence." I smiled widely at the others, then beckoned to Aiven. "Everyone else, get back to devouring the castle's best offerings. That's an order."

Aiven strode to join me, and we walked around the side of the castle, towards the stables. Once we were out of sight of the others, he took my hand in his. "I didn't think you'd choose me."

"Well, now you know my secret. I'm a fool for big men in small shirts."

He looked down at his tight white shirt and grimaced. "I didn't have time to change properly. The Mistress of Household threw this shirt at me and told me to get to the pavilion while they still had fresh food. I think they must have panicked once we arrived, and put everything on the table."

"I must say, I don't mind the consequence." As Aiven pretended not to be embarrassed, a thought occurred to me. "Oh gosh, Aive... did you want to finish eating? I didn't think. I'd just spoken to Dr Galar about father's instructions, and I wanted to get away. We can go back!"

"Settle down." Aiven patted me gently on the head. "You've only just recovered from a dizzy spell. Think about your own needs, not mine. Do you need more rest, maybe? Are you hungry, Fierre?"

I thought of my dream, where I had eaten as many raven buns as I liked and never got fat.

"No," I said.

The look on Aiven's face told me that I'd said it far louder than I intended to.

WE RODE PRESSED together on one horse, down the narrow trail that led into the centre of the Isle of Hairstin, and once we were a little distance from Dunhairstin, I turned back to take in the castle's majesty. Although I'd seen it numerous times as a boy, the gap between my last visit and this moment made it seem new. Memories of visiting the isle flooded back, and it was not the castle, with its walls of grey cloudstone, that stood out to me, but the experiences it had afforded me: the hikes to the forbidding slopes of the Black Peaks and the rides to the translucent pink water of the Fae Pools, still burned into my memory.

Every time I set foot on this isle, I felt as if magic were hanging over it. Perhaps it was the mist that swirled above the dark mountains. Or perhaps it was something intangible; something that couldn't be given an image or a name.

"I can see you know Hairstin like the back of your hand," Aiven said, as we turned off the path and onto a barely visible trail, cutting between hills on our right and farmland and small lakes on our left.

"When I came here as a child, we were visiting my grandfather. Before his death, of course; to say goodbye. Now it's not him dying, but…"

My voice gave out, and Aiven's hands tightened around my waist. In that moment, I felt very glad that I had asked him to ride on the same horse.

Despite the chill of the misty afternoon, I enjoyed the ride past the lakes, for every so often the cloud cleared enough to offer a slice of blue water, unrippled, reflecting the black pinnacles of rock that towered above us. Woolly cattle raised their heads to stare at us. A few of them approached us, lowing as we passed, and I grinned as I took in the long hair that fell over their eyes.

"I suppose you need a thick coat to survive up here in the winter," I said, turning my head so that Aiven could hear me.

"Good thing you don't live here, then." Aiven smiled. "God missed your chest when he was giving out hair."

"No need to gloat. We can't all be strapping young men."

"I think you're perfect the way you are."

Suddenly, I became very interested in the landscape. I turned to face ahead.

How could Aiven say things like that with a straight face? No one could really believe that I was perfect. Not truly. And even if he did, it had to be because I was slim and looked like a Dannatyne prince—if my body changed, and became bigger and softer, he'd lose interest. *Perfect* was a full-time job, and one that I suspected I was failing at.

The next turn around a hill revealed a bank of cloud, and where the land dipped, the cloud became so heavy that I could barely see. I slowed the horse and let it trot at a cautious pace through the low-lying clouds, pushing through their grey mass one hoofbeat at a time. Cold air embraced us, but it lifted after the greyness began to thin, and soon we emerged into a patch of clear sunshine, our faces shocked by the flood of warmth.

"Stirring saints," Aiven whispered. "I didn't picture it like this."

Before us, four pink pools sat at the foot of four rocky outcrops, a waterfall pouring down from the mountain above them and tricking into tributaries until it flowed into the pools. The steady tinkle of water surrounded us with song.

"How did you picture it?" I said.

"Less pink. And less beautiful." Aiven dismounted and helped me down, lifting me carefully onto the ground. "It's like someone was trying to imagine the exact sort of place where faeries might live, so they painted these pools… and the picture sprang to life."

I glimpsed rocks at the bottom of the nearest pool. The pink water was so clear that I could see through it, and I noticed that some of the rocks were large and lumpy, others small and round, and others still skinny and pointed. That was how nature made things: in different shapes and sizes, jumbled together, with no separation between large and small.

How could you know which stone was perfect, if none was exalted above the others?

Aiven tied up the horse and walked to the edge of the nearest pool. I joined him, and we gazed down silently into the water. Where the sun streaked the water, golden lines fell across the rocks below, criss-crossing each other in a web of light.

"Do you think the faeries really come here?" Aiven said.

"There's no such thing as faeries, Aive."

"Oh." He looked down. "I thought we were supposed to pretend."

"Well, maybe there is such a thing as the Fae when people believe in them. They exist in our minds. It's like anything, really. If everyone around you believes that there's one way to be special, and tells you it all the time, you start to believe it too. And if they tell you that it's *your* job to be special, you start to believe that it must be.

Soon it no longer matters whether they were right—you believe it, and by believing it, you make it so."

Something warm embraced my shoulders. I realised that it was Aiven's arm.

"Are you all right?" he murmured. "You don't sound happy."

"Oh, you know me. Guzzle a bit of sea water, get prodded around by a doctor, and I'm right as autumn sun."

"I thought Sethune was going to kill you, for a moment. He was looking down your throat, staring into your eyes, lifting up the lids, and you weren't responding. It was scary, Fierre. Then he asked for salt, and mixed it into a glass of water. He tipped the salty water into your mouth, and you woke up, spluttering. We all thought he was a genius, then. Though I still worried. He fed you a piece of bread, and you smiled and went back to sleep. Your chest was rising and falling with normal breath, then, and even Galar didn't want to interfere."

A silence fell, while I took all of this in.

"He fed me bread?" I said.

"That's what you're worried about?" Aiven's voice swelled in force. "Not the fact that you were unconscious for some reason that we can't discern? Not the fact that you can't remember any of it? Not the fact that you've been having dizzy spells and shivering for weeks now?"

I stared at Aiven. His expression changed from angry to guilty in the space of a few seconds. "I'm sorry. I just... worry about you."

The breeze swirled between us. I heaved a deep breath, repressing everything I wanted to say. "We shouldn't be having this conversation here. The faeries can hear our words." I gestured at the nearest pool. "I've come here to wash off my favours, and I hope you're going to keep me company, Aive."

"There's nothing to wash. If the church demands it of you… if your father expects it of you, this granting of…" He let his voice trail off for a moment. "There's nothing to cleanse," he said quietly.

"There's always an invisible line. Father draws it in his mind. I must offer up my body for the crown, but only *exactly* as much as he deems appropriate." I smiled tightly. "And the position of that line is always shifting."

Aiven looked down. The clenching of his hands told me that he was repressing a response. "I don't like the thought of you passing out and swallowing water in there," he said, at last.

I shrugged, and began to untie my enserre.

Aiven's strong hand gripped mine. "Your father must know you've done the rituals already, at the palace."

"Of course he knows," I said. "He asked me to do this so he could humiliate me in front of my lairds. Now, if you don't mind, I'm going to get it over with."

He let go, then, and stepped back. I finished unfastening the strings, and had unwound my enserre halfway down my chest before Aiven said: "May I?"

He held my gaze, and I blushed. "It's my job, isn't it?" he added. "As Star."

"Very well, then."

I stood as still as I could while he took the end of the cloth from me and began to unwrap me. This felt different. It was raw, and new. Before, at the rituals, there had been a priest watching me, and other observers, and the sunlight pooling around me and making me the focus of all eyes. Everything had been tangled in the ceremony of the occasion, keeping Aiven and I from staring openly at each other. Now, there was only the two of us beneath the sky. The low-hanging grey clouds shielded us. I had the strange feeling that god had kept this clearing for us alone, and my body for Aiven's eyes only.

He didn't kneel, this time, nor tie any ribbons. He didn't need to do anything but peel off my garment. We both knew that this had taken on a different feeling, I was sure, and we didn't need fancy golden ties. Aiven gently undid the last few feet of cloth and suddenly I shivered. It wasn't the cold that unsettled me, though—I felt like I was showing myself to Aiven for the first time, like I had never been this bare before.

I wanted to be naked, and I wanted to be covered again. I wanted him to see me, and I wanted to hide my flesh and make excuses for it. I wanted to melt into nothingness, and yet I wanted to be solid and fallible before him.

Aiven folded my enserre, then removed my necklace and placed it carefully on top of the garment. When he was done, I took a step towards him. "It's my turn."

The confusion on his face was very sweet. I began to unlace his shirt, and comprehension dawned in his eyes. "Fierre—"

"There's a prize for men who swim fully clothed. It's called an uncomfortable, waterlogged ride back to the castle."

He gave a sigh, and it was clear to both of us that it wasn't a protest. My hands moved faster down the front of his shirt. I should have savoured the process and taken in every inch of skin as I undressed him, but I was so conscious of my nakedness and of my inability to hide any reaction that I hurried.

I didn't dare to look at him. If I let my gaze linger on any part of him for too long…

He waited for me to move first, and I walked slowly to the edge of the nearest pool and dipped my feet into the water. A chill covered me, and I knew that I would jump out again if I didn't move, so I plunged into the pink water and paddled out, picking my way across the rocks on the bottom.

The cold hit me like a closed fist. I gasped.

Before I knew it, Aiven was climbing in after me. He wrapped his arms around my waist and held me, and I felt the warmth of his body flooding through me, chasing the cold away.

"There's a ledge over there," he said, nodding to the far side. Awkwardly, still hugging, we crossed the pool and perched ourselves on the ledge. Aiven let go just long enough for me to sit, then wrapped his arm around my shoulders.

"You're so warm all the time," I murmured, nestling into his body. "How do you do it?"

"Eating a horse's share at breakfast, when I can get it."

"Well, personally, I'm glad for the horse's loss."

It wasn't just Aiven's body temperature that made him warm. It was the comfort he offered me through his kindness; his gentle way of speaking; his strong support, no matter what I'd done. Aiven's strength made me feel safe, not afraid—that quiet inner strength that he showed in every gesture was far more important than skill with a blade or a hammer.

Now, I was beginning to feel warm. Not just in my flesh, but inside, where all my emotions were twining and weaving into a single web. I felt that I should untangle them, and yet, somehow, with a certainty that was hard to admit, I liked the warm mess that Aiven created inside me.

"Thank you," I said.

"You don't need to thank me for holding you. I'll do it any time."

"Thank you for saving me, again." I paused, feeling a surge of heat in my cheeks. "Thank you for always being there to save me, Aive."

Aiven lifted up my hair and kissed the top of my forehead, just below the hairline.

"I promise you, I always will. I just hope that one day, you won't need me to save you."

"Because I'll be less pathetic," I said.

"Because you'll be healthy, and safe, and happy, surrounded by the kind of bliss that you've always deserved."

I don't know what possessed me then—I think it may have been some sort of licentious demon with little care for self-preservation, because I turned my face to Aiven's until we were close enough to feel each other's breath. Without thinking about anything, I kissed him briefly on the lips. He tasted like homemade wine: a little strong, a little salty, and exactly what I wanted. The taste of him slaked my thirst, and yet, paradoxically, it renewed my desire.

I wanted more. I *needed* more.

"Fierre," he said, into my mouth.

I pulled back. My face turned hotter, and I wriggled away from Aiven. I couldn't believe that I'd done it, right now, without any warning or indication. Desperately, I searched his face for a reaction.

He looked as if he wasn't sure what to say. For a moment, I thought he was going to kiss me back. But then he turned sideways and wrapped himself around me, encircling me properly with both arms, gripping me to his chest and holding my torso as if he didn't want to let me go. I could feel my body stirring, warning me that Aiven's touch did something dangerous to my lower parts.

I thought of Aiven lying in bed, pressed against me, and then of seeing him roll over in the morning, exposing all of himself... I swallowed. His body was right here, against me. I could reach down and touch him, and see what happened.

I wanted to say: I've thought about you, many times, while I was with other men. Just two nights ago, I pretended it was your warmth I could feel, your voice I could hear, your chest and thighs against mine, while I lay with my legs above my head. I fantasised about having you inside me while Kinnaid fucked me senseless.

But I didn't say anything.

I was supposed to be *getting rid of* my lust in this water, for saints' sake.

Instead of reaching down, I moved my hands upward slowly, to cup Aiven's jaw. We looked into each other's eyes.

"Can I kiss you?" Aiven whispered.

I replied by pressing my mouth to his and kissing him so hard that my lips hurt from the pressure.

Hunger overtook my sense. I didn't just want to kiss him, and touch him, and do other things that I was trying not to think about: I wanted to make him mine, and mine alone: my gentle but strong Aiven, who always caught me before I fell. I held onto him now, and I think I must have poured all of my repressed feelings into the kiss, because I forgot about the water, the sun, and the breeze on my cheeks; I simply breathed Aiven's scent into my consciousness. His fior-chridhe smell was life itself.

Aiven let go of my torso. He withdrew, and I felt the shift in position at once, accompanied by a renewal of the cold.

I looked into Aiven's face. He was hesitating—I could see that much.

For a moment, the shock of what I had done seemed to envelop the both of us, holding us in place, and I wondered if we would be immovable forever.

Then Aiven kissed me with all the hunger that I had been feeling; he held the back of my neck and pulled me hard towards him, and I moaned shamelessly at his touch. He ran his hand down my back. His mouth still tasted like homemade wine, and I had just enough time to recognise that before he licked my upper lip and planted swift kisses along it. Aiven's hand lingered at the base of my spine, as if he could only be daring with his mouth.

I launched my body at his. He caught me in both hands, his palms cupping my arse, and as I pressed myself on top of him and returned the kiss, I thought that this was how it was meant to be: Aiven's hands under me, and his tongue in my mouth; as much of Aiven touching me as was physically possible.

When we let go, our bodies didn't seem to want to detach from each other.

"Oh god. Fierre. God." Aiven put his hand to his mouth, covering it. He stared at me, wide-eyed. After a long moment, he removed his hand. "I'm so sorry."

"Don't apologise," I said.

My words came out in a raspy whisper.

Aiven stared at me. I could see the realisation dawning into his eyes that I had enjoyed it just as much as he did. I was feeling the same shock, but in reverse: despite the fact that he had just been all over me, I couldn't quite believe that Aiven liked me enough to kiss me back.

Aiven *wanted* to kiss me.

A memory of Aiven kneeling came back to me. Oh god. I had made him tie ribbons on me while I was naked. I had never asked him how he felt about me. I had begged him to hold me in the tent at night, and I had wriggled backwards against him. I had pressed my arse to his groin.

Oh, cartwheeling god… had I actually been torturing Aiven this whole time?

"I don't want you to do anything you'll regret." His voice softened to a quiet murmur. "How do you really feel about me, Fierre?"

I thought of all the ways I could describe how I felt about Aiven. None of them were enough. Instead of trying to answer, I reached down and put my hand on his cock.

"This is how I feel," I said.

Aiven closed his eyes, and a look of desperation transformed his face. If he was desperate, it was nothing to what I was trying to repress. The feeling of his hot skin beneath my fingers made me want to plunge my head beneath the water and wrap my mouth around his cock. I would slide down until it hit my tonsils, and even then, I probably wouldn't come up for air—I would probably keep sucking his cock until I drowned. It seemed like a pretty good way to go.

Fortunately, Aiven spoke before I could move.

"I wanted to kiss you for so long, I thought I was going to die from keeping it in. If you don't stop touching me, though…"

He was staring at me as if he was taking in my features for the first time.

"I'd like to hear you finish that sentence."

My words rang out in the chilly air.

He leaned in, without trying to take my hand off his cock, and grabbed hold of my arse. His lips found mine as if we were dancing the easiest dance in the world. When I opened my mouth to allow his tongue in further, I felt like we were rehearsing something that was only minutes away from bursting into full colour. I didn't protest when he switched angles and kissed me from slightly higher, pushing down against me.

He was halfway through kissing me again when a voice carried across the pools.

"So, this is the man who came back from the dead."

The pair of figures must have emerged from the cloud bank while we were kissing. They stood at the edge of our pool, gazing down at us. I broke away from Aiven and sat up straight on the ledge, hoping they weren't scrutinising my body.

On the left, a man with grey stubble clutched a long staff. On the right, a man in a black cloak peered at me. At once, I recognised the man from my flash of memory.

"Lighiche," I said.

The man in the black cloak nodded.

A silence engulfed us all, until Aiven splashed to the other side of the pool and climbed out to stand, naked, before the two men.

"If you harm Prince Dannatyne, you'll have me to answer to," he snarled.

"Easy, now." The older man smiled. He let his gaze drift from Aiven to me, and his eyes became more serious again. "Your friend suffers from the same illness as his father."

"Excuse me?" I said.

"There's no hope for your father, Prince Dannatyne.

But there can be for you." The man scratched at his grey stubble. "Come to us at Clan Sethune, and our doctors will tell you more. But inform nobody that you're coming. We won't have the old king killing more of our sons and daughters. Meet us under the full moon, a night hence, at the green forest a little way north of here. Bring no weapons."

"Where in the forest will we find you?" Aiven said.

The older man smiled.

"You won't find us," he said. "We'll know when you arrive."

He said a few words to the younger man in their native tongue, and they turned around and strode into the cloud bank, disappearing into the mass of grey. I climbed slowly out of the pool, slipping over to Aiven's side.

He turned to me. We stood, frozen, for a moment, before he took my hand and slipped it between his. There was nothing more to say. The spell was broken.

Thirteen

Fierre

THE SILENCE THAT shrouded us all the way back to the castle came as a relief, for I didn't want to talk about what had just happened—not the feeling of Aiven's lips on mine, not the feeling of his chest pressing against me, not the feeling of his cock beneath my fingers. I was glad that he couldn't see my face as we rode. Our interruption from the Sethunes gave me the perfect cover for silence: I could pretend that I was thinking about the doctor and his clan elder, and their strange warning.

In truth, I wanted to talk to Aiven. I wanted to ask him exactly how long he had wanted to kiss me, and whether he wanted to do it again. I wanted to ask him if I'd made a terrible mistake in throwing myself on him. But I was scared to say anything at all.

As we rounded the last of the mountains before the castle, the chill faded a little, and Dunhairstin came into view through a swirl of low fog, its grey cloudstone walls almost merging into the weather. Moonstone, sunstone, starstone, cloudstone: the four royal stones of Eilean-òir might be beautiful, but the cost of quarrying them seemed excessive to me. Perhaps that was what made them royal. A needless expense, flaunted for all to see.

I thought of Cameron and Annis, dashing out with sickles to defend their potato fields, and my stomach lurched.

"Do you want to go to the Sethunes tomorrow night?" Aiven said, into my ear.

I slowed the horse.

"Maybe," I said. "Maybe they can offer an opinion that'll help me. But Dr Galar should be the best medical mind we have. I mean—I don't know—it's all so dashed confusing." I drew a deep breath. "I'd like to hear what the Sethunes have to say. One of them revived me, after all. And if they do know something about father's illness..."

It was hard to spell out the rest of it.

"Do you think it's true that this island is safe, even if you were ride to the green forest in the evening?" Aiven said.

"Father always said there were no bandits here. No guards needed." I paused. "So, you think I should go, then?"

"I don't want to influence you," Aiven said. "You can make up your own mind."

We slowed and brought the horse to a stop, and Aiven dismounted first, helping me down and lifting me in both arms onto the ground. I blushed as he set me down. He must have known, as well as I did, that it was different now when he touched me—that his firm grip reminded me of what we had done in the pink water of the faerie pool.

"Excuse me, Sky," someone called out.

I spotted Browne striding towards me, her forehead wrinkled. "Your father asks to see you now," she added.

"I thought we were waiting till dinner."

"He's woken from his rest. He's not in the best of moods when he wakes up, Sky."

Browne's expression led me to suspect that she had been on the receiving end of my father's tongue more than once.

"Your scar…" I began.

She nodded.

I gave Aiven a quick look. We left the horse with a stable-hand and moved through the castle to my suite. When I told Aiven that he could go, he lingered by the door, blocking my way in. "Are you sure you don't need me for support?"

"I'd like nothing more." I smiled gently. "My father won't tolerate it. If he asks for me alone, he means me alone."

"Be careful," Aiven said.

I thought about telling him that being careful around my father was about as useful as walking warily towards a coiled adder. You could approach with soft steps, but the creature would still sink its fangs into you, right through your layers of skin and bone.

In my chambers, I changed out of my enserre and into the family tartan that the castle staff had provided, tying my sash carefully and belting my kilt as tightly as I could. I examined my waist in the mirror. Not small enough for my father to approve, I was sure. I did my best with the positioning of the sash. By the time Browne escorted me to the back of the castle and showed me to the Suite of Kings, I'd managed to push down my thoughts.

The door of the suite opened onto an empty chamber. Or so it seemed, at first; the sparse decorations made my gaze flit around, searching for something to fix on. A small table offered a death's-match board with a few pieces laid out. I would have spotted those bright renderings of kings, lairds, captains, and soldiers even in darkness, whittled as they were from walrus ivory and whales' teeth. The pieces of the strategy game stood as if in the middle of a campaign, but only one chair had been pulled out, and a single cup rested on the table top.

Had my father been playing against himself?

"I see you've come to Hairstin despite my wishes."

The voice reached me faintly, but I couldn't have mistaken it if I tried.

"Step into the light."

That cold and high tone gave each word a sharp resonance, like diamonds breaking. Through the doorway to the next room, I spied a pale gold light, and I walked towards it like a moth to a familiar flame.

"Dear boy," my father said.

It hurt every time he said that word. *Dear.* I could hear the mockery in that one little syllable, reminding me what he really thought of me.

I approached the chair on which he sat and knelt before him. As I looked up at the arms of the chair, I realised that it was actually a throne, with thick arms, a padded seat, and a headrest topped with a gold sculpture of two prancing deer. My father must have ordered it to be made once he moved here.

"I can recall how youthful you looked just a few years ago." He clicked his tongue. "Is that a line at the corner of your right eye?"

I rubbed at my eye with my finger. I couldn't feel anything there, but my father could probably see everything; he had turned the golden lamp on the cabinet beside him so that its light now bathed me instead of him. I had to squint to make out his figure. I didn't like what I could see: those wrists looked twig-thin, and that slender torso had narrowed to a sickly slimness. Where his face had once been sharply beautiful, the lines now protruded in a jumble of hard edges.

"I'm not the one you should worry about, Your Majesty," I said, hearing the ring of his title, stiff and cold. If I called him *father*, he would strike me across the cheek, or roll up my shirt and set to work with a birch rod. I didn't like to remember how I had learned that.

"News reached me," I added. "Is it true that your health is declining rapidly, Your Majesty?"

"Declining? What a mouthful of worms you spit." The collar of his shirt fell forward as he sat up, revealing a cavity above his collarbone. "You're the Prince Regent now. You should look to your own failings. I left you in that godforsaken palace because you're a burden, and it's about time you learned to live up to your heritage. Beauty. High standards. Proper conduct. I see you haven't managed the first, and reports tell me you haven't come within a field's length of the last two." He barked out a laugh. "Did you bathe in the Fae Pools, like I ordered you?"

"Yes, Your Majesty."

"And how many men did you have to scrub off yourself?"

A clank of armour alerted me to the presence of four guards in the shadows near the walls, on either side of my father. How had I missed them? I drew a breath, choosing my next words carefully.

"I've endeavoured to give favour only to men of influence, as you taught me."

"I didn't teach you to give it to all of them."

I winced. He rose, inch by inch, until his figure towered over me, and I could see how painfully thin he had become—even thinner than when I last saw him, drifting across the water in a boat and holding his arms still while I waved goodbye.

"How can I please you, Your Majesty?" I said. "Your good health is my desire."

"You can present yourself to me."

We stared at each other, he gazing down and I gazing up at his angular face. The light just touched the edges of his hair, providing him with a gilded aureole like a saint in one of the old paintings.

"You can see me from here," I said.

"Remove your shirt and tartan, Fierre. Show me how you've kept your figure."

"No."

The word echoed in the chamber. I knew that it was pointless to refuse—that he would do what he liked, as he always did—but I wanted him to know that I didn't consent. I wanted him to look my objection in the eye.

"Remove them for him," my father said, glancing at one of the guards.

The man didn't hesitate. How long had he been following my father's orders, up here? I stared at the guard, willing him to stop. He had the good grace to drop his gaze and fix his regard on my chest instead.

When he grabbed my shirt, I flinched.

The sound of ripping filled the whole chamber. I felt the fabric tear—felt the cold air on my bare skin as heat rushed through my cheeks. The guard tore the shirt harder, until it ripped to mid-way, pulling the tartan off me, letting it drape down over my kilt.

"More," my father said.

The guard couldn't look me in the eye as he ripped my shirt twice. The threads gave way easily to his hands. He tore the broken shirt from me, pulling the sash with it, and stepped back with his armful of clothes.

"Kneel, Fierre."

"I refuse."

"Make him kneel." My father didn't raise his stare to the guard this time.

A shove in the back sent me sprawling forward. I landed hard on the stone. The guard kept his hand in the middle of my back, and my father descended from his throne and walked slowly over to me, taking my chin in one hand.

"Pretty," he said. "You were always pretty. But you're a slut." He exhaled quickly. "Sluts like you have to work hard to look perfect. Stand up before me."

I gritted my teeth and hauled myself up.

"I can see the problem here." My father ran a finger along the bottom of my ribcage, tracing the length of the lowest rib, pushing hard against my skin. "The shape of the rib should be more prominent. And here," he pinched my hip hard, without warning, making me flinch. "Stuffing yourself for the coronation, were you? Eating all the delicacies you liked? It's a funny name, delicacy—those little treats do the opposite of make you delicate. You should know that."

"I didn't eat what I liked!"

"Did you think you could do whatever you wanted and face no consequences?" He tried to pinch me just below my armpit, but couldn't find enough flesh to hold.

"Your Majesty, I promise, I've been fasting and eating the tiniest amounts, just like you taught me."

"I should put you naked in the stocks and let everybody look at you. My son. He can't even get one of his royal duties right. A disappointment, just like I knew he would be." He dug his fingernail into my chest on the left side. I winced while the pain grew, his nail's ragged edge cutting deep into the thin flesh. I wanted to cry. I kept silent while he held it there before giving a final push and scraping it downward, trailing the sharp nail over my chest, serrating the skin.

His palm pressed against my stomach before lifting away.

"All I wanted was for you to be beautiful," he whispered.

I waited, then: waited for him to slap me across the face; but no movement came, and a sob broke the silence. I stared. The guards around me didn't seem to know whether to step forward or not. They had probably never seen their king crying like this, but their discomfort was nothing to mine, for I stood transfixed by the tears tricking out of my father's eyes, watching them make silvery paths down his cheeks.

A churning began in my stomach. I felt the full force of his words, stirring me up. All he had wanted was for me to be beautiful—it had to be true. He was my father, after all.

And I had failed him.

I reached out and placed a hand upon his shoulder. When he didn't bat me off, I moved forward to embrace him, wrapping my arms carefully around his robe, making sure not to squeeze his body too tightly. The narrowness of his waist shocked me; in all the years I'd gazed upon his elegant figure, I couldn't remember seeing him this thin. There was barely a handful of fat on his body to scrape together. *An example*, a voice in my head intoned. *The image of a true king of Eilean-òir*.

"I'm sorry," I said. "I tried my best."

He turned his face away from me. After a long pause, he rested his head in his hands and sobbed. Guilt churned harder in my stomach.

"I'll do everything I can to lose what's left. I swear to you, Your Majesty, I'll make sure that I eat even less."

"I'm sure you will." My father turned his face away.

Something in me wanted to grab him hard, to shake him and tell him that I had Galar's help and I could really do it, if I tried.

I could assure him that I would take that cerise potion every night if it meant that I could make him proud.

I didn't say any of it. I watched as he wiped his eyes with his hands, unable to stop a fresh trickle of tears from spilling out.

Silence stayed with me as I left, making my footsteps louder. The guard who had ripped my shirt and pulled it off locked eyes with me as I approached the door. I wondered if he felt satisfied to see me go, or if he wanted to pull the rest of my clothes off. When he held out the torn shirt and the tartan sash, his mouth twisted slightly at the corners, and I knew that he had enjoyed the whole scenario.

I didn't take the clothes from him. I decided that I would rather walk through the whole castle shirtless than let him have another smirk at me.

The corridors seemed colder than before, though maybe it was just my bare skin. The guards put in a good effort to avoid staring at me and almost succeeded. I made it back to my suite without encountering any of my lairds, thanking god for small mercies as I opened the door.

I sat down on the edge of my bed. My body was shaking, and I couldn't tell if it was from the cold or the feeling that my father's sobs had caused. I clutched my stomach and waited for warmth to return. When it didn't, I pulled on a new shirt and tugged the long sleeves down to my wrists. The table in my room bore a platter of blackberries, raspberries and strawberries, as well as a bowl of snowfruit, and one look at the white skins of the snowfruit reminded me of how I'd allowed myself one cup of snowfruit juice for each meal before the coronation, and how I'd lain awake at night, desperate for sleep to carry me away from hunger. I could still feel the burning sensation in my gut when I woke before the dawn—the bitter taste in my mouth as I gulped water, hoping that the fluid alone would be enough to dispel my desire.

Food. It was always food. If I was stronger, like my father, I wouldn't crave nourishment; I'd be able to get through the day on a few bites or a drink.

All those years I'd struggled to meet his rules: first, *three small meals*, even if the small plates left me hungry— even if I had to shake salt onto my wafer of bread in the morning to give me the energy to get through the day— then *two small meals*, more salt, and a cup of the brew made from a thin broth of salty beans, so I could bear the hunger until evening. Then, at last, I'd begun the fast for the coronation, smiling at everyone I saw as I walked around the palace, even if I was cracking on the inside.

I'd thought it was enough. I'd thought that I could whittle away those last bits of fat and attain the perfect body. I'd imagined that my father would break into a smile when he saw my figure.

But I wasn't beautiful enough.

I picked up the snowfruit at the top of the bowl and peeled back its skin slowly. Removing a segment, I felt the firmness of the fruit between my fingers. Half ripe.

I chewed it slowly, making the most of each bite. I ate two more segments before I stopped myself and went searching for the bottle of cerise liquid. Carefully, I unstoppered it.

The potion hit the back of my throat and slid down. I put the bottle and the fruit back on the table. The sickly sweetness in my mouth preceded the sudden explosion, as stars burst inside me and my stomach swelled and crackled, the force building inside me, and I slumped into a chair. I tipped all the snowfruit from the bowl on the table and brought the empty bowl to my lips, straining to vomit.

Only air came out. I strained, feeling my stomach writhe. Nothing. The small portion of snowfruit had no momentum behind it; my mouth opened, but to no avail.

I stared at the cerise liquid inside the bottle. A thimbleful, immediately after eating, Dr Galar had said. But he'd instructed me only to take it if I ate more than his recommended amount, and this time, I hadn't scoffed any cakes or biscuits. I clutched my stomach and strained again, but nothing rose inside me.

The bottle seemed to dare me to do it. *Just a thimbleful more*, it whispered, *and then another. Keep trying.*

I drank more of the potion and set it down. This time, there was no delay before the effect. The liquid hit my already-churning stomach and made it churn harder, and I clutched at the table. Heat ripped through my body. I retched, and brought up a tiny piece of snowfruit, catching it in the bowl.

It wasn't enough. My father's tear-stained face floated in my mind. I should be able to shed the last bits of fat, if I only tried hard enough.

I held the bottle to my lips and tilted my head back, swallowing as much of the potion as I could. When the churning increased, I nearly fell over. I gripped the corner of the table and breathed hard, trying to brace myself. The rest of the snowfruit I had eaten rose inside me and flew out, and I barely caught it in time. I managed to get the bowl to my lips before the next churn of my stomach brought up a few meagre fragments of my last meal. I strained, opening my mouth, waiting.

There had to be more. I wasn't going to let myself give up this easily. I closed my eyes and strained harder.

At last, one huge heave saw me throwing up every scrap left inside me before something red infused the spittle from my mouth. It looked like blood.

The sight of it made me reel backwards, dropping the bowl. My face felt newly hot; my heart knocked angrily inside my ribcage and my stomach strained like it was going to burst open. Maybe I was going to die, here, in my father's castle.

But it didn't burst. I tasted acid and knew that I had finally purged all the food from my body.

In the tiny mirror on the wall, I examined my face, and at first, I looked completely normal. It was only after I drew closer that I noticed the red dots around my eyes – dozens of tiny dark splotches scattered over my skin, beneath the eyes and around their sides, like someone had angrily thrown a jar of red ink in my direction.

Or like the devil had marked out my sins.

I gasped and put my fingers to my face, tracing the red spots. This was all my fault. I'd tried to cheat my body by purging everything from it, with no care for my stomach or my throat, and now my punishment was here. Everyone would stare at me and ask why my eyes looked like a demon's. Would I have to lie?

Maybe the marks would go away. I rubbed at one of them, hoping silently for a sign. Nothing happened. The same tiny splotch marked the skin below the corner of my left eye, along with a whole trail of others.

The thirst hit me a minute later, and I poured myself a glass of water and focused on drinking. I couldn't dispose of my chamber pot quickly by giving it to the staff, as I had done in Castle Aonar. Who knew if my father had instructed them to spy on me?

I opened my window, but it offered no convenient garden below. Only a courtyard stretched before me, and I could hardly empty the pot there. I let the fresh air chill me for a moment, allowing it to clear a little of the vomit smell. By the time I shut the window and set the pot down, I felt strangely weak, and I wobbled a little as I made my way back to the table.

Why did my head feel so light? It hadn't felt like this when I collapsed in water. It hadn't felt like this at the banquet back in the palace, either; I'd never been quite this far gone.

I reached for the table too late. My fingers closed on empty air. For a split second, I felt my knees tremble, and then they gave way entirely.

I clutched at the chair on the way down and my fingers scraped the wood, incurring a painful tear on the underside of my thumb. More blood, I told myself, to join the blood in the bowl, the red mess I had brought up from my gullet. A private punishment.

I slumped onto the floor and rolled onto my back. The ceiling stared back at me. Its wooden beams offered no aid.

The lightness in my head transformed into a grey mist. I closed my eyes. The pain and heat and discomfort in my body faded as my sight did, leaving me in a state beyond sensation.

"Fierre! Are you in there?"

I heard Aiven's voice faintly through the suite door,

well before I heard him trying to prize it open. At least he had the courtesy to wait a minute before throwing his shoulder against the wood. Time seemed to rush, however, without a care for my wellbeing; I dreamily welcomed the darkness that covered my vision. All I wanted was to lie here, supine, breathing.

"Fierre!" Aiven shouted, much closer to hand.

Each breath came slower until my lungs almost stopped. I had the vague sense of Aiven dropping down beside me. As he grabbed my shoulders and shook me, I smiled weakly. At least, I thought I did. My lips didn't seem to move. Aiven prized my teeth open and pushed his lips hard against mine, exhaling into my mouth. It was funny: I had all his breath inside me, yet I couldn't seem to breathe. Maybe I'd die kissing Aiven, I thought, as I drifted off into a thick and sticky blackness, pushing towards the viscous centre of the darkness.

Fourteen

Aiven

I EXHALED WITH every bit of force in my body, expelling all the air in my lungs into Fierre's mouth. Pulling back, I drew in more air. I breathed out again. I breathed in. I pressed my lips to Fierre's and held him close. I pulled back. With every movement, I hoped for him to splutter back into life; any moment now, he was going to cough violently into my mouth and sit up, clutching my arm.

But he wasn't coughing or spluttering. He wasn't even opening his eyes. His breath came weakly, like the tired panting of a dog that has given up on trudging home.

"Come on!" I shouted. "Come on, Fierre!"

He couldn't die. I wouldn't allow it.

In the chamber pot on the floor, pieces of food floated in a sea of pale liquid, and I spotted a burst of red colour spreading slowly through the liquid. Was that blood? And if so, what had happened here?

I shook Fierre slightly by the shoulders, shouting his name again. For a moment, he went so still that I thought he'd stopped breathing entirely—then he shuddered, coughed, and blinked his way back to life.

"Oh gosh, Aive," he whispered. "Did I ruin your dinner?"

I laughed and clasped him to me. I must have sounded hysterical, but I didn't mind. All that mattered was Fierre's body moving underneath my hands, and his eyes, big and open, staring up at me.

"Stay here." I realised how ridiculous my order sounded after I said it: Fierre looked in no state to sit up, let alone run off for a jaunt around the castle. "I'm going to fetch you some things."

I propped him up in a chair and ran out, making sure to close the door behind me. It didn't take me long to find the kitchens. When you'd been a Master of Compliance for years, you knew how things were run at a castle, and I slipped through a low archway to enter a small chamber where a cook and three kitchen-hands sat around a table. They looked up from their pie as I entered.

"Excuse me," I said. "I have urgent need of your help, for the Sky."

Armed with bread, salt, and a jug of water, I sprinted back to Fierre's suite. I found him slumped forward in the chair, his eyes closed and his arms dangling. Trying not to panic, I mixed salt into a glass of water and raised it to his mouth, pushing his lips apart just as I had watched the Sethune doctor do yesterday. Some of the liquid spilt from his mouth and trickled down his chin, and I tried a second time, propping his lips open more forcefully now and praying for him to swallow. The liquid slipped down. He moaned slightly, and I put down the glass and tore off some of the bread.

I wasn't sure exactly when Fierre woke, but it must've been sometime between my turning away and my turning back. He stared at the bread in my hand and flinched.

"No," he muttered.

"You're ill, Fierre. Just a few bites."

"No!" His voice rose to a shout. "I don't want it."

"You're going to die! Fierre, I promise, this is to save your life! It's how the Sethune doctor saved you—this is his physic I'm copying. Please." I knelt down before him, still clutching the bread. "Please do this for me."

"I can't," Fierre whispered.

"Please."

"Aive, I can't eat it."

"Fierre!" I shoved the bread at his mouth, but to no avail. I could feel tears prick the back of my eyes. If he lost consciousness again—if he went still and didn't blink his way back to life once more—I didn't know what I would do. I *couldn't* live with that.

If I had to make him hate me, it would be better than seeing him dead.

He turned his face away from me. I felt something surge through my body, a strange and powerful feeling that held me. Slowly, I realised that it was fear.

He wasn't going to open his mouth. And I couldn't bring myself to wrench his jaw so hard that I hurt him. Searching around for something to persuade him with, I found the only words I could think of.

"Please, Fierre," I whispered. "I love you."

I felt him go still beneath my hands. Those dark eyes locked on mine, and he stared as if he had never seen me before.

Without hesitating, I held the bread out to his lips. He opened his mouth and let me slide it in. Still staring at me, he chewed until the last bite was gone.

I was so relieved that I didn't realise what I had said until a minute later, when Fierre had settled back into a calmer state and taken two more sips of the salty water, and was still staring at me. A lump rose in my throat. What had I done?

Had I just ruined my chances of remaining by Fierre's side?

I looked around for anything to distract him. My eyes fell on a bottle with a cerise potion inside it, sitting on the table.

"Did you drink this, Fierre?"

"It's medicine." He sounded strangely defensive. I held up the bottle, looking at the amount of empty space at the top—more than a few sips were missing.

"And what exactly does it remedy?"

"Dr Galar says it will put things right. It's not easy, Aive, you know… eating just a little. Sometimes, you crave a lot of energy. But you have to be good. Dr Galar is teaching me to be good."

I unstoppered the bottle and smelled the contents. The scent of hazelnuts drifted up to me.

"How much did you drink?" I said.

"He said to take a thimbleful after I'd eaten too much."

"And how much did you take?"

"I'm tired, Aive." Fierre leaned back against the chair. "I don't want to talk about it. I took your physic—isn't that enough?"

"You're right." I patted him gently on the shoulder, not wanting to risk a caress. The memory of slipping into the pink water of the Fae Pools and holding his naked body in my hands came all too easily. "Rest. You've earned it."

He leaned on me as he rose, and I walked him to the bed, where I left him undressing. Nothing about his manner made me worry, but I asked to check his pulse one last time. It came rapidly, but a little slower than before. I hoped that he would sleep peacefully now.

The lairds and ambassadors had gathered in the antechamber outside the dining hall, and Rossane looked up as I entered. MacArlay and Kinnaid followed suit. The stone room suddenly seemed chillier; the air seemed to thin.

"The Sky needs his rest," I said, keeping my voice calm. "Allow me to join you in his stead."

"And he trusts you alone with his condition?" Rossane said.

"He trusts me with anything," I said.

A long pause stretched, while Rossane looked at me like a tiger considering a foal. Eventually, he gave a small nod. I didn't miss the sardonic look on his face, nor the annoyed look on MacArlay's. Carefully, I led the way into the dining hall.

I was ready for a grim affair of heavy wood and dim lighting, but the glow of candles welcomed us all to a long table of honey-coloured oak where dishes sat in wreaths and silver plates gleamed, while a hearty fire crackled in the hearth at the far end of the room, lending a warm light to the hunting tapestries on the walls. We made a modest party, with the king unwilling to join us and the castle offering no noble company. I tried to encourage the staff to eat with us, but none of them seemed willing to risk their master finding out that they had violated hierarchy. Most frustrating of all was the absence of Galar. I glanced up every few minutes, hoping to see him walk through the door, but his chair remained empty throughout dinner.

Afterward, I made to head back to the corridor, intending to sneak around the castle and look for Galar, but I had scarcely reached the door when I felt a hand on my forearm.

"Come, now, Star. What's the rush?"

I looked into MacArlay's face. There was absolutely nothing welcoming about it.

"Why not stay a little while and join us for the grapple?" he added.

"I didn't know you were grappling," I said. "Is that wise, so late?"

"Surely, a little competition between friends is always wise. And we should get to know each other, shouldn't we? What better way to know your strength of character than with a bout in the castle grounds?"

MacArlay spoke loud enough for the ambassadors to hear, even at a distance from the table. Rince stared in our direction, and the ambassador for Sarleven could not hide her interest; it was the most animated I'd seen her since we left the palace.

"We welcome you as our equal," Kinnaid said, looking at me. "Why not show us that you return that welcome?"

Rossane's tiger-like manner had returned. I sighed. If there'd been any hope of excusing myself, it had flown into the ether with that question.

"Of course," I said. "I'd be delighted."

We trooped out into the grounds, guided by the staff to the clearest part of the back gardens. Under the low-hanging moon, the grass wore a silver sheen, and I heard the blades rustling around my ankles. The bitter cold of the breeze didn't stop Rossane from rolling up his shirtsleeves and stepping into the wash of moonlight, turning to face us.

"Are you going to ask me to fight you, my laird?" I said.

"Stirring saints, no." Rossane's mouth twisted savagely. "But I'd love to invite Laird MacArlay for a bout."

My chest tightened. I glanced across at Kinnaid. His

expression gave nothing away, though I could see that he was watching MacArlay closely.

"Of course," MacArlay said.

Before I could intervene, he walked over to Rossane and stepped up to within an inch of him. The two men faced each other down, one tall and furnished with lean muscle, the other broad and powerfully built.

"You've been on top of the wrong things lately," Rossane said.

"I do as I'm commanded." MacArlay's lips pressed tightly together.

"You share my duties, my laird. Be careful that you don't share anything else—anything that you would be wise to leave untouched."

"Oh, I'm careful, my laird. You'd be wise to be more cautious, yourself. Word gets around of your particular talent for crossing lines."

Rossane's smile turned dangerous. I wanted to remind them that there was no judge standing by to make sure that they followed the rules, but Rossane lunged before I could speak, and I realised that he was well aware of that fact. So was MacArlay, judging by his quick lunge. They had chosen this location because they knew that it afforded them the opportunity for violence.

And I had agreed to take part.

MacArlay wrapped his arms around Rossane's chest and wrenched him sideways, but Rossane slipped free of his grip and tackled MacArlay in return. The two of them darted and shoved, performing an awkward dance, landing a few blows on each other's upper bodies, struggling to prize each other off. At last, MacArlay threw Rossane back and swung his fist, crunching it hard into Rossane's stomach.

Rossane reeled, retreated, and took a few breaths. He winced, but didn't pause for long. MacArlay had scarcely begun to advance when Rossane ran forward and ducked his outstretched fist, tackling him beneath the ribs and throwing him down. The two of them rolled over and over, MacArlay struggling to pin Rossane to the ground.

"One of them's going to smash the other in the jaw, if they're not careful," I said, as MacArlay landed a blow next to Rossane's head.

"In your experience, Master Grian, do men usually grapple at night without a judge because they wish to be careful?"

Kinnaid's voice sounded slightly wry. I glanced to my left. He wore the tiniest of smiles.

"They should call it off," I replied. "It's not even a real contest, my laird. They're not fighting for anything."

"Oh, you can fight for something without declaring it aloud," Kinnaid said.

We watched as Rossane manoeuvred himself on top of MacArlay and landed a punch on his face. I heard the sickening crunch of the blow landing. MacArlay seemed to weather it fine, untangling himself and rolling sideways from under Rossane. He jumped to his feet and swung downward; Rossane ducked just in time.

"Get down," Rossane shouted, lunging at MacArlay. "And stay down, if you like your face whole."

His words sent MacArlay running at him. It was perfect, I admitted to myself: he had provoked MacArlay at just the right moment. All Rossane had to do was dodge and wheel to take hold of MacArlay and throw him down, forcing him to yield.

Rossane dodged. He wheeled, and grabbed MacArlay by the shoulders.

Instead of throwing him down, he kneed MacArlay hard in the crotch.

I clapped one hand to my mouth, involuntarily, as MacArlay crumpled. Rossane stood over him. A smirk curved his mouth. He seemed on the verge of making some witticism when a boot struck the back of his knees—MacArlay had kicked upward and sent Rossane flailing and tumbling to the ground. Rossane didn't have time to avoid MacArlay's punch. The sound a fist hitting a jaw was no less sickening the second time.

It should stop now, I told myself. Rossane should see sense and remember that this was meant to be a grapple. If he pushed it further, MacArlay might decide that he wanted to fight as dirty as Rossane, and I didn't like the thought of where that might take things.

Relief poured through me as Rossane rolled away from MacArlay and stood up. I waited. Slowly, MacArlay rose, too. The two men shared a moment of stillness, eyeing each other. When Rossane moved, I almost believed that he was going to shake MacArlay's hand.

He kicked MacArlay in the crotch with so much force that MacArlay fell.

"Enough!" I screamed.

The ambassadors were murmuring, but a greater noise came from behind them. A decent portion of the castle's staff had gathered and were watching from a few feet away, some staring aghast at Rossane, others peering with curiosity at MacArlay's prostrate form. *Excellent*, I thought. *Entertainment for everyone*. Never mind that half the countryside would be talking about how Fierre's lairds were fighting each other for his favour.

"I agree with the Star," Kinnaid said, stepping up to my side. "Give it up, my lairds, and make way for the next bout, before the night grows colder."

"Exactly," I said, taking MacArlay by the arm and helping him aside.

"We asked you to take part, Star, after all. Let's not disappoint our audience."

I looked up quickly and met Kinnaid's stare. He smiled coolly at me. I'd forgotten that I would be grappling until now, and the stares of the crowd took on a different feeling.

"I'm sorry?" I said.

I knew exactly what he meant. This was my last attempt to stave off the inevitable.

"No need to be sorry, Star. I'm inviting you to grapple with me."

I hadn't thought that anything could make Rossane and MacArlay forget their differences, but for a moment they seemed united in silence. Everyone was staring at me. Even Rince was peering over.

"As you say." I stepped into the wash of moonlight, where just moments ago, Rossane had been kicking MacArlay in the groin. "A fair fight."

"When two people come to blows over something worth winning, can a fight be anything but fair?"

I wasn't sure if Kinnaid was speaking sincerely or mocking me. His calm, slightly amused face gave nothing away.

"You know, it's funny, I never saw you wearing any bright garments before—anything made with those pretty dyes from Archland. You never had much of an income, did you? Not even though you were Master of Compliance. And yet as soon as the Sky is crowned, he makes you his Star... one has to wonder what you gave him, for this change of fortune to suddenly fall into your lap."

"I've no idea what you mean," I said.

"Do you want to know what I gave him?"

"Not particularly."

"He does like to receive," Kinnaid said.

I didn't bother to reply.

I felt slightly unbalanced, even as I took up an even stance. Yet my gut told me that Kinnaid wouldn't kick me in the balls in front of two Rocks of the Glen, two ambassadors, and a crowd of palace staff, even if he wanted to. He didn't strike me as the type who resorted to brutish violence.

He circled me, and I moved to face him all the way. It was a simple move, but one that positioned him immediately as the active party, the leader, the man who set the pattern of the fight. He was setting up a contract between us and laying down the terms in his favour. The same slight smile hovered on his lips.

I broke the contract by dodging sideways, feinting backwards, and surging forward again, grabbing him around the upper body and pushing hard. Kinnaid stumbled, tottering back a few steps. He regained his footing quickly and circled me again.

"Were you expecting a quick win?" I said.

Kinnaid kept his eyes locked on me.

"I don't fight because I need to win," he returned.

"You must think I'm going to ask you why you fight at all." I rushed forward to grab him around the waist. "But I don't care."

He let me shove him, taking the force of my body without any resistance. By the time he stumbled and came back at me, I was spent, but his hands seized me with untempered strength, and I tottered and fell. I kept hold of him, and we dropped together, rolling over the grass in a tangle of arms and legs. I elbowed him hard, but he held me tightly and pushed me under him.

Quickly, he dug his hand into the grass, scooped something up and flung it in my eyes. Grit forced me to blink, and blink again, but no water was on hand to flush it out; I put my fingers to my eyes and touched specks on the skin just below my eyelashes. Dirt smeared my fingertips. I blinked, trying to get the grit out of my vision. Kinnaid heaved me upward and held me on my knees, gripping me from behind, his right hand sliding up to my throat.

He didn't press down but kept up a firm pressure. The warning that he could snap my neck at any moment was obvious.

"You might not care why I'm fighting you, Star," he said. "But I'm going to tell you anyway." He cut off my struggle easily with a knee to my back. "There are some things that never change, no matter how much you grapple."

I elbowed him backwards, as hard as I could. A shout told me that I had hit his ribs, and a moment later, his hand tightened around my neck.

"It's for us to fuck Prince Dannatyne. It's for you to clean him up and hold his hand afterwards." Kinnaid's breath gusted hot against my ear. "Forget it, and you'll get more than dirt in your eyes."

He shoved me forward with one hand and let go of my neck with the other. The push sent me sprawling into the grass. I felt the dirt go deeper into my eyes until grit pricked at the very corners. Behind me, somebody laughed. It sounded like Rossane.

I jumped to my feet and turned to face Kinnaid. He was smiling coolly, and as I approached, he held out his hand to me. I couldn't tell if the crowd had seen him fling the dirt in my eyes, but I was willing to bet that they hadn't seen the best part of it. I shook Kinnaid's hand silently and walked past him.

"You can leave, ambassadors," I said. "Show's over for the night. But the kitchen-hands might be kind enough to find you some more wine."

The crowd of staff behind them, thankfully, understood their cue and began to scuttle off. I didn't feel I had the right to give them orders, not being their employer, but I didn't know if the ambassadors would be insulted without a little more comfort and hospitality after the long journey, and I wanted to do the right thing for Fierre. All the same, I felt guilty as the staff headed back into the castle.

I left Kinnaid, Rossane, and MacArlay standing apart from each other in an awkwardly spaced triangle, and followed the staff through the castle doors. Keeping my pace moderate, I avoided touching my eyes or wincing until I was inside; once I was out of their view, I hurried to my chamber and poured a glass of water. I splashed it into each eye, repeating it several times until the last specks of dirt washed away and the rubbing of grit was gone.

Kinnaid wanted a response, I told myself, putting down the glass with a thump. He wanted me to lash out at him, to bloody his jaw and prove myself to be the uncouth lowborn they all thought me to be. I wasn't going to give him the satisfaction. Kinnaid seemed the kind of man who could wait to strike a blow; well, I could wait, too.

It's for us to fuck Prince Dannatyne. It's for you to clean him up and hold his hand afterwards.

I had to ignore the sting of those words, just like the sting that lingered in my eyes.

A knock sent me straightening up, brushing myself down, and hurrying to open the door. I wasn't sure if I expected Kinnaid, coming to add further insult to injury, or Rossane—but I certainly didn't expect the Ambassador for Sarleven to squeeze herself though the doorframe.

"Excuse me, Star," she said. "Mistress Tarleigh. I don't believe we've met."

"Ambassador." I gestured to her to come in. There wasn't much point. She was already filling the entranceway.

"In my country, when a man has been beaten up, somebody checks on him."

Ah. So that was how nobles showed sympathy. By twisting their sentences into knots to avoid saying anything directly.

"I hear that in Sarleven, you also light fires for those who land a first punch," I said.

Tarleigh raised her eyebrows slightly. "You know a fair bit about country rituals."

"I'm a farmers' son, mistress." I never got tired of watching the reaction to that.

"Well, you should know we don't have many pretty things in Sarleven. We're not Archland, Star. Nor are we blessed with Eilean-òir's minerals. Ours is a colder, flatter, harsher land, with no lick of hidden sparkle beneath its soil. But we're good at defending it. So we rely on our ships to trade."

And on the threat of what your soldiers might do when they disembark, I thought.

"And you, in Eilean-òir… you have beautiful things that we wish to purchase," Tarleigh added.

"Can a diamond really be worth a ship?"

"You sound so surprised, Star. It is the universal desire: the lust for lustrous things. Do you mean to tell me you have no appreciation for beauty?"

"I wouldn't try to trade for it."

"There is a famous story about a beautiful temple in Sarleven. Some even say it contains a lesson."

I wasn't sure that I'd done anything to deserve a late-night parable from a diplomat, but as I began to open my mouth and find an excuse to send her away, I had a flashback to the tooth-grinding thoughts that I'd been having just before her knock interrupted me. I closed my mouth again.

"You know, we're not like you in the courtroom, either, with your divine ruler. The church draws a line from the state in Sarleven. As a consequence, we're not so gentle-fingered with all things holy."

"I've heard that fighting over religious artefacts is common in Sarleven."

Tarleigh smiled, as if she didn't need to acknowledge it. "Many summers ago, there were two noblemen who wanted to possess a beautiful temple at the border of their lands. It was almost unfair, this temple. Each wall dripped with silver; the ceiling was sculpted with imported marble; the floor doubled as a mosaic about our god's birth. When moonlight slipped in, the temple drenched itself in divine illumination. These two lords each swore that their own ancestors had fashioned this building.

"One of them marched his guards up to the temple. The other responded by encircling the soldiers with his own men. They began to shoot arrows at each other, and one lord's soldiers had to retreat, but he ordered them to come back at nightfall and shoot some more. For weeks, it went on like this. One volley and another. Arrowheads dinted the temple walls. Chunks of marble broke off. Pieces of mosaic splintered and rolled across the ground.

"Then the explosions started. Yellow powder and black, fizzling nightfire. Lobbed into the midst of the guards at night to explode in shatterings of skull and bone. The defenders replied with powder of their own and sparks flashed across the starless sky. Within two weeks, the battle was over, and the lord who attacked at night had won the temple.

"He waited for the next dawn to spread and then gazed upon the rubble that lay before him, a single pillar left at the back of the smashed building.

"You see, they had blown up the whole temple that night, in their fighting. Out of their greed and entitlement over this beautiful thing, they ended up destroying it by accident."

Silence settled upon the room. I met Tarleigh's eyes.

"Is the lesson for me, ambassador?"

"I think it is a lesson for Laird Rossane, Laird MacArlay and Laird Kinnaid. Wouldn't you say?"

"I'd love to agree with you. But I'm afraid they wouldn't listen, even if your anecdote danced in front of them in a kilt, doing highland kicks."

"Then you must take care, Star, and intervene."

"Intervene?" My voice echoed off the chamber walls.

"If they come close to destroying your own temple. Or whatever it is that you hold most beautiful. I couldn't say. Excuse me."

Her boots rang all the way down the corridor, until the last echoes were gone.

I moved to the mirror and examined my face. The irritation in my eyes had mostly faded now. If only the irritation in my head was so quick to make itself scarce.

Tarleigh's final remarks had touched on the very thoughts I wanted to avoid.

Maybe I was a bad person for wanting to get back at Kinnaid. But I'd deal with that when the time came. For now, there was something much more important that I had to do: someone I had to visit.

I left my chamber and made my way toward the kitchens, listening to my boots echo as I walked down the stone corridor, until I found an attendant who wasn't hurrying somewhere.

"If you please," I said, "would you take me to Dr Galar's chamber?"

The woman hesitated, trying not so subtly to look me over.

"It's on a matter of urgency for the Sky's health," I added.

As she nodded and began to walk, pointing to the way ahead, I thought about Fierre lying still in my arms, taking tiny, shallow breaths, and I quickened my pace; the attendant sped up her steps and we jogged into the shadowy depths of the corridor.

Fifteen

Aiven

THE SCROLLS COVERING the table told me that Dr Galar had more than a few friends. Even if they hadn't been tied with the glossy ribbons of well-to-do families, the battered parchment would have revealed that they were not his own jottings. I had untied enough messages as Master of Compliance to know when I saw a scroll that had travelled a distance by air and bumped into a few trees on the way.

"May I help you, Star?"

Galar gestured to the smaller table near the front of the chamber, where empty chairs were pushed out from the dark wood. Potions and herbs dominated the table's surface.

I took the nearest chair, breathing in the pungent aroma of a leafy plant that had sprawled over the edges of a plate.

"I have a few questions about Prince Dannatyne. Would you indulge me?"

"Of course." Galar's voice came out brighter than usual.

"I'm not sure how to say this, but Prince Dannatyne has had a serious collapse."

"I see. That is bad luck. And you wish me to arrange for some physic, I presume?"

"I'd love that, doctor, except there's one problem." I carefully restrained myself from putting emphasis on my next words. "It appears that your physic may have caused his collapse."

Galar froze. To his credit, he recovered quickly. "Are you a doctor, Master Grian?"

"We both know I'm not." I smiled calmly. "But I couldn't help noticing that Fierre had been drinking from a bottle of cerise liquid before he collapsed. He described it to me as a medicine you'd given him. Do you think you could explain to me how this physic works?"

Galar steepled his fingers together and eyed me with a searching stare. "As you know, Star, it is my observation that the prince suffers from hysteria. I prescribed this medicine for him as a way of alleviating his symptoms."

"And his low body heat? His dizziness? His passing out at unexpected moments? Does the medicine help with those?"

"It aids with the full range of hysterical symptoms." Galar's voice sounded soothing, at first, but I detected a note of steel beneath the silk.

"I hope you'll forgive my inquiries, Dr Galar. As you pointed out, I'm not a doctor. It falls to me to ask you, then, why Prince Dannatyne became ill after taking the medicine you gave him. If it was intended to alleviate his symptoms, then, surely, he shouldn't have collapsed?"

"A little harsh medicine can be useful for a hysterical temperament."

"Are you certain that hysteria is the cause? Perhaps my creativity is lacking, but I can't imagine how hysteria could lower a man's body heat."

"Stress comes to bear upon the situation, as well." Galar regarded me with a lizard-like focus, unflinching. "Hysteria and stress are particular risks for the highest of nobility, you must understand. Both conditions tend to plague those with fine breeding. And princes are most at risk: young men of royal families bear such a fear of growing into their responsibility as future kings. When they are not fretting in hysterics, they grow melancholic with stress, and a strong course of physic may be needed to keep them in check."

I regarded Galar for a moment.

"Does the prince need to be kept in check, in your opinion?" I said.

"We all have duties and responsibilities in Eilean-òir, Star. It is my privilege to help the Sky to fulfil his."

"Duties? Could you enlighten me, doctor?"

"A duty to the realm: to stand up as a symbol of grace and remind us of the divine right of kingship. A duty to remain graceful in comportment and elegant in figure. A duty to be beautiful, not for any common reason, but to show the people what perfection looks like." His nostrils flared. "You understand?"

"I understand." I pushed back my chair. "Thank you for your time, doctor, and for your candour. You've shone a light on many things."

Galar shook my hand and followed me to the door. He nodded politely as I left. There was a coolness about his smile, but he didn't speak, and I strode down the corridor without looking back.

There had to be a library in this castle. I stopped the next attendant and asked for directions, following her instructions until I arrived at a slim door flanked by two guards. The men took one look at my face and bowed.

"Star," the guard on the left said. "You're most welcome, but all who read here must be accompanied by one of us."

"Of course." I hesitated. "How did you know who I was?"

"You fought courageously against Laird Kinnaid," the other man said, then quickly dropped his gaze.

I guessed that some of the watching crowd had seen Kinnaid fling dirt into my eyes.

"Thank you," I said.

"I wish Kinnaid had been the one to get kicked in the balls," the first guard muttered.

With supreme effort, I managed not to smile. It was a close thing.

The library of Dunhairstin Castle boasted shelves overflowing with books—so many books that I felt jealous, and even a little resentful, for Fierre's father obviously didn't read these tomes. Dust lay heavy upon the covers and pages. I noted the words at the end of each row of shelves, telling me that books about "History", "Sculpture", "Philosophy" and more lay within, and I ambled along until I found a row marked "Physic". It took a good quarter-hour of pulling out books until I found one that served my purpose, and plonking myself down in the chair next to a narrow window, I read it under the watchful gaze of a guard. I took notes in my head, keeping my efforts to the salient points.

The sky had darkened by the time I left, and I mused awhile in my chamber before settling into an uneasy sleep. The next morning found me going over my reading from last night in my head, etching several phrases about hysteria into my mind.

I ate breakfast quietly with the rest of our party and

let Fierre converse with the lairds. A smattering of little
red dots marked the skin around Fierre's eyes, yet neither
Rossane, nor MacArlay, nor Kinnaid seemed to care: every
laird wished to serve him food, touch his arm, or wipe his
cheek. Once he'd finished smiling through the small talk,
the ambassadors swooped in to discuss foreign policy,
and after a long bout of whispering with Ambassador
Rince about dyes for garments, wolf balm for healing,
and something called weathergrain, Fierre made time
for the ambassador for Sarleven, who possessed a list of
demands that was longer than a hermit's patience and
delivered them in a firmer voice than the one she'd used
with me. From what I could glean, Fierre didn't like the
idea of wasting money that could be spent on improving
the taxation system, and he didn't need a raised voice to
make his priorities clear. It took a good while before they
finished a discussion on jewel exports, and Fierre turned
to me with an apologetic smile.

"Gosh, Aive, I've kept you waiting."

"I'll wait however long you need. If you want another
half hour, I'll sit quietly over here, nursing my shadiest
thoughts."

"Another half hour talking politics, or a walk with
you?" Fierre took my arm, smiling, and we left the hall
together, heading into the castle grounds. "You're so
warm, Aive."

"You've never told me that before."

"Ha, ha." Fierre clasped my hand in his. "Was there
something you wanted to ask?"

I drew a deep breath. Checking quickly over my
shoulder, I ascertained that no one was following us.

"I've been thinking about the Sethunes' offer, and I
think we should go. Ride tonight and meet them at the

green forest north of the Fae Pools, under the full moon, just like they said. I'll be at your side the whole time—I won't let them speak to you alone."

Fierre stared at me. "I was going to say the same thing."

"You were?"

"I think I want to know. Whatever it is that's killing father, and maybe making me ill... I need to know it by name and nature. Because it might end up killing me, too."

Perhaps we both knew it already. But he was right. Name and nature—they made a difference.

I stroked his hair. "You're brave."

"You're the one who gives me courage."

How beautiful his voice was, all of a sudden. How soft his eyelashes looked, in the mid-morning light. But I couldn't tell him that. What if I had already taken a step too far, in the pools?

Just a sack of flesh to so many people. I couldn't let him feel like that again.

"Then it's settled," I said. "After dinner, we ride."

Fierre beamed, and stopped walking. It took a moment for me to realise that I had tightened my grip around his hand. He didn't wince or draw away from me, however; he looked up into my eyes, until I felt that the whole world had softened around me and become a kinder, gentler place.

I studied the red dots around his eyes. Up close, I still couldn't tell what they were. I wanted to know that he was safe, and yet I scarcely knew what to ask him: what affliction to name. Pressing my other hand to Fierre's palm, I sandwiched his soft hand between both of mine, and he went still, allowing me. Eventually he rubbed his fingers up and down against mine, but neither of us let go until laughter reached us, and the familiar bugle of Laird MacArlay's voice reminded us that we were not yet alone.

PALE MOONLIGHT STRIPED the grass in the evening, and as I crossed the grounds to the stables, I looked up and saw a crescent moon dangling in the sky, its shape a bright curve of silver against the vast blanket of indigo. I hoped that it would fatten and swell to fullness by the time we reached the forest.

Fierre gripped the reins of a black horse—probably one of his father's team, for it had a well-rested and sated look. I guessed that ours were sleeping off their journey in the stables.

"Shall I get another horse?" I said.

"No." Fierre swung up onto the horse's back. "I'd rather you sat behind me."

I pretended to be cool and collected as I climbed up behind him. He flicked the reins and we set off at a cracking pace, leaving Dunhairstin Castle in the distance within minutes, our bodies pressed closely together as the horse cantered on. I wrapped my arms around Fierre's waist, and since I couldn't see his face, I hoped that he was comfortable and happy.

We passed through the hills at a steady canter. The Fae Pools glinted like circles of glass, emerging from the darkness, their colour lost to the encroaching night. Fierre slowed the horse's pace as we pressed further north, glancing from side to side.

"I'm going to let her trot for a bit."

He didn't have to add that we were nearing our destination. I could read it in the stiffness of his shoulders.

The forest looked deep emerald in the darkness. As we

approached, moonlight splashed a few trees with silver, revealing the bright lime green of their leaves. No wonder the Sethunes had called it the *green forest*—you could hardly miss this place in broad daylight. We dismounted and tied up the horse at the edge of the forest, looking around for any sign of a torch, listening for any sound of a footstep.

"I have to tell you something, Fierre," I whispered.

"Oh?" He shuffled closer to me, and I felt his fingers interlace with my own.

"When you were asleep, I went to see Dr Galar, and I asked him—"

A whistle cut off my sentence. The sound came sharply, and I looked up, expecting to find one of our hosts nearby. But there wasn't one Sethune. There were at least a dozen Sethunes stepping out of the trees, moving to encircle us, their boots slipping silently over the grass. I couldn't spot the man with grey stubble or the doctor who'd revived Fierre; every face that the moonlight touched was unfamiliar. My fists balled at my sides.

If we'd come here unarmed to become the eager bait in this clan's trap... if anything happened to Fierre... I would never forgive myself.

"Full moon," a bearded man said, stepping forward.

He jabbed a finger at the sky, and I looked up. The silver crescent had fattened to a ball.

"We kept our promise," I said. "Will you keep yours?"

"Aye. No peeking, though." He beckoned to another man, who stepped forward, holding two lengths of cloth. Except, no, it wasn't a man—those were feminine features, and the curves of her chest were not what I had expected. A woman, on a clan mission at midnight? What sort of family *were* the Sethunes?

It took a few seconds for me to realise that we were about to be blindfolded, but Fierre seemed to have worked it out already. His hand squeezed mine. We didn't struggle as the Sethunes tied the cloth over our eyes and separated us, leading us by the arms.

"We won't hurt you, Sky," the woman said.

"Nor you, Star," another woman chimed in.

Another woman?

I soon had a different issue to focus on. The sensation of walking blindfolded was like wandering through a pitch black sea to an unclear destination—at best, uncomfortable, and at worst, disorienting. I was more worried for Fierre than for myself. Would he panic, or feel alone? Would he be reminded of his previous blackouts and reach out to hold me, only to find that I was no longer within reach?

I wanted to tear off my blindfold and throw my arms around him. Yet I had a feeling that the Sethunes wouldn't take kindly to me breaking our agreement.

The crunch of twigs under our feet told me that we were walking through the forest, and only when the sound of singing burst forth from up ahead did the Sethunes guide us to a halt. A pair of hands removed my blindfold. I looked across for Fierre at once and found him blinking, teetering slightly on the spot, but apparently unharmed. A sigh of deep relief washed through me. It took a moment for me to remember that I was on the land of Clan Sethune, and I should be taking in my surroundings.

The harmony of sound swelled, and I gazed ahead to find a group of six singers cradling candles in small brass holders, staring at Fierre and myself as they layered their voices. They made a dance of high melodies and low thrumming tunes, and the flames in their palms flickered at the gust of their breath. Together they wove a single, braided song that seemed to match the forest, an ancient and haunting power that merged with the bark and leaves behind us. When they stopped, it was as one entity, and they kept gazing at Fierre and I long after the sound had faded.

I felt something cold brush my palm and looked down. Fierre's hand pressed against mine. At once, I clasped that hand and held on tightly, hoping that he knew I would keep him safe.

"Well?" a man said, striding up to stand beside the singers. "What do you think? As the song said, we welcome you to our home, the seat of our clan, the heart of our family—the home of medicine in Eilean-òir. Will you step through the doorway of Clan Sethune, Sky and Star?"

I saw a stone archway behind the singers, barely illuminated by the candles they held. Beyond it, a cornucopia of lights welcomed us: candles glowed at the doors of tiny houses and around the base of a spreading tree. Torches added a stronger glow from brackets on a low wall running back from the archway, bordering the village path. I could see no towering castle, no building that gloated over the rest from a lofty height, yet the orange haloes above the candles made this tiny village look blessed.

"I shall gladly step through your doorway," Fierre said.

"You'll meet our leaders soon enough." The man who had spoken smiled.

Fierre glanced at me, but I stayed silent, for I didn't know what this plural, *leaders*, meant. Wasn't there only a single laird running Clan Sethune? I hoped that the riders weren't bloodthirsty, for I couldn't imagine how we could fight off a bunch of angry nobles.

"Allow me to give you a token of our good will," Fierre said, pulling something out of his pocket. "A little something from Clan Dannatyne, if you like."

As he held the item up in the moonlight, the silvery glow washed over a medallion carved with the crown. I drew in a breath. These were rare, I knew; even the Sethunes, on this far-flung island, had to know this honour. You only got a royal calling-coin if the Sky was marking his visit with an offer, promising his hospitality in return for your own.

The man who had spoken to us bowed low.

"Thank you, Sky," he said. "We feel the weight of your promise."

He led us past the singers, through the archway and into the village. I gripped Fierre's hand and he squeezed my palm, darting a look at me. In his eyes, I read fear, but also sorrow, and I wondered what his father had said to him back at the palace. This pall of sadness had covered him since yesterday evening, and I didn't like it at all.

The singers and the riders fell into step behind us, and as one, we followed the man who had greeted us, walking steadily towards the end of the village. Candlelight glossed our faces. I felt Fierre's fingers press tighter against mine.

"Maybe it's better not to know," he murmured. "Maybe there's something broken inside me, and I'll die... just the way father is dying."

I stopped, for a moment, and held his palm between both of mine. The whole group stopped abruptly behind us, but I didn't care. I focused only on Fierre's face.

"I don't believe that," I said. "I don't believe you're broken, or that the dizziness is your fault. But no matter what the cause is, we'll face it together."

"We?"

"I'll be right by your side. Always. Even if they tell me you're cursed, I won't leave you." I smiled at him. "I'll let the demon take me, so you can walk free."

"Did you mean it?" Fierre whispered.

"That I'd face a demon for you? Every word."

"No, I mean… before… when you said you loved me."

I looked into his face. The silver light turned those big eyes into shining pools, like the faerie bathing spot we had passed on the way, and I recalled how I had felt when I said the words—*Please, Fierre. I love you.* I remembered the hot wave of panic that had swept through me while Fierre was refusing to eat, and how much more terrified I had felt when I realised what I had allowed myself to say. But there was no hiding, now. Fleeing the truth would leave him sorrowful and alone. I couldn't bear to see that.

"I love you," I said. "If I could say only one thing on my deathbed, it'd be that I love you, and I always will, even in the afterlife. But I guess I'm saying it now. While we're still alive."

While your hand feels soft in my grip. While your pulse still finds the power to sing in your chest, creating a song more beautiful than the music here.

Fierre ran his thumb over my forefinger.

"I'm afraid to say how much I want you," he said.

"Then don't," I said. "Just hold my hand."

Together, looking anywhere but at each other, we walked on up the slope.

Sixteen

Fierre

I HADN'T IMAGINED that Clan Sethune would have a grand castle with soaring towers, stained glass windows, or a glimmering lake. They were a family of highland doctors, after all. I'd pictured them with *some* kind of castle—a little one, perhaps, of unadorned stone—but father had never said a word about them. He'd answered my questions about the families that were worth money and power to the crown, the clans with armies or mines or well-stocked vaults.

As the Sethunes showed me into a tiny dwelling at the end of their village, I wondered if I should've asked more questions about the poorer families. I felt stupid. And acutely aware of my own ignorance. My gift must have reminded them of my position, and I'd probably made them feel uncomfortably obliged to welcome me in.

And then there was the matter of the red dots around my eyes.

Could everyone else see them? Were they all pretending not to notice? What about Aiven—was he disgusted by my appearance?

It was awkward all around.

The only thing that didn't feel awkward was Aiven's hand in mine, with his warm fingers wrapped around my own. His palm felt like a compact sun, radiating heat. *I love you*, he had said, and I'd been afraid to say exactly what I felt, unable to find the words to do it justice. I clung onto him now and hoped that he understood.

The man who had spoken to us gestured ahead, and as we passed through the doorway, I followed the line of his pointed finger to where two chairs sat at the end of a small but comfortably appointed room. A few of the riders followed us in, but most of them stayed outside. I heard a cough at my shoulder, and recognised the *lighiche* who had met us at the Fae Pools: the same man who had brought me back to life.

He muttered a few words in his native tongue.

"He says you can approach the Clan Elders now," one of the female riders said, stepping up to us. "Follow the carpet, and no need to kneel."

If there was one thing I was glad for, in this little hall, it was the blue carpet that unscrolled all the way to the far end. The stone of the floor looked rough enough to scrape my sandals. Aiven and I walked hand in hand to the two people sitting in the chairs, coming to a halt, and the man on the right placed his hand over his heart. The woman in the left chair made the same gesture, over her sash, and both smiled. It made me feel dashed funny, as if someone had poured something warm into my stomach.

"Welcome to Clan Sethune, Sky," the woman said. "It's our pleasure as clan chiefs to host you here."

"Clan chiefs?" I echoed.

"I have the delight of sharing my duties with my wife." The man winked at the woman beside him. "When she's not managing the doctors' training, she's seeing to the farmers' needs. I prefer to train our riders to defend us, and teach our clan songs and stories, but sometimes, we do each other's jobs, and we're no' the worse for it. You'd know something about managing a bunch of people, now, wouldn't you?"

Before I could reply, the man who had greeted us outside hurried up and handed my calling-coin over to Lady Sethune. She held it up to the nearest candle and examined the crown marking. Setting it down on her knee, she stared at me.

"We're honoured, Sky," she said, quietly, and her voice was like polished stone. "Your father's never offered us hospitality."

"I may not be perfect, but I'm doing my best not to turn into my father," I said.

"I can see that." She ran a finger over the calling-coin.

Her husband clapped once and the riders scurried past him, into an adjoining room whose door seemed to blend into the wall, barely visible unless you looked for it. They returned with a plate, on which three bottles clustered around a pair of glasses. An amber liquid filled the first bottle. A deep honey-coloured liquid filled the second, while the third was half-full of a pale golden drink that sparkled.

"Before we speak of medicine and healing, Sky," Lady Sethune said, "a proper welcome is in order. Every guest of the Sethunes must drink the clan whisky before they take an audience with the lady and laird. And here, we have three kinds of whisky, for the three kinds of person that cross our doorstep."

"Oh?" I raised an eyebrow. I hoped that I looked nonchalant. I wished that father had said *anything* about the Sethunes' hospitality—like whether or not they were known to poison their guests.

"This one's for a parent to drink," Lady Sethune said, tapping the bottle of pale golden whisky. "A mother or a father, no matter how many their children, alive or passed away, must sip our first whisky."

"And this one can only pass the lips of an experienced guest." Laird Sethune touched the bottle of honey-coloured whisky. "Someone who isn't a virgin, but is yet childless."

"Lastly…" Lady Sethune tapped the bottle of amber whisky. "A whisky for virgins to drink."

Several of the riders smiled, but there was no cruelty to the smiles—no animosity, nor even a hint of shaming. I recalled some of the northern lords cracking the occasional irreverent joke at court, often requiring a back-and-forth dialogue that drew the listener into the humour. This ritual of whisky drinking, with its cheeky question-and-answer process, struck me as something like the same banter.

I stared at the amber-coloured liquid, wishing, for a moment, that I could take a sip.

"Er," I said, "well, if it gets us an audience with you, I supposed we'd better take a dram, eh, Aive?" I noticed that Aiven's hand had gone limp in my grip.

"Yes," Aiven said. The word barely made it out of his mouth.

"So which one will it be, Sky?"

Lady Sethune gazed at me. Everyone else in the hall—the riders, the doctor, and Laird Sethune—seemed to be staring at me with the intensity of a midwinter blizzard.

"Er," I said, "I suppose I'll take the whisky for experienced guests. I'm childless, but, well… this might suit."

I took the glass that Lady Sethune poured and raised it to my lips, trying to avoid looking at Aiven. I didn't want to see his expression. Would he be embarrassed to hear me admitting my night-time doings before the whole hall? *Sluts like you have to work hard to look perfect*, my father had said. Those words seemed to ring in my ears.

The whisky tasted sweet and soothing, like a summer wine. It took a few seconds before the afterburn kicked in and I coughed, clutching my throat. Lady Sethune grinned, and Aiven patted me on the back. I still didn't dare to look at him.

Well, I'd done it. Feeling my cheeks burn, and being pretty sure that it wasn't due to the whisky, I kept my head down as I placed the glass back on the plate.

"And which one will you take, Star?" Laird Sethune said.

Aiven took a tentative step forward.

"Er," he said.

"Don't be shy, now. We've all drunk one whisky or another, in here." Laird Sethune winked. "Some of us have to drink a different one a year later."

The jocularity didn't seem to reassure Aiven. He pointed to the amber whisky, and his voice came out softly. "That one."

He didn't look at me as Laird Sethune poured him a glass. Nor did he look at me after he had downed the whisky—the whisky meant for virgins.

My mouth had been hanging open for some time before I realised and closed it. Aiven stepped back beside me, his head down.

The echoing clap from all present told me that our welcome was complete, and I reached out for Aiven's hand again. He took it, still not looking at me.

Aiven was a virgin. The statement seemed to ring in my mind, even though no one had spoken it. Aiven had never slept with another man, or a woman, or anyone of any nature—and yet he'd said that he loved me. In the Fae Pools, he'd cupped my arse with both hands and dotted kisses along my lips, and then he'd kissed me hard, pushing down against me. He hadn't seemed like a shy virgin when he'd looked at me, in the water, right after I put my hand on his cock and silently dared him to touch me.

"Sky," Lady Sethune said, and her smooth voice brought me back to the present. "Shall we speak of your health and prospects, alone?"

I squeezed Aiven's hand with all the force I could muster.

"If *alone* means with my Star of the Sky, my lady. We do everything together."

"Everything. That *is* impressive." Lady Sethune rose. "Riders of Clan Sethune, take up your posts outside the door. Unless there's a fire racing up the hill, I don't wish to be interrupted. You understand?"

The riders nodded and made their bows, retreating quickly. We were left standing before Laird and Lady Sethune, who put the whisky down on the small table to their left. Laird Sethune rose too. I was suddenly aware of their height—almost a match for Aiven's—and I felt like a pixie who'd wandered into a group of giants.

I drew a deep breath and tried to find the right words to broach the topic of my illness. Fortunately, Lady Sethune didn't have any inhibitions.

"I've been told my son Keir has met you already. Once while you were clothed, and once while you were bathing." She inclined her head to the doctor, who nodded nervously. He shrugged off his robe and folded it, revealing a Sethune family tartan, bright red lines crossing over deep blue cloth.

"We thought it only fitting that you speak with the most skilled doctor in the whole clan," Laird Sethune added, with a roguish gleam in his eye.

"Indeed? You must've done a cracking job," I said, smiling at Keir.

"Not him!" Lady Sethune laughed, and Laird Sethune guffawed with her. "No, turn around, if you will, Sky, and meet our doctor-in-chief!"

Aiven and I turned as one, letting go of each other and then joining our hands again. A woman met our stares, seemingly unperturbed by the fact that the ruler of the land was standing before her. She wore a clan tartan, too, with a sash over a plain shirt and a kilt in the same style as the men, and she bowed deeply towards me. I had the distinct impression that I was being sized up, but I didn't mind. Something about this woman was plain and straightforward, like her clothing.

"Sky, my name is Oighrig." The pronunciation, *Oyrick*, made me think of oysters. "Daughter of the clan chiefs. I spoke to your father, once, after he arrived on the Isle of Hairstin, though he didn't like what I had to say. It falls within my ability to offer you advice now." She glanced over at Lady Sethune, who nodded. "But I ask something in return. Our family wish to make a petition to you. I'm no haggler—except when it comes to herbs for a quality pipe—but I'd ask for a reply before you leave. That's all."

"Well, I can't see the harm in that," I said. "And even if I wanted to, I couldn't refuse. It's a Prince Regent's duty to hear every case that is put to him and provide a fair and honest answer."

Oighrig smiled, but her mouth did not curve all the way. "You really aren't like your father, Sky," she said.

It was the best compliment anyone had ever given me.

Laird Sethune gestured to the left wall of the chamber. Tartan cushions made a ring around a cluster of burning candles, and on the wall above, a painting showed a woman with a scalpel in one hand, speaking earnestly to an old man.

"If you'll sit with us on the floor, then my daughter will share her knowledge. We all break bread as equals. We break news as equals in Clan Sethune, too," Laird Sethune said.

I led the way, sitting down, and a wave of relief poured over me as Aiven took the cushion next to me. He rubbed my shoulder gently. The presence of four Sethunes with a history of medical knowledge suddenly seemed less daunting, with Aiven at my side.

Keir spoke first, and though I didn't understand a word of his native tongue, I understood the serious look in his eyes.

"He asks if you want to know the truth," Lady Sethune said. "He says that any Sethune doctor has sworn to speak honestly, but for our own safety, when advising a member of the royal family, we demand that the patient must wish to hear our counsel."

What exactly had my father done to these people? Or had it been my grandfather? *We won't have the old king killing more of our sons and daughters*, the Sethune with the grey stubble had declared at the Fae Pools... how exactly had my father reacted to these doctors?

"You're safe to speak freely, with me," I said.

"And you truly wish to know why you are ill?"

Oighrig Sethune sat directly opposite me, and her voice

hit me like an arrow to the chest. Of course, I wanted to know, and I didn't want to know at the same time. How could I explain that to her?

"Shall I list all my symptoms?" I said.

"No, Sky. I shall list them for you. You are cold, to the point where you fear you could die from a mild chill. Sometimes your toes feel like blocks of ice, as if they might snap off in the night. Your head feels light and weightless, leading to dizzy spells. You collapse suddenly, every so often, without even a hint of warning. Often you feel irritable, without knowing why. You wake in the night, several times a week, and cannot get back to sleep. No matter how much you fast, you always feel swollen, and your body seems too fat. Am I correct?"

I stared at her, forgetting the laird and lady who were sitting with us.

"How did you know all that?" I breathed.

"Because I've treated your father. And from what I hear, you suffer in the same way."

"Dr Galar tells me that I need to work hard to live up to the standard of a prince," I said. "But I think he actually knows what's wrong with me, and he doesn't want to trouble me."

The distinct sound of Aiven clearing his throat followed my reply.

We all started. Aiven looked apologetically at me, dipping his head just a little. "Fierre, I've been meaning to tell you… Dr Galar spoke with me before we left."

"Oh?"

"He gave an opinion on your health."

I didn't like the way that Aiven was hesitating. It had to be really bad, surely… if Aiven, of all people, was pausing…

"What did he guess? Terminal case of being pretty and good at conversation?" I tried to get the falsely bright note out of my voice.

"He claims you suffer from hysteria," Aiven said.

I frowned. It wasn't the worst thing I could have heard. But why couldn't Galar have simply told me that, too? I was about to say as much when Oighrig snorted.

"Convenient, that the Sky of Eilean-òir should be hysterical," she said. "A pleasing explanation for a doctor who does not wish to treat his patient." She looked me directly in the eye, and I saw a little of the cool stone of Lady Sethune in the daughter's gaze. "Have you cross-checked his opinion?"

"I have." Aiven's voice cut through the air like a knife. We all stared at him. "That is, I took the chance to look up hysteria in the library here at Dunhairstin. I knew that the former king was supposed to have the best collection of books in the realm." He drew a deep breath, and turned his attention to me. "There's no mention of hysteria before your grandfather's time. No record of any such condition affecting a line of noblemen. And, more to the point, hysteria seems to be a very vague entry, described in the most general terms. I could find no mention of any your symptoms: no recorded instances of dizziness, passing out, cold, irritability, interrupted sleep, or discomfort. The author speaks of stress and leaves it at that."

"And who is the author?" Lady Sethune said.

"That's the most curious thing, my lady. The entry on hysteria bears no signature. The initials of the doctor who contributed the record are entirely missing."

The doctor-in-chief and her mother shared a glance.

"Well, I can give you my medical opinion, unbiased by

coin or rank," Oighrig said, staring at me again. "You aren't hysterical, Sky. You're starving."

I searched for words and found none. A silence hung in the air of the little room.

At last, I laughed, and the sound burst from me like a wineskin breaking.

"Of course I'm starving," I said. "You don't get to look good in an enserre by eating whatever you like."

"Or anything you like," Oighrig said.

"But those symptoms are of a different order," I said. "Getting cold. Feeling dizzy. Feeling weak. Passing out. It's not about *food*—it's stress, and a matter of the mind."

"Do you think that food plays no role in the workings of your mind?"

I opened my mouth and closed it. Oighrig Sethune stared straight back at me, without shifting an inch on her cushion.

"Well…" I began.

"Sky, it gives me no joy to tell you this. A starved mind is like a weak fire. It runs on half the fuel, or less. Imagine that your body has a small supply of wood in its garden— it can't afford to burn a big fire. So it burns a smaller one. Your temperature drops. You can't get warm, no matter how many blankets you wrap yourself in. And your body maintains that weak fire, keeping you permanently cold until it receives more fuel to burn. That's how it still has some wood to keep your heart beating, your lungs pumping, and your blood circulating." She looked me directly in the eye. "That's how you're not dead, Sky. Your body is running efficiently on almost nothing."

I stared right at her, not bothering to look away out of politeness.

"But the dizziness," I said. "The fainting."

"Even a very efficient fire fails, sometimes. The flame goes out. One moment you're stable, and then suddenly you're falling, unable to find any energy, unable to leap back up. You don't know why your fire is burning so low. Well, I can tell you why, Sky. You're not putting any food into your body. You're asking it to run with no wood at all."

I looked down, now, with shame burning in my cheeks.

"It's not your fault, Fierre," Aiven whispered. "Didn't Galar ask you to eat less?"

I couldn't manage to reply.

"And as for the sleep, do you feel hungry when you wake, Sky?" Oighrig said.

"Of course." I considered, for a moment. "But I feel hungry all the time."

"Your body knows that. It won't let you rest unless you eat more, to fuel it through the night. You lie awake, tossing and turning, wondering why you can't drift off into blackness."

It all made sense. I didn't like it, but I saw, all too easily, how it fit together as one mosaic. Yet I wanted to snatch at excuses, to find a way to disprove her.

"It might be true. But I feel so annoyed when someone keeps me from food. Surely that's not the body, but the mind," I said.

"When you've little to eat, your brain must treasure and depend on every morsel," Oighrig said. "You have no patience for interruptions because you cannot afford to miss those scraps."

I thought of how I had slammed my plate down and snapped at Mistress Browne when she had interrupted my tiny meal of oatcake, back in the palace. The memory didn't make me proud.

"Fierre," Aiven whispered, leaning closer to me. "Tell her about the potion you drank last night."

"What?" I felt heat surge fast through my neck and face. "I told you, Dr Galar gave it to me so that I could put things right and stick to my regime."

I looked across and found Aiven's face inches from mine. He was staring at me with a blend of compassion and severity that made me feel even more ashamed of myself.

"Er…" I turned back to the doctor-in-chief. "My personal attending doctor, Dr Galar, has been aiding me with a very restrictive diet. He knows that I'm greedy and I struggle with wanting more food. So he's provided me with a special medicine. It's a cerise liquid that smells like hazelnuts, and I drink a thimbleful if I overindulge."

Oighrig stiffened on her cushion. Keir tensed, too, and stared at me.

"What happens after you drink it?" Oighrig said.

"Well, I, er… I expel the contents of my stomach, and then I feel very thirsty."

A heavier silence hung in the room, and I could feel the shift that happened after I spoke, a swift change that saw Lady Sethune glancing at her husband, and Oighrig Sethune glancing at her brother. Whatever I had just revealed about Galar's treatment, it had cooled the mood.

"I thought your doctor incompetent," Lady Sethune said. "But I see now that he is something more than that."

"My lady?"

The Sethunes looked at each other and seemed to confer silently, passing some understanding between them, lady and laird, daughter and son. I tried to tell myself that the situation couldn't be as bad as it seemed. The grim look on every face warned me otherwise.

"The red dots around your eyes," Oighrig said, at last. "They match…"

I leaned forward, but she hesitated.

"Did they appear after you used this cerise potion?"

"How did you know?" I said.

The Sethunes shared glances again.

"I fear this is a matter of the crown's security," Laird Sethune said. "Perhaps even the crown's very essence. Your life itself."

"We would ask you to stay the night in these humble surrounds and converse with us tomorrow before you leave. We may not be gilded and glinting as a royal palace, but we know how to offer the embrace of the land at Clan Sethune." Lady Sethune smiled. "Tonight is Starfall, the festival of spring moonlight. Our people will strike up a song for the moon and stars and revel until dawn in the forest, raising their glasses to the silver beams that light up the night. You may dance with them, and sleep the day away tomorrow, and when the four of us have conferred with all the senior doctors of Clan Sethune, we will come and find you, and give you our advice."

"And make your petition," Aiven said.

I had to hand it to him. He never stopped thinking like a Master of Compliance, even when he sat in a tiny village near a forest on a far-flung island, listening to a promise of midnight revels. He never forgot anything important.

Right now, he ran his fingers over my knuckles, reminding me that he was right here by my side.

"Yes," I said. "I will hear your advice *and* your petition tomorrow. I appreciate your kindness, laird and lady, in putting us up for the night. Now…" I squeezed Aiven's hand, and felt his warm skin. "Show us to our quarters, and we shall see about this revel."

As Keir and Oighrig moved out of the chamber and Lady Sethune gestured to us to follow them, I allowed myself a deep breath. The air outside tickled my face, cold but not cruel. I looked around in every direction, searching the village, and from somewhere beyond the houses I heard the plucking of a stringed instrument and the soft tap-tap of a drum. Unlike everything I had just heard, it was beautiful, and soothing, and right.

Seventeen

Aiven

THE DANCERS WHIRLED around us and laughed, and I tried to keep my balance on the soil, holding onto Fierre's hand. Glasses were thrust into the air and whisky tinkled everywhere. Starfall certainly wasn't the kind of festival that priests told you about, but then, I suspected that the customs of the island clans were scarcely known to the rest of us, like peaks shrouded by fog. I felt more than a little foggy myself after my first drink, and I declined the second, withdrawing from the crowd of dancers and guiding Fierre to a spot on the fringe.

He didn't speak. That alone made me uncomfortable. For Fierre to be standing in a forest clearing, surrounded by revellers, plied with drink, with the light of the silver moon falling like a blessing upon the whole scene, and for him to stand quiet and aloof... something had to be troubling him.

Fortunately, we both knew what it was.

I'd expected something like this. A nebulous idea of the kind of illness that Oighrig Sethune had described had been swirling in my head for some time, yet to hear all its spike-tipped specifics laid out one by one was something else entirely; and if those details made me flinch, how must Fierre feel when their points pricked him?

I slipped my arm around his shoulders and moved close to him. Moonlight striped his face as he turned, glossing it with silver. I had never seen anything so beautiful. In his big, dark eyes, the torches of the revellers flickered and blazed.

A woman ran toward us, thrusting out a glass.

"No, thank you," I said. "We've had quite enough."

"It's virgin's whisky!" the woman cried.

Hot shame swelled inside me. The woman's smile widened, and her face was full of honest cheer. None of them *meant* to shame me, I told myself; Laird and Lady Sethune's ritual had clearly been one of those examples of far-northern 'humour' that had manifested into custom. I had simply been the victim of excruciating and unfortunate timing to have encountered it while with Fierre.

The woman in front of me hadn't been inside the chamber—no one here had seen me drink the amber whisky.

Except for Fierre, that was.

Oh god. It was still so humiliating.

"I'm sure it's delicious. Pour your friends a glass for us, if you like," I said.

"By the hanging moon, you can bet I will!"

The woman danced away, leaving us in uncomfortable silence. I couldn't bear to watch Fierre digest the news he had just received from the Sethunes by himself, shutting his doors to me and locking in the pain. I grasped his hand and made to lead him away, and he came easily, not asking me where I was taking him.

Once we entered the trees, the shouts of the revellers lessened. The dark coolness of the forest shrouded us, giving us the illusion of privacy for a moment. Fierre's cold palm felt tiny in my grip.

"It's going to be okay," I whispered.

I wasn't sure why I was whispering, because the village was busy throwing a pagan dance and no one was paying us the slightest bit of notice, but it felt right.

"Darling Aive," Fierre said, leaning to the side and resting his head against my chest. "I could almost believe that."

"You can recover. Now that you have the information about what's wrong—and soon you'll have more—you can heal. I know you can."

"I don't know," Fierre murmured.

"It probably won't be easy. But we can do it. We can figure it out together. Because it's not poison or a curse, it's a lack of food; and we can remedy that."

He was silent for a long moment, and as the silence stretched and stretched, I wondered if I had offended him by speaking too bluntly. But then I felt his hands close around my back, and I knew that he wasn't offended at all. An emotion much more serious than annoyance had suffused his gaze.

"I'm afraid of food," he whispered.

I looked down at his pained expression. "You can learn to be friends with it again."

"Do you really mean that?"

"I know it."

Fierre hugged me tightly and nestled further into me. "I can't believe it, but when you're the one saying it… I want to believe. Thanks, Aive."

"I'll be here every bit of the way, because I love you.

Even if you turn into a little demon when you get into a faery pool," I said.

I felt him tense against me. His head remained on my chest. After a pause that felt like an eternity, he whispered, "I care for you, too, you great pillar of muscle."

I pressed my lips to his forehead and quickly drew them away. I hadn't been thinking. Of course Fierre wouldn't feel ready to say he loved me. Fierre wouldn't even want me to touch him, right now, when he was sad. But as I watched, he turned towards me and kissed my chin, and strained on tiptoe to kiss me on the lips. His tongue ran over my lower lip. I couldn't mistake the feeling of his hand as it slipped down my back.

"Fierre," I murmured, still half-believing that we could be overheard, despite the revellers. "I don't want you to feel obliged to do anything... to be close to me." I caressed his hair. "I'll be here when you need me, no matter what. No obligations. No bargains."

"Who said anything about bargains?" He kissed me quickly, then drew back to stare at me. I felt a warm spot on my mouth where his lips had been. "What I felt, in the Fae Pools—what *we* felt, because I think you felt it, too... it was real."

He knelt, slowly, and laced up my boot. I hadn't even noticed that it'd come untied. As he rose again, his face came close to my groin, and I tried very hard not to move.

"I want to give myself to you tonight, Aive," he said. "Of my own choice."

Silver beams showered over us, and I was dimly aware that moonlight had snuck through the canopy to paint us in its glory. I didn't care how beautiful it was. Nothing could distract from the weight of what Fierre had just said, and the look in his eye, firm and unmistakeable.

"Can I touch you?" I said, quietly.

"You can touch any part of me you like."

I couldn't control myself, then. My hand moved to his arse, and I grabbed him and kissed him, tasting him as my tongue met his, breathing his scent deep into my nostrils. He smelled like summer berries, just ripening, a little sweet without being cloying: a perfect blend of juice and seed, barely contained. He whimpered. Paying attention to the new warmth of his neck, I pressed kisses from his chin down to his collarbone, feeling him shiver with each one. I liked the way he lost control. There was no mistaking his feeling now.

I grabbed his arse harder, and he wrapped his arms around my middle.

"Why don't we go back?" he whispered, after a moment.

As one, we looked through the trees, not towards the clearing where the villagers were still dancing, but the other way—toward the houses.

"If you're sure," I whispered back.

We slipped through the trunks in silence, conspirators in our new pact. The sounds of the revel grew fainter and fainter behind us, and I concentrated on the trees illuminated by moonlight ahead. Only when we burst out of the forest and into the little village again did I realise that I had no idea where the Sethunes had stored our things, or where we were supposed to sleep.

My brain had been so stuffed with concern for Fierre, after the meeting, that I had forgotten to ask about the most basic arrangements. To my relief, Keir Sethune rose from a bench outside one of the houses and strode to meet us.

Without a translator, Keir merely pointed uphill, to somewhere beyond the laird and lady's house. We followed him, turning off the main path onto a tiny track that looked as if it might lead to a dark and dangerous place. For a while, it was certainly dark, and I trod carefully on the soft earth, keeping a firm grip on Fierre's hand. At last, the doctor brought us to a stop and pointed ahead into a rainbow of lights.

A little cottage emerged from the clutch of dark bushes, its front door illuminated by a series of hanging lanterns. The porch was studded with pots in which bright flowers bloomed. I could see lights inside the front windows, most likely more of the coloured lanterns, judging by the pink and green glow emanating from different sides of the cottage; our horse was tied up to the porch railing, pails of food and water within its reach.

Whatever I had expected, it hadn't been this.

The Sethunes might be frank of speech, but with this accommodation, they were telling Fierre that they respected and welcomed him. They could have chosen a very plain dwelling for us. They could have chosen their most dilapidated rooms. But they had not.

"Thank you," Fierre said, and though Keir did not reply, he looked pleased.

He handed Fierre a key and set off at a stride down the path again.

Fierre waited until his footsteps had faded before stepping onto the porch. He tapped one of the dangling lanterns and beamed. "Dashed pretty, don't you think?"

"Yes," I said.

I wasn't looking at the lantern.

"Let's see what the doctors have prescribed us." He turned the key in the lock and walked through. I followed him carefully, taking off my shoes just outside. The pink and green lights in the front room revealed a tastefully spare chamber, with a little table and chairs, a Sethune tartan rug, and several bottles of whisky. I didn't like to raise the question of whether they were the same bottles we had drunk from earlier. The whole memory was too embarrassing.

Passing into a narrow corridor, we moved out of the range of the pink and green lanterns and into a purple glow. The first door to the right offered a tiny kitchen with plates of food and jugs of water laid out on a table. Through a door on the left, I spied a small room with a desk and a shelf of books, bathed in red light. Finally, the double doors at the end of the corridor opened onto a room awash with golden glow. Fierre and I stopped at the same time, bumping into each other.

"Well," Fierre said, "they didn't skimp on the bedding."

Before us stood the largest four-poster bed that I had ever seen crammed into a small room. The curtains had been bundled up, leaving us a clear view of the smooth golden sheets. A sumptuous cover of black velvet had been rolled up, as if the bed was inviting us to lie down. The scent of honey permeated the room and twin golden lanterns poured a sheen over the furniture.

I coughed. All of a sudden, the privacy of our circumstances felt real. No camp this time… no guards waiting outside, no ambassadors hanging around, no lairds hovering to snap at Fierre's ankles. No limit to our time, either. We had no need to rush back anywhere, as we had rushed back from the Fae Pools; we had the whole night to ourselves.

I want to give myself to you tonight. Fierre's words echoed in my head, bright as newly-polished crystal. *You can touch any part of me you like.*

He might not have said that if he'd known what I'd

daydreamed about, several times, since I'd accidentally looked up his enserre in the ritual bathhouse.

My hands felt clammy. I swallowed and took a deep breath. As Fierre walked into the room, I tried to look calm.

"Do you think they brought in the saddlebags while we were in the forest?"

"Must have," I murmured. The bags were positioned on a small cabinet, next to a vase of roses. The deep scent of the roses perfumed the chamber, combining with the gold light to make me feel as if I were entering a boudoir from some other world—the kind of world that Fierre could slip into so easily, as if he belonged there; the kind of world that I shouldn't set foot in.

"Come on," Fierre said, sniffing one of the roses and grinning at me. "What are you waiting for?"

I couldn't answer honestly, so I stepped through the doorway and shut the door. I flinched as it made a loud thump.

"It's okay," Fierre said. "There's no one to hear us."

The statement hung between us like an apple, ready to be plucked. Fierre seemed to realise it, too, because he turned away and picked up his saddlebag without meeting my gaze. "I think I need a moment in the bath chamber," he muttered. "Stay here, will you, Aive?"

He made his way over to a door that I had missed until now, and I glimpsed a tiny adjoining chamber before Fierre shut it, leaving me to stare at the solid wood.

Perhaps I should've said something. Or done something. I should've hugged him as soon as we entered the bedchamber and made him feel safe. Maybe I should've said more to comfort him about the Sethunes' diagnosis.

Maybe I should've lied, and told him that it was a

fleeting illness. Yet I knew, deep down, that I could only tell him the truth about the things that mattered.

Maybe I shouldn't have kissed him in the Fae Pools. He was a prince, after all, and I wasn't a noble by even the most generous standard. Even being his best friend didn't bridge that gap. Princes saved their favour for those born in the world of silver and gold, everyone knew.

I had overstepped a line, and I hadn't deserved to.

Watching the bath chamber door, I sat down on the edge of the bed. I waited. I watched the door some more, and tried not to listen to the sounds from within. I began to think that Fierre could be crying, or that he wanted to be alone. The porch would be comfortable enough. I could call out, now, and tell him that I'd sleep outside and give him some privacy.

The door swung open. In the glow of the lanterns, Fierre's body transformed into a gilded figure, like the image of a holy martyr in a classical painting.

He stepped forward and became a man again, and now I saw the three ribbons tied at his neck, waist, and ankle: the three ribbons that I had tied there, some time ago.

They were the only clothing he wore.

I followed the lines of his body down from his neck to his feet, and swallowed.

He looked like he wanted to speak. That was good. I was on the verge of saying something very foolish indeed; much better to let him speak first. Maybe he would say that he liked me. Maybe he would finally tell me that he loved me. I swallowed again.

Fierre took a deep breath, raised his gaze to my face, and said:

"Are you really a virgin?"

Eighteen

Fierre

THE SEA-BLUE LIGHT in the bathroom bathed me from the crown of my head to my toes. I stared into the mirror as I stripped down, watching myself in the glass, wishing that I looked slimmer and more elegant. I had to stop thinking about that. *Think about Aiven, sitting in there. Think about Aiven kissing you hard in the forest. Think about how his voice sounded when he said he loved you, deep but trembling.*

I fished the ribbons from my bag and found the tiny bottle of oil. I tied the ribbons onto my body first, fumbling with the knots—it was dashed hard to make a bow, yourself, without your best friend there to help you, and even if the bow on my ankle still looked a bit wonky after three tries, I did my best.

The stopper on the bottle of oil came out easily. I blushed as I poured a little bit of oil onto my fingers and spread it around.

This could all be a terrible mistake. Aiven might not want me, after all.

Certainly, he had said that he loved me. But since he was a virgin, he might not really know what that meant. Maybe he loved the deep bond of our friendship, but the prospect of getting into bed with me made him feel sick. Maybe he didn't even know what he wanted.

Then again, he *had* grabbed my arse like he was snatching the last piece of bread from a loaf.

I had to make sure. If I charged ahead and didn't test the water first, I might drown our friendship… in waves of my own lust, if I wasn't careful.

That was enough metaphors for now.

I checked my appearance—ribbons in place, hair falling down low on my forehead—and then I finished the last bit of preparation, pushing my fingers in deep. My fingertips felt cold and slippery. Once I was slick enough inside to feel self-conscious, I washed my hands and coated them with the fragrant perfume that the Sethunes had left on a ledge. It smelled faintly of honey. That must have been what made the bedchamber smell so nice; I'd thought it was some kind of magic the islanders had worked. Everything up here seemed to blossom with mysteries and secrets.

The door felt heavy under my hands. I pushed it hard until it swung open, and stepped through into the golden light. Aiven sat up on the edge of the bed. He ran a long, scrolling look from my neck to my feet.

I wanted to ask him if he was completely sure that he loved me; if he really wanted to touch me, and if he wouldn't regret it. The words stuck in my throat. I opened my mouth and willed them to come out.

Instead, I said, "Are you really a virgin?"

Aiven's face crumpled slightly. He shifted on the bedsheet, looking down. After a long moment he said, without raising his eyes, "You're wearing the ribbons."

"I couldn't believe it, you know. You didn't seem shy when I jumped on top of you, in the pool. You seemed ready for it."

"I never thought I'd see you in the ribbons again."

We were going to talk at cross-purposes forever if I didn't give in.

"I wanted to wear them for you," I said. "Because when I put them on, I remember where your fingers touched my skin... how your fingertips felt, even just for a second."

I stared at Aiven. He looked at my ribbons, one by one, then brought his gaze up to my face. He swallowed.

"I really am a virgin," he said. "Sorry—I know it's not the answer you want to hear. I know it must be disappointing, after all the men you've slept with who could sweep you off your feet. I mean, not *all* the men. I'm not saying there's a lot. I just mean... I'm not everything you want."

"That's where you're wrong." I took a step towards him, then another. "You *are* everything I want. I didn't know it until I was Prince Regent, and I'd made a right hash of things by making you Star. But you being a virgin, it feels... new. And bright. And different." I paused, and looked him directly in the eye. "That's why I want to be sure that you mean it when you say you love me."

"Fierre," Aiven said, and his voice came out husky and raw.

"Do you really want this? Or are you just trying to be nice?"

"I promise you, I've never wanted anything more."

I reached the bed and felt his breath gust against my naked chest. The look on his face told me that he wasn't going to protest. Slowly, I lowered myself onto the bed, using my arms to prop myself up so that I was kneeling over him, but without putting pressure on his body. I brushed my naked chest against him. He made to roll up the bottom of his shirt, but then his hands dropped.

His fingers gripped my buttocks hard, and this time, I didn't need to question anything. Aiven's breath strained, like he was just holding himself back from pulling me down onto him.

"I like that you're a virgin," I whispered.

"And I like that you're not."

I let him touch me gently, allowing a silence to stretch between us, then I leaned forward until my lips nearly touched his left ear.

"Aive," I whispered. "I want to make your first time special. I want to make sure that when you think about it, years later, you remember every detail, from the smell of me to the touch of my hands."

He exhaled hard, tightening his grip on my arse.

"That looks halfway done," I said, gesturing at his partially rolled-up shirt. "Surely, a Master of Compliance shouldn't leave his tasks half-finished."

Aiven pulled off his shirt, exposing a solid chest with a few small scars and the kind of arms that could carry a large load of barley, or... well, a prince. His skin shone in the light, browner than mine thanks to the open fields. The sight of his upper body made me hungry, but it was nothing to how I felt when he pulled off his pants, granting me full view of his calves, thighs, and everything else below the waist.

I was so caught up looking at Aiven's naked body that I didn't notice the way he was looking at mine.

"God," he whispered. "You're so beautiful."

The words jolted me. They were familiar, fresh from the lips of many, many men; and I realised that I didn't want to hear the same old line. Not from Aiven.

"You wouldn't say that if I put on weight," I said.

"I don't care if you're small, or mid-sized, or bigger than me. I don't care if you double your weight. I don't care, Fierre. I just see you."

"You can't mean that."

"I see your smile, like the sun's come out. I see the way you laugh, and I hear the quips you make—faster than anyone I've met. I see the way you help people, and the way you really want to do the right thing. I see the side of you that makes quips, too... the side that I wish I could keep for myself alone." Aiven took my hand and kissed it. "All of that makes you beautiful. Thin or fat: it doesn't matter. I love the shape of you, no matter what, because your soul shines through it."

Tears brimmed over the edge of my eyes. Where had they come from? Just a moment ago, I had thought I had everything under control.

"I love you too," I whispered.

Now Aiven's eyes glistened. I kissed him, before either of us could cry any more, and felt like I was devouring his mouth. I pressed my lips hard into his and pushed my chest down against his skin, until I felt his warmth.

"Sit back," I said, "if you do want to touch everything."

Aiven obeyed me, pushing himself back until he sat against the bedhead, propped on the pillows. Something about seeing him naked and waiting made me desperate, and I slipped a hand down to try to cover my erection.

Too late.

Aiven didn't seem to care, though; he took it all in, wearing the same look of awe as before.

I positioned myself above him and placed my knees on either side of him, straddling his body without pressing down. Guiding his hands to my waist, I let him trace the curve of my hips and the length of my thighs, then I ran his hands up to my arse and left them there. He closed his eyes. I kissed him, and he moaned softly.

"I suppose we should kiss a bit more, or stroke each other... or something like that," I said.

Aiven's eyes blinked open.

"Do you want to?"

"No," I said.

It took a moment, but he stared at me, and I guess that he'd realised what I meant.

I crawled up and positioned myself higher up his body. Aiven moved his arm. I looked down and saw him gripping his cock, which was jutting upward. He held it in place with one hand.

"If you're sure," he said.

Slowly, very slowly, I positioned myself so that I was just on top of his cock. I rubbed myself against him.

"You're torturing me," Aiven whispered.

Good. It seemed only fair that he felt a little pain, before I took his entire cock inside me and tried to survive it.

"I love you," Aiven whispered.

I slid down onto him and fought hard not to cry out. *Fuck,* I thought. I had known it was going to hurt, but I hadn't been ready for the way it felt as I stretched around the head of his cock. Aiven was on the larger side of the scale, out of all the men who'd fucked me, but he didn't know how sensitive I was. I felt embarrassed that his size had caught me off-guard, so I suffered in silence. Thank the stirring saints for the oil. It helped me enough that I could pause, adjust to the feeling of fullness, and push a little further before my body started to strain again. It hurt like nothing else. But oh god, it felt so *good* at the same time. I kept going down until Aiven was entirely inside me, and then I clamped my hands onto his shoulders.

He was looking at my face. Dimly, I observed that this wasn't usual. Men didn't typically focus on anything above my hips, at this point.

"Are you in pain, Fierre?"

"That's sort of the point." I dug my nails into his shoulders. "Do you mind if I, ah, stay still for a moment?"

"You can…" His voice came out breathy, as if he was struggling too. "You can wait as long as you like."

He kissed me while I tried to get comfortable. Just like when he had kissed me in the Fae Pools, he tasted like homemade wine, and I drank up the salty taste of his mouth.

I'd been fucked by big men before, but none who were quite so tender, and none who kissed like this. I felt like I would take anything from Aiven.

The pain receded, and I began to slide upward. I moved slowly, at first, up and down, getting used to the feeling of Aiven's cock. He moved his hands to my back and caressed me gently, moving his palms around, as if he was afraid to hold onto me. I started to ride him faster, but I overdid it slightly and gasped, weathering a sudden burst of pain.

Aiven stared at me. He didn't say a word.

"Does it feel good?" I managed.

"I think this must be what heaven is like. You, fused with my cock."

I searched for a sign of a joke, but he was sighing, his head thrown back in bliss. "Do you mind me being on top of you?" I said. "I wasn't sure if, um… if you'd want it this way."

"I like looking at you." Aiven took a firm hold of me for the first time, gripping my waist. "Fierre…"

"What?" I said, nervously.

"Can I hold you down?"

I nodded. He pulled me down from where I was riding him and held me so firmly in place that I almost cried. But *stirring saints*. The sensation. Suddenly, I understood what Aiven had meant. If the afterlife didn't feel anything like this, I'd ask god to send me back.

"This is dangerous," Aiven muttered.

I raised an eyebrow. Or at least, I thought I did. I wasn't sure if my face was doing anything I intended it to, as my lower muscles were doing ten times their usual work.

"Dangerously good. The saints probably want me to stop."

"Don't you *dare*."

Aiven smiled, and squeezed my hips. "Tell me at once if anything hurts."

He thrust upward, filling me entirely. I could feel his cock pushing my limits, going deeper than I had thought possible, and I focused on holding onto his shoulders, trying not to resist. I wanted to see how it felt if he kept going.

And he did. Hands on my waist, he kept me locked in place and fucked me from below, watching my face all the while, searching my eyes for a signal to stop. I made damned sure I didn't signal.

Aiven's breath came in shorter gasps, and his voice moved up a pitch. The sound of his new moans drove me over an edge I didn't see coming, and I cried out and reached down to cover my cock.

I didn't make it in time.

By the time I stopped jerking, Aiven's chest and stomach

were streaked and glistening. I clapped one hand to my mouth.

"Don't worry about it," Aiven said, slowing his movements.

"I don't usually... it's, um... it's usually the other person who... first..."

"It's fine," Aiven said, and his voice dropped low again. "I might sort of like it." He rubbed my back gently. "We can detach ourselves, if you like."

"Keep going." My voice came out firmly.

"Fierre..."

"Keep fucking me," I said.

Aiven's hands tightened around my waist again. Now, with my body drained, it was easier to watch his expression, and the clenching of his jaw as he thrust faster and faster into me. The sheer force of those muscles made me cling onto him. I wanted to see him let go.

As he neared the peak, a guilty expression covered his face, and he grabbed my shoulder. "I should stop."

"No," I said.

"Fierre, you don't have to..."

I looked down at his face. Poor Aive. My permission wasn't going to cut it, I could see.

Gently, I leaned down against his ear and whispered something dirty enough to turn holy water black.

It worked. Well, I knew it would work. But that didn't stop me from feeling a little smug as Aiven thrust up into me one last time, filling me completely. I felt less smug a moment later when a burning sensation flared inside me, and I climbed off Aiven slowly and lay facing him, letting the heat flow down inside me, feeling the burn slowly lessen.

Aiven was staring at me, I realised. I kissed him softly on the shoulder and dared to meet his gaze.

He didn't try to touch me down there; didn't try to inspect what he'd done, or mess around with my body. He just looked at me like he'd never seen me before.

"Fierre," he said.

He kissed me slowly, opening up my lips, making my mouth his own just like he had made my body his. The soft sweep of his tongue over my teeth felt like a balm. He pulled back, stared at my face some more, and kissed me around the eyes, touching his lips to the red dots on my skin—my punishment for overindulging in the cerise potion. He didn't say a word about them. Without hesitation, he pressed his lips to my cheek, then my neck, my collarbone, my shoulders, and finally, my lips again. He planted a line of kisses along my upper lip and stared at me.

"You don't have to taste all of my face," I said. "I'm not going anywhere."

Aiven laughed and brushed my hair back. The warm honey of his laugh seemed to match the colour of the room. In that moment, I realised why everything had felt different to sex with any other man. It wasn't only because Aiven's questions and remarks were born of care, instead of duty... though that was part of it.

"You were looking at my face the whole time," I said.

"Did it bother you?"

"No," I murmured.

"I'm glad. It's my favourite face in the world."

I kissed him hard. He froze, letting me.

"I don't mind if you want to shove your fingers in me, you know," I said, into his ear.

"Do you want me to?" Aiven sounded shocked.

"Er, well... maybe don't shove. No one's done it gently before."

It took a moment for Aiven to realise that I was asking him to. He climbed over to lie behind me and slid two fingers very slowly into me, opening me up, and I felt something dripping out of me. Aiven kissed me as he fingered me, until all of it was gone. He rose quickly, left the room, and returned a moment later with a glass of water. I lay still as he dipped his fingers into it and slipped them into me again.

I shivered at the cold. "I'm sorry," Aiven murmured.

Of course he was apologising. Even when he was doing exactly what I wanted, he was apologising.

"Don't be sorry," I said. "I like the feeling of your fingers inside me."

"Fierre, when you say things like that…"

"What? What will you do?"

Ever so slowly, Aiven pushed a third finger into me.

"Is that too much?" he said.

"I wonder if we could fall asleep like this," I said. "You, lying here, with half your hand inside me."

"*You* couldn't fall asleep like that."

"You'd be surprised."

Aiven laughed, and snuggled up to me. "Don't tempt me, Fierre."

We lay in silence for a while, until I insisted on cleaning his chest, using a towel from the bath chamber to wash and dry him. When I was done, he readjusted his pose to drape an arm around my stomach. The instinct to take his hand and move it to anywhere else surged strongly through me. He could probably feel the fat on my stomach—the last remaining bits that I hadn't been able to lose. There wasn't much of it, but it felt like a spectacular reminder of my failure, a horrible thing to show him.

Yet I didn't move Aiven's arm. I allowed myself to grow accustomed to his muscle against me and to the warmth of his palm, and to feel covered by his embrace. If it was anyone else, I would've twisted out of his grip.

I wasn't just bare of my clothes, but bare of all protection, of all the barriers that lent an illusion of grace to my pathetic body. It was absolutely fucking terrifying.

"It did feel special," a voice thrummed in my ear.

"Aive?"

"My first time," Aiven said.

I let myself grin like an idiot, knowing he couldn't see me.

"You're beautiful inside and out."

"Didn't expect you to be so perverted," I said.

"That's not what I meant!" I could *feel* him blushing, through the sound of his voice. "I just meant—I loved it. Feeling all of you. Your softness, your warmth, but also your inner self... your spirit isn't soft at all, but made of solid oak."

He stroked the back of my neck with his other hand. The firm muscle of his thigh pressed along my own thigh, and I'd never felt so safe, after sex: not even half this cherished.

"Do you want the room to be darker, to sleep? A little warmer?"

"No," I said. "I have everything I need, here." I wriggled slightly backward, so that my arse pressed against Aiven's groin, but this time, there was no tension between us, no prickly alertness from holding back. "Good night, Aive."

He pressed one last kiss to my neck.

There had to be candles in those lanterns, but I didn't get up to blow them out. I let the golden light burn and fill the room. Perhaps when we fell asleep, the wicks would founder at last in the candle-wax, sated and spent; the faint scent of honey would linger all the way through the night, and in the morning, everything would still smell sweet and rich, as if life was meant to be a dissolution of evening and dawn, wax and smoke, a melting of borders that birthed something unnamed: something undefinable.

Nineteen

Aiven

MY FIRST FEELING, when I woke, was discomfort; not panic, exactly, but a gnawing concern. The sheets didn't feel like my bedsheets at Dunhairstin Castle. The cover came halfway up my thigh, messily draped, as if I hadn't been bothered to smooth it out in my usual neat style. The whole room smelled like honey, but not like the clean scent of honey-cake—the echo of fragrance mingled with a hint of smokiness in the air.

My arm was stretched out to the side, as if I'd been holding someone.

For a moment, I lay on the pillow, my eyes closed, and then the memory hit me like a bucket of quarried stone, and I sat up and stared at the empty bed.

I'd been sitting, last night, but I hadn't been alone. Fierre's face flashed before my eyes, screwed up in pleasure. I felt the grip of his body around my cock, as if I were living the moment again. *Keep going*, he'd said, right after he came on my chest. *Keep fucking me.* I remembered the feeling of his soft body straining to take

254

all of me; the pressure of his arse on top of my thighs; his vulnerable sounds as I pushed three fingers deep into him.

It didn't seem real.

And maybe it hadn't been real. The space where Fierre should have been offered no sign of him. I wondered if someone had come to call for him, but since the Sethunes would be sleeping off an all-night revel of whisky and dancing, that seemed unlikely. There was no reasonable explanation for my memories.

For a long moment, I tried to convince myself that I'd imagined coming inside my best friend.

My best friend, who also happened to be the Sky of Eilean-òir.

The door creaked open and Fierre tiptoed in. A diamond choker encircled his neck. It glittered and threw tiny beams of silver across his chest. I was so entranced by the sight of his face that it took me a few seconds to realise the diamond choker was his entire outfit.

Too late to pretend I was asleep.

If I hadn't been awake before, I had just become *very* awake.

"Good morning," Fierre said, slipping onto the bed.

I put one hand on his forearm. It was the only bit of him I dared touch.

Last night had truly happened, then. We had really gone beyond our friendship to cross every line between us. We'd been fully joined, fully coupled… and I hadn't just hallucinated the moment when he whispered *I love you*.

What had I done?

Had I snatched a prince away from his obligations? Were Rossane and MacArlay and Kinnaid going to kill me now?

Or would Fierre be giving out court favours tomorrow, pretending this never happened?

I stopped dwelling on my anxieties a second later, because I made the very good choice of looking at Fierre again.

"Wow," I said, letting my gaze flow down his body.

Fierre beamed. It was the kind of bright smile he always saved for me, but now, it felt different. And yet I still couldn't believe that it was real: that someone so beautiful was sitting right there, beside me, naked, and gazing in my direction. That he was looking at me as if he wanted to be here, and his body seemed to agree.

Visibly.

"*Wow* yourself." He leaned over and kissed me on the cheek, then leaned down to smell my neck. "It's simply not fair for anyone to smell this good after waking up. It's like you get blessed with rose petals while the rest of us roll in mud."

"Oh?" I said.

Fierre lay down on top of me and rested his head on my upper chest. The red dots around his eyes had faded to a weaker colour, I was relieved to see. He rubbed his nose in my chest hair and sighed deeply. "We've wasted so much time, you know. I could have been smelling you in the morning for years."

My mind immediately leaped to several things that I could have been doing to Fierre in the morning for years, but I decided to keep my mouth shut.

"At any rate," Fierre added, "as prince, it's my duty to conduct a full inspection." He pressed his nose a little lower down my chest and inhaled: a long, deep breath. "Now, this is a good start."

He slipped down slightly lower. I felt hazy with

disbelief as I watched him rub his whole face into my chest. I couldn't believe that someone as pretty and sweet as Fierre could like the smell of someone as ordinary as me. But here we were, and his nose was tickling my hair.

"Mmm." He dropped down lower, and lower… and then suddenly, much lower. I realised what was happening just before he stopped.

"Fierre," I said.

He looked up at me. I looked down at him. It was quite obvious that I was going to have to grant or deny permission.

"Um," I said. "You don't have to do this."

"What if I really, really want to?"

When I didn't say anything and stared at him through a haze of disbelief, he dipped his head and slid his mouth over my cock.

It felt like someone had lit a fuse inside me. Stirring saints, I was going to explode—and not in the obvious way. My heart felt like it was going to burst inside my chest as Fierre removed his mouth and then began licking downward and up again. I dared to look at him, and instantly regretted it. The sight of him gazing pleadingly up at me, as if he'd like to keep doing this forever, nearly finished me.

"Do you have to taste so good?" he whispered, between licks.

"Mmph," I said, unhelpfully.

Fierre stopped, kissed the tip of my cock, then took the whole thing into his mouth and held it there. His lips felt searingly warm. Too warm, and yet perfect, like heated honey. I couldn't think, because his lips were around me, but I couldn't take more of this, either.

"Fierre," I said, "we should stop."

"Stop?"

"I'm going to come."

He gazed at me for a second; then he rubbed his cheek up and down the length of my cock, kissed it a little more, and began to use the other cheek.

"Fierre." He wasn't listening to me. "I can't do it like that. Not with you *there*. It's… disrespectful."

Fierre looked up at me.

"To you," I added.

"That's a shame. I was hoping you'd disrespect me all over my face."

"*Fierre.*"

"Fine." He slid down further and kissed my balls, giving me a moment's reprieve, if an achingly sensitive one. I'd barely adjusted to the sensation when he moved again and began to run his tongue along my inner thigh, leaving a wet trail. Fierre's tongue gave orders to nobility, I reminded myself. It was a tongue that decided laws, charmed ambassadors, and told army commanders what to do… and now it was making a path back upwards to my cock.

"You don't have to do this," I tried, one more time.

"I know." Fierre licked one side, all the way along, and I shuddered with pleasure. "I'm doing it precisely because I want to." He licked the other side and watched my reaction. "But if you want me to stop…"

His soft hair tickled my stomach. We looked at each other. The raw desire in his gaze made my hands tremble.

"I don't want you to stop," I said.

Fierre leaned down immediately and parted his lips, not halting his descent until he had swallowed my entire cock. I gasped. It was too much sensation at once, and I twisted the sheet, trying desperately to keep control. He kept his head down, letting my cock press into his throat, letting it touch his tonsils and probably rub him raw. At last, he came up for air, and the full force of his puppy-dog eyes hit me at once.

"I'm doing it the way you wanted," he said.

"I didn't mean—"

Before I could reply, he took my cock into his mouth again and held it at the deepest point he could manage. I could feel myself losing control. However much I tried to resist, the feeling of his lips around me made me grip the sheet harder, overwhelmed by pleasure. Words swirled inside me. I wanted to get them out. I wanted to tell him how much it meant that he thought me worth the grip of his hands, the touch of his tongue, and the full devotion of his gaze—and how powerless I became when he was kissing me.

Kissing any part of me.

If I could just hold out a little longer, maybe I could say it all.

Fierre pulled back for a moment and looked at me again. He had to know what it did to me when he gazed up at me like that.

"Don't try to be so nice," he said.

"I can't help it." I didn't even know why I was apologising.

"Just do whatever you want to my mouth." He held my cock with both hands and took all of it again, and I couldn't stop my body's reaction as his lips tightened around the base. My legs jerked, and my hands—which had been clenched in the sheet—found their way to his hair. I touched those soft dark locks, and my last bit of restraint fell away.

I came down his throat.

Fierre kept his mouth over me, and didn't seem in any hurry to remove it. His lingering made me nervous. At last, he slowly withdrew and slid up on the pillow beside me. I could feel heat surging through my cheeks, and I searched his face for any sign of discomfort, seeking even a hint of disgust.

He smiled, and even I couldn't mistake that for displeasure.

I stroked his hair, running my fingers through the fine strands. I wanted to thank him for giving me a gift I didn't deserve, but that seemed rather pathetic to say aloud.

"Can I return the favour?" I said.

"I don't want that. And, ah…" Fierre blushed a pretty shade of red. "It wasn't a favour. Actually, it was more of a long-held dream."

"What can I do to please you?" I sounded so damned stiff. I felt weird, and guilty. I was sure that he could tell.

"Let me do that to you tomorrow morning. Only next time, in a different position," Fierre said.

"A different position?" My mind was fuzzy.

"I want to suck your cock while you're standing over me, yanking my hair."

Oh no. How could he say something like that? I was suddenly, undeniably, embarrassingly turned on by the thought of standing over him. Trying to cover myself up, I reached down, but my body betrayed me.

"Does this mean we get to go again?" Fierre said.

He was grinning.

"If you want," I said, and then nervously added, "We can try."

Fierre climbed on top of me and slid his whole body over me, angling himself slightly. I read the invitation and grabbed him around the waist, pulling him up over me, and he wriggled against me, twisting out of my grip for a moment. Had I hurt him? But no—he was still grinning, and as I pulled him back against me, he looked extremely smug.

This was what he wanted.

I hefted him to the side, stood up, and picked him up quickly, gripping his arse in both my hands. He gave a little sound of surprise and wrapped his legs around my back. The way he was clinging to me, voluntarily; the way I could feel the curves of his buttocks against my palms; it all sparked something inside me. Watching his expression, I carried him backwards through the room.

I was ready for any protest; for any sign that he didn't like it. But his face lit up immediately. He kept his arms locked around my neck, holding on as I carried him into the corridor and then into the study, where I laid him on the wooden desk.

He gazed up at me, breathing hard.

All of a sudden, I could see the face of royalty staring back, like gold and pearls in an open box.

"You're a prince," I said.

"Thought you would've noticed that before now."

"You're royalty."

"Did you sleepwalk through the rituals? You seemed pretty awake when you were kissing my ankle."

Fierre had a way of talking that bubbled over you, soothing you like a particularly charming brook, and I had to remind myself not to be distracted by it.

"You're a prince, and I'm the son of two farmers," I said. "I haven't got a single drop of noble blood in my veins. I know how to use a foot-plough; I can dig trenches; I can carry two sacks of barley in each hand, for god's sake!"

"Does that mean you're going to lift me again?"

"Fierre, I'm not joking."

"I liked the part when you lowered me onto the table like I was a lamb."

"You don't have to risk this. I want you to know that you don't have to descend to my level just because we're here, in the middle of a barren island, miles and miles from the throne. You might regret it later. I don't have any armies to offer you, or mines full of gems. I don't have anything you can trade."

I stopped, exhaling. Fierre's smile had dimmed a little bit. He reached up and touched my shoulder, rubbing his way down my bicep.

"Do you mind if I mention my past?"

"Of course not," I said.

"It's just that… I've slept with a lot of men, Aive. All of them were noble. And most of them satisfied my body in some way, but not the same way that you do." He shifted on top of the table, but he didn't look away. "I felt like I was asleep my whole life. When you push into me, when you're inside me… it's like I'm finally awake. You see me for who I really am, with all my stupid little habits and weaknesses, and you still want to pour your love into me. Right into me." He smirked, then, after a moment, looked earnest again. "You kiss me, and it's never a reward or a payment. Your hands feel rough and then smooth, like stone that's only glazed in certain places… it's as if you could plane down all my desires and then rough them up again, until I'm proud of each one." He sat up and brought his face up to mine. "I want you to fuck me like you're writing your name in permanent ink, so that I always have a piece of you to carry around inside me."

I looked at him for a long moment. A bird trilled, somewhere outside the shuttered window.

I traced a finger over Fierre's lower lip.

"I want to be so deep in you that we're joined, even after we finish," I said.

I kissed him, tilting his head back and sliding one hand down his neck, feeling the pulse flutter in his throat. He didn't tense or pull away, but opened his mouth to me. This was what he wanted, I now knew—for me to carry him around, heft him about, and then push my way into his body in whatever manner I liked.

And I wanted to please him.

Last night, Fierre had done all the work. I wasn't going to let that happen this time.

I broke the kiss and turned him onto his front, pushing him against the table. His moan came out softly, as if he had stifled it on purpose. There was so much lust in that sound that I didn't hesitate to press my hips down against his, so that my cock fit between his buttocks, reminding us both of how it felt when there was no distance at all between us.

Fierre made another noise of appreciation. I reached up to tug at his diamond choker, pulling it tightly against his neck, and felt a rush of excitement when he gasped.

"Oh," Fierre said, softly.

I pulled at his choker again, repeating the movement a few times, and then, with a sudden flash of inspiration, I reached down to smack him on the arse. He went still. I wondered if he was horrified. But then he said "More," in a low, desperate tone, and relief swept through me.

I smacked him again and kissed the back of his neck, just above the choker. Positioning myself over him, I was suddenly glad that I didn't have any clothes on. One less thing to worry about. Fierre pushed his arse up against me, making his feelings very clear.

"Wait," I said.

"Are you joking?"

"Sorry." I smiled, knowing that he couldn't see me. "We forgot something important."

When I returned with the oil, Fierre was still lying naked on his front, his hands grasping the edge of the desk. The sight of him like that was almost too much to take. I quickened my steps, set down the oil and got to work. By the time he was readied, my desire had risen so high inside me that it seemed to sit in my throat, waiting to burst out.

The gasp he gave as I entered him was full of surprise, and the sound turned me on even more. If Fierre hadn't expected me to fuck him from behind with his cheek pressed to the desk, I was happy to surprise him. I didn't slow as I pushed into him but went all the way down, not stopping until I was completely inside and our bodies were touching skin to skin.

It would have been nice to stay in that position for a few moments, to let him adjust.

Don't try to be so nice, Fierre had said, minutes ago.

I pushed all the way out and into him again, and he cried out. His fingers tightened on the edge of the desk. I pulled his hips upward and fucked him deeply, listening carefully all the while to make sure that those were sounds of pleasure. I was going to make sure that I was *not so nice*, but in the way that he wanted.

It seemed to be working, because as I took control of his body, he relaxed in my grip. All the tension left his back muscles. He breathed in a way that I hadn't heard before: a sound of pure starlight, as if he'd abandoned all restrictions.

I loved the way he sounded. I loved the sight of his head thrown back, his mouth parted, visible to me from above;

264

and I loved the slight hitches in his breath whenever he was taken by surprise.

I slowed just a tiny bit and allowed him some respite. He murmured something, and I realised that it was my name. In the lull, I rubbed my palms over his lower back and felt the smoothness of it, the kind of delicacy that could only manifest in someone who had never done rough work in their life. I didn't envy him. Working on the farm, under the blazing sun, was my pride and pleasure. But it meant the world to know that Fierre didn't mind our differences—that he felt, as I did, that smooth and rough skin were alike in beauty.

I ran my hands slowly up to his shoulder blades and back down, massaging his fine skin, and heard him give a satisfied moan.

Then I sped up my pace and slammed into him, until my body smacked against his. He cried out my name, loud and clear this time. I fucked him harder, showing no mercy, listening to his shuddering, broken noises and trying to match my thrusts to his moans—two thrusts per moan, then three, until he lost even the ability to shout my name. He came seconds before me, going limp against the desk.

I ran my fingers down his back. I finished inside him with a hard thrust, slapping him across the arse as I came, making sure he felt a sting. My whole body sang with pleasure—not the fleeting, physical kind, but a bliss that stored itself in my very bones.

In the silence, I listened for any sound, straining for any word from him.

Fierre's breathing came fast and ragged; he took a long time to settle into a calmer pace, the syncopation of his breath giving way to a single rhythm.

"That was…"

I waited. When a silence stretched again, I thought about flipping him onto his back.

"I, um…" he said.

Still hesitation. Had I misjudged, and pushed him too far? Had he wanted me not to slap him—should I have caressed him gently instead? I made to touch his back again, then withdrew my hand, waiting.

"I don't usually like to make comparisons," Fierre said. "But that was the best fuck I've ever had."

I beamed, rolled him over, and kissed him on the lips. He kissed me back hungrily, gripping my neck with a force that took me aback. I wanted it. I was about to say something very unsuitable for a prince to hear when a knock sounded at the door, and a piercing voice called out: "Message for the Sky and Star, if you please!"

LAIRD AND LADY Sethune knew how to show off the fruits of their territory. The basket they left for us could have fed four people; it overflowed with blackberries, dourberries, bannocks, browntop rolls, miniature spiced apple cakes, barley quickloaf, and small jars of honey, butter, and cream. The messenger was content to shout his invitation to a meeting through the door. I suspected that by the time we finished breakfast, we'd have to roll our way to the village, but I wasn't surprised when Fierre shouted his agreement back through the wood.

We washed together, filling the bucket from a small spring outside the cottage. It felt shockingly intimate to be pouring water over myself in front of Fierre. It felt even more shocking for me to be scrubbing his body with my hands, foregoing the sponge in favour of my fingertips and cleaning his stomach, his lower back, and the soft skin at the top of his thighs, just beneath his buttocks—but I wasn't complaining.

We nearly didn't make it to the meeting.

I scoffed a handful of berries after I'd dressed and then picked up a spiced apple cake and poured cream across it, drizzling it with honey. I was about to offer it to Fierre when I caught the look in his eye.

He edged around the table. I could've been holding a dagger or a bottle of poison; a crossbow would hardly have produced a more alarming effect.

"There's a lot of good-looking food," I said, lifting the cake to my own lips and taking a bite. Damn, but it was sweet and rich, with that special dense quality you only got in northern cakes. "You don't have to eat it. But if you want some, just tell me, and I'll slather it for you."

"It does look nice," Fierre said.

He pronounced the word *nice* as if it were a snake that might rear and bite him.

I didn't say any more but focused on eating my own breakfast, slowing down a little so that I didn't rush him. From the corner of my eye, I saw him pick up a browntop roll and trace his thumb across the glazed top, and he held it for a long time before putting it back. He shot a glance at me. After another long period of hesitation, he sat down in the chair beside me and reached out toward the basket.

His fingers closed on a blackberry and he raised it to his mouth, then stopped. He held it just an inch from his lips.

"Galar gave me a strict regime." He caught my eye, and searched my face for a reaction. "But maybe one berry won't hurt."

When I said nothing, he put the blackberry into his

mouth and chewed. Relief rushed through me like a torrent, though I tried not to show it. Fierre's fearful expression transformed to unadulterated joy as he tasted the fruit—then, all too quickly, to guilt. He looked at the basket. "Maybe I could eat a bite of bannock."

"You could," I said.

He tore a piece off a bannock and examined it. I took the jar of butter and the small knife and held them up, as if asking a question. Fierre stared at the items in my hands for a long time before he nodded, and I scraped the butter across the piece of bannock very slowly, giving him the chance to change his mind. He put the food into his mouth more hesitantly this time and chewed it for a long while, but when he closed his eyes, the bliss on his face emerged stronger than before.

I couldn't imagine how hungry he must be, every day, if a tiny morsel of buttered bread made him this happy.

I proffered the basket, but Fierre shook his head. Guessing that a slice of quickloaf might be pushing things too far, I plucked a single blackberry from the top of the cluster. I didn't just pass it to him, this time, but brought it all the way to his mouth myself, watching for any sign that he wanted me to stop.

His gaze locked on mine with such concentration that I thought he might refuse.

Instead, he parted his lips and accepted the fruit. I pushed it further into his mouth and felt his lips close around my finger. His tongue stayed still. I withdrew my finger slowly—though I would much rather have kept it in the warm velvet of his mouth—and let him taste the blackberry.

After that, he ate two more. Then another two, and another two, until he finished the blackberries and declared himself done. "If I keep going, I don't know what I'll do."

I understood that sentiment all too well.

We walked back to the village hand in hand, towards the little house where Laird and Lady Sethune had received us, and as the sun shone on our cheeks, it seemed to offer a new light, a kinder and more precious radiance than the sun that had greeted us yesterday. Perhaps it was just my imagination. I slipped my fingers between Fierre's, interlocking our hands. Perhaps I was sleepwalking through a dream, and it would last this way until I stepped into the royal palace again, at which point I would wake with a sudden, violent jolt and find myself alone again.

Twenty

Fierre

THE MEMBERS OF Clan Sethune needed no candles or torches outside their houses this morning. The highland sun peeked through the clouds, showering enough light over the village to reveal the carvings of names on doors and the letters scored in the centre of the wood. In the absence of expensive decorations, flowers bloomed in tiny pots beside some homes, while vines and creepers draped others, and the breeze blew through the village, filling the air with notes of fresh leaves, bedewed earth and newly opened roses.

I'd been focusing on the taste of my breakfast—the deep sweetness of the berries, the creaminess of the butter, the perfect density of the bannock—and struggling to stave off guilt. The only thing that seemed to work was guiding my mind back to earlier memories, and the feeling of Aiven's hands rubbing water over me, slipping beneath my arse and running over my thighs... and even before that, to the hard press of Aiven's body against my back as he pinned me to the desk... the delicious pain of him slamming into me, and his voice, oh god, his voice. *I want to be so deep in you that we're joined, even after we finish*.

I held onto his hand, now, and stepped over the threshold of Laird and Lady Sethune's house. The door bore a carving of a marten's head, an animal I recognised from their crest in father's book of clans.

Symbolic of healing, I remembered. Its furry face and pointed snout seemed to throw up more issues.

Could I really be healed, until I felt happy when I looked at food—until I ate it without panicking or looking for a potion?

What about father? Was he going to die here, on the Isle of Hairstin?

I parcelled up these questions and tied them tightly, facing the room ahead. The clan chiefs sat on the cushions again, with Oighrig and Keir flanking them, and the guards shut the door behind us, leaving us to approach. I gripped Aiven's hand tighter.

"Take a place with us," Lady Sethune said.

Sitting on the floor made the prospect of the conversation less daunting, and I was grateful for it. It also levelled my authority, and I was aware of that, too. As I thanked the Sethunes for their hospitality, I noticed that Keir's hands were twisting his sleeve, while Oighrig looked as stiff as a priest at an orgy. They both stared at me.

"Sky, we want you to know the truth about your doctor," Lady Sethune said.

"Here's the problem, my lady. I've suspected since our first conversation that I already do."

I had expected the shocked looks.

"Dr Galar has been starving me, and keeping me in a weakened state; and mentally, well, I suppose it's a bit like when the clouds roll over the Isle of Hairstin. A sort of fog of the mind, if you like. But you've blown through my head like a wind, and now I see the clouds lifting," I said.

"Not just starvation," Oighrig cut in, her voice rising. "What he's doing to you, it includes that potion. Self-induced purging, I call it. I'm sorry to inform you that the cerise liquid is a rare emetic."

"In non-doctor speech, mistress?" I said.

"Pardon me. It was invented by our doctors to give to victims of poisoning, to make them throw up."

"You can't think that Galar has been treating me for poisoning?" I cried.

"I'm afraid I don't. Dr Galar knows very well that the only thing in your stomach is food—and precious little of it. Tell me, Sky, have you noticed the red dots around your eyes?"

I put a finger to the skin under my right eye, as if I might cover it. Nervously, I stared back at Oigrig.

"I could hardly miss them."

"That's the thing about burst blood vessels. They mark you like the devil's paint, for a day or two. Then... they fade." She must've seen my anxious expression. "They disappear after a few days. But they're a sign that your body was straining to vomit—that you were under a great physical pressure."

"Dr Galar didn't warn me." I heard the weakness in my voice.

"Why would he? He's been manipulating you to bring up your food. And the toll of *that* on your body... well, if you keep it up, Sky, it could damage your throat, strip the coating from your teeth, even wear a hole in the lining of your stomach and leave you unable to digest your food. You would die swifter than your father, who's been withering away in a state of deprivation for a long time. You would die before you reached the age of forty—of that, I am sure."

A silence filled the room, and as I worked through her assessment, the quietude curled at the corners and became an encroaching thing, pushing back upon me.

"What I can't understand," I said, shelving my pain for the moment, "is why he'd advise me in this way."

"Indeed. What could motivate a doctor to hurt their patient?" Hard lines carved Oighrig's brow.

"My dear, think of the world we live in. Think of what we're all taught before we're knee-high," Lady Sethune said. "The Sky of Eilean-òir is the symbol of god. To look on him is to look on the image of our lord's beauty and grace. At some point, along the way, someone decided that *beauty* should mean *thinness*, and *grace* should mean *frailty*, but neither is true. You see, my dear, in the original text that establishes the Sky's role—the Book of Gold, which predates all those books that our courtiers and priests favour—the author only stipulates that the Sky should be *elegant* like god. And the word *elegant*, back then, derived from the idea of something that was well chosen." She paused. "The Sky wasn't meant to be thin. Or sickly. Or half-starved. No, the very first Sky was someone who had demonstrated the right qualities to be *chosen* for his role, so that he could run the realm well, just as god should rule the world with beneficence."

I was staring at her all throughout this speech, so I didn't miss the satisfied way she folded her arms. "Forgive me, my lady, but how can you be sure?" I said.

"Because, Your Majesty, I was curious. Have you not heard about curious women? We are said to be quite dangerous, although I'm inclined to think that the real danger lies in a lack of reading." A triumphant smile tugged at the corners of Lady Sethune's mouth. "Our clan has preserved one of the few remaining copies of the Book of Gold. I read it from cover to cover. There wasn't an example in its pages that had anything to do with the Sky's physical appearance, and yet there was plenty about the Sky's work ethic and the dedication he should bring to his duties. How odd, no?"

I stared in silence, now, unable to find words for what I felt.

"So, you see, contrary to what the court may have decided, our god was not always a god of starvation."

"Aye, that's right," Laird Sethune put in.

"Why some might wish to starve the Sky, I shall not *dare* to presume. But the truth, as I see it, runs like this. Bodies can be beautiful at any size, and graceful in any shape. And good health is more than size—it includes rest, contentment, and a deep peace of the mind." Lady Sethune's voice acquired a diamond sharpness, and I had the feeling that she could've lacerated anyone who got in her way. "Sky, I speak as a doctor when I tell you that you deserve to be free of this tradition of self-scrutiny. The court's idea of beauty is killing you faster than any amount of fat ever could."

Her words seemed to swirl around in my mind, battering its walls. I was grateful when Aiven's hand seized mine again and covered my palm with warmth, calming me.

"My lady," I said, "have you any other recommendations?"

"My daughter's medical advice is for you to eat more, slowly and steadily adding to your daily meals, and never consult Dr Galar again."

"And…?"

"Sky?"

"I can hear the beating wings of something else you want to say," I said.

She smiled, and there was something of that diamond edge to her mouth. "My other advice is that of a clan chief, not a doctor." She paused, and looked directly into my eyes. "If you want to discover who's doing you harm, then you must do one more thing. Find out who pays Galar."

"The crown supplies his fee," Aiven said.

"The crown alone? Can you be so sure, Star? Have you found out who his friends are—who he meets with, who he writes to, when you're not looking?"

Aiven said nothing. I sensed that the encroaching silence would return if I wasn't careful, and I wanted to end our meeting with the thanks the Sethunes deserved. "My lady and laird, I consider myself privileged for your wisdom and compassion today. Is there anything else you would add?" I looked around the little circle.

When Laird Sethune spoke, his voice came out gravelly and broken. "If you find our advice to be sound, and you decide that Dr Galar is unfit for your service, we ask that you would recognise our family's generations of training. Reinstate us as doctors. For too long we have suffered under your father and grandfather's bans, unable to earn fair money anywhere outside of the Isle of Hairstin – and as you can see, we live humbly and well, but we cannot teach others from here."

I stared at him. My lips seemed to have frozen like a pair of stubborn icicles.

"They *what*?" I spluttered, at last. "My father and grandfather did what?"

"A shadow ban. Made orally in law, but not written

down for anyone else to see. They showed us clear enough how it would work if any of us tried to get to the mainland and seek employment there." His eyes clouded with sorrow. "My first daughter learned that the hard way."

"Two years in heaven, now. Shot in the chest with an arrow as she climbed onto a mainland beach." Oighrig made a sign of prayer by pressing a hand to her forehead, and the other Sethunes did the same.

A long time ago, they dared to pour their words into your grandfather's ear, before he sent them on their way, Galar had said. But when I'd heard him say that, I'd imagined a dismissal from court—not exile—and certainly not an order to shoot on sight.

"We believe that the kings were pressured to outlaw us," Lady Sethune said. "We knew not from whom, suspecting some courtier or other, but now that you've told us of Dr Galar's behaviour..." Her mouth tightened. "Well," she said, after a moment, "my advice remains. Follow the trail of money and see where it leads."

"My lady, you have my word." I rose, beckoning Aiven to do the same. The Sethunes followed suit, standing before us. "If what you say turns out to be true, both with respect to my own healing and to Dr Galar, then I will reinstate your family and overturn the ban. Not only by spoken word, but in writing." I extended my hand. "Let's shake."

"Aye." Laird Sethune shook it firmly, and Lady Sethune did too. "More than that—let's drink on it," the laird added.

"If you can handle something that's not for virgins," Oighrig said, winking at Aiven.

"Oh, he can," I said.

Every single Sethune seemed to look at me at once.

"Can handle any kind of drink, that is," I said quickly.

Laird Sethune gave a nod, but I thought I caught a hint of a smile from Oighrig.

Guards were summoned, and clan whiskies were brought. This time, a fourth bottle joined the others, and it shone red as blood in the light from the windows.

"Oath whisky," she said. "One drink, and you're sworn under Sethune rules to never break your word. I hereby swear that what I have told you today comes from my best knowledge and judgment, as a doctor and as a chief. I swear that I mean you no harm."

"And I swear to honour my promise to you," I said.

The clink of our glasses hitting the platter again at the same time was a very pleasing sound, and we drank as one, downing our drams with a single swallow each. I didn't need to cough, this time, since the whisky was as smooth as a baby's head, and it lacked the punch-to-the-eyeball aftertaste of an island drink. Thank god. I didn't wish to fall on my face on the way out. I accepted a bow from Keir and Oighrig Sethune, shook hands with their father, and tried to look as though I was calm and regal as I made my goodbyes.

In truth, my insides were dancing some kind of stomach-disrespecting jig, and my head churned with a force that was not despair, but more like anger.

A Sethune boy waited outside with our horse. I wobbled a little as I approached it; perhaps my breakfast had not been enough. Aiven grabbed me and boosted me up until I could swing myself onto the horse's back. He jumped up after me. His hands wrapped around my waist, firm and steady, and I felt his lips touch the back of my neck.

A bolt of joy shot through me. I wondered if the

Sethunes had seen Aiven kiss me, but then we were cantering away, and it didn't matter.

As we rode, I allowed the birdcalls from the trees and the soft baaing of sheep fade into the background of my mind. I sank into my thoughts. For the first time, I saw my regime of tiny bites and hungry hours for what it really was. *Self-scrutiny*, Lady Sethune had said—and yes, that was it, because now I saw how I'd been inflicting this on myself. I was the prince of Eilean-òir, but anyone would be hard pressed to tell! I'd acted as if I had no choice but to starve, as if my life would only be worth something when I was tinier, and then tinier again, and so on with no stopping point in sight, so that I could earn some value by shrinking to a wafer.

I thought of the day that father had showed me the crown for the first time, placing it in my chubby little toddler's hands, pointing out the prancing deer. "See how thin they are," he'd said. And I'd seen, all right. I had never forgotten his remark.

It had been impossible to stick to his regime, growing up. But I'd tried. Every saint in heaven knew I'd tried, until I'd cried into my pillow at night, hollow and yearning.

When I was twelve, he had taken me to mother's tomb in the crypt and ordered an artist to paint me standing beside the headstone. He had wrinkled his nose as he looked at the painting. The artist had asked if the tomb looked large enough.

"It's the size of the boy that troubles me," my father had said, walking past the artist.

He had taken me by the arm and pinched the fat of my forearm until I cried.

"Paint him smaller," he had spat at the artist.

Had any courtier ever challenged him whenever he

spoke of beauty? Or had they been the ones to plant the idea in his head in the first place? If the Sky's expected *elegance* had changed from worthiness to rule into frailty of form, where did the problem take root?

I felt a sharp and sudden anger about the days I'd lost pinching my arms and waist and thighs, feeling for the fat that my father had warned me to lose. So many minutes spent before mirrors, readjusting my clothes. So many days spent dreaming of bread and cake, obsessing over the mere thought of another meal, instead of simply eating a raven bun and forgetting about it.

They had trained me this way: my father, the nobility, and the whole milieu in which they lived. They had raised me to think of thin as beautiful, to see a starved body as a prince's kind of beauty—as something to aspire to. But Lady Sethune had said that beauty could come at any size. And health was not sustained by starving, was it?

Nor was it perfected by throwing up in a chamber pot.

"How do you feel now?"

Aiven's voice sliced through my thoughts like a knife through a raven bun. I weighed my answer. It didn't seem right to lie to him.

"Angry," I said. "And you?"

"I'm glad that we know the truth, but I'm raring to lay Galar on his backside and teach that fraud a lesson." Aiven paused for a second. "Unless you had something... gentle in mind."

"I'm angry at the whole lot of them. My father, the court, Galar. And not just those people, but the way it all comes together: the way the whole culture's built to make me less of myself. To make me take up less space. To force me to be a needle when I could be a sword, or a glint of colour when I could be a whole damned rainbow.

And while my light's dimmed—I can hardly shine it on others. I can hardly help them when I'm occupied with the full-time job of shrinking myself." I drew a deep breath. "That's why I'm seething."

Ideas were already jostling in my head. The people I'd met all along this journey had sown their labour for this realm. Now, they need to reap its rewards. Money could be part of it, but money alone wasn't enough. Food, and steady crops. Ways for children to learn. Ways for villagers to become masters of their own lives. And what of women, who lacked even the right of inheritance— what would women like Oighrig wish for in reforms?

"You're a rainbow to me." Aiven's hands moved to reach the full way around my waist. "And everyone will see it, if you let yourself take up the whole sky."

As we galloped towards the palace, it occurred to me that he was right. The realm deserved enough food, and even princes deserved to eat. Some people had barely enough oats and potatoes to see them through the winter. I'd had every luxury, but I'd lived in a prison that others had made for me, with my own mind as jailer.

If I was going to fix every kind of deprivation in Eilean-òir, I had to find the courage to show my beliefs: to arc across the whole sky in a glory of colour, and begin to set things right.

I galloped into the palace grounds, urging the horse on.

Twenty-One

Aiven

We stepped into a circle of tense faces, the light from the windows of the dining hall showing the expressions around us in sharp detail. Rossane's jaw clenched. MacArlay's brow furrowed into deep crevasses. Kinnaid shifted on the spot. Beside them, Ambassador Rince and Ambassador Tarleigh waited, their countenances drawn and tight, their backs straightened.

Surely, we hadn't been gone long enough to merit this sort of reaction. We probably *should've* explained where we were going, and as I looked around the group, I half-expected an outburst about our trip—an exclamation, or the sudden barking of a question. But then I noticed the way that Rossane glanced at MacArlay, as if he were hoping that the other man would speak first.

It wasn't anger filling the room.

"Sky, I hope your diversion has rested you." Kinnaid stepped forward. "We received the news this morning from a carrier bird, an ugly tawny thing with a broken beak. Hattray's bird. Bringing word from the palace." He dipped his gaze for a moment. "I regret to tell you that a member of your court—that is, a member *without* a position—has drawn steel." He cleared his throat. "You were wise not to elevate a public brawler. Laird Crawshall has taken possession of the palace and is holding it unlawfully with his clan army."

I started. Beside me, Fierre let out a small gasp.

"Was any blood spilt?" Fierre said, at last.

"Eight guards died trying to defend it. The others saw which way the wind was blowing, after that, and galloped off to the next town. Sky, we hope you understand... we did not wish to rush off until we had your command," Rossane said.

Now I understood the frowning and the jaw-clenching. We weren't the ones whose activities were under scrutiny. Fierre waved his hand in a dismissive gesture.

"You did well to wait." He paced to the window and back again, seemingly lost in thought. The fiery look that he had worn as we reached the palace flashed across his face, and I held back the urge to draw him aside and ask what he was thinking.

"I made you two Rocks of the Glen." Fierre's gaze swept to Rossane and MacArlay in turn. "You have two of the realm's most capable armies, but more than that, you're men of honour—men who stake your reputations on serving the crown with great nobility of spirit. Your houses have won glory in ages past. I ask you to win it again, now, by taking back the royal palace and clapping Crawshall in irons. And know this: if you bring him to me together, united in your efforts to recapture Eilean-òir's seat of kings, I shall reward you beyond anything you can imagine."

Rossane bowed at once and dropped to one knee,

placing a hand over the left side of his chest. MacArlay copied him seconds later, looking up at Fierre. As they swore their loyalty in silence, I hoped that Fierre knew what he was doing when he promised a reward *beyond anything you can imagine.*

I had a feeling that each of these men had a very good imagination.

"Send word to your armies now. The rest of us will ride slowly, a day behind you, and wait at Castle Aonar for your news. When the siege is broken, we will join you, and you shall drink your fill of glory. Ambassadors," Fierre turned to Rince and Tarleigh, "you will stick with me."

Rince's face wilted in relief. The tension in the room seemed to break as Rossane and MacArlay rose again and everyone began to talk. I rubbed Fierre's shoulders before anyone could get near him, and he looked up at me with such thankfulness that I was tempted to kiss him on the lips. But I felt the gulf between what I wanted to do and what I *could* do, publicly, without any kind of relationship declared.

"Do you trust those two?" I said.

I didn't need to specify who I meant.

"I'm not a complete idiot." Fierre gave me a small, confident smile. "I trust them to put ambition and fame first."

"Be careful of promising them too much."

"Oh, I have an idea about that."

We were cut off by the arrival of two kitchen-hands with platters. They hovered just inside the doorway, staring at the group of excitedly talking lairds and ambassadors. I raised my voice and shouted above the throng: "Excuse me!"

Everyone turned to stare at me. I realised, suddenly, that I'd never used my position to shout before.

"Lunch is served, I believe," I said. The kitchen-hands nodded. "And it seems that we'd do well to eat heartily before we ride. Laird Rossane and Laird MacArlay, you have a long way to go. Why don't we all share a final lunch in the castle, before our Rocks of the Glen take back the seat of kings?"

"Great idea, Grian." Rossane shot me a supercilious glance.

No one objected, and after Fierre sat down at the head of the table, I made sure that I took the chair on his right. Dr Galar slipped into the room just in time to take the seat on Fierre's left, leaving everyone else at a slight remove from the prince. I smiled to myself.

Rossane shovelled stew into his mouth and wolfed down bread as if he had a fire at his heels—which, in a way, I supposed he did. While the others set about their meal, I turned to Fierre. I could see the strain in his neck as he regarded the plate of scones before him, but he caught my eye and managed a smile, and in that smile, I saw determination.

"Would you pass me a scone, Aive?" he said.

I reached out and took one of the dense balls of tate scone, passing it in my palm to Fierre. He gripped it between his thumb and forefinger and raised it to his mouth. For a long moment, he stared at it.

"Star," Dr Galar said.

I looked across at him.

"I believe your prince has his regime to consider."

"Indeed," I said. "My prince's health comes first. And a starving body should be fuelled. Sky, do you feel hungry?"

Fierre gazed at the scone for another few seconds.

"Yes," he said, at last. "I rather think I do."

"Well, then. No one could reasonably object to you eating."

"Sky," Galar began, "as your doctor, I would respectfully guide you to eat what is sensible."

"Respectfully, I think I'll eat when I'm hungry," Fierre said. "That seems sensible to me."

He broke off a piece of scone and placed it into his mouth. Chewing it, he wore a blissful expression, and he closed his eyes for a moment and savoured the taste. When he opened them again, he reached for the butter.

"Sky—"

"Excuse me, Dr Galar," I said. "I'll thank you to be quiet while the Sky is eating."

Galar stared at me as Fierre continued to demolish the scone. If looks could kill, I would have been diced and crushed into a fine purée, but I smiled stubbornly back at him and took a scone myself. I broke off a piece and took the butter dish from Fierre. I could feel Galar's gaze searing into my cheek.

The sight of Fierre beaming at me as he held up his last crumb of scone made it worthwhile.

I escorted him to the side when we finished lunch, steering him clear of Galar. Once we were far enough from the others not to be overheard, I leaned close to Fierre.

"I have a few choice words for the doctor," I said.

"I trust you to choose them well."

We looked at each other, and I couldn't resist the urge to hold his hand. I traced my thumb over his knuckles before I left. He looked as if he were teetering on the spot—as if he might change his mind at any moment. But he didn't, and I strode out, following Galar down the corridor.

The doctor moved briskly, and I hurried to stay a few feet behind him. I thought about calling out his name. Instead, I slipped to the side as he took the stairs, shadowing him to his chamber.

I blocked the door as he made to close it behind him. His look, when he turned, reminded me of a bear surprised by a hunter.

"I thought we should have a little chat, doctor," I said.

Galar glanced at the door, and his lips pressed tightly against each other, but after a moment he stepped back, leaving me space to enter.

I made a straight line for the desk. Galar scurried across to join me. He hovered near my elbow as if he would like to take a step further and block my path, but only one of us had the physique of a grappler, and he obviously knew it.

"Interesting amount of letters you've got there." I plucked one of the pages from the desk's surface. "Are these signed orders for funds?"

"You're speculating, Master Grian." Galar made to snatch the paper from me, but I whisked it above his reach. "My physic only requires a modest fee from the crown."

"But these aren't from Fierre, are they? They're signed by someone else. And what a surprise, this signature has a *K* at the start. I can make out the other letters. *K... i... n...*"

Galar leaped for the page and almost seized it. I folded it and tucked it into my pocket. "Too late," I said. "Now, let me guess, what could Laird Kinnaid want with you?"

"Merely private transactions, of no interest to the Star of the Sky."

"I'm afraid you're wrong, doctor. Laird Kinnaid paying for the potions you supply to Fierre? That's of great interest to me."

"Laird Kinnaid cares for the prince's body and soul. That is all."

"Oh, I suspect he thinks a lot about the prince's body, but I don't think it's for reasons of health. And as for his soul... does a man who owns half the realm's mines really know what a soul is? How much does he pay his miners? And how much does he earn from cutting lumps of coal out of the earth and selling them?" I sat on the edge of the table and eyed Galar. "I'd say there's a lot of money in Clan Kinnaid. A lot of money that Laird Kinnaid is eager to keep. And if the Sky were to go changing the laws about and taxing him, and giving some of that money to the poor, well..."

"Excuse me," Galar said, "but I fail to see what this has to do with Laird Kinnaid providing a little fee for the items in my physic." His eyes narrowed. "If, indeed, he was."

"It seems to me that when a prince cannot think clearly because his mind is half occupied with dreaming of food... he's easier to manipulate. He can't go dreaming up policy changes and making our realm fairer when he's running on half the fuel." I liked the sharp efficacy of the phrase that Oighrig Sethune had used. "And if the Sky is distracted, hungry, and irritable, then it's easy to maintain the status quo. Money for the rich. Labour for the poor."

I picked up a few more papers from the desk. Each page offered a list of items with prices, signed by Kinnaid. Putting them down again, I turned my gaze back to the doctor.

Galar's stare had turned wild. He snatched at the papers, and I reached inside myself for all the courage I had, trying to fend off the sticky mass of fear that clung to my mind. Then I lunged and threw my arm across the table, sweeping all the pages into one corner and gathering them, then clasping them to my chest. "Now, doctor," I said, "think about your future. You're a thinking man. Does a noose seem fair, to you—should it be *you* who swings for treason?"

A long pause punctuated the air between us.

"Or," I said, slowly, "would it be just if you made a confession about Laird Kinnaid's orders, and sent him to answer for his crime?"

"I can go free, then?"

"Whoever said anything about *free*?"

Galar lunged for the pages in my hand, and I threw my arm out and grabbed him bodily, hauling him onto the desk and pushing him down. He struggled, kicked, then ceased to twitch. I stared down at him, taking care to straighten the pages against my chest.

"I take no delight in cruelty," I said. "That's why I'm making you an offer. In return for an honest, signed confession, you may live. You cannot work as a doctor. You must stay on the Isle of Hairstin and train under Clan Sethune's guidance until their chiefs are satisfied that you can treat patients fairly. Then you will sign a written pledge to do no harm, to accept no money but an honest fee from your patients, and to never starve anyone again. You may petition the prince to return to the mainland then. See how generous he feels when his mind is relaxed and his health fully restored."

"And if I don't wish to train under Clan Sethune?"

"Well, then. Your other choice is to remain here and do no training at all. Live off the land; scrounge a little fruit and barley where you can find it. See how long it lasts for you." I slid off the desk and made a small bow from the neck to Galar. "Goodbye, doctor."

I had almost made it to the door when Galar said, in a small, broken voice, "You really do work for him, don't you?"

Turning, I met his gaze.

"I mean the Sky. There's no benefit in this for you, is there?" His eyes roved around my face. "You're doing it for him."

"He's the Sky to me in more ways than one," I said. "When I look ahead, he fills the whole horizon."

The firm bang of the door echoed as I walked down the corridor. I let my steps ring. It felt good to know that Galar would have heard the slam.

Fierre's guards let me into his chamber, which offered me nothing except a faint trace of lavender scent. Perfume, I realised. That was odd. Fierre never wore perfume around me—he found the smell of it overpowering, he had told me—but when he was trying to impress someone he was afraid of, he dabbed a bit of it onto his neck and wore it like armour. There was only one person in the castle that Fierre feared.

I took the corridors at a stride, and when I reached the Suite of Kings, I almost ran into a pair of armoured guards.

"Gentlemen," I said. "I'm usually quite a patient man. But I'm afraid to tell you, I used up all my patience in my last encounter. You have two choices. You can let me in, or…"

They leaned slightly forward, waiting.

"Or you can find out what the other choice is," I said, rubbing my fingers slowly across the knuckles of my right fist.

The guards pushed the door open and stepped aside. I wasted no time in the first chamber, after a glance showed me that it was empty. The sound of voices carried from the next room, and I hurried to the door at the end.

"You know, in your heart, that everything I've said is true." Fierre's light voice had taken on a desperate tone. He knelt on the floor before a great throne with its padded seat, its sturdy frame, and its gilded deer prancing on top, at the end of the next room. Against the pomp and display of the throne, his father's body looked tiny, a child in a grown-up's seat. Yet there was nothing naïve or childlike about the look on the king's face.

"Please, Your Majesty." Fierre took one of his father's hands and pressed it between his own. "If you come back to court with us, you can eat, little by little, and maybe you'll even feel warm again and sleep through the night. No more false physic. You can try to heal, with me."

Fierre's father gazed at him with utmost disdain.

"Have you forgotten that the monarchs of Clan Dannatyne are vessels of god?"

"It's convenient, isn't it? We present ourselves in a way that no one else can match. We live up to the myth, to maintain our power. But it's awfully convenient for the church, too, isn't it? Have you ever thought about that? About how all things holy remain untaxed? Perhaps one family ought not to be divine."

"This is how we are, Fierre."

"It doesn't have to be like this. As I said, father… you can heal."

The king looked down at Fierre, removing his hand from his son's grip.

"You're asking me to get fat," he sneered.

I took the opportunity to step through the doorway, clearing my throat, and both of them turned to stare at me. "What is fat, anyway?" I said. "You say the word like it's an insult, my laird, but doesn't fat protect our organs? Doesn't it keep us warm? Aren't we born with it on our bodies, and aren't we supposed to have it?"

The look I received from Fierre's father could've cut somebody in two. I forced myself to stand my ground.

"You're poisoning my son's mind," he said.

"No," I said. "Your son's too clever to be poisoned by anyone, now that he's informed." I shot a look at Fierre. "Your son ate a whole scone at lunch. Did you know that?"

Fierre's father crumpled in on himself, shrinking back against the throne. "You used to be so beautiful," he said, gazing at Fierre.

"I…" Fierre began. He looked at me, and I felt a sharp burst of anger upon seeing the pain in his eyes.

"He's beautiful now," I shot back. "He'll be beautiful when he gains the weight he needs to. He'll be beautiful as he changes, and changes again, and fluctuates like the tide at evening." I strode up to stand next to Fierre, looking down at the former ruler. "Your son shows courage, facing his illness. Will you do the same?"

"Come and join us," Fierre said, rising to his feet. "It won't be easy. I think healing is something you have to fight for—and keep fighting for, until the forces that seek to obstruct you eventually back down. But I'm a fighter. And as I fight for myself, I'm going to start fighting for this realm, too. You could be part of that. A crucial part."

His father looked from one to the other of us and sighed. The chamber was cold and empty, and for a moment, I thought that he was going to make a choice that would take him away from this castle—this hollow retreat—this suffering.

"Goodbye, Fierre," he said.

Fierre stifled a sob as he kissed his father on the forehead. They stayed there for a long moment, until his father grabbed him by the arms and pulled him close. When he let go, both of their faces glistened with tears.

"Goodbye," Fierre whispered.

We made it out of the suite before he began to shake. We were halfway down the corridor when he clasped my hand, and I pulled him into my embrace. I held him, breathing in the lavender perfume on his neck and the subtler sweetness beneath it, the natural perfume of his skin.

I kissed him on the neck, then the cheek, then the lips, until his shaking gradually stopped and his breathing calmed.

"You tried," I murmured.

"It was my last hope."

"You offered him kindness. That's all anyone can do."

He kissed me open-mouthed, then, and the wetness against my cheek told me that he was crying again. I held him there and let him cry. I would hold him forever, I thought, if it showed him that he was safe: cherished and warm and loved, no matter what path his father had chosen. When we walked on, it was as a couple, our arms linked.

Twenty-Two

Fierre

On an ordinary day, the residents of Inveroak would've rushed forward to get a glimpse of their prince. Rose petals would have been strewn, cheers would've been shouted, and hands would probably have been shaken for an embarrassingly long time during a royal visit. Despite being the nearest town to the palace, Inveroak rarely saw nobility.

As I dismounted, I looked around to find a smattering of nervous faces. Heads peeped from behind shutters and poked out of doors. Evidently, the locals had decided to make themselves scarce in case any of Crawshall's men rode back from the palace and decided to do a casual spot of head-lopping-off. I couldn't exactly begrudge them the hesitancy.

Once Aiven made his way around the town square, our reception changed. He gave honest, straightforward explanations to honest, straightforward people, calmed farmers with talk about crops, comforted children and discussed trade with merchants. His sandy hair fluttered in the cold evening wind, and I thought to myself that he was a bit like a golden star, shedding light on everyone as he did the rounds. By the time he finished, more people had emerged from their houses to greet us. I would've liked to think that they were there to greet the Sky of Eilean-òir, but I suspected that they were drawn to Aiven.

"If you please, mistress," Aiven said, "the Sky will gladly speak with you." He steered a woman in a ragged cloak over to me, guiding her by the arm. Her wrinkled face smoothed itself out as she gazed at me, and I detected a touch of awe.

As usual, I wondered what I had done to deserve it.

"Fierre, this widow will shelter us for the night. She says she has the best capacity in the town for our party, with three empty rooms."

I supposed that inns weren't exactly plentiful in Inveroak. I flashed the widow a smile. "Thank you kindly, mistress. Are you sure you can accommodate us?"

"If ye don't mind sleeping close-packed, like trout in a skinny net, then yes. I'd love to brag to my nephew about hostin' the Sky for a night." She winked at me. "Beggin' your pardon, but he glimpsed ye once as ye were riding through, a year ago, and he's been sweet on ye ever since."

"I'll make sure I wash in the river exactly when he's doing his laundry."

The widow guffawed, and I slapped her on the back, prompting her to laugh even harder. Opposite me, Aiven rolled his eyes.

It felt good to have a little humour as we set up for the night. It'd been a long ride. The tension from not knowing how Rossane and MacArlay were faring at the palace had spread over us like a scratchy blanket, rubbing against us every few minutes. I tried to shake it off as I directed our riding party to their new quarters, but to no avail; Ambassador Rince wanted to ask the townspeople if they had any news of the fighting, and I had to reassure him that Aiven had already checked. Rince agreed to share a room with two guards, both of whom looked starstruck to be near him.

I dispatched Kinnaid to sleep with the remaining guards while Mistress Tarleigh agreed to share our hostess' room. That left Aiven and I to take the small room upstairs, a hideaway that was really a disused corner of the house's attic, with a sloping roof and a window overlooking the garden. A bowl of fruit welcomed us on a tiny table. After putting his bag down, Aiven opened the window and let in a stream of air.

I joined him at the windowsill. The night breeze buffeted my cheeks.

"Do you think they'll win?" Aiven said.

"No chance of losing. Rossane and MacArlay's armies will overwhelm whatever guards Crawshall has in place. Besides…" I drew a lungful of cold air. "I've told them how to open the secret passage that leads from the grounds into the Heart Hall. They'll come out in the middle of the palace, swinging their blades."

"Stirring saints." Aiven gave me a shocked stare. "You didn't tell me about that."

"I had the idea as soon as they told me the news." Feeling the full force of Aiven's shock, I added, "And I felt a little ashamed. You wouldn't do something like sneaking your force in by a back passage."

"I'd do what it took to win, for you," Aiven said.

I wrapped one arm around his waist, and he pulled me close and enfolded me in his warmth. We looked down into the night sky for some time, before I turned my gaze to the garden below. In the dimness, I made out the tops of trees and bushes, their silhouettes brushstrokes against the canvas of the grass. I thought of Rossane and MacArlay's soldiers climbing through the secret passageway, dim shapes sneaking into the heart of the palace, unsheathing their swords in the darkness.

"It won't be long until morning comes," Aiven said. "Maybe we'll get some news."

We undressed and climbed into bed. Aiven stripped naked while I donned my usual shift, the two of us huddling together for warmth. The drape of Aiven's arm around my stomach still made me nervous, but slightly less so than before, and I fell into sleep sooner than was my habit. I woke to a chilly silence. Stars pierced the sky outside the window, darning the blackness with gold silk.

My stomach churned. Hunger jabbed inside me, sharp as a tooth.

For once, I didn't want to drink water and try to roll back into bed. I walked to the table and plucked an apple from the bowl.

The green skin felt smooth against my palm. It looked so innocent—the colour of leaves and stems—a little piece of nature in my hand.

You're not putting any food into your body, Oighrig Sethune had said. *You're asking it to run with no wood at all.*

I couldn't believe I'd confessed to her that I felt hungry when I woke in the night.

Your body knows that. It won't let you rest unless you eat more, to fuel it through the night. You lie awake, tossing and turning, wondering why you can't drift off into blackness.

I ran a finger over the top of the apple. Just one bite...

surely, I could start with one bite. But I couldn't bring the apple to my mouth. Every time I looked at it, I remembered how Galar had cautioned me not to eat any more than the smallest meals, and how my father had dug his fingernail into the flesh on my chest until he marked out my fat.

"I can help you," a voice said.

I glanced across. Aiven was sitting up against the bedhead, looking at me.

"Oh, drat it. Sorry, Aive. I didn't mean to wake you."

He climbed out of bed and crossed the room, seating his naked form in the chair beside me. I did my best not to stare. Aiven's unclothed body made that very difficult. I hoped he knew how inconvenient he was being.

"Here," he said, and lifted the apple to my lips.

He held it there, in front of my mouth, without moving his hand. I stared at him for a moment, and I felt the love radiating from his eyes, but beneath it, there was a layer of worry in that gaze. I wondered how much time Aiven spent fearing for my health.

Slowly, I took a bite of the apple.

Sweetness hit my tongue. I took a second bite, revelling in the taste of the fruit. Juice dripped down my chin, and I was about to mop it up when I felt Aiven's fingers brush over my lips and downward.

He wiped the juice off with his forefinger. His eyes locked on mine as he raised the finger to his lips and licked it, running his tongue along the length.

I blushed. I took another bite and lay the apple down.

"Are you still hungry?" Aiven said.

Reluctantly, I nodded.

"Then eat the apple. Right down to the core."

I knew that he was asking me, not instructing me. Yet

the sense of his advice was too much to ignore. I let the juice drip as I took bite after bite, let Aiven keep wiping it from my chin and licking it from his fingers. He kissed me when he finished. I could feel shame creeping up on me—shame for devouring a whole apple—but I put the apple core on the table and stood up.

"Would you comfort me?" I said.

Aiven pushed out his chair and stood up. I wrapped my arms around his waist and leaned into his naked chest. He curled one arm around me.

"Like that?" he said.

"That's a reasonable start."

Aiven took in my expression.

"We'd have to do it silently," he whispered. "Unless you want to put on a show for all your guards."

I kissed his neck and tasted the slight saltiness of his skin. I thought about trying to keep silent while Aiven was inside me. I tried to imagine myself holding in every sound.

"I can't," I said. "That is, I don't think I'm capable."

"We can go back to sleep, if you want."

I walked to the bed and slipped under the covers. "I don't want to sleep," I said.

Aiven came and lay beside me, taking the spot where I had been. He faced me, propping himself on his side. The uneasiness that had crept over me since Rossane and MacArlay rode to fight still lingered, but when Aiven was near me, I could relax and breathe again.

I looked at his fingers, still shining with dampness.

"Fuck me," I said.

Aiven's breath hitched. "I want to, but like I said…"

"We could do it if you put your hand over my mouth."

He stared into my eyes. A smile played around my lips.

I waited to see if he'd reproach me.

When he didn't, I leaned closer and rubbed my cheek against his chest, then looked up at him. "I promise not to bite your fingers when you get rough."

It was funny: you couldn't always read Aiven's emotions, but right now, I watched his will crumble against the force of pure lust. It was like seeing a mountain implode in front of your eyes.

His big hands flipped me onto my front. I loved the way he positioned me gently against the pillow, making a contrast with the sheer strength of those hands. First a push, then a careful alignment. He began to tug my night-shift upwards, and I held my arms out so that he could pull it over my head.

A warm touch greeted the back of my neck. His lips... god, the way he kissed me, daubing heat down my spine; it was more effective than any physic.

"Stay there," he whispered.

After he readied me, I thought he was going to take a moment's pause. I was caught by surprise as he pushed into me, clapping his hand over my mouth at the same time.

"Remember your promise," Aiven whispered into my ear.

He didn't stop to let me adjust but kept pushing in one smooth movement, all the way in, until I moaned into his palm, trying to keep as quiet as I could. Aiven's hand tightened its grip, pressing against my mouth.

The feeling of Aiven restraining me was a gift I'd never known I wanted.

I slept well that night, better than I had for a long time. I couldn't say if it'd been the apple or Aiven that put my mind at ease—the juice of the fruit in my mouth, or Aiven kissing me furiously while he thrust into me. In truth, I suspected that it had been both. For the first time, I was starting to believe that I deserved them both: happiness and food. I didn't have to deny myself the sweetest things in life any longer.

AT BREAKFAST, EVERYONE sat quietly around the small table. By mid-morning, we were pacing around the square, listening for hoofbeats or a whinny on the wind. The messenger rode in just after noon, tethered his panting horse, and ran straight over to me.

"The armies of Clan Rossane and Clan MacArlay have triumphed, Sky!"

The cheer that went up from the guards behind me nearly drowned out my thanks. As the townsfolk trickled over and absorbed the news, they too began to cheer and clap, and the whole square came alive with merriment. I didn't look at the crowd. I was too busy staring at the messenger's anxious expression.

Aiven stayed by my side. Kinnaid joined us, and I guessed that he had noticed the messenger's look too.

"Is something amiss, master?" I said. "A sour note in the victory tune?"

The young man looked down. "Sky, your Rocks of the Glen have captured Laird Crawshall alive."

"Surely, that's good news."

"He refuses to confess. He's demanding to speak to you in person, to explain himself before he can be charged."

I shared a look with Aiven. I could see him mentally sharpening his dirk.

"Perhaps we should hear him out." Kinnaid spoke evenly.

"Is that your advice, my laird?"

"I'm not saying let him go free, Sky. But he may have something important to say—something that implicates others."

"Not you, though, I'm sure," Aiven snapped. "You're always free of implication."

I stared. Aiven's jaw had clenched, and his right hand had balled into a fist. He was gazing at Kinnaid like a wolf staring down a packmate.

"You sound angry, Star. I've no notion what you mean, but surely we can all be courteous to each other at such a difficult time for the Sky." Kinnaid smiled. "After all, he's been through so much." His hand found my shoulder and rested there.

Aiven's gaze swung to Kinnaid's hand and his mouth twisted into a scowl. "You'd do well to keep a distance where it's appropriate, my laird. Don't you think?"

"And you'd do well to remember what I told you when we were grappling," Kinnaid shot back.

Kinnaid and Aiven had been grappling? That was a surprise. And not the happy kind of surprise, either, where you feel warm about the news for the best part of an hour. I cleared my throat and watched both men jump to attention.

"I'll meet with Crawshall," I said. "But Aiven will accompany me."

Relief and gratitude mingled on Aiven's face, but he shot another glare at Kinnaid. For his part, Kinnaid maintained a nonchalant air. I wondered what had come between the two men; whatever it was, I knew that Aiven didn't hold petty grudges.

It would have to wait. I remembered the fury of Crawshall's lunge when he charged at Aiven in the Heart

Hall. I remembered the way he had flung his sword out and strode across the floor.

"Let's get this over and done with," I said, looking up at Aiven.

He nodded, and took my hand. The warmth of his fingers folded around me. I knew that he was with me, no matter what.

THE PALACE WORE a sombre air despite the shower of golden light that glossed its sunstone walls: even the late afternoon sun couldn't wash away the red flecks on the slab of black rock, reminding me of the fighting that had taken place outside the palace, spattering its very foundations. I knelt and said a prayer on the blood-dappled ground. The ambassadors gaped as they took in a pair of men with arrows in their chests who lay across the steps. I felt a little weak myself, even though I knew these corpses had once been my enemies. Ambassador Rince nearly fainted when he saw the bodies up close, and in the ensuing bustle, in which Ambassador Tarleigh scooped up Rince and carried him into the palace in her sinewy arms, no one seemed to notice my moment of weakness.

It was a relief to see the corridors empty and the statues and paintings largely intact. I found Rossane and MacArlay in the Heart Hall, surrounded by their soldiers. The two lairds looked up when I entered.

"Clan Rossane has seen off the usurper, Sky." Rossane elbowed his way through to me.

"And Clan MacArlay cut down just as many Crawshall soldiers." MacArlay swaggered forward. He held out an unsheathed sword, laying it in my hands before I could refuse. Dark spots marred the steel.

"I cut the last two resisters down myself," MacArlay said. "We pinned Crawshall down between us. The bastard's foaming at the mouth in a cell below the old throne room—we've put half a legion of guards down there to watch him. Can't be too careful."

"You both did splendidly." I looked from one to the other. "And your rewards will come sooner than you think. Laird MacArlay, will you take the ambassadors aside and find them some clean rooms? Rooms with no arrowed corpses strewn around, if you don't mind. I have someone to see."

I passed the sword back to MacArlay. He took it with a look of slight disappointment, and Rossane stepped forward and teetered, as if he would like to ask something of me. I swept past them both before they could speak.

Aiven stuck by my side as I headed through the castle, winding through the corridors until I reached the stairs that led down to the cells. He blocked my way to the top stair. "Let me go first."

"There's a whole heap of men in armour down there, Aive. I think I'll be safe."

"Please." He grabbed my arm. "Just in case."

I nodded, and he descended the stairs, keeping his body between myself and whatever awaited us. A pair of guards greeted us and led us down the row of disused cells. We passed many more guards, stopping outside a chamber whose solid door offered a firm barrier. Only a barred window afforded us a view.

I leaned close and glimpsed Crawshall's powerful figure stationed on a chair in the centre of the cell, his hands tied behind his back. A gag covered his mouth.

"His weapons?" I asked the guards.

"All removed, Sky."

"Very good." I looked over at Aiven. "Got your dirk, Aive?"

"Of course." Aiven looked surprised.

"Well, then. Do we have some paper and ink at the ready?"

The guards fetched me the materials for the confession, placing the quill, inkpot, and parchment in my hands. I shared a long look with Aiven for a moment, then nodded to the guards.

They opened the door, and the creak of rusty hinges ushered us in. The nearest guards stared, as if waiting for my command to file in. They could keep waiting, I thought, as I closed the door.

"Fierre," Aiven murmured, without taking his eyes off Crawshall.

"Don't worry about me," I said, and then, realising that that was about as likely as a heatwave in the highlands, I added, "Trust me."

I placed the parchment, quill and ink on the floor in the corner of the cell and walked across to Crawshall. He eyed me like a bull lowering its horns, waiting to charge. When I stopped within inches of his chair, he grunted something into his gag.

I heard Aiven object, but I untied the gag before he could stop me. I stared down at my prisoner with what I hoped was a refined, regal, yet ultimately benevolent look.

Crawshall spat in my face.

Aiven shouted a reprimand, but I wiped the saliva from my cheek and lips and kept my eyes fixed on Crawshall. "That's not very polite, my laird," I said. "You haven't been very polite lately, have you?"

"Apologise for spitting on the Sky," Aiven shouted.

"I did much more than spit on him a year ago." Crawshall laughed as Aiven looked furious. "Feeling jealous, are we?"

"We're not here to talk about your manners, my laird, fascinating though they are. We're here for your confession." I continued to stare at him, imploring my hands not to tremble. "My Rocks of the Glen said you wished to speak to me—well, then, pour out your monologue. I shall be your captive audience. Or rather, you'll be my captive, and I'll be your audience. But I suppose we can let the term stay."

Crawshall wriggled in his chair and glared at me. "Unbind me first."

I knew what Aiven would be thinking, and yet I stepped around Crawshall and began to untie his hands. Partway through, I glanced up and saw Aiven's horrified stare. I looked determinedly down and finished freeing Crawshall.

"There." Crawshall flexed his fingers and held his arms out in front of him. "That's more like it. You want to know why I took your palace, Dannatyne? Why I dare to consider myself a leader above the Prince Regent of Eilean-òir? I bet you're dying to know."

"Oh, raring for it."

"It's because you raise the dirty produce of farms from the soil, where it belongs. Hay belongs in a field. Potatoes belong in the ground. Don't they? But you'd pluck a farmers' son from his cottage and make him your Master of Compliance. You'd raise him further and parade him around as your Star, flaunting him before us all—as if we didn't have the right to rule—as if we didn't have the blood to earn a place at your side!"

"Interesting," I said. "As far as I'm aware, I'm the one who rules." In the pause that followed, Crawshall's face told me that he had realised his error, but I cut off his spluttering. I could argue against what he'd just said— passionately refute the idea that farmers were *dirty produce*—but I knew Crawshall didn't care about that. "I don't think you wanted a place at my side to assist me. Did you think that being my right-hand man would mean you could manipulate me until you ruled the realm in my stead?"

"I didn't—"

"Get up, Laird Crawshall."

He rose, and suddenly, I was aware that he towered over me.

"There are some lairds in the highlands who cater to their people fairly and carefully. But not you. You're a man of the sword. You take what you like, when you like, so I've heard. And you took what you wanted from me, without due care. Now you're angry because Master Grian has captured my heart, and you're afraid that he may stop you from exploiting all the things you like… not just my body, but your people's bodies. Their arms, that lift sacks of grain. Their feet, that work a plough. Their backs, that strain all day for your clan's resources, which you store and fail to distribute. Am I right?"

"You little—"

"As your prince, I command you to write down everything you've just told me about your motivation and sign it as your confession. I'll hand you the paper and quill myself. Once it's been safely conveyed to the guards, I'll grant you a life sentence in prison, to be reviewed after twenty years—rather than an appointment with the hangman." I gazed up at him. "Agreed, my laird?"

Crawshall looked at me for so long that I could've sworn he was considering it. I could practically feel the tension emanating from Aiven behind me. My face was damp with the remnants of Crawshall's spittle.

I remembered Crawshall spitting into my mouth, last year, and telling me I liked it. I remembered him wetting his fingers after that, trailing them down my stomach, and saying, "It won't hurt." And I remembered how much it had hurt as he'd pushed into me with no oil.

He was silent now, as the seconds crept by. At last, he extended his hand.

As I made to shake it, he grabbed my arm and pulled me against him, spinning me so that he could pin me with my back against him. His muscular arm found my throat. He held it there, exerting a pressure, locking me in place while Aiven rushed over.

"Don't even think about it, Whyte," Crawshall snarled. "Yes, I know your real name."

"Let him go."

"Attack me, and you'll regret it."

"I'm not going to attack you," Aiven said. "I'm going to kill you, my laird. And I promise you, I won't regret it for even a flicker of a moment."

Aiven punched Crawshall so fast that I had just enough time to duck—not that I needed to: the punch hit square in the middle of Crawshall's cheek, fist crunching bone with a sickening thud. I twisted out of Crawshall's grip. As Aiven knocked Crawshall to the ground, I saw the flash of a blade and watched Aiven's dirk slash towards Crawshall's throat.

But Crawshall hadn't gained his reputation for savagery by giving up. His fist ploughed into Aiven's stomach, sending Aiven stumbling backward. He pressed the advantage by knocking Aiven to the ground, and the move triggered something inside me. I ran at Crawshall without thinking—all I could see was Aiven, lying on the floor.

I knew, in the split-second before I hit Crawshall's chest, that he would raise his arms, but I wasn't prepared for the force of his shove. As I tumbled, the floor rose to meet me.

"No!" Aiven shouted, launching himself at Crawshall again.

His arm made a blur above me, hacking at Crawshall. There was a sharp pain jabbing my left side, but I forced myself to my knees and hauled myself up against the wall. I tottered towards Aiven and Crawshall.

Crawshall's hand seized Aiven's and his free hand reached for the dirk. They tussled, pushing hard against each other. Aiven threw Crawshall back and whipped the dirk around, and Crawshall grabbed hold of Aiven's wrist just before he could slice. They went back and forth, back and forth, Aiven gaining a little ground and then losing it.

"Blood tells, in the end," Crawshall hissed. "Give up, now. I'll overpower you."

Aiven's hand dropped suddenly. He drew it back, then jabbed his dirk hard into Crawshall's stomach.

"Not if I gut you first," he said.

Crawshall bit Aiven's neck, and Aiven roared, threw him off, and kicked him in the shin. As Crawshall fell, Aiven caught him, stabbed him once in the neck, then withdrew the blade and let him fall.

The look in Crawshall's eyes as he hit the floor was one of white-hot fury.

"I told you, my laird, I won't regret it for a moment," Aiven said.

He flung himself down, dug his blade into Crawshall's stomach again and dragged it downward.

After a few breaths, he rose to his feet.

I hobbled to his side, and we stood and watched while Crawshall writhed and then went still. Blood spilled from his neck and gushed from his stomach, pouring crimson over his kilt. The sight sickened me, but I was so glad that Aiven was safe, so relieved that both of us were alive, that I didn't look away.

Aiven swept me into his arms and then began to pat me down as if he were inspecting me for hidden marks.

"Are you unharmed?" he said.

"Aside from a nasty bump, I think so." I rubbed his face. "Thank god you're good at standing up to rabid noblemen."

"I can't believe he dared to attack you." He stared down at Crawshall. "And me," he added, as an afterthought. "It's just a pity we didn't get his confession written down and signed, for the public's sake."

"What are you talking about, Aive?" I gestured at the quill, inkpot, and parchment that lay in the corner of the cell. "We have his confession right here."

Aiven stared at the blank scroll for a long moment.

Slowly, he looked back at me.

"You know," I said. "The confession he made about opposing my new program of reform. The statement we're going to share with everyone. You remember that."

I sat down and began to write. I was aware of Aiven watching me in silence, and of Crawshall's blood dripping further onto the floor. When I'd inked the last line, I gazed at the space where the signature should go.

"I'm going to need the last letter we have from Crawshall, Aive," I said, sticking the quill back in the inkpot. "And I'm going to need our best calligrapher, before we gather the court."

Twenty-Three

Aiven

THE COURT OF Eilean-òir murmured as it assembled on the grass. It might be a mild day, and the grass might be soft, but it was unusual for the nobility to meet outside, and lairds didn't like unusual situations—especially those that involved someone more important than themselves. They eyed each other and shifted on the chairs that filled the western garden of the palace.

Once, I would have been sitting at the very edge of the group, but today I stood by Fierre's side, keeping as close as possible without touching him.

There wasn't a single red spot near his eyes. The burst blood vessels must have faded entirely. I searched for the dark blossoming of new ones, and found none.

"How do I look?" Fierre whispered.

I ran my gaze over him, enjoying the sight of his new enserre. Silver crystals twinkled in a pattern below his hips, covering his groin. At first, my eyes jumped to the bright sparkle of the gems, but after a moment my interest transferred to the fabric of the enserre, a fine creation with one crucial difference to the usual style.

It was little more than a window. Through the translucent layer of silvery cloth, I could see everything that wasn't covered by a crystal: the dots of nipples, and a swathe of smooth skin, soft and kissable. When he twisted sideways to show me the rest of it, I caught a view of his backside.

There were significantly fewer crystals on his backside.

"Um," I said. "Well…"

"That good? Two whole syllables' worth?" He was grinning, and the sight of that grin made me feel as if the clouds had been lifted from the sky. Fierre often asked how he looked with an anxious expression on his face, as if he were certain that there was something fundamentally wrong with his body. Today, he was cracking a joke.

"Every man out there would fight the others in a tournament for your favour," I said.

"Am I that dangerous?"

"If they catch a glimpse of the back of your outfit, they'll start a riot right here."

"You don't need to worry about that." Fierre flashed me a smile. "I had the back made for you alone."

He stepped forward and raised his hands in a gesture of welcome, and the court quietened. The move positioned him directly in front of me. I tried very hard to think about political matters, about the task at hand, about anything except for the portion of skin visible below his hips and how much I'd like to run my tongue down from the base of his spine, picking off each crystal one by one.

A ray of light caught the crown on his head. Its pearls and stones gleamed. This was the first time Fierre had worn it since his coronation, I realised. He seemed to move more easily in it now, as if it no longer weighed so heavily upon his brow.

"My lairds." Fierre projected his voice. "We gather here today to honour the two men who worked hard to save us. I call Laird Rossane and Laird MacArlay forward. Come hither and kneel, my lairds."

Rossane got there first. Even when it came to ceremony, he raced MacArlay with impressive speed. MacArlay lowered himself down beside his rival and the two of them bowed their heads to Fierre.

"Let everyone witness that I name these two men Defenders of the Monarch, a new title, created to capture the glory of their protection of the crown!"

Applause burst forth from the crowd, and as the two lairds rose, Fierre touched each on the upper arm. "With an annuity of five hundred marks in return for their ongoing devotion," he added, loud enough for only them to hear.

"Sky, you honour me beyond expectation," MacArlay said.

"Keep your expectations low, and you may receive more honours." Fierre smiled at him.

"My devotion to you occupies the highest ledge in my mind," Rossane said, edging closer to Fierre.

"The second-highest, surely," Fierre said.

Rossane looked at him nervously. His gaze dipped down to Fierre's sheer garment. "What should come first, Sky?"

"Your obedience," Fierre said.

He turned to face the crowd and gestured to Rossane and MacArlay, waiting until the crowd burst into applause again. The sound washed over us like wine.

Fierre waited until the lairds had taken their bows before motioning them to the side. When they made to return to the group, he shook his head, leaving them to awkwardly take up a position in full view.

"You must all be wondering why Laird Crawshall committed so treacherous an act," he said. "Wait no longer, my lairds. For I have his confession, signed and clear as day."

At Fierre's nod, I stepped forward and held up the scroll that I had been clutching. Untying the blue ribbon from it, I rolled out the parchment and displayed it high above my head, listening to the gasps of the crowd as they pointed at the writing and the signature. It might be too far away for them to make out the words, but they could certainly tell that it *was* a confession, stamped with the Sky's seal on the bottom-left corner.

I kept my hands steady, holding the parchment flat, until Fierre nodded to me to lower the scroll.

"Laird Crawshall demanded that the poor of this realm starve. He knew of my new document of laws, lovingly prepared for the people, and he worked his treason against the crown itself. He hurled his anger at the embodiment of the divine—the Sky himself. He sought to plunge his dagger into my heart." Fierre broke off, as if the statement had made him lose his courage. A ripple of shock ran through the crowd. I heard Fierre heave a deep breath, clearly audible across the grass.

"But Clan Rossane and Clan MacArlay stood against him. They reminded us all what our system of clans is for—not just support for the prince, but protection of the people. They brought down the usurping army for the safety of all. And I can stand here before you today and declare that with the support of our clans, my new declaration of laws—the Harvest of Eilean-òir—will go ahead." He drew a deep breath, but this time, I knew it wasn't for show; the shaky inhalation wasn't loud enough for the crowd to hear. "The people will see better health, more schools, enough food to go around, coin to meet their needs, and secure employment. Our farmers and craftspeople and merchants have sown and toiled for centuries on this gilded isle. They've seen the fruits of their labour plucked away, and silently borne it. Now, their harvest is due."

He beckoned to Rossane and MacArlay, who edged over to join him.

"Sky," MacArlay muttered.

"Your laws—" Rossane began.

"Five hundred marks," Fierre said.

Both men fell silent.

"Raise your hands to applaud the men who stand for reform, and the nobility of spirit of this entire court! Together, we nourish the realm!" Fierre exclaimed.

The applause came louder this time, though I glimpsed a few confused faces amongst the lairds, and I guessed that some of them were wondering how a duty to the crown could allow for funding the prosperity of the poor.

"But there is something more, my lairds." Fierre's voice pierced the air and brought every gaze to his face. He stepped forward from the slightly shaded grass into a patch of full sun, and from the gasp of the crowd I guessed that the light shone through the front of his outfit. The crystals glittered, but they barely covered the necessary parts. It was unfairly erotic, the way he shifted on the spot in his enserre; somehow, it was more erotic than if he'd been naked. Every movement made you hope to catch a glimpse of what lay beneath.

The lairds seemed to have forgotten their concerns for a moment.

"The usurper Crawshall wrapped his arms around my throat. He choked me, and as I felt him squeezing the life out of me, I heard him shout: *you're mine*. Because Crawshall desired me for himself. In his confession, he tells the world that he intended to imprison me in his castle."

I had to hand it to Fierre. He didn't let his voice waver. If you weren't listening for the slight hitch in his breath, you couldn't tell it was a lie.

The court murmured in shocked undertones.

"He wanted to use me for his own boorish desires. The laird of one of our biggest clans! A man who should know how to care, love, and provide!"

Louder murmurs, now. Rumblings.

"He wanted to master me and keep me for himself. But I wish to show you all today that no man can oppose true love and joy. And I know that all the other clans of this realm support the happiness of their prince, as they show loyalty to the crown, and to god!"

He beckoned to somebody at the back of the crowd, and I saw guards escort a man and woman around the side of the chairs. As they walked closer, their faces came into the sun. I recognised them. They were the most familiar faces to me in the whole world.

"Finlaye and Rhonar," Fierre called out. "Come and stand by me."

What were my parents doing here?

When Fierre had told me about stitching up Crawshall with a personal motive, I'd listened carefully. If he'd said anything about my mother and father, I would've remembered. I was hardly likely to forget the names of my commoner parents coming out of Fierre's royal mouth.

Was he going to make an example of them? What had he meant about love? Were my parents going to be questioned about their marriage?

"Darling boy," Rhonar said. "You look…"

Her eyes ran down Fierre's outfit. Not even my mother could fail to notice that he was a few crystals away from giving the crowd an unforgettable show.

"…unique," she finished.

"Did you bring it?" Fierre said.

"Of course." My mother passed something to Fierre. He folded his fingers over it quickly and grinned. He glanced at Finlaye, then turned to me.

"I declare here, before the court, before my guards, before your parents… that you're the key to my future. The key to my lock." Fierre lowered himself onto one knee and held out his hand, unfolding his fingers. In his palm nestled a single acorn—the same acorn I had given him just before his coronation. I stared at it. I couldn't work out why it was there.

"Aiven Grian, will you marry me?" Fierre said.

And suddenly, it all made sense.

Something pricked my eyes. I put a hand to my right eye. Slowly, I realised that I was feeling tears, but I didn't mind—I didn't even mind that I was crying in front of the assembled nobility of Eilean-òir. I looked down at Fierre's earnest face.

"Yes," I said. "A thousand times, yes."

Fierre leaped up, pressed the acorn into my palm, and wrapped his arms around my waist. The feeling of his body pushing against me and the sight of his practically naked figure beneath the enserre should've sent me struggling for control, but a wave of joy moved through me and filled me so utterly that I had no room for anything but pure bliss. At any moment, it was going to burst out of me and spill all over the grass, flooding the garden with my happiness.

I kissed him on the lips, then froze. I'd forgotten, for a brief moment, that we were in front of a crowd. But did it matter any more? Was I allowed to kiss Fierre now?

The issue was solved when Fierre reached up on tiptoe and kissed me without restraint, plunging his tongue into my mouth and angling his head to get the most out of the opportunity. I grabbed hold of his arse and hefted him up, and he gave a little whimper of surprise. I kissed him back ferociously. He tasted so good. How did he always taste like summer berries, so temptingly sweet?

The shift of his buttocks beneath my fingers made me realise that I'd been holding him for too long, and I broke the kiss and put him down. The applause hit us a second later. I felt dazed, but Fierre's broad smile righted me again. Whether the crowd was clapping because they approved, or because they wanted to please Fierre, I didn't know, but somehow he had done the unthinkable: he had prompted a public display of support.

We were going to be married.

My mother edged towards me, holding out a box. From the other side, my father approached Fierre. We took the boxes, and Fierre smiled comfortably and waved his around.

"Well," he said. "Open yours."

My fingers fumbled with the latch. Inside the box, a square diamond gleamed in the middle of a silver ring. Fierre opened his box to reveal an identical ring, glittering bright as a spring moon.

"Husband and husband-to-be," Rhonar said, nodding her head in approval.

"Aye, and don't you go messing it up," Finlaye added.

"Father!" I said. "You can be sure I'm going to give Fierre all my love."

"I was talking to the prince," Finlaye said.

Fierre laughed and stepped forward to hug him. My father froze. For a moment, I thought that he might push the Sky of Eilean-òir away out of sheer awkwardness, but then the two of them embraced so firmly that it caused a prickle at the back of my eyes again. I wiped away a tear and felt a hand take mine.

My mother hugged me, and then the four of us beamed stupidly each other.

When my parents returned to the crowd, taking the boxes with them, Fierre made sure that they sat in the front row this time. I kissed him on the brow. Taking his ring, I slid it slowly onto his finger, taking my time to push it all the way down to the end. He put mine onto my finger much faster, grinning as he did.

"Let me be the first to congratulate you," a voice said, from the side.

I had almost forgotten that the new Defenders of the Monarch were standing there.

Laird Rossane moved towards us, his smile a rictus, and he extended a hand to me. As I shook it, he whispered into my ear:

"You're a lucky little bastard, aren't you?"

I smiled forcibly back, then leaned over to his ear.

"My laird," I said, "if you ever lay a finger on my future husband again—or cross anyone else's boundaries—I'll cut off that finger, right after I slice off your cock, and I'll feed both appendages to the palace hounds. I'll strip your title and your annuity from you as quick as you can say *rapist*. Then I'll give you a job in the royal choir, singing for your supper. I've heard that eunuchs have beautiful voices." I stepped back, to where the others could hear me, and added loudly, "Pleased to have your support, Laird Rossane."

He gritted his teeth.

Slowly, with a jerkiness that suggested he was forcing his body to move, he made his way to Fierre and shook his hand very gently. He turned back to flash a last look at me before joining the crowd.

When I made to shake MacArlay's hand, he muttered: "I heard you already."

Fierre hugged me again and then stared into my eyes, as if he could not stop looking at me. He held up his hand and pressed it against mine so that our rings rubbed together. I kissed him on the brow and beamed. My cheeks hurt from smiling, but I didn't care. I would smile until my face turned numb if it meant that all this was real, and I was truly going to marry Fierre.

"I think it's time we sent the court home," Fierre said.

The after-party took a little while to peter out, with scones, cream, and berries served in the Heart Hall, along with copious amounts of raspberry wine and a fizzy strawberry drink that turned some of the lairds excitable. After several glasses smashed, Fierre directed the guards to begin escorting the lairds to their horses. My parents caught my eye from the corner where they were lingering, and seeing that Fierre was embroiled in another conversation with Mistress Tarleigh, I allowed myself to slip over to them.

"Sorry we didn't tell you, love," Rhonar said, squeezing my forearm. "He swore us to secrecy. Couldn't even tell the sheep when I was traipsing around the farm."

"I'll forgive you this once." I smiled.

"We're so proud of you," Finlaye said, wrapping his hand around my shoulders. "First, a job as Master of Compliance. Your own room in the palace. Then it's Star of the Sky, and every laird in the land looking up to you.

And now y'can go no higher. Marrying *him*." He nodded in Fierre's direction with such seriousness that it looked as if he were indicating a god. "Does that make you a Prince Regent as well? Prince and prince?"

"I believe it's prince and consort. But I suppose I'll find out." My smile was widening by the second—I couldn't help myself. "Thank you, dad and ma… for never judging me."

"We do judge you," my mother said.

I swallowed.

"We judge you and find you perfect," she added.

"Aye," my father said, "that's right. We scored you carefully, and you got full marks. Our son's done what no other Whyte could—made a name for himself in the realm."

I wanted to tell him that it didn't matter what people thought of you, only that you were true to your values and kind to all those who weren't cruel. I wanted to tell him that a pair of farmers could be as honest and kind as any laird. I wanted to explain that the wind of fame was nothing if it blew no compassion to others, but before I could find the words, I felt a tug at my arm.

"It's true, then? Your name's really Whyte?"

Ambassador Rince bobbed on the spot. His cheeks wore a familiar red tint that many of the other guests were sporting after drinking the fizzy strawberry drink. I tried hard not to laugh.

"I see the truth has flown around the whole court, then," I said.

"Whyte's a farmer's name—isn't it? Like Blacke and Browne. But not Red, or Purple, tee hee!" Rince swayed and grabbed hold of my arm. "You Eilean folk love your colours! Why would you change an honest farmer's name,

320

Master Aiven? Master Whyte… Master Aiven Whyte…"

"Because honest farmers aren't so well appreciated by the prince's court." I steadied Rince with one hand. "When I became Master of Compliance, I puzzled over a new name until my father finally cracked it. Grian, he suggested. It means *sun*. You couldn't find a better reminder of our family's work, out in the fields under the sun all day—even though it made me sound fancier, it tethered me to where I'm from. It's an old word, though, *grian*. From the Salt Tongue. I wanted to make sure no laird would stumble across the meaning and connect it with me." I smiled gently at Rince. "Not that that was ever likely. Lairds don't banter with farmers."

"Grian. Somewhat fitting for you, wouldn't you say?" Rince jabbed a finger into my chest.

"I won't dispute it," I said.

"Because, as we all know, the sun's in the Sky all day. Ha, ha, ha!" Rince threw his head back and guffawed, then promptly toppled over. I jumped and caught him just in time before he hit the grass. When I rose, with him clutched in my arms, I could feel the heat in my cheeks, and I wasn't sure if it was from my leap or from what Rince had said.

It brought back a recent memory which I had engraved into my mind… a particularly lustful part of my mind.

I led my parents and Rince away, showing them to the guards who were escorting the lairds from the palace. My mother gave me a final hug, and my father hugged me tighter still. I watched them go with a smile. Rince tottered behind them, supported by two guards and muttering something about big women and wishing to be carried firmly.

As I joined Fierre again, I saw a flicker of red at the

fringe of my vision. A glance showed me a blaze of red hair and a familiar tartan, and then it was gone: disappeared through the door of the hall.

"Excuse me," I whispered to Fierre.

In the midst of a fresh bombardment from Mistress Tarleigh, he didn't reply. I wove my way slowly through the remaining crowd, taking care to smile and greet the lairds I knew and nodding to those I didn't know, making sure that nobody could think I was in a suspicious hurry. Once I emerged into the corridor, I stared around.

Nothing but brown, black, and blonde hair greeted my eye. Then I glimpsed a flash of red at the far end of the hallway, and a figure disappearing around the bend.

I began to sprint. Someone called out to me, but I didn't listen. I rounded the corner and increased my pace, my breath pounding in my ears.

Twenty-Four

Aiven

THE MEDICAL SUPPLY room of the palace held the unenvied position at the end of the corridor on the second floor, closest to the stairs. It meant that any doctor who chopped or mixed medicines had to endure the sound of guards and staff clomping past as they worked, yet it also meant that the supply room was close enough to the stairs for the doctors to dash to any part of the palace. For my purposes, it meant that I scarcely had time to catch my breath at the top of the staircase before sprinting after my quarry.

His red hair disappeared through the open door, and before he could lock the room, I threw myself at the narrowing gap.

Kinnaid stared at me. He looked surprised to see my face, but surprise quickly gave way to anger, and he shoved the door hard, ramming me with the wood. I held my position.

"Curious business, mining," I said.

"I don't know what you're talking about, Grian, but you should leave your betters to their work."

"And why would you be working in a room that only doctors use? You can't really expect me to believe that you need a poultice for matters of diplomacy."

I pushed the door hard and it swung back, hitting Kinnaid in the thigh and knocking him a few steps into the room. Pressing my advantage, I stepped in and slammed the door.

"As I was saying, mining's a curious business." I strode over to Kinnaid. "Digging up the earth. Taking things out of it—coal, in your case—and selling it to people. Strange, to be selling something you don't own. Doesn't seem like it should be allowed. Yet mining makes big money... not for the labourers doing the digging, of course."

"I don't see what this has to do with you."

"Now, if it's big money, there's a lot for you to win, and there's also a massive amount for you to lose. You can't have a ruler who goes around taxing you, or worse, shutting down coal mining in Eilean-òir to save our land. That'd be a pain in the arse. To keep the profits big, you need to control your king—or your Prince Regent, as the case may be." I was aware that my lips had curled into a snarl. "Keep him compliant, so that he lets you ravage the earth unchecked. Keep him tired and hungry, with his mind shrouded in fog, so that you can take and steal all the coal you need."

Kinnaid made a dash for the nearest shelf, but I ran to block his way, seizing him by the wrist. "My laird, I'm not finished."

I manoeuvred him back to the centre of the room. His eyes blazed, but he hesitated, watching me. My death stare must have been working.

"Let me tell you a story, Laird Kinnaid. Your father had an idea. He saw Prince Dannatyne's grandfather—the king at the time—doing his yearly fast for the mid-autumn festival. And he saw how distracted and compliant the king was during the fast, when he was so hungry that he could think of little but food. The king's reasoning was poor. His attempts at conversation were weak. Already worn down by a need to stay slim for the sake of Clan Dannatyne's image, he was tipped into starvation. Your father saw a solution to his own problems: if he could keep the king in that state, he could dig more mines and profit from them, without the king ever stepping in and interfering." I tightened my grip on Kinnaid's wrist. "Your father persuaded the king that the doctors of Clan Sethune were frauds, swaying him to exile them and ban them from practicing. He installed a doctor in the palace who would starve the king. A nasty arrangement—don't you think?—but the perfect way to worm into his brain as if it were a rotten apple. When the king died young, Clan Kinnaid's doctor treated Prince Dannatyne's father next. He starved him, as well."

Kinnaid tensed. I saw him dart another glance at the shelf.

"And when your father died and you took over as the head of Clan Kinnaid, it was all there for you. A system to continue. Dr Galar's predecessor must've been ageing by then, and he appointed Galar to take over." I smiled, but there wasn't an ounce of mirth in me. "Hear any mistakes? Can you correct me, my laird? Or is every word I said true?"

Kinnaid broke free and lunged for the shelf, and my body responded just in time for me to block him, but not fast enough for it to be flawless. My shoulder crunched into his chest and he stumbled and hit the shelves, scrabbling for a hold. His hand swept along the shelf before it found purchase, knocking jars and bottles to the floor, sending clouds of herbs and seeds into the air. Amongst the spilt ingredients, pieces of paper scattered on the floor. I caught a handful of them and read as many words as I could before Kinnaid punched me in the stomach.

Weathering the blow, I regained my footing.

"Seems like you paid Dr Galar an awful lot," I said, waving the paper in my hand.

"The mines are my family's legacy. It's our right to keep Clan Kinnaid running, whatever you may bleat—that land we mine belongs to *us*."

I stepped over a piece of broken glass, towards Kinnaid. "You've made one fatal error," I said. "The land doesn't belong to you. It isn't Clan Kinnaid's to claim. It's nobody's, and everyone's. This whole realm must nourish its land if we're to survive. You had the choice to earn your fortune an honest way, tending to the land, maybe grazing a few animals." I drew a deep breath. "Instead, you chose to rape the earth."

Kinnaid snarled and ran at me. I ducked his lunge, bobbed back up, and punched him in the jaw. He rubbed his jawbone.

"You act as if you're so bloody righteous," he spat. "Sitting on top of your hill of morals. All peasants are the same. I did what I had to do."

"For duty? For others?" I chuckled. "No, my laird: for yourself."

He snatched at my arm and pulled me toward the table at the back of the room. I pushed back with every ounce of determination in my body, ignoring the cracking of glass beneath my boots, focusing only on out-muscling Kinnaid. I got him onto the table first and pinned him down, only to feel a hard ache in my side as his fist pummelled my ribs. He pushed me back, grabbed a jar off the shelf and hurled it at me, sending yellow dust into the air as it smashed behind me.

"You're desperate," he said, and his voice thrummed like a taut wire. "I bet you haven't got a clue how to satisfy Fierre."

My fists clenched. Fierre's name, coming from Kinnaid's lips… that hurt more than a punch to my ribs.

"Oh, did you think you were the only one to call him *Fierre*?" Kinnaid laughed: a short, sharp sound. He circled me, stopping near the shelves on the opposite wall. He wanted me to stumble, I told myself; he wanted a chance to kill me. I had to ignore those taunts.

"I fucked him with my dagger-hilt, and he bent right over and waited for it. Just like a bitch in heat." Kinnaid smirked. "Totally submissive. I bet he would have let me use the other end of the dagger if I'd asked."

Don't make any sudden moves, I told myself. *Don't rise to the bait.*

"He likes to be pinned down and used like a whore— did he tell you that? But I suppose he only enjoys the touch of a nobleman. Real power." He shrugged. "You couldn't give him that if you tried."

"You speak rashly, Laird Kinnaid."

"Don't worry. I made sure he knows who to call on, if he needs pleasure. I left him nice and wet."

"There's no point trying to incite envy, my laird. I have no reason to be jealous of you."

"I bet you'd love to know how he looked when he opened his legs for me." Kinnaid raised an eyebrow. "Don't you want to know the names I called him?"

"I have no questions for you, my laird. Only a message."

Kinnaid looked suspicious. "Which is?"

My fist connected with his nose at the same moment that the door creaked open. I didn't have time to turn and see who was witnessing me punch Kinnaid's lights out. I decided to let it be. I grabbed Kinnaid by the shoulders while he was stumbling to regain his footing and hefted him sideways, throwing him against the desk. I landed another punch before he could recover. He ducked my third punch, but I kneed him in the balls so hard that I almost felt sorry.

Almost.

I remembered Fierre collapsing in my arms after a dizzy spell. I remembered breathing into Fierre's mouth, hoping and praying that he wouldn't die.

I punched Kinnaid in the jaw again and hauled him by the collar onto the desk. I was about to land the killing blow when a voice cut through the room.

"Not at your hands, Aive."

I stared. Fierre picked his way across the glass and herbs, stopping a little way from the desk. He ignored Kinnaid and looked directly into my eyes.

"You've done brilliantly," he added. "But I need him alive, to possess his mines."

I lowered my fist. Still looking at Fierre, I dropped Kinnaid's collar and heard his head thunk against the desk. Shock lingered in Fierre's eyes, but he reached over to wipe something from my cheek. Crimson smeared his fingers. I realised that I must've been bleeding for some time, though I hadn't noticed; ignoring Kinnaid's blows, I'd focused purely on beating him into silence.

Right now, I probably looked like a feral animal.

"Guards!" Fierre called, and a clatter of armour and boots broke the moment. Soldiers traipsed into the room, kicking the smashed glass, herbs, and pieces of plants aside.

"Take Laird Kinnaid down to the cells," Fierre said. "Make sure you take his dirk from him and leave him without so much as a pointy stick. Then lock him up, and permit him no visitors. I want him alive when I visit."

"Sky, if you'll hear me out—"

"I heard everything you said, Laird Kinnaid."

Fierre shot Kinnaid a diamond-sharp look. I hurried to move off the desk.

As the guards hauled Kinnaid to his feet and marched him away, Kinnaid reached for Fierre, and Fierre shifted quickly out of his grasp.

"You were wrong, my laird," Fierre said, watching Kinnaid's mouth twist in anger. "I don't need a nobleman. I don't care how much a man's estates and assets are worth. I care how much he thinks *I'm* worth."

The guards pushed Kinnaid through the doorway and out into the corridor. I heard the clop of their boots on the stairs. After a long while, the echoes died away, and we were alone in the supply room.

"Are you hurting?" Fierre wiped a little more blood off my cheek. "Tell me he didn't break anything—if he dared to hurt your bones…"

"The only things shattered are bottles and jars." I flexed my arms and checked for wounds. "At least, I think so."

"Come on." Fierre held out his hand, and I took it, letting him lead me to the door. "There's a cake with your name on it out there. Not literally. I'm saving that level of embarrassment for the actual wedding." He flashed me a smile, and it was weaker than usual. "But I had it made with that raspberry sauce you're always banging on about."

"I wish you hadn't heard anything that pit viper said."

He kissed me on the shoulder, and it occurred to me

that Fierre was a lot stronger than people thought; a lot stronger than he looked to people who only saw the surface.

"Let's talk over cake," he said. "I think you've earned more than a mouthful of it."

THE HEART HALL had nearly emptied by the time we returned. Fierre took a platter with a half-demolished golden cake on it and carried it to a table. I brought a knife over and cut two slices. It felt a little decadent to be eating alone in the middle of Eilean-òir's most famous hall, but I supposed that now we were going to be married, we could do that. *Husband and husband-to-be*, my mother had said. I passed Fierre a piece of cake with the knife, holding it in place with my fingers, watching nervously as he took it from me.

I hadn't really expected him to eat it. Yet as I watched, he took a bite, his lips covering both the golden cake and the drizzle of raspberry sauce across it. He closed his eyes. When he opened them again, he was beaming.

I kissed him on the lips. As I took his hand in mine, I felt his fingers trembling.

"I'm proud of you," I said.

"And I'm indebted to you. Thank you… for getting to him in time, for holding him off from leaving…" He drew a shaky breath. "How did you know that he was the one paying Galar?"

"I meant to tell you, but I clean forgot. I don't blame you if you want to punish me." I rubbed my forehead. "When I exiled Galar for you, he was swimming in letters from Kinnaid. They looked like signed orders for funds. And there were more of them in the supply room."

"Ah." Fierre looked down. "I'm glad you got to Kinnaid. I'm only sorry you had to learn… had to hear…" He broke off again, and seemed to wrestle with something.

"You don't have to explain," I said.

"After we argued in Castle Aonar, Kinnaid kissed me. I wanted to pretend he was you. Once we started… I asked him to call me Fierre while he…" He trailed off. Again, a pause. "I kept thinking of you," he said, quietly, at last. "While he was inside me, I wanted it to be you. It wasn't the same, but I closed my eyes and pretended."

I could feel tears welling. I had to stop them.

"Aive, are you mad? Say something."

I wiped a tear from my eye and looked into his face.

"I can't believe you want me," I said. "It still feels like a dream. When you proposed, I thought someone was going to step in and take it away from me a second later."

"You're going to be my husband," Fierre said, a twinkle in his eye again. "I'm not letting you go. Not a single hair of that fragrant chest is leaving me."

I broke off a piece from my slice of cake, feeling the stickiness of the raspberry sauce on my fingers, and I held it out to Fierre's lips. He stared at me for a moment. His lips parted, and I pushed the cake onto his tongue, feeling the warm velvet of his mouth close around my fingers.

"I'm not letting you go either. I'm going to be here, offering you cake, until the end of my days," I said.

Fierre beamed. He swallowed, then kissed me. The sugary, fruity taste of the cake still clung to his lips.

"I think we should celebrate our betrothal, don't you?" he said.

Betrothal. I still couldn't believe it. If we celebrated in private, maybe it'd seem real, then. If he still wanted me, then maybe I could finally believe that I deserved him.

Twenty-Five

Fierre

JUST WHEN YOU think you're done with speech-making, crowd-dazzling, and arresting a traitorous laird after a medicine-smashing fray, another thing comes along and throws you off your horse. That's life, I suppose. At least, this time, it was a distraction that pleased me.

The solid, confident figure of Oighrig Sethune blocked the doorway of the Heart Hall, and on her arm was a willowy blonde woman in a smock. Oighrig strode towards me, cheerfully ignoring the guards' entreaties to wait.

"Go and wash up, Aive," I said, rubbing the last spot of blood off his cheek. "In my suite, if you like. I won't be long."

Aiven gave me a hopeful look and retreated.

Oighrig thanked me and quickly recounted her family's happiness. It was strange to see a Sethune in the palace after we'd knelt on the floor of her parents' small house, during our solemn discussion, but now that I'd reinstated them all as doctors, perhaps it wouldn't seem strange for much longer. The neat combing of Oighrig's hair into a bun and the fastening of a clan pin on her sash told me that she'd made a singular effort to look presentable. She put an arm around the shoulders of the blonde woman with her.

"My wife, Sky. Ailsa Blacke—now Ailsa Sethune."

"Charmed." I gave Ailsa a warm smile. She muttered her thanks, nestling into Oighrig's embrace like a dove.

"If you please, Sky," Oighrig said, "I'd like to offer you my services, and Ailsa's."

"Is she a doctor too? Goodness, you do know a lot of clever people."

"No, Sky." Oighrig laughed. "She's a cook, though she's right clever. I'm the one who means to offer my medical services, if you would be so good as to employ me. I'd be honoured to work near the palace."

"How about within its walls?" I'd made my decision as soon as she entered the Heart Hall, but it was much more satisfying to watch her beam in surprise now. "I could use a doctor to take over from Galar as my personal source of physic. Not to starve me, mind."

"I'd seek to increase your food, safely and steadily." Oighrig bowed. "It's my honour to accept, Sky. Laird and Lady Sethune will be honoured, too." A smile curled the corners of her mouth. "My mother'll do her nut. Begging your pardon. She used to say we'd never be let back on the mainland's soil; just imagine her hearing this!"

"And your wife," I said, to cut off her flow of delight, which was beginning to embarrass me, though not in the worst of ways. "Is she seeking employ in the kitchens?"

"I'm happy enough cooking at home," Ailsa said. "But if I may make so bold…"

I waited. She glanced at Oighrig, and the two of them shared a look.

"We heard about your affection for Master Grian. And we thought that it might make the Quickening harder. What with him being jealous and all. *If* he were," Oighrig added, quickly. "But you see, Ailsa and I, being both women…" She inclined her head, as if this needed to be pointed out. I held back a laugh. "We have no easy way to make a child. And Ailsa here, she wants to raise a baby while I work. We had this idea that, if you were interested, we could save you the trouble of favouring one of your court families above the others. What I'm saying is…" She heaved a breath. "You could try to make a child with Ailsa."

"I see." I felt a familiar heat in my cheeks. How was it that I had stood mostly naked before all the noblemen of my court without blushing, but now, I was reddening like a roseship? "I'll think on the proposition, doctor. But I have a feeling that it'll prove useful to us all. As for the present…" I gestured at the guards hovering nearby, who still looked nervous about the women's proximity to me. "These gentlemen will show you to your new working quarters. Er… actually, we might do that tomorrow. The supply room needs a bit of cleaning up. And I think we can find you a space worthy of a Sethune."

Oighrig beamed, shook my hand, and said a number of things about increased intake of grains and the importance of fat that made me feel warm inside. *Warmer*, that was. I hadn't quite finished blushing over her proposition.

We parted, and I saw that the Heart Hall was empty, except for the kitchen staff who were clearing the plates away. No more people to greet. No more lairds to charm.

No more obstacles standing between me and my newly betrothed.

My footsteps seemed to ring louder in the corridors

than they usually did. Maybe it was due to the staff being busy in the kitchens, and the emptiness of the hallways, but I had a feeling that my own nervousness was creating the echo.

The breeze blew gently through the windows in the Skyward Suite, making the curtains billow and wafting a scent of heather from the gardens. A purple sheen caught my eye. I noticed Aiven sitting at my desk, draped in a lavender robe from my collection. The silk barely covered three quarters of his chest, leaving a generous swathe of skin on display.

I cleared my throat.

He raised his eyes to mine. Without speaking, he held up a wad of pages. The first page bore the heading:

THE HARVEST OF EILEAN-ÒIR

My throat tightened.

"Ah," I said. "You've read it, then."

Aiven rose and walked around the desk, advancing with my manuscript grasped in his hand. His silence made me even more nervous.

"Fierre," he said, softly.

"Whatever you think, just out with it. If it's bad, I'd rather know now than proceed with something half-baked."

"Fierre…" Aiven drew a breath. "This is going to reshape the realm."

"You don't hate it, then?"

"Two schools built in every town." He flipped over a few pages. "Clean houses. No more taxes for farmers, so they can keep all their food to eat or sell. Funds to train apprentices. Safe premises for smiths and merchants.

Money to see the people through a bad season, and a project to build them safer dwellings. A program to guide all students to seek out their vocation—not merely a job for coin, but their true calling." He flipped through a few more pages. "A code of ethics for all doctors practicing throughout the land, and stable pay."

"Well, I had a bit of personal motivation for that one."

"A shift away from spending money on decorative dyes from Archland, and towards trading with Archland for healing plants and weathergrain, the crop that can—"

"Survive all seasons," I finished.

"It goes on. And on." Aiven waved the pages. "Equal rights for *women* in marriage and succession. Do the lairds know about this?"

I was silent.

"And there's a note here about the potential to change the rule that only an heir of Clan Dannatyne can inherit the crown." Aiven looked directly at me. "That'd take away the need for each Dannatyne king to be a vessel of god. To be distinguished by his body. To starve."

"One thing at a time," I murmured. "It's merely a note."

"Very clever." Aiven glanced at the *Harvest* again. "And a vast reduction in the quarrying of royal stones, down to a bare minimum. The closure of coal mines, with a promise to protect and cherish the earth, and an ongoing investment in safe fuel. That's why you wanted to repossess Kinnaid's mines? To make sure his enterprise never succeeds?" He stared into my eyes again. "To find a cleaner way?"

"I tried to phrase it subtly, but I suppose nothing gets past you."

"Fierre, this is simply…"

He waved the manuscript at me one more time and then

his hand dropped, dangling it at his side. He was staring at me like he'd just read a book made of gold, inscribed with faery ink.

"I know it's an awful lot to do," I said. "I hope you don't think I'm charging in naively and waving my sword at the lairds. We'll have to do it bit by bit, I'm certain; but if we make a start now, and work at it month by month, year by year, I think we'll see more progress than anyone expects. The rich only notice progress once it's underway." I smiled gently. "I'd like to get a head start."

"You're the prince this country deserves," Aiven said. "One day, you'll be king, and unlike every other king in this realm's history, you'll have earnt it."

I swallowed. Yet the thought of my father passing away was no longer as painful as it once was. I would face that day when it came.

"You know," Aiven said, "you could save a bit of money for the people if you reduced your household expenses. And the lairds' expenses." There was a twinkle in his eye. "A former Master of Compliance could show you where to trim and cut. Of course, it might mean fewer necklaces for you, and fewer enserres…"

I closed the space between us and ran my hand over the exposed swathe of Aiven's chest.

"Well," I said, "I hope you've enjoyed this one, then."

His gaze ran from the top of my enserre down to my waist, and then lower.

"I'm torn. Ever since you stepped onto the grass and the sun shone through that fabric, I can't be sure whether I like looking at it or whether I'd like to peel it off your body."

"We were meant to celebrate my betrothal," I said. "You figure it out."

He placed the manuscript on a chair and lifted me onto the desk. I wasn't ready for his hands under my arse and back, but I decided at once that I liked it. I wriggled when he put me down, shifting myself into a flat-out position with my back against the desk. Paper crumpled beneath my shoulders and legs. A couple of pages fluttered up and fell, and Aiven caught one.

"What's this?" he said, frowning at the scribble.

"Drafts for the *Harvest*."

"Ah." He seized a clump of pages from the corner of the desk. "I hear drafts are useful for resting your head against while your husband-to-be makes love to you."

"And when exactly did you learn that?"

"Right now." Aiven lifted my head, keeping the crown in place, and stuffed the wad of paper beneath it. He took his dirk from where it was resting on the desk and pressed the blade against the top of my enserre.

"Stay still," he said.

He held the fabric an inch or so above my skin. With a single movement, he sliced from my neckline to my navel, ripping the enserre into two. It fell away to the sides, and he pulled the ripped garment downward, letting the tear continue. The enserre ripped all the way to the crystals at my groin. I felt the air of the chamber against my skin, and all of a sudden, I was conscious of my naked body.

"I loathe these crystals," Aiven muttered.

"Too bright for you?"

"No." He dropped his dirk, lifted me, and rolled me onto my front, so that my chin hit the draft pages of my manuscript. The paper cushioned me. Aiven traced a line down my spine to the place where the crystals remained. "They're in my way."

He pulled at the garment, and when he dropped

something shiny next to my face, I realised that he'd ripped one of the crystals right off the fabric.

"Only eight to go," he said.

And then... I thought, quickly imagining the possibilities.

He untied my sandals last. As soon as he had me naked, he kissed my lower back. I smiled into the paper, glad that he couldn't see my face. I expected to feel his fingers trailing lower.

Instead, I felt his tongue touch the base of my spine.

I had scarcely time to say "oh" before it moved lower again, and I wriggled against the desk, my hands scrabbling to grab hold of the corners. Oh, capering god. When had Aiven decided he wanted to do this?

He pushed deeper into me with his tongue, and I forgot to ask.

I was a quivering mess by the time he finished, yet not spent—only roused to the point of desperation. He lifted me again and turned me onto my back, carefully checking that the paper was piled beneath my head and spread out under my body.

It took us both a moment to notice that my stomach and legs were streaked with ink.

"Your words," Aiven said, running a finger over a black stain on my thigh.

"Do I look ridiculous?"

"I think you look even more beautiful, wearing your laws." He grinned and shrugged off his robe, treating me to a view of everything. I wanted to make good on my idea of sucking his cock while he yanked my hair, but there'd be plenty of nights together to come, I told myself. And mornings.

Aiven pinned my legs back as he oiled me. He entered

me with one hand cupping my jaw, holding me tenderly, as if he wanted to make sure he could stare into my eyes. He needn't have worried. I wasn't going to look away—not while he was gazing at me with a look so loving that I felt as if the room suddenly lost its colour; as if the hangings and paintings and ornaments all fell away, leaving only the two of us.

He kissed me on the lips as he pushed all the way into me, and this time, I didn't have to stifle my moan. This time, I could make all the noise I needed to.

And I needed to make a lot of noise.

He sank all the way in and held his body there, keeping up the pressure, forcing me to close my eyes. I exclaimed something that I was fairly sure I could never repeat. A moment later, I called out his name and felt him breathe out sharply against my forehead, just beneath the band of my crown.

"You have to do this to me every day," I managed. "Every day that we're married."

"Fierre—"

"And you have to keep it there, just like this."

"*Fierre.*" He sounded desperate.

"I want you to remind me how much you love me. Make me feel it in each muscle, so that I'm thinking about you all week as I move around."

Aiven pulled back until he was almost all the way out of me, then slid in hard enough to make me gasp. I kept my eyes shut, enjoying imagining his face.

"And every single morning I'm going to kiss you." I exhaled shakily. "In different places. To remind you that I love every single bit of you, and that I'm glad you saved me."

Something wet splashed onto my forehead. I opened

my eyes. Aiven wiped the tears from his cheeks, but it was too late—I had already seen the shining trails.

"Leave it," I said, as he made to wipe the tear from my forehead.

"I'm sorry."

"Why ever should you be?"

He moved slowly in and out of me, kissing my neck as he did, striking that sensitive strip along the right side where a single brush of his tongue could make me into a weakling. I clenched my muscles around his cock, and heard his intake of breath.

"I can't believe I get to hold you," he whispered.

"Well, believe it."

"I still can't understand why you want me."

"You're strong, and handsome, and kind. And terrifying when you protect me. I'd be mad not to want you. It's more than want, though… I need you, Aive. I need you like water."

"Then let me wash over you, every day."

I smirked. "Will you wash over my face, if I ask nicely?"

"Fierre! Saints' sake, I was trying to be poetic."

"I can't help it if your mouth is accidentally filthy." I let myself be serious for a moment. "Honestly, Aive, I can't believe you want *me*, either. I never thought that anyone would want me. I knew they'd all want the prince, but I didn't think they'd want the dolt of a man underneath— the one who used to check his reflection in the mirror and hate what he saw—the one who thought he'd never be good enough."

For his father, I almost added.

"You're more than good enough," Aiven said. "You don't need a mirror to tell you that. Just look at me, and I'll remind you."

I gasped as he hit a spot inside me that sang like a lute string through my flesh. He shifted into a fast rhythm before I could recover, and I clung to him desperately, hooking my hands around his neck, letting him grip my ankles hard and push my legs back. He knew exactly what he was doing to me, because he kept hitting that spot mercilessly, reducing me to a wordless creature. When he leaned down to kiss me, I whispered into his mouth:

"I love you."

The words were simple. But he looked at me in a way that was anything but simple.

"I love you more," Aiven said, breathing shakily.

He kissed me on the mouth and slammed into me. He was kissing me still when I came, gasping. The look of pleasure that flitted across Aiven's face told me that he'd been waiting for me to reach the end, and in an instant, he picked up his speed, fucking me until his whole body tensed and he froze, cried out, and pushed slowly into me one final time. He let go of my ankles and moved his hands to my shoulders, holding me tightly, looking at me as if he never wanted to break our gaze.

When he finally let me go, he blinked, and tears fell from his eyes again.

"Aive," I said, wiping his cheek. "Aive, what is it?"

"I was so afraid you'd die in my arms, that day in Castle Aonar. But now you're here in my arms, and you're alive. So alive."

I kissed him on the nose.

"I intend to live for a very long time," I said.

He rolled onto his side, lying next to me on the desk, and I draped my left hand to the side, stretching my arm out. My fingers brushed against something smooth. I looked across. I'd clean forgotten that the staff had brought me a bowl of oatcakes sprinkled with salt for good luck. I reached into the bowl and seized one of the oatcakes.

My fingers rubbed it gently, feeling its round shape. There had to be at least a dozen of those in the bowl. In the years past, if someone had offered me a bowl of oatcakes, I would've refused the gift at once—and if it'd been left in my chamber, I would've glanced across at the bowl every minute.

"Here," I said, passing the oatcake to Aive. "What do you think?"

He took a bite, closed his eyes for a moment, then nodded. "Well made."

I rubbed against him, nestling into the warmth of his body, and as I plucked another oatcake from the bowl, it occurred to me that the realm was like the object in my hand. Most of it was baked flat, with only a few grains of salt on top. But that was going to change. There would be challenges ahead, but we could take them on—Aiven and I, and the Sethunes, and every person who chose to join us. We could make sure that there weren't just a few people on top of everyone else.

"Thinking?" Aiven said, and I realised that I had been silent for a while.

"Mmm," I said. As I thought back over the law I had drafted about providing coin through the bad harvests, I bit down on a corner of the oatcake, plunging into the details. Only when I'd chewed through the rest of the oats did I realise that I had eaten the whole oatcake—not out of desperation to feed myself, nor out of defiance and anger. I had eaten it without thinking. And now that I had finished, the panic that I had grown accustomed to feeling didn't rise in my chest.

There were still mornings when the mirror mocked my form. There were still some afternoons when I turned my plate away, and some nights when every bite demanded penance. But there were also moments, like now, when I forgot what that old fear felt like.

I laughed. The sound echoed off the walls. I threw back my head and laughed some more, revelling in my mirth.

"Fierre, what is it?" Aiven said.

I smiled into his chest.

"It's nothing," I said.

It was true, I thought, looking at my empty hand, where the oatcake had been. Today, it *was* nothing. But it meant everything in the world that it was nothing.

I slipped another oatcake into my mouth, chewed it, and kissed Aiven. The taste of butter merged with the taste of his lips, and for the first time in a very long while, I wasn't hungry at all.

Author's Note: Trigger Warnings

This book depicts a character suffering from an eating disorder. It depicts a range of behaviours associated with an eating disorder, including both physical and mental aspects, and includes two graphic scenes of purging.

Additionally, there are some depictions of violence, slut shaming, and bullying. There is one scene of sexual assault early in the book, and one brief depiction of sexual assault a little later.

About the Author

Darcy Ash is the author of *The Two Hungers of Prince Fierre*. She often writes about queer relationships, illness, and characters from low-income backgrounds. She can regularly be found dreaming about travel.

FIND US ONLINE!

www.rebellionpublishing.com

/solarisbooks

/solarisbks

/solarisbooks

/solarisbooks.
bsky.social

SIGN UP TO OUR NEWSLETTER!

rebellionpublishing.com/newsletter

YOUR REVIEWS MATTER!

Enjoy this book? Got something to say?

Leave a review on Amazon, GoodReads or with your
favourite bookseller and let the world know!